To an

school chum

Bernadette Brown

SHORTY'S
S T O R Y

(The Author)

Ron Herrett

Hope you enjoy reading
it as much as I enjoyed
writing it !. !.

June 11, 2013

SHORTY'S
STORY

Ron Herrett

Library of Congress Control Number: 2012903675
ISBN: Hardcover   978-1-4691-7538-6
                 Softcover   978-1-4691-7537-9
                 Ebook   978-1-4691-7539-3

This book was printed in the United States of America.

To order additional copies of this book, contact:
Xlibris Corporation
1-888-795-4274
www.Xlibris.com
Orders@Xlibris.com
107537

Dedication

I would like to dedicate this book to my parents, Murray and Edith (Purdy) Herrett. They raised a large family with a lot of hard work and very little money. My father always explained what he was doing and why, a lot like the main character in this story; Shorty Stout. We never had a lot but it was enough. My mother kept us fed and clothed with long hours of hard work. We never ate fancy but we ate good, I wore hand-me-downs most of my life but I was clothed. I wish they could both see what they helped me to do.

Also I would like to mention my daughters Wendy, Marla and Lisa, who gave me four grandsons; Matthew and Devin in Nova Scotia and Tyler and Travis in Alberta. I set out to write them a story for Christmas and it turned into this book. Hope you enjoy reading this story as much as I enjoyed writing it.

Chapter 1

SHORTY STOUT WAS one of the top cowhands working on the Axe. The Axe is a cattle ranch in southeastern Alberta, where normally there are about two thousand cattle roaming the range. They also raised enough horses for ranch use. Now, if you are curious about the name of the ranch, the Axe, I'll tell you. The owner's name is Xavier Forrest, and his wife's name is Angela. The name they settled on was the A-X (A bar X). You can see for yourself why it soon became known as the Axe.

The owners are a good couple to work for. They believe in a man working for a dollar, but they don't push anyone too hard; in fact, the boys work a lot harder than they are expected to. Where a good cowhand gets forty dollars a month, the Axe pays their hands fifty, and the boys feel they should work harder to earn their pay.

The Axe has a good, snug bunkhouse for the hands to live in, and they are expected to keep it reasonably clean. Well, I've seen women-kept houses that weren't as clean as that bunkhouse! The floor is swept every evening after work. There is a wooden chest built onto the end of each bunk and a sliding drawer under most of them. There are several clothes racks on the wall (where there is room) to hang extra clothes on. The hands are treated with respect, and they treat the owner's property with respect. The boys try to outdo each other in keeping everything clean and neat.

On most ranches, the food is good and plentiful. On the Axe, the men are fed almost royally. There is the usual beef, beans, and bread. The cook makes pies at least once a week, and there are always fresh cookies. The turnover isn't very high, because no one wants to leave once they find a place like this to work. The Axe doesn't have to go looking for hands or advertise for help.

Shorty was drifting through late last summer and stopped in for a meal and a place to sleep overnight. In these times, most ranches had a spare bunk for the drifter or other travelers. On the Axe, any drifter that took advantage of the hospitality offered wasn't very popular, but the owners very seldom had to ask anyone to leave. If a man didn't seem inclined to pitch in and help with what he could do, the hands usually explained the situation to him, and he soon drifted on.

When Shorty arrived at the ranch, he got a good meal and a comfortable bunk for the night. Early the next morning, he was outside, working at anything he could find that needed to be repaired. He was good with an axe, saw, hammer and nails, or just about anything else you might want him to do.

When the hands first saw him, he was fifty feet off the ground, at the top of the windmill. It had been clanking and screeching for weeks now, but most cowhands who were comfortable in a saddle, wouldn't go near that tower unless under a direct order, and on this ranch that very seldom happened. Shorty had taken with him a can of grease and some strips of sheet metal for shims. Before the boss knew what was going on, Shorty had that windmill purring like a kitten and pumping water like it really enjoyed it!

The ranch was always kept clean and neat, because the hands were proud to keep it that way. After Shorty had been around for a few days, everyone noticed the difference. Not only was the windmill quiet, but there was not a hinge squeaking or a gate dragging or anything out of place. The buildings had not been run-down, but they now looked so good and everything worked so smoothly, the hands could hardly believe it! Shorty was a thinker and figured there was usually an easier way to do almost everything.

On the third day, Shorty was working in the vegetable garden after having cleaned up the flower beds the boss's wife had around the place. The foreman, Chuck, was talking to the boss about how impressed he was with Shorty's work. Although the ranch wasn't short of hands, the boss didn't think he could afford to let a man like this slip through his fingers. The two men didn't notice the boss's wife coming up behind them until she said, "If you don't hire that man right now, I will! We probably have the best bunch of men on this ranch that you could find within a hundred miles. I have to ask someone to help me with the garden work. Not one of them will refuse, but they won't go out of their way to do it unless asked. I don't think one of them would go near my flowers, present company included. In the few days he's been here, Shorty has the whole ranch looking better than it ever has. Now, are you going to hire him, or do I?" The boss looked at his foreman and said, "You heard the lady. Put Shorty on the payroll as of one week ago!" So that was how Shorty Stout came to be working on the Axe.

Maybe we should take a few minutes here and find out a bit more about this guy called Shorty. When he was just a baby, someone pinned the handle 'Aloysius J. Stout' on him. He has always given his name as 'Al Stout.' Now when he gives his name as Al Stout, usually someone smirks and comes out with 'Short 'n' Stout.' The name stuck. He answers to Al, Short, and Shorty. If you met up with him, you might wonder about his handle. He stands six foot two and weighs in at one hundred and eighty pounds. Hardly a 'Shorty.'

He was born with light hair, almost blond, but it has darkened over the years until it is almost black. He wears a neat mustache on his upper lip. He usually wears low heeled, cavalry-type boots, as he does as much work on foot as in the saddle. He doesn't talk a lot, but what he says is worth listening to. He is good with almost every hand tool you might ask him to use. He can ride and rope with the best and is an excellent shot with both rifle and handgun. He can think his way out of almost any problem you might throw at him. He believes every person should be treated with respect, unless he proves otherwise. Very few people have ever heard his proper name, very few ever will. If pressed hard enough, Shorty will reveal his full name, but no one this side of his family ever heard what the 'J' stood for.

Well, as our story continues, spring has arrived at the ranch. After a long winter, when people didn't get out to do much socializing, there is usually a dance at the schoolhouse on the outskirts of town. It was twelve miles from the ranch, but just about everyone in a radius of twenty-five miles attended these events. Some people didn't go to dance but just to meet neighbors and relatives they hadn't seen since Christmas or even last fall. Since it was a long ride, or drive in a wagon, most people brought along a lunch and arrived about suppertime. They would meet family and friends to visit, before the crowd got too heavy.

A dance was an important social event in ranching country because people lived so far apart. Everybody was dressed in their best, and all were slicked up and shaved. Many a romance started from a meeting at the little schoolhouse. All of the eligible young, and not so young, ladies were here, as well as most of the single and married cowboys. As always in these times, the men were on their best behavior. No one would ever dare to insult a lady, married or single!

When the music started, there were a few tunes played with no one dancing, as no one wanted to be the first on the dance floor. Very soon a couple of ranchers or townsmen would grab their wives to get the ball rolling. That was all it would take to get the boys asking the girls and the dance was underway.

There was a man and a lady playing fiddle, three men with guitars, and one banjo. A few ladies would take turns at the school organ to help the musicians. Before very long a gentleman arrived with a squeeze-box. If someone took a break, another person would pick up the instrument, so there was always lots of music.

Shorty arrived with a bunch of hands from the Axe. He was pretty good on his feet and never lacked for a partner. The schoolteacher was very popular, not only was she a good dancer and single, but because she was also a very pretty young lady. She had a wonderful personality, which a lot of people commented on. Everyone was enjoying themselves so much; nobody kept track of the time. Most of the young children were tucked in and asleep, in ranch wagons all around. Well, all good things must come to an end and so with this social event. When a rooster began to crow, people realized it was time to call it a day (or maybe a night).

Since this dance took place on a Friday evening, it was now Saturday morning! Shorty, along with everyone else, enjoyed kicking up his heels. He very seldom drank alcohol, and on the rare occasion that he did, he never had more than two drinks. He had seen too many people who overdid it, and at the very least, made big fools of themselves.

On the Axe, the men worked five days a week, except in the busy season when they worked six, and occasionally seven days. The busy spring season hadn't started yet, so Shorty decided to get off the beaten trail and do a bit of exploring on the way back to the ranch. Each weekend, the hands took turns checking the range and worked out the rotation to suit themselves. Sometimes a man would work a couple of weekends in a row, so he could have more time other weekends for himself.

Shorty was off the main trail to the east, heading in the general direction of the ranch. Farther east were a few big hills, which in some places would be called small mountains. It was a beautiful day and he was enjoying himself looking over new country. Suddenly he pulled his mount up short! He sat in his saddle, trying to decide if he had heard something, or if his ears had been playing tricks on him. He sat still as a stone, looking around and listening. After almost ten minutes of silence, except for a few birds and other natural sounds, he decided he hadn't heard anything important. He was just about to continue riding on when he heard it again. It sounded like an axe striking wood! It was quite a distance off, but he was sure of it now. Still in no hurry, he reined his horse in the direction the sound was coming from.

The land had a few small trees and bushes on it, but the farther he went, and the closer he got to the hills, the bigger the trees were. About ten minutes of slow riding and listening, brought him to a spot where he could see farther ahead. He could see a team and wagon and two people in the distance. As he got closer, he could see the bigger person was dressed in overalls, shirt, and a man's hat. When he saw the long dark hair, he realized it was a lady dressed in men's clothing. The second person was a boy of about seven or eight years. As he approached, the woman seemed startled to see him. They stopped what they were doing, which was using a crosscut saw to cut a fair-sized tree, into stove lengths. They left the saw in the cut and looked at this stranger who was interrupting them.

As Shorty looked around, he could see the axe that he had heard earlier, and he could see that some of the wood had been split and tossed in the wagon. After a few seconds of hesitation, Shorty removed his hat and said, "This is pretty heavy work for you and this young man, isn't it, ma'am? Don't you have a man to help with this type of work?" As he was speaking, he could see that the boy was definitely the woman's son. They resembled each other too much to be anything except mother and son.

Now it was her turn to hesitate. After a good half minute, she spoke, "Really, sir, I don't think it is much concern of yours what we are doing, but no, I don't have a man to do the work except Matt, here. My husband died about a year ago. If there is work to be done, we do it!" She didn't have an edge to her voice and wasn't in the least sarcastic, she was politely stating a fact.

Shorty felt terrible and could feel his face burn. "I'm sorry to hear about your husband, ma'am," he said. "I meant no offence to you. I just don't think a lady should have to work so hard. Would you mind if I stopped and gave you a helping hand for a bit?"

She looked around for a few seconds and then she said, "If we could afford to hire some help, we would. Money is in short supply right now, but if you want to give us a hand, we are in no position, and not too proud, to accept your offer to help." Shorty got down from his horse and walked a few steps to a bush which he wrapped his reins around. He took off the light jacket he was wearing and tossed it over the saddle. He went back to where the lady and her son were standing. "Howdy, ma'am," he said, "my handle is Stout, Al Stout. I was just on my way back to the ranch when I heard your axe and decided to investigate." He reached out toward her and they shook hands.

"My name is Dawn Ryan and this is my son Matt," she said. Shorty shook hands with Matt also. "Pleased to meet you both," Shorty said, "now if you don't mind, I'd like to help you with your work." He walked over to the crosscut and was about to start using it by himself. Mrs. Ryan took hold of the other end and made ready to go back to work. Shorty looked at her and said, "I can handle this myself, ma'am, if you would like to rest up a bit." She looked him in the eye and said, "You offered to help us with the work, Mr. Stout, now start helping! I'm not going to sit back and watch someone else doing my work."

They took up the saw and began cutting wood. After a few minutes, Shorty stopped work and said, "Ma'am, I don't want to offend you, but is it OK, if I explain a few things to you? I'm not saying you're wrong, but most jobs are easier if they are done the proper way." "Mr. Stout," Dawn said, "You offered to help us, so you would have to try very hard to offend us. As for being wrong, most of what Matt and I have done has been done wrong. Just about everything we do is by trial and error. Most of what we do is done the hard way until we find a way that works for us. If I'm doing it wrong, feel free to show me the right way. We would both appreciate having someone teach us what we don't know, Mr. Stout."

Shorty looked all around for a few seconds. "Is there something wrong, Mr. Stout?" Dawn asked. "Well," Shorty answered, "I was just wondering who this 'Mister' feller is you're talking to. That isn't my name."

Mrs. Ryan smiled as she looked at him. Shorty said, "Ma'am, you can call me Al, Short, or Shorty. My name isn't Mister." Dawn looked at him and asked, "Why would someone call you 'Shorty'?" "Well, ma'am," he said. "When I tell someone my name is Al Stout, some people smile and say, 'Short 'n' Stout,' and the name stuck. Now, can we go back to work?"

They stepped back to the tree, and Shorty said, "Now ma'am, when using a crosscut, the first thing is to have the log off the ground and if possible, at a comfortable height for working. Now, I'm going to lift this log and I want you to stand this piece of wood under it, about eight feet back. Fine, let's get started. Now, don't push down on the saw, just let the weight of the saw do the cutting. Also, don't try to push the saw back to me, I'll pull it my way, then you pull it your way. Now isn't that easier than before? "You're right Mr . . . . er Al," she said, "it does work much easier"

As they worked with the crosscut, young Matt tossed the sawn wood onto the wagon, then climbed up and piled it neatly. It wasn't a very long time until they had the wagon loaded. They laid the saw across a log and sat down on a block of wood. Mrs. Ryan said, "We brought along some lunch because we expected to be here all day. You're welcome to share what we have." "Well, ma'am," Shorty replied, "I sure don't want to refuse your hospitality and I am getting a bit hollow."

They sat under the trees and ate their lunch. It wasn't fancy but wholesome and filling and there was plenty of cold water to go with the food. As they were finishing their meal, Shorty said, "Ma'am, if it's OK with you, we could saw up a bit more wood and it would be ready for another time. Then you and Matt could come and get it when you need it or have the time to spare." Dawn agreed that would be fine. They spent another couple of hours sawing wood, while Matt piled it in rows so it would keep drying. When he thought they had enough wood cut for another load, and Shorty could see that both Mrs. Ryan and Matt were getting tired, he called a halt. "There," Shorty said, "You have at least enough wood for one more load. I think it's time to call it a day and save a little work for another time."

As he loaded the saw, axe, and lunch basket on the full wagon, he said, "Ma'am, if you would like, I could go along with you and help unload this wood. I'm heading in your direction anyway so it's not out of my way." Dawn said, "Mr . . . . Al, I think you have done more than enough to help us. You must be tired after all the work you have done. We don't expect you to do any more."

"Well, Ma'am," he said, "I consider it a real privilege to work alongside a pair of hard workers like you two. If you want me to leave, I will, but unless you say it real plain, I'm going to be riding in the same direction anyway, so I'll just stop in and help unload this wagon. All right, Rolllll the wagon!"

It wasn't a long drive to where they lived in a small cabin backed up against a hill. Besides the house, there was a barn big enough to shelter more stock than he could see and a couple of smaller outbuildings. A lean to woodshed was attached to the back of the house. Mrs. Ryan had stopped the wagon by the woodshed and started to unhitch the team. Shorty gave her a hand and then led the horses to the barn. There he took the harness off and hung it on pegs inside. The horses were turned into the pasture behind the barn. He checked the water trough, but it was almost full of water, which had to be carried about a hundred feet. This water came from a small stream that came from the hills behind the buildings. When he saw everything was fine, he headed back to the wagon. "OK, Matt" he said, "you toss down some of that wood and I'll bust it up for you." It was mostly straight-grained pine, so it split quite easily. Matt would throw off some wood then hop down and carry the split wood into the shed and pile it in neat rows. The building was open on three sides, except for a few upright posts holding up the roof and woodpiles.

Mrs. Ryan had a good fire going in the cook stove and was getting supper ready. Before the wagon was emptied, the cook called out that supper was just about ready. Shorty helped Matt toss the rest of the wood in a heap beside the woodshed. Then he and Matt washed up in a pan of water beside the door. When they went in, the food smelled delicious. There was a pot of reheated beef stew and a pan of hot biscuits. After working all day in the fresh air, all three had a good appetite. The stew disappeared in a hurry along with most of the biscuits. Then, Mrs. Ryan brought a pot of tea and some cold milk for Matt. Everybody was tired including Shorty. They talked a bit as they finished their meal, then Shorty said he'd better make tracks back to the ranch. Mrs. Ryan spoke up, "You must work at the Axe, since that's the way you are headed. Have you been there long?" "Nope," Shorty replied, "I've been there seven or eight months. Do you know the owners?" "Well," she said, "everybody around here knows them and we hear about them when we get to town, which isn't very often. We're five miles from town and it's about seven to the ranch. We don't get to either place too often."

As Shorty climbed aboard his horse, he asked Mrs. Ryan, "Would it be OK if I stopped by some other time and give you a hand? It wouldn't be any bother and a meal like we just had would more than pay for all the work I'd do." "Well," she said, "It's a free country and we can't stop you from riding where you want. I can't see why you would want to come way out here in God's back pasture to help us, but I'm sure Matt appreciates your help as much as I do. Good night Mr . . . . er, Al."

Sunday morning on the Axe was usually very quiet. After a week of hard work, everyone was ready to take it easy and rest up for the coming week. Most of the hands spent the day washing and patching the clothes they had worn all week. If their saddle gear needed some attention, this was the day it got it. Nobody did any ranch work that wasn't absolutely necessary, but there were always a few light chores that had to be done, even on Sunday.

When Shorty got his housekeeping chores done, he headed out to the tool shed. He was already thinking ahead to what was needed at the Ryan place. He had noticed that the corral needed some work, and there should be a fence around the buildings to keep range cattle out. He saw half a dozen drawknives hanging on the wall. He also noticed a froe for splitting out shakes. This wouldn't be necessary right now, but probably in the near future it would be. There were other tools here he might want to borrow later, but he would ask the boss, or the foreman, about borrowing the drawknives for next weekend. He had the next weekend free also, so he planned to help out at the Ryan place.

As usual Shorty worked hard all week, sometimes doing as much as two men. He never wasted a move. Almost everything he did, he did so smoothly it seemed almost effortless. Toward the end of the week, he met up with the boss in the yard. He asked about borrowing some tools for the weekend. "Shorty, you can borrow anything you want from this ranch except my wife," he said with a smile. "Take whatever you want as long as it's back here when we need it. By the way, what do you want those drawknives for?" "Well," Shorty answered, "I want to peel a few poles for a project I have in mind. I'll make sure everything is in good shape when I bring it back." "No problem Shorty," the boss told him, "Just feel free to use whatever you want anytime. The work you've done on this place since you came more than pays for anything you want to use."

Early Saturday morning, Shorty was on the way to the Ryan ranch. He had two drawknives and his bedroll tied behind his saddle. When he arrived at the ranch, Mrs. Ryan and Matt were already hard at work. He looked in the shed attached to one end of the barn, to see what was there in the line of tools. Besides the crosscut, there was a bucksaw and a peavey. He said to himself, 'These just might come in handy.' He walked over to where Matt and his mother were working. "Ma'am," he asked, "Is it all right if I borrow your team, wagon, and your son for a few hours? I also need a few tools from your shed."

"You are welcome to whatever you need," she said, "but if you think you two men are going off to the hills to have a good time by yourselves, you are badly mistaken. You aren't leaving here without me. By the time you have the team ready and the tools loaded, I'll have a lunch packed for us."

Shorty and Matt got the team harnessed and hitched to the wagon and loaded the tools. Matt had tossed a forkful of hay in the wagon to sit on and also so the tools wouldn't rattle around. At lunch time it was also something for the horses to eat. With the drawknives, they had put in the crosscut, bucksaw, axe, and the peavey, just in case it was needed. By this time, Mrs. Ryan had a lunch ready. Shorty suggested to Mrs. Ryan that maybe she should take along the overalls she had worn the previous week. If she insisted on working with them, the overalls might come in handy.

They headed back up into the hills that were covered with trees. Shorty was looking for a thicket of closely growing trees. He wanted them small and straight for fence rails. When they found the right spot, he stopped and tied the horses to a tree. "Now Matt, I have an important job for you to do" Shorty said, "I want you to look for a special tree for me. It should be no less than ten inches on the stump, with a big limb sticking out at least three feet above the ground. It should be quite straight for at least twelve feet. If you can find two Matt, that would be even better. Now, don't go too far and get lost, but I think you're too good a woodsman for that. Just remember to look behind you often, so you know what the area looks like for coming back. If you find something, tie this red rag on a branch as high as you can reach, close to it. We'll start cutting and peeling these poles for fence rails."

Shorty started cutting the small trees with the axe, as it was faster than the bucksaw. Mrs. Ryan took a small hand ax and cut off the few branches that were on the trees. When they had a lot of small poles cut, about four inches on the butt, Shorty got a drawknife and began peeling the bark off. Matt's mother put on the overalls Shorty had suggested she bring along and started peeling poles too.

It was a couple of hours before Matt arrived with a big smile on his face. "I found two trees like I think you want," he said.

"There is even a place we can get the wagon almost to them."
"Good work, Matt," Shorty said, "I think it's about time for a break, so we'll go check them out. We might as well take the saws and the axe, and if they are suitable we'll fall them, so they will start drying. Bring those drawknives too, Matt."

"While I was looking around, I saw two big buck deer, too," Matt told them. "I was less than a hundred feet from them before they saw me." "You must be a good woodsman to get that close," Shorty replied, "Just remember where you see animals as most keep to one area. Someday you might need some meat, and you will know where to get it."

It was about a five minute walk to where Matt had found the first tree. It was perfect for what Shorty wanted. The tree had been crotched or doubled when it was small. Another tree had fallen in the crotch and damaged one side. As the tree grew and healed, one side grew at almost ninety degrees from the main trunk, for about two feet, then grew straight up again. The damaged side didn't have nearly as big a top, which was fine. Shorty notched the tree and then Matt's mother helped him cut it down with the crosscut. Shorty had cut a slim pole for Matt to push the tree over with. When it came down with a swish and a slight bump, Shorty took Matt's pole and pried the butt of the tree back up on the stump. Then he took the axe and started cutting off the limbs, while Matt and his mother began peeling off the bark with the drawknives. When Shorty finished limbing the tree up past where he wanted, he left the top on.

He asked Matt, "Do you know why I put the tree back on the stump and left the top on?" "Well," Matt said, "I guess it makes it easier to peel." "Right," Shorty said, "It does, but it also lets it dry faster. With the butt off the ground, it can't suck any moisture from the ground. With the top drawing the sap from the trunk, the tree will be dry in a short time. Now, where is that next tree?" The next tree wasn't as big or shaped quite as good, but it would serve the purpose. This tree was cut down. Peeled and left to dry the same as the first one. As they walked back to the wagon, Matt asked, "What are we going to use those trees for?"

"I like to know a man who isn't too proud to ask questions," Shorty said, "It means he wants to learn. Well Matt, those trees are going to be gate posts, one for the corral and one for the fence we are going to build around the yard. We'll dig holes and set those poles up straight, and those limbs will hold the gate up off the ground. If we had a long iron bar to drive in the ground that would be fine, but this will work good too. Now let's get those fence rails loaded and eat that lunch. My stomach tells me it's time to put on the nosebag."

As they ate lunch, they talked about what they were going to do at the ranch. The most important things had to be done first, and all agreed that the fence around the place was the top priority. After lunch, which the horses had too from the back of the wagon, they moved to a grove of bigger trees. Shorty picked out the ones between six and eight inches on the stump for fence posts. These were dropped and cut into seven foot lengths, then peeled. One end was set on a stump or another post, so they would dry faster. The wagon was loaded with fence rails, so the posts were left to dry, which would make them a lot lighter to handle. The tops of the trees were limbed until too small for fence posts and then a small top was left on to dry them. When dry, the tops would be used for smaller posts or firewood. Very little effort would supply them with firewood and nothing was wasted.

By the time they had a good supply of fence posts cut, it was getting late in the day. The tools were loaded up and the work crew climbed aboard for the trip home. The trail was mostly downhill and the horses hadn't been working very hard, so they didn't mind the extra weight. Back at the ranch, the wagon was stopped where most of the fence rails were to be used. The team was unhitched, unharnessed, and turned into the pasture. Usually when a horse is unharnessed, the first thing they do is have a good roll, to get rid of the feel of the harness, and to scratch any itches they might have. This time was no exception as both horses rolled, or tried to. A horse will usually roll completely over at least once. Horses will try to roll several times and if not successful, will stand up, lie down on the other side and try again.

After a good roll, a horse will get back on its feet, shake the dirt from its coat, and go about its business.

While Mrs. Ryan was getting the stove heated up and cooking supper, Shorty and Matt started digging postholes for the fence. Where the gate was going to be, at the spot where most of the wagon tracks were, they dug a hole on each side about fourteen feet apart. These holes had to be bigger and deeper to put the gateposts in. The hole for the main gate post, which would carry the gate, had to be especially deep. There would be a lot of weight on this post and Shorty didn't want it leaning over. Most ranches had two long logs with a crosspiece on top; this made it easier to hold the posts straight. Braces could be put in the top corners to hold the arch square. When Shorty came over the next time, he would bring the posthole digger from the ranch but in the meantime, they could get a start on digging the holes.

Shorty paced off the distance he wanted the posts to be and got Matt to push a small stick in the ground to mark the spot. It is much easier to keep a fence solid and tight if it is straight and for a wire fence this is especially important. It wasn't quite so critical for a pole fence, but it looked much neater if it was straight. Before they got themselves in too deep of a hole, they were called to supper. They both washed up before going inside, to a meal of baked beans, bread, and cold meat. When they were almost filled up with this, there were hot biscuits, tea, and cold milk. For desert, there were doughnuts, made the day before. Shorty was surprised at being served doughnuts. He had thought he was full, but he put away a few doughnuts with another cup of tea.

"Ma'am," he said, "you could do good, making and selling doughnuts, 'bear sign' to most cowpokes. They never get enough of them. If you were in town, you could make a living selling coffee, tea, and doughnuts." "That might be," she said," but we don't live in town and we don't plan to. Matt and I have worked hard for the past year to keep this ranch going. As long as we are able, we are going to be here. Someday, this will belong to Matt, but right now we are partners. I don't think he would be any happier in town than I would be. Thank you for the suggestion, but here we'll stay. If you like my doughnuts so much, I'll try to have fresh ones made before you arrive."

"Well, ma'am," Shorty said, "thank you for the meal, now I better get outside and work some of it off digging postholes. If you don't mind, I brought my bedroll with me and I'll bed down in the hay later. That way I won't be wasting time riding back to the ranch tonight and back here in the morning." All three worked for a few more hours before calling it a day. They then sat on the front step and talked for a bit before turning in.

Chapter 2

EARLY THE NEXT morning, Shorty was out repairing the corral fence. A few minutes after he started, there was smoke from the house. A short time later, he was called to the house for breakfast. It consisted of home grown, home-smoked bacon, hot biscuits and tea and cold milk. "I'm sorry we don't have any eggs," Mrs. Ryan said, "but a coyote got the last few chickens we had. I haven't figured out how to get a few more to get started again."

"This is a fine meal even without the eggs," Shorty replied, "It's the kind of meal to stick with a person and give him enough ambition to work." After breakfast, Shorty and Matt dug a few postholes and repaired a few shaky spots in the corral fence. There were lots of small jobs to be done even though it was Sunday. They worked at several light projects until Matt's mother called them in to dinner. After a good meal, they spent a few minutes talking over what had to be done before leaving the house. As they crossed the yard, Shorty asked Matt, "Did I hear you mention that your ma had a birthday coming up soon?" Matt replied, "Yes, her birthday is about two weeks away. I wanted to get her something nice, but we have no money. What little we have has to be used to buy things we really need."

"Well, Matt," Shorty said, "since we can't buy something for her, how about we do something to make her work easier? We've got to be careful she doesn't get wind of it, though. Now, you go get a couple of those small ends we cut off those fence rails. Then we need some lumber. Are there any boards around here?" Matt replied, "Yes, there is a big pile of boards to one side of the hayloft. My Dad brought them home a couple of years ago." Shorty said, "OK, Matt, let's go get a few, and then I'll explain what we're going to do."

They went up in the loft and, sure enough, there were a lot of boards of different lengths and widths. Shorty told Matt, "We need that four-inch board and a long-eight inch without any big knots," These were carried down to where they had room to work. Matt went outside but was soon back with some fence rail ends. "Now, Matt," Shorty said, "You help me hold these while I cut them at the right angle." Shorty cut two small poles with a very long slash. Then he put the cut ends together evenly and cut the other ends square and about thirty inches long. Next he cut two pieces of the four-inch board about three feet long. "Now, Matt," Shorty said, "You get that can of nails and the hammer from the shed, and we'll get to work."

Shorty nailed two of the poles to each end of the narrow board. This made a rough but serviceable sawhorse. They repeated the operation and soon had two sawhorses. A couple of short boards made a workbench to work on. A small scrap of lumber was nailed to one end. "This is just temporary, Matt, so I didn't drive the nails all the way in," Shorty explained, "that makes it easier to take them apart. I think I saw a carpenter's plane in the house. You go get it, and I'll have a job for you to do."

Shorty cut a piece off the eight-inch board just a bit over three feet long, then cut two pieces three feet long. He realized he needed more lumber, so he went for another eight-inch board. Matt was back with the plane by this time. "OK, Matt, we're going to make a sink for your ma. Now, put this board against that small piece and use the plane to make it smooth." When Matt had the first piece smooth, Shorty marked a line on it while Matt smoothed the other two pieces. Matt held the first board while Shorty sawed it at an angle across the middle. Then using one piece turned around for a guide, he cut the exact angle on the other end. Then the piece with two angles was laid on top of the second one and cut so both pieces were exactly the same angle and length. Shorty used the plane to round off the long edges of the angled pieces, and then he rounded both corners on one side of the long boards. These were nailed together to form a flared rectangle three feet long and about twenty inches wide at the top. Then Shorty trimmed and fitted two long pieces in the bottom or narrow side of the rectangle. A couple of strips of wood were nailed on the bottom, from side to side to keep the bottom boards from sagging.

Matt spoke up then, "Won't the water leak out through the cracks?" Shorty answered, "You take this up the creek where your ma won't see it. Put it in the water so it will stay wet. When it swells up, it won't leak a drop. First, I better bore a drain hole in one corner. Wood is easier to work with when it's dry." When Matt returned a few minutes later, Shorty told him, "When we were up on the hill the other day, I think I remember seeing a wet spot. It might be a spring. Let's go see." They went up on the hill behind the house. Sure enough, there was a wet spot with a patch of reeds growing in it. They had brought along a shovel and pick and set to work. There was a rock ledge on the low side of the spring hole. It didn't take them long to clean out the dirt and loose rock. With twenty minutes' work, they had a hole thirty inches across and about the same depth. Matt went to the house to get a can to bail out the roily water. They dug out a little more gravel and a few stones until it was solid rock. The water seemed to be coming from a crack in the bottom of the hole and there was also a crack in the ledge on the downhill side.

Shorty explained to Matt, "We can widen this crack down a few more inches so we can run the water out. After we get a pipe in here, we'll seal it up and put a cover over the spring to keep it clean." Matt then asked, "How are we going to get the water to the house? Are we going to build a sluice or something?" Shorty answered, "You're thinking, Matt. That would work, but there would always be dirt falling in the water. I have a better idea. Let's go back to the barn." Shorty told Matt, "You climb up there and slide down a bunch of narrow boards." Matt soon had a lot of boards standing on end. He even found some one-inch edgings in the lumber pile.

When he got back down, Shorty said, "Look here, Matt. What does this look like?" Shorty had laid a three-inch board on their worktable. He then put a three-inch board on edge on each side and laid another on top. This left a one-inch wide, three-inch-high rectangle in the middle. Matt was all smiles now. He said, "We're going to build a wooden pipe. There is one problem, though; that hill isn't straight, and a wooden pipe won't bend much." Shorty said, "Well, when we join the pipe we can angle the boards and put a bend in the pipe. We don't need a pipe this big, so we can use these edgings to make a smaller hole. A one-inch pipe will run more water than anyone needs in a house. We'll build a couple of sections of pipe so you know what to do, then you can build more while I'm at the ranch next week." Shorty used two three-inch boards and two one-inch edgings to make a one inch square pipe. "Matt," Shorty said, "When you build them, don't nail too close to the ends. We will have to trim them as we put them together. Do you know where we can find a hollow tree at least a foot through at the stump?" Matt answered, "Yes, there's one up the creek where I took the sink. I can cut it and bring it down here next week, so it will be ready. I think I know what it's for. I bet you plan to put our pipe in the middle of it to run from the hill to the house." Shorty said, "Right Matt! We'll pack moss around the small pipe to keep the water cool in summer and so it won't freeze in the winter. You sure are learning to be a thinking man, Matt. Now, it's about seventy-five feet from the spring to the house Matt, so eight sections should be enough pipe. Try to keep them out of sight, so your ma won't suspect what we're up to. Now I have to head back to the ranch so you look after things here. I'll bring that posthole digger next time and we'll get more done on that fence."

The next weekend, late Friday evening found Shorty at the Ryan spread with a posthole digger and a one handled knife, called a froe. After saying hello to Matt and Mrs. Ryan and having a cup of tea and a few fresh doughnuts, he was ready for some sleep. They all decided to head back to the hills in the morning to get some fence posts.

They were away from the ranch just as the sun came up. At the site where the posts were drying, they finished limbing the tops and cut the last ones to the proper length. Shorty had brought the draw knives and he suggested maybe the ranch could use a bunkhouse. Mrs. Ryan and Matt thought that was a good idea but decided there probably wasn't enough lumber to build one, and no way to buy more.

To this Shorty replied, "There is plenty of lumber right here, in the round. We could build a log bunkhouse. It would be cheaper and warmer too. Matt, you go look up some of those gullies and see if you can find some tamarack trees. They make a good base log and will last a long time. While you're gone, your ma and I will start dropping some of this jack pine."

They cut over a dozen trees and then Shorty took the axe and started to limb them, while Mrs. Ryan began peeling them with the drawknife. The trees peeled a lot easier, with a lot less effort, as it was getting on toward early summer. Shorty left the trees long with some top on each one. They used the peavey and sometimes the handspike together to lift the butts off the ground. It would probably be a few weeks before they got the time to start on the bunkhouse, but in the meantime, the logs would be drying. These pines were long with very few limbs, so it would be possible to get two or three logs from each tree. When it came time to haul the logs, they would be cut to the proper length right here to make them easier to handle. The trees they had cut were no bigger than ten inches on the stump, so when dry they wouldn't be too heavy to load.

Matt arrived back with the news that he had located a grove of tamarack not too far off. He said they were about a foot through and straight with very few branches except for the crown at the top. By now it was time for a snack, so the tools were laid aside. With a good appetite from working in the fresh air, the food disappeared quickly. With lunch out of the way, the wagon was loaded with fence posts, and the smaller tops put on last for firewood. These would be dropped off near the woodshed to be cut into firewood when time permitted. They spent the rest of the afternoon finishing the postholes and putting in posts. By the time supper rolled around, they had more than forty posts in the ground. This was due mainly to having a lot of the holes almost deep enough the previous weekend.

After a filling supper and a few more doughnuts, Matt and Shorty went outside. Shorty suggested they build a sluice to run water to the barn, so it wouldn't have to be carried. They got some long three and four-inch boards and began nailing them together. The four inch was nailed to the side of the three-inch board; this made a trough of equal height on each side. They went up the creek about two hundred feet to be sure of enough fall for their purpose. They carried the sections out and laid them almost end to end, overlapping a few inches. Then, with an armful of sharpened pole ends, they began to set up the sluice. They drove one stake in the ground at about a thirty degree angle. The sluice was put under a small fall in the creek, with the other end held against the leaning stake. With just enough slope to keep the water moving, another stake was driven in to make an X, narrower at the top. Matt went to the barn and got a corner of board, which was tacked in the sluice to stop the water flow. The next section was held under the first in the X and held by one person as the other drove the stakes. Enough water seeped through the stopper to allow them to see that the correct grade was kept. One nail was driven in the posts where they crossed to keep them in place. When they got to the barn, the sluice was almost three feet off the ground. A short section of sluice was built of eight-inch boards and placed at right angles under the main sluice. One more section completed the run to the water trough. Instead of stopping and starting the water, Matt suggested taking a small corner off the stopper and letting a trickle of water run all the time. Shorty bored a hole near the top of the trough, cut a vee in the side of a short board and nailed it under the hole. A short piece of sluice was nailed in this. Shorty told Matt, "Later we'll put on a couple of sections to run the water away, so it won't get so muddy. Right now I think it's almost time to hit the hay." Next morning as usual, everyone was busy with the morning chores. Matt normally milked the cow and fed the one calf she had. It was a young heifer, so in a couple of years there would be two milk cows. He also made sure there was water for the stock, which wasn't going to be a problem in the future.

After a good breakfast, the boys were back outside and busy. They worked at the fence for a while and at a few other smaller jobs, until Dawn called them in for dinner. After the meal, as they worked, Shorty asked Matt, "How are we going to get your mother away from here next weekend? If we could get her away from the ranch, even for half a day, we could get that sink and water hooked up and surprise her. Have you got any ideas? Does she go visiting very often, or even into town?"

Matt's answer was this; "She doesn't go visiting much because there is always so much to do here. We only go to town about once a month to get what we need. We don't have much money to spend, so there isn't much we can buy. Hey, it's just about time to plant the garden! Maybe we could send her to town to get some seeds. She won't go for a few seeds though, what else do we need?" Shorty said, "Well, we could use a few pounds of nails, two and a half and four inch for the fence. We could also use a few lengths of pipe for a stove when we get the bunkhouse built. We should be able to make up a big enough list that she would go to town for it. You could mention a few things we need and start a list, but don't let her go to town until Saturday. Tell her there might be something I want her to pick up, when I get here."

The boys were all smiles now, thinking they were going to have a chance to surprise Matt's mother. The work seemed to go a lot faster, now that they had a plan they thought would work. Soon it was time for Shorty to head back to the Axe. The week on the big ranch was hard, but the time seemed to fly by. It seemed like only a couple of days until it was Friday again. About noon, Shorty met up with the boss's wife in the yard. "Ma'am," he said, "I've been meaning to ask you for a favor. Would you sell me a couple of your older hens and that stove-up rooster?" She smiled and said, "Are you going to start your own chicken ranch, Shorty?" "No, Ma'am," he replied, "I've been helping out at the neighbour's place for a bit. A varmint got their hens and I thought I'd get them a few to get a flock started again. A few of those older ones would lay a bit and hatch out a few settings to get them started."

"Shorty," she said, "The chickens will be heading for the roost right after supper. At seven o'clock, I'll have a few chickens in two sacks by the door of the coop. You pick them up and take them with you. Would they be worth fifty cents?" Shorty answered, "Ma'am, they are worth a lot more than that. You take this dollar and we'll call it square. I sure do thank you for your help. Now, I better get back to work before the boss sees me loafing and fires me!" She laughed and said, "Yes, Shorty, I'm sure there's a real danger of you getting fired."

With the day's work done and a good meal under his belt, Shorty saddled up, fastened the two sacks together with a nail, hung them on his saddle, and headed for the Ryan ranch. He thought the sacks were heavy for a few chickens, but figured they must be big ones. When he got to the ranch, just before dark, Matt helped to carry the chickens to the chicken coop. When they opened the sacks, they found there were four chickens in one sack and three chickens and a rooster in the other. All looked to be young, none more than two years old. "Seems like the boss's wife made a mistake Matt," Shorty stated, "I asked for a few older ones just to get you started again. I'll have a talk to her when I get back. Now, let's go see if we can talk your ma into disappearing for a few hours tomorrow."

Shorty and Matt told Mrs. Ryan what they needed. Shorty also suggested another roll of tar paper, for when they started on the bunkhouse, as there was only a part roll in the shed. Mrs. Ryan told them; "I don't think I should leave here with so much to do, but since you've been here Shorty, we've gotten so much done, I might be able to spare a few hours. Besides, we need some more things to work with if we're going to get anything done. OK, finish up the list and I'll make a trip to town." Matt and Shorty could hardly keep a straight face when she said she was going to town. With her away, they would have at least half a day to get running water in the house, as a surprise for her birthday.

At daylight, Matt and Shorty were outside getting the morning chores done while Mrs. Ryan prepared breakfast for all three of them. When the work was accomplished, breakfast was waiting to be eaten and they wasted no time talking when there was good food to be eaten. The boys harnessed the team and then worked at the fence until Mrs. Ryan was ready to leave for town. As soon as she was out of sight, Matt ran up the creek to get the wooden sink. It was a lot heavier now that it was soaked up with water. Shorty built a couple of triangular brackets which he fastened to the wall. The sink was placed on these and securely fastened. He put the left end of the sink about thirty inches from the corner of the room. This left room for a shelf to set things on at the end of the sink. For the drain, he made a pipe of four three-inch boards and fastened it under the hole in the sink. The first piece was about six inches long and the next section was about three feet long, cut at an angle to give it a down slope. Matt had bored a lot of holes through the wall where Shorty had marked. A hole was broken through to allow the drain to pass to the outside. One more long section would be put in place to run the waste water away from the house. When time permitted, a hole would be dug and lined with stones for the water to collect in and eventually disappear. When not busy helping Shorty, Matt was carrying sections up the hill toward the spring. When the sink was in place, Shorty helped Matt widen the crack in the rock where the outlet was going to be. He asked Matt to whittle a plug for the end of the pipe, so water wouldn't run continuously while they worked. Shorty took the pick and started digging a trench down the hill toward the house. He thought a trench a foot deep should keep the water from freezing. If the pipe didn't lie flat in the trench, he would angle the joints, so it did. From a distance it would resemble a stretched, out flattened staircase. It wouldn't be pretty, but water would flow through it! When he came to the bottom of the hill, he stopped digging. The hollow tree that Matt had brought from up the creek was brought to the site. Shorty had made a hole in the wall, high enough to allow a bucket to sit in the sink for filling. Four stakes were driven onto the ground and the hollow log was placed between them. With one end resting on the hill, Shorty held the other end while Matt nailed a crosspiece under it. The last section of pipe was slid through the middle, already fitted and trimmed, to complete the job. Matt had collected several sacks of dry moss, which was packed loosely in around the pipe. Shorty bored a few holes in the bottom of the hollow log to allow any leakage to drain out. This pipe was connected to the last one on the hillside, and the pipe was complete. The pipe was supported on the ground where it left the hill and where it went through the wall. The hollow log was supported in the cradles that were built for it. Where the pipe came out of the spring, moss was packed around it and then clay from the creek was packed on the low side. The soil was scraped away from the spring and a square of boards placed around it, other boards were cut to fit as a cover and then a double layer of tar paper was put on top to seal it. The top would be covered with soil later. Everything was ready for a test run! Matt removed the plug from the upper end of the pipe and they both hurried inside to see the results. Clear, cold water was splashing into the sink and running down the drain. They both sampled the fruit of their labour: the water was clear and cold, but had a definite woody taste.

Matt said, "Maybe if we leave the water running, it will wash the pipes out and it will taste better. First though, I'm going to see if this plug will work in here." He pushed the plug into the pipe and the water stopped, except for a few drops. "Well, Matt," Shorty said, "I think your mother will be pleased with this, don't you?" Matt grinned and answered, "I'm sure she will be. Now I won't be carrying in water and spilling it on the floor. Nobody will have to carry water to the house now!"

They were both feeling good with the results of their work. "Now Matt," Shorty said, "let's go make one more section of drain pipe and dig a hole for the waste water." When the spot was marked off, Matt set to work digging while Shorty built a set of shelves to fasten to the wall at the end of the sink. There were four shelves, a foot wide and twenty inches long. A flat surface, as wide as the sink and eighteen inches long was level with the top of the sink, with the shelves against the wall above it. Shorty was only a short while finishing the shelves and then he went outside to help Matt. Shorty told Matt, "I'll keep digging here. You go put the dirt back in the trench over the pipe. Pile it up as much as you can to keep it from freezing when it gets cold. When we get this hole dug, we'll line it with rocks and cover it over too. Your ma should be back before long and hopefully we can have it all finished before then. We won't cover the spring in case she wants to see it."

They both worked hard to get everything done before Mrs. Ryan got back from town. They were inside having some cold biscuits and colder water when they heard the horses and wagon. Matt's ma drove the horses to the barn as most of the material would go in the shed. Matt and Shorty hurried outside to help unhitch and unharness the team. They both kept talking to keep her with them until they were ready to surprise her. They each carried a box of the supplies from the wagon to the house and set them on the table.

Mrs. Ryan heard water running and looked around. She got a shocked look on her face, and her eyes got shiny and bright. She started to cry, threw both arms around Shorty's neck and then she really began crying. It was now Shorty's turn to be shocked! He awkwardly put one arm around her and patted her back gently, as if he thought she might break. Shorty said, "I'm sorry if we did something wrong, we thought you would be pleased with what we've done."

Between tears and sobs, Mrs. Ryan said, "Oh Shorty, don't you know anything about women? We always cry when we're happy. Right now I think I'm the happiest woman in the world. You have done so much for us since we met you. I don't know how I'll repay you." With tears streaming down her face, Dawn kissed Shorty on the cheek. Shorty was so shocked he almost fell over.

"Now ma'am," Shorty stammered, "Don't go blaming all this on me. Matt here did just as much work as I have. In fact, he's been working hard through the week when I'm not here and keeping things out of sight so we could surprise you." Shorty reddened and said, "Seems like we did!" Dawn called Matt over to her and put her arms around both her 'Men,' and cried some more. Both Matt and Shorty were red faced. After a few minutes, her crying began to ease off.

Shorty suggested, "Ma'am, if you'd like we could show you some of what we've done." Mrs. Ryan backed up a step, looked Shorty in the eye and said, "Shorty Stout, I don't want to hear you call me 'ma'am' again! My name is not 'ma'am!' My name is not 'Mrs. Ryan!' My name *is* Dawn! From now on, you will call me Dawn! Do you understand me? If you call me 'Ma'am' again, I'll run you off this place with that shotgun!" Shorty was shocked and red faced. "Yes, m . . . Dawn," he said, "I'll try." With that, Mrs. Ryan, Dawn, took hold of Shorty's left hand and Matt's right and they went out to show her their latest project.

Dawn asked, "Where did you get the pipe to run the water through?" They took turns explaining how they had built the pipe without her knowing about it. They had also built the wooden sink and cleaned out the spring in secret. Matt explained how he had told Shorty that he wanted to get something nice for her birthday, and Shorty saying they might be able to make something for her. Dawn started crying again and said, "I think this is the nicest birthday gift I have ever received!" She cried for a few minutes then asked, "Shorty, where do you get all of your ideas for everything you do?"

SHORTY'S STORY | 35

Shorty's face got red and he replied, "I told you ma . . . , Dawn, this young man has a lot of good ideas, too. I've been teaching him to think and he's been doing a real good job of it. A little bit more experience and he'll be better than me with his ideas. I'm not very smart, but I figure there is usually an easier way to do most jobs, and I'm too lazy to use my hands when I can use my head to make a job easier. It sure beats doing everything the hard way!"

Dawn took her men by the hand and led them back to the house, "You two sit down while I get us some supper," she told them. Matt and Shorty sat at the table and talked to Dawn as she got a meal ready. Everything seemed so much easier with a steady supply of fresh, cold running water. After supper they did some more work on the fence around the yard. Shorty thought maybe they should go up in the hills and bring down the gate post trees, as they should be fairly dry by now. Dawn suggested making a lunch in the morning to take along. They could have a picnic, while still getting some work accomplished. Everybody had been working so hard lately, they all decided one lazy day wouldn't put them too far behind.

Next morning, after a breakfast of bacon and fresh eggs, they hitched up the team and headed for the hills. When they reached the spot where the gate posts were, work got underway. Shorty marked where the trees were to be cut and he finished limbing the tops, while Dawn and Matt cut them off. A horse was used to pull the logs to a good spot for loading. When this was accomplished, the small top pieces were loaded on top, destined for the woodpile. Since the pine logs they had fallen for the bunkhouse were in the immediate area, Shorty suggested cutting some of them to the proper length while they were here. At that point, Matt spoke up, "What about the tamarack we were going to cut for bottom logs for the bunkhouse? Maybe we should cut them, so they will be drying too. Even dry they are going to be heavy." "You're right Matt," Shorty said, "I forgot about them. Sure is a good thing somebody can still think around here. You take the axe and lead the way, I'll bring the crosscut and bucksaw and Dawn can bring along the peavey, in case we need it. This way nobody has a heavy load to carry."

It was only a short walk to the tamarack grove that Matt had found a couple of weeks ago. Shorty looked them over and decided which two he wanted. He took the axe and cut a long slim, but stiff pole about fifteen feet long. He then used the axe to notch the trees, so they would fall where he wanted them to, without hanging up or damaging any young trees. He told Matt, "You put that pole under a limb where it won't slip and just hold it. Dawn and I will use the crosscut. When I say push, you lean on that pole. OK, here we go!"

The saw was cutting well and it only took a few minute's work until the tree was ready to fall. With Matt pushing, the tree was soon on the ground where Shorty wanted it. He and Dawn used poles to lift the butt off the ground, while Matt put a section of dead tree under it. Matt then used the bucksaw to cut off the bigger limbs while Shorty used the axe on the smaller ones. Dawn used the axe to get the bark started peeling on the butt and then she sharpened a limb like a chisel. With this she could peel the bark off faster than with a drawknife. Now that the trees were growing faster, they peeled much easier than earlier in the season. Dawn could peel the tree almost as fast as Matt and Shorty cut off the limbs. When she got up to where the log was knotty and small, Shorty told her that was fine, as the top was only going to be used for firewood anyway. The next tamarack was treated to the same operation and the job was soon completed.

Shorty said, "When we come back to get them, we'll unhitch the horses and bring them up. When we get the last of the limbs off, the horses will pull them one at a time down to where the wagon is. There, we can cut them up and load them. Leaving the top on will dry them out in a short time." They went back to where the loaded wagon sat and had a cold drink while they rested a bit. "Tomorrow I think I'll get the manure spread on the garden and get the ground worked up," Matt said. "Now that we have the seeds, we should get the garden planted." Dawn told Matt, "I can help spread the manure, you can work the ground up and we can both do the planting. It shouldn't take very long with both of us working." It was getting late in the afternoon, so they decided it was time to head for home. The wagon had to be unloaded to be ready for the garden work. After a good supper, Shorty left for the Axe and a week's work there.

On Tuesday he met up with the boss's wife in the yard. "Ma'am," he said, "did I get the wrong chickens the other night? When I got to the neighbour's place, I had all young-looking chickens. I just asked for a few of your older ones to get them started." Angela smiled and said, "Shorty, you've been helping them a lot lately. Why shouldn't I help out, too? This way they have a good head start. Not only do they have a good supply of eggs, but by fall they will have chickens for the table also. Shouldn't we both be able to help our neighbours get ahead?"

"Well, ma'am," Shorty replied, "I'm just trying to help out, so I guess there's no harm in you doing the same. There sure isn't enough of this helping others if you ask me. It doesn't hurt a bit to help others." "You've got it right there Shorty," she said, "The Bible says to help your fellow man, but most folks are too busy helping themselves." Shorty said, "That's right ma'am. At least we're making a small start by helping others. I'm sure we're not alone at this, although it sure seems like it most times. I sure do appreciate your help." Shorty went back to his work, and as he worked, he kept thinking of what still should be done for Matt and Dawn Ryan.

Out on the range, Shorty had noticed a few cattle with the R-R (R bar R) brand. They weren't plentiful, but he had seen a few dozen head scattered here and there over the range. One day he was riding with Gus, one of the older ranch hands. Shorty saw a few more of these R-R cattle and he asked Gus, "Who has the R-R brand Gus? I've seen a few cattle wearing that brand, but I haven't heard much about it."

Gus answered, "That belongs to the widow Ryan. When she and her husband first came here, they registered that brand. He wasn't much of a rancher or a farmer. He could do a bit, but wasn't real handy at much of anything, seemed to be more of a city feller to me. When we're branding and see a cow with the R-R brand that has a calf, we slap the same brand on it. The boss is pretty strict about that. If a hand swings a wide loop here, the boss gets real upset. He believes in being honest, and to tell the truth, the R-R gets to put on calves belonging to Axe cows quite often. Around here you ride for the brand, but you don't swing a wide loop." Shorty said, "Thanks for the information. I believe in being honest myself, and keep a tight loop. Let's ride Gus!"

Shorty worked out the week on the big ranch and on Friday evening, he headed for the R-R. There was still plenty of work to be done there. When he arrived, he found that Dawn and Matt had the garden all planted. After a good night's sleep and a good breakfast, Matt and Shorty started on the gate posts for the main gate. The gate opening was going to be twelve feet high and fourteen feet wide. First, they got the tree with the jutting limb, situated directly in line with the hole. Next the hole was deepened to accommodate the end below the limb. Shorty wanted the limb to be about a foot above the ground. They carried over three long, untrimmed fence rails, about fifteen feet long. These were fastened together at the small end with a chain and a rope was tied to the chain. A pulley with a long rope threaded through it was secured to the chain, also. A shallow hole was dug at the base of two of the poles. With Matt and Dawn pulling on the rope and Shorty on the third pole, all three were stood up to form a tripod. The rope Dawn and Matt had been pulling on was fastened to a fence post. One of the horses was hitched to the long rope and the other end was securely fastened to the top end of the gate post. With the tripod directly over the hole, Dawn led the horse in a straight line away from the anchor rope. The gate post rose up until it was suspended in the air over the hole. Shorty and Matt, with a short rope tied to the butt, guided the gate post into the hole in the proper position. Dawn backed the horse slowly, until the post touched bottom. A twist with the peavey to turn the projecting limb to the proper position and the job was completed, except for backfilling the hole. Shorty and Matt rolled rocks into the hole and these were tamped in tightly with a small fencepost.

When the hole was half filled in, Dawn backed the horse until the rope was slack and the horse was unhitched. Dawn went back to her work until needed again.

Shorty went to the shed for a ladder while Matt went to the house for some string. While Shorty steadied the ladder, Matt went up and drove two nails into the post near the top. The nails were at about ninety degrees to each other. He hung the string on the first nail and Shorty tied a couple of nails on the bottom. If the string was the same distance from the pole at the top and bottom, the pole was straight. Shorty nudged the pole a bit and the string was moved to the second nail. When the pole was straight enough to suit, Matt shoveled soil into the hole while Shorty compacted it with the fencepost.

To set up the second post, the tripod was 'walked,' over to the other hole. This was accomplished by moving one leg and then another, until the tripod was in the correct position over the second hole. The anchor rope was refastened and they were just about ready. The anchor rope kept the tripod from pulling over until the weight was pulling straight down. Again Dawn led the horse as Shorty and Matt guided the pole into place. When it was solidly tamped in place, the tripod was 'walked' to the center of the opening.

The space between the gate posts was measured and the top log was trimmed for length. Where the inside edge of the uprights came, Shorty sawed one-third of the way through and the outside end was split off and squared. This made a flat surface to sit on top of the gate posts. Shorty had measured and trimmed one post to match the height of the other. Dawn led the horse again to pull the top log up into place. Matt was up the ladder with a board, hammer, and nails. When he had the log in the correct position, he nailed the board solidly to both logs to hold them securely. Meanwhile, with a long board, Shorty pushed the other end into position and Dawn lowered it into place. Matt moved the ladder and fastened this end also. Shorty chopped out a peg sixteen inches long, while Matt bored a hole through the top log and into the upright. Then

Matt drove this peg in solidly. The process was repeated on the other gatepost.

Shorty then went up the ladder with a two by four. This was placed against the top log and the upright and marked with a pencil. Shorty then sawed a notch two inches deep and used a chisel to make it flat and square. The two by four was trimmed to fit snugly and nailed securely in place. This process was repeated on the other end and a solid, square arch was completed. The projecting stub of limb was trimmed for length, shaped square and flat on top and a hole was bored two-thirds of the way through. The hinge log was trimmed, so there was a half inch clearance between it and the top log. Matt had bent a light iron strap around the top and bottom of the log and bolted it in place, to prevent the log from splitting. A hole was bored in the center of the hinge log, top and bottom. An iron rod of the proper length was driven into the bottom hole. Matt measured the distance and bored a hole down through the top log. A rope was tied to this log about one quarter of the way down and the end of the rope was tossed over the top log. With Matt pulling on the rope and Shorty lifting, the smaller log was soon upright and lowered until the pin was placed into the waiting hole. Matt went up the ladder and drove a pin through the top log into the hole in the hinge log. Now that the heavy work was done, the gate could be finished with little effort.

Shorty decided to bore holes and pin the horizontal poles to the upright hinge pole. He used the axe to square the face of the hinge pole and marked where the holes would be. He trimmed a four-inch pole for the latch end, while Matt was boring holes in the ends of the horizontal poles and the hinge pole. He also bored holes in the short upright at the latch end as Shorty was making wooden pins. Three short poles were notched into the horizontal poles and nailed. The gate had been constructed on the ground then it was held into its proper position and securely pegged. Matt had found a small light chain in the shed and this was bolted near the top of the hinge pole and fastened to the bottom of the gate at the latch end. Supported in this way, the gate couldn't sag. It was a heavy gate but it swung easily. All that was required now was a latch to hold it shut. That could wait for a bit as the fence wasn't completed yet. Right now the triangle was telling them dinner was ready. A good morning's work had been done, now it was time for a break.

Chapter 3

DAWN HAD A good hot meal prepared and the boys were ready for it. While they were enjoying their dinner, a couple of rumbles of thunder could be heard off in the distance. Very soon it was close enough to make the dishes rattle and then the rain began to fall. Dawn looked out the door and said, "the chickens are still outside, so I guess it's going to rain for a while. This warm rain should give the garden a good start. If this lasts for a few hours, what are you men going to do this afternoon?" Shorty looked at Matt and said, "Well, Matt, do we have any inside jobs that would keep us under cover this afternoon?" Matt replied, "I guess we can always find something to do, but most of what we have to do is outside."

Dawn had a sly smile on her face as she said, "I have a small project that will keep you out of the rain for an hour or two. I would like to have a better wood box. Would it be possible for you to build one in the wall, so it could be filled from outside?" Shorty looked at Matt, "What do you think, partner. Can we do that for your ma?" Matt had a big grin on his face as he answered,

"Yep, I think between the three of us, we can come up with something." They all agreed the new wood box should be close to the stove.

Shorty took a few measurements and matt wrote them down. Since the stove took sixteen-inch wood, they would build the wood box twenty inches wide inside and thirty inches high. Dawn thought if it was narrower at the bottom, it wouldn't take up so much floor space. With all the specifications written down, the boys headed for the barn, trying to dodge raindrops on the way.

With their sawhorses set up, they began to saw and hammer in tune with the thunderstorm. They soon had a box twenty inches by two feet on the bottom. Both sides flared until it was twenty inches by three feet on the top. Matt covered the outdoor side with tar paper held on with strips of wood. This sealed the cracks, so wind wouldn't blow through in cold weather. The wood box was soon completed, except for a cover. They carried the wood box over to the woodshed and began measuring again. The exact dimensions were transferred to the wall of the house, where the wood box was to be located. It was quite a job to get the handsaw started, to cut a hole in the wall, but it was soon accomplished. When the hole was ready, they began pushing the box through the wall. With a bit of trimming, it was soon in place. Shorty asked Dawn for a few strips of heavy cloth, which he folded a few times and held them on the top edge of the box while Matt tacked them in place. This made a seal to keep out drafts. After a wide board was trimmed to fit and slid through the wall on top of the box, a seal was tacked on the outside top as well. The wide board protruded about two inches on each side of the wall. After a few more measurements, Shorty went to the barn to build two lids. When these were set in place, Matt tacked on a strip of leather for a hinge. Strips of wood were nailed against the box and the wall to seal the joints. The wood box was now complete! Matt and Shorty went outside, lifted the lid, and filled the new wood box from outside.

Dawn was more than pleased with the results of their work. "It's so much better than I thought it would be," she said. "How do you manage to do everything so well and still make it look so easy?" "Don't blame me for all this," Shorty answered. "Remember, this was your idea, and I have a good partner here to help. My pappy always said if a job is worth doing, it's worth doing right. I don't know if I do things right or not. I just do it the best I can. I've shown Matt a few things, but the most important thing I've shown him is how to think for himself. If a man stops and thinks, he can come up with a solution to most problems. I think there is an easier way to do most things, and if I think about it, I can usually find it. Matt is going to be a good thinker too, I'll bet."

Everyone was pleased with how the latest project had turned out. Since the rain had stopped, Shorty and Matt gathered up their tools and went outside. It was past mid-afternoon by this time, kind of late for starting a new project, so Shorty said to Matt, "What would you say about looking for a good spot for the bunkhouse?" Matt thought that was a great idea and said, "Maybe if we decide where it's going to be, we could bring down a load of logs tomorrow. With everything ready, we could do a bit in the evenings!"

They stood in the yard and looked all the area over carefully. Shorty said, "We don't want it too far away, but then again we don't want it too close to the house, either. What would you say about putting it over by that little hill?" Matt also thought that was the best spot. They decided to start work right now to get the area ready. They took a pick, shovels, and even a hoe. First, the site was measured off and small stakes pushed into the ground to mark the corners. There was a bit of slope to the ground, so it would have to be leveled. The soil was loosened with the pick, then scraped and shoveled to the low side. Rocks and small stones were placed on the low side to help hold the soil. They would have to dig into the bank a few feet past where the cabin would be set, to allow for drainage. As they worked away, Matt suggested, "Why don't we dig a couple of more feet into the hill, then extend the roof on this side? That would give us about six or seven feet for storing wood or anything else that needs to be under cover. Maybe we could build a hole-in-the-wall wood box here, too." "Now that's thinking, Matt," Shorty said. "I was kind of wondering how we would keep some wood dry for the bunkhouse. I thought of extending the roof on the front to make a porch and to store some wood. Let's do some more digging."

As they dug farther up the hill, the wall of earth got higher. When it got to be five feet high, they decided that was far enough. As the soil was moved to the low side, the flat area got wider. They planned to have the bunkhouse ten feet by sixteen feet inside. This would give them room for four or even six bunks if that many were needed. Shorty got a piece of paper and drew a rough sketch of the floor plan for the future bunkhouse. They planned on having two double bunks, one on each side at the back. This would leave about four feet between the bunks. A window would go near the middle of the long wall toward the house. The door would go in the center of the end wall, with another window to the left of the door. A table would set between the windows, giving it lots of light. A stove would be placed in the middle of the room, so it would warm the whole place evenly. With this rough plan, Shorty could figure how many logs of each length were needed. This would save a lot of waste, and shorter logs were a lot easier to work with.

Shorty and Matt marked off where the cabin was going to be again as all the markers had been removed. With the extra space on the high side, most of the logs could be piled there, where they would be close. The shorter ones could be piled at the front and back ends. As they say, time flies when you are having fun, and here it was supper time again.

After supper, Matt thought about the tamarack logs they had cut and drying up in the hills. He said to Shorty, "Some of those logs will be hard to get the wagon close enough to load. Maybe we could pull them out with a horse to where we could load them," Shorty then said, "We could probably build a scoot sled to haul them out with. That way they wouldn't be getting dirty and scraped up." Matt said, "OK, how do we build a scoot sled?" Shorty asked Matt. "Do you know where to find a couple of small trees with a curve in the butt? There should be some growing on a sidehill where they get bent over, then try to grow straight again. We need two, about five or six inches through and about eight feet long." Matt thought for a bit then said, "I think there are some up the creek where I got that hollow tree. I'll get the bucksaw and go up and look around."

They took the axe and bucksaw and went up the creek; it didn't take long to find a couple of trees suitable for what they wanted. Ten minute's work had the trees cut down and limbed, ready to carry out. Since the trees weren't very heavy, Shorty took the butts on his shoulder and matt carried the tops. They dropped them on the ground by the barn, where they were handy to the tools. Shorty showed Matt how to shape the ends, while he went to the shed to look for some hardware. He found a couple of bolts and a couple of iron rods; he also got a small auger to bore the holes. The curved ends were held together where Matt had beveled them and a hole was bored through both. The bolt was driven through and tightened securely. Next a pole about five inches in diameter was placed on the runners about four feet from the curved ends. A hole was bored through the top piece and half way through the bottom pieces. The short rods were driven into these holes until almost through the bottom. The rods fitted tightly and protruded from the top a few inches, which would help to hold the logs or wood on the sled. A short piece of wood was nailed across the curved ends one foot behind where they had been bolted. There in front of them sat a completed scoot sled!

Matt looked at it for a minute then asked, "How do we keep the logs on the sled? It looks kind of small to me." Shorty grinned and said, "We don't put the whole log on the sled Matt, just the butt. When we finish limbing them, we bring the sled to the butt of the log. We put the butt on the bunk, bring the chain back under the bunk, over the log and back under the bunk and hook it to the other end of the chain. When the chain tightens up, it holds the log on as it pulls it. At the next log the chain is slacked off, the log is put beside the first and hooked up again. The pointed ends of the sled will go around stumps, rocks, trees, roots, or whatever gets in the way. Only the top of the log drags in the dirt, and it is going to be firewood anyway. When we get the logs to the wagon, we can cut them to the proper length. Now, if you don't have any more questions, I think it's time to hit the hay so we can get some work done tomorrow!" Matt grinned and said, "Nope, no more questions . . . for now. I'll probably think of some later!"

The next morning saw Shorty, Matt, and of course, Dawn, on the way back to the hills to haul the first load of logs for the bunkhouse. As they hauled the logs, with one horse, out to where they could be loaded on the wagon, they placed them on small sticks to allow for easier sawing. While Shorty and Matt were getting more, Dawn began to cut them where Shorty had marked them. She was able to saw them almost as fast as the boys could haul them out. Since most of the tree had been peeled, except for the top, the logs were surprisingly dry and light. They were fresh smelling and a light golden yellow, with hardly a mark on them. They would make a beautiful and warm log bunkhouse. Dawn thought if the bunkhouse was built bigger, she might want to live in it!

When they got all the logs hauled out to where they could load them, Shorty got out his plan to figure out how many they would need of each length. Dawn had a lot of them cut already, so it didn't take long to finish cutting the rest. When the wagon was loaded, they tossed on a few of the firewood pieces to lay the logs on. The logs were clean and nice and they wanted them to stay that way. When they got back to the ranch, they piled the logs on sticks on the storage area side of the future bunkhouse. As they finished unloading, Shorty said, "We forgot our tamarack base logs, Matt. Maybe you and I could go back and get them while your ma rustles up some chow. It shouldn't take long as there are only two trees."

Shorty and Matt went back to get the tamarack logs while Dawn got some supper ready. Back in the hills, Matt got the scoot sled alongside the first log while Shorty limbed it with the axe and chopped off the top. Using a small pole, Matt pried the log onto the sled. He hooked the chain around it and pulled the sled up even with the second log. Shorty had it limbed and topped by the time Matt got it on the sled too. Since it was downhill and the butt was clear of the ground, one horse could pull it easily. Without the sled, the butt would dig into the ground and one log this big would be all one horse could pull.

When they got to the wagon, they realized it was going to be a big job to get these heavy logs loaded up. It was decided to haul the tamarack home on the scoot sled. With two horses hooked to the sled, being mostly downhill to the ranch, there would be no problem to get there. Only the top of the logs would be scuffed up from dragging. Next time they came for logs, the wagon would be waiting for them. After a good hot supper, it was time for Shorty to head back to the ranch as he had another week of riding the range ahead of him.

About the time the boys were ready to hit the hay, the foreman came in. He told them, "Next Thursday is the first of July. The boss is giving everybody the day off. He said anyone that wants it can have Friday off too. A few of you might not be in any shape to work anyway! I hope all of you appreciate this as I haven't worked many places where a man got a day off and got paid for it. The boss and his wife appreciate how hard you work all week and this is their way of showing it. If I find anyone taking advantage of the ranch, you will answer to me! Now, have a good time and try to act like the gentlemen that I know you are. By the way, I'll be back here on Friday to keep the lid on this place."

Most of the boys had expected to get Thursday off, but Friday too was a pleasant surprise. They knew there was going to be a lot taking place in town. There would be a lot of contests to enter. Usually the hands from each ranch got together to show everyone how good they were. There were no prizes, as most of the ranches were pretty well matched. What one ranch lacked in one area, they made up for in another. Cowboys doing their trick riding and roping were the main attractions. There were lots of contests for teams to enter. There was log sawing, wood splitting, log tossing, and many others. Most contests had three-age levels:

ten and under, ten to fifteen, and adult. Not many boys over fifteen would enter a child's contest anyway. They felt they were an adult by this time and most people agreed that they were.

There was a greased pig catch for everyone under twelve. Half a dozen young pigs were coated with lard and turned loose. This event created a lot of noise as pigs squealed, children screamed, and most of the crowd cheered everyone, including the pigs. Sometimes this contest lasted for hours until the pigs got rolled in the dirt enough that someone could hold on to them. Young and old looked forward to this event.

The first of the week, Angela drove over to visit Dawn. When she got close to the buildings, she could see a big change in the place. When Dawn came out of the house, she heard Angela singing;

> Shorty Stout has been about,
> And everything's just dandy;
> He can do 'most anything,
> Because he is so handy.

Dawn asked her, "Where did you hear that song and how did you know Shorty has been here?" Angela replied, "I heard the boys singing this song on the weekends when Shorty is away. There is a lot more but I haven't heard it all. I'll ask some of the boys to write it down, sometime. As soon as I saw how much work had been done here, I knew it was Shorty's work. We've been wondering where he's been spending his weekends. He did the same on the Axe and it wasn't a bit rundown. Does he know we are sisters?" Dawn said, "I don't think so. I've never heard it mentioned, and I know he never did."

Angela told Dawn, "I came over to see if you were going to town for the first of July. All the hands have the day off and will be in town as this is always the biggest event of the year. There will be all the usual contests, a box social, and a dance in the evening." Dawn thought she had too much to do, but Angela finally convinced her to go into town with her. Angela said, "I didn't know this was where Shorty was spending his weekends. He did say he was helping a lady and her son. I'm going to convince him to collect this 'young man' he's been helping and take him to town. I'll be along later to pick you up. Now, what contests are you going to enter besides baking?" Dawn replied, "Shorty is really impressed with my doughnuts, so I'll enter that one, maybe I can come up with some other ideas later."

Work went on at both ranches as the First of July was getting closer. Most people were excited as in these times there weren't many celebrations held. Very soon it was Wednesday evening and the next day was the First. Everybody was taking a bath, washing clothes, shining boots, and many other things to get ready for town and the First of July celebrations. Angela had been talking to Shorty and convinced him to take this 'young man' he'd been helping, to town with him. Early the next morning, Shorty with a borrowed horse and saddle, was on the way to the R-R. He asked Dawn if she was going in but she said she had too much to do at home. She gave Matt and Shorty a package of doughnuts to take with them. They rode into town and found a place to leave their horses and unsaddled them. They began to check out some of the things that were going on around town. There were lots of people displaying the things they had for sale. Even this early, the town was a busy place and it was bound to get a lot busier. The street would soon be lined with people selling everything from apples to xylophones. In between there would be tools, toys, and livestock. Sometimes a lot of money would change hands on the First of July holiday. About ten o'clock the games and contests began. There were footraces for the younger ones, as well as many other games. Matt entered the footrace for ten and under. The distance was two hundred yards. Some boys took off fast, but soon ran out of steam. Matt finished twenty-five feet in front of the boy in second place! The prizes were fifty cents for first, thirty-five for second and twenty-five for third. Matt now had some money in his pocket! He wandered over to where the baking contest was set up. There were pies, cakes, cookies, doughnuts, bread, biscuits and many other kinds of food, to be looked at, tasted and judged which one was the best. Matt knew if his mother was here, she would probably get a prize for her bread and biscuits and a sure first for her doughnuts. Nobody made doughnuts like Dawn Ryan!

There were a lot of things to look at, taste, and a lot of people to talk to. He was waiting for the other contests to start, later in the afternoon. He wanted to try the wood sawing contest with bucksaw and crosscut and the wood tossing and possibly a few others. Matt and Shorty, along with a lot of others, walked over to the Church and bought a light lunch. The money helped support the Church and there was no shortage of food. When everyone was through eating, the greased pig catching began. What a commotion this raised! There were kids and pigs going in every direction! Matt probably could have caught a pig, but felt he was too old for that. The pigs and kids raced around for more than an hour and it was hard to tell who was squealing the loudest, kids or pigs. Finally the last pig was caught and penned up. Now, it was time for the other contests to start!

First Matt tried the wood-tossing contest. Two ropes were stretched out on the ground about fifty feet apart. The judges told everyone, "You must stay behind the rope. Where the stick first hits the ground is your mark, no matter how far it rolls or bounces afterwards!" There were about a dozen boys for this contest. Matt waited until last and he threw well past all the other marks. The prizes were one dollar, seventy-five cents, and fifty cents. Matt had just won another dollar!

He entered the under fifteen contest also. Some people thought he shouldn't, but the judges said it was up to Matt, as he was competing against older boys. Matt came in third against boys twice his age! This made him feel pretty good. Next was the bucksaw contest, where each person cut two thin slices off a six-inch log and Matt got first prize in this contest. He entered a few other contests and got at least one prize in each of them. Working hard on the ranch was really paying off now!

Next was the box lunch auction. The men and boys tried to buy the lunch made by the girl they wanted to talk to, or their wife if they were married. No one was supposed to know who made them, but usually they found out ahead of time. Most of the lunches sold for between two and five dollars and there were only a few left. The auctioneer picked up the next one and read the tag, "Fried chicken, fresh bread, and doughnuts. Who will start the bidding at three dollars?" Someone started at fifty cents, another said, one dollar and it was soon past the three dollar mark originally asked for. Matt and Shorty were watching, but weren't too interested as neither knew that Dawn was in town. Matt asked Shorty what time the dance started that night. He answered, "At eight." There was such a commotion, with people talking and others trying to sell things Matt couldn't hear. He said, "I couldn't hear what you said!" Shorty repeated it a bit louder, "At eight."

Suddenly the auctioneer shouted, "Sold to that tall cowboy over there for eight dollars!" pointing directly at Shorty. Both he and Matt looked shocked as Shorty had bought lunch number seven for eight dollars. A short time later all the lunches were sold. Shorty knew he had to eat lunch with the lady who had made it. The money went to the school, so it wasn't a total loss. He gave the money to Matt and asked him to go pick it up for him. When Matt came back he was very excited. He told Shorty, "It's ma's lunch! Her name is in the basket. I didn't think she was coming to town today!"

Soon Dawn appeared and they found a spot to eat their supper. Dawn asked Shorty, "How did you know that was my lunch when you bought it?" Shorty answered, "I didn't. I didn't even buy it. I was just talking to Matt and all of a sudden it happened." As they were eating, Dawn told them she got first prize for her biscuits and second for her bread. The doughnuts would be judged right after supper. When they had finished eating, they moved over to the food display again.

The judges told everyone, "We're stuck for a winner of the doughnuts. We have narrowed it down to four contestants, but we need some help. If there is a good judge of doughnuts anywhere, it has to be a cowboy. We have cut the doughnuts in small pieces.

We want all the cowboys to come up and try them. Take one piece from each plate and then we will decide who the winner is." The cowboys did as asked. They sampled the doughnuts and then moved back a bit. The judge then picked up a number card and asked, "Who votes for number one?" Two or three hands went up. Who votes for number four?" Two or three hands went up again. Next came number seven. Four hands went up. The judge asked, "Who votes for number twelve?" The hands in the air looked like a field of hay, and a huge roar filled the area. When the judge got everyone quiet again he said, "Well, I guess that means we have a winner, now who is the best donut maker in the area?" A helper turned the plate over and the judge read the name; "Dawn Ryan!" She had won another first prize!

Everyone moved over to where the wood tossing and sawing was to take place. The wood toss was first. Shorty took first, Gus got second, and Slim got third; the Axe cleaned up on this contest. Next was the log chopping contest. Again the Axe took all the prizes, with Shorty getting first. Next up was the crosscut contest. Shorty and Gus got first while Slim and Red took third, another ranch got second. The last was the under ten crosscut contest. Half a dozen teams of boys took their turn. Matt wanted to enter but didn't have a partner. He looked at his mother and asked her to partner with him. She looked at the judge and he said, "Go ahead." Dawn said, "It wouldn't be fair." The judge repeated, "Go ahead" Again Dawn said, "But it wouldn't be fair!" The judge told Dawn, "Go ahead. The boy wants to try, so help him out. He has no other partner but you. Dawn tried to protest again but the judge said, "Even if you don't have much of a chance, you could at least try. Cut the log!"

Dawn and Matt picked up the saw and got ready. They were both trying hard not to smile too broadly. The judge hollered "*go*" and started his stopwatch. The saw was singing through the log as they pulled the saw until their partners hand almost hit the log. A steady stream of sawdust poured from the cut. When the piece fell from the log the judge called out, "The best time by more than a second!" The crowd cheered and yelled for more than a minute! When everyone was quiet again, he said, "I don't believe it! Try it once more." Dawn and Matt got ready to make another try at cutting the log. When they were ready, the judge called, "Go." Again the saw seemed to melt through the log. This time they sawed half a second off their original time! The crowd really went wild this time. The cheering and clapping went on for five minutes! The judge looked at them and asked, "How did you do that? Women don't use a crosscut saw!"

Dawn smiled and said, "This one does! I tried to tell you it wouldn't be fair! I meant it wouldn't be fair to the other contestants, not us. You see, Matt and I have been using a crosscut together for more than a year. We cut all of our own firewood. We did have a good teacher to show us the right way, for the last few months." The judge said "I'd like to meet this teacher of yours. Is he here?" Shorty stepped forward and said, "I've been giving them a few pointers and they caught on quick. As you just saw, they did it on their own." The judge said, "How about you two giving us a small demonstration?"

Shorty and Dawn picked up the saw and got ready. Shorty held up two fingers and when the judge said "go," they pulled on the saw. When the first piece fell from the log, they put the saw back on top and started again, without a pause in the action. Shortly the second slice fell to the ground and the crowd roared. When the noise finally died away, Dawn said to the judge, "Let the other best times have the prize. It wouldn't be fair to them if we kept it!"

The judge looked at the crowd and said loudly, "Did they win this prize fair and square or not?" The crowd roared, "Yes!" When Dawn could speak, she said, "Matt and I will donate this prize to the school!" All the Axe hands decided to do the same! The judge said, "Well, folks, this has been a fine demonstration of sawing and generosity. It's just about time for the dance to start. Don't forget, there will be fireworks at dark, everybody enjoy yourselves!"

Matt got Shorty aside where he could talk to him. He said, "Shorty, I've been thinking of buying a couple of hogs to raise.

There's a man over by the barn that has some to sell. He has some brown ones, some white ones, and some black and white ones. What would you recommend? I kind of like the black ones!" Shorty said, "Well, Matt, I never raised a lot of hogs myself, but I helped butcher a few. I always found the brown ones had a lot of hair and it was harder to get off when they are butchered, also they don't seem to grow as fast. The white would be a good choice. If you want my opinion, from my limited experience, I would go with the black and white, the more black the better. They seem to grow faster and they are a lot easier to get the hair off than the brown ones." Matt said, "Most of the pigs he has are over fifty pounds. He wants a dollar a head, so I'm going to get two if he still has them."

The dance soon got underway and everybody did enjoy themselves. Shorty had the first dance with Dawn and then Matt danced with her. He wasn't really good, but he tried hard and learned quickly. At dark the music was moved outside, so everybody could watch the fireworks. When the show was over, everybody moved back inside, and the dance got going in earnest. Even the people who weren't dancing enjoyed the music. A few of the men outside had been passing around a bottle or two, ever since it had gotten dark. Most men were careful about how much they drank, but there were always a few who overdid it. Loud voices could be heard from outside and a couple of men stationed themselves at the door to keep out possible troublemakers but one of the drinkers got past the guards and arrived inside. Someone told him, "Rowdy, you better behave yourself or you will be put outside. Everyone is having a good time and we want no trouble from you!"

Dawn Ryan was one of the finest looking ladies on the dance floor and she was in great demand as a partner. At this time, she was dancing with Shorty. Rowdy Ripley pushed his way through the crowd toward Dawn. He tried to push Shorty away so he could dance with Dawn, but Shorty stayed between the two. Rowdy looked at Shorty and said, "You got to eat with this woman and now you get to dance with her. I want to dance with her, too."

Shorty said, "If you ask her politely, I'm sure she will allow you to dance with her. That will be entirely up to her." Rowdy said, "I want to dance with this s . . ." The first part of Rowdy's body to hit the floor was his shoulders! His feet were a good four feet from where he had been standing. Most people never even saw Shorty's fist move. He was standing casually and the next second his fist connected with Rowdy's jaw. The music stopped suddenly!

Shorty asked, "Will someone help me carry Rowdy outside? I think he slipped or fainted." Two men took his arms and Shorty put his hands under Rowdy's knees. They carried him outside and laid him on the grass. After a few minutes, he started to come around. He asked, "What hit me, a fence post?" Someone said, "You're lucky I didn't have a fence post or I would have hit you with it. Shorty stopped you from making a fool of yourself."

Shorty helped Rowdy to his feet and said, "No hard feelings, I hope!" Rowdy felt his jaw and said, "No hard feelings? My jaw has lots of hard feelings! I probably won't be able to eat for a week!" Everyone within hearing laughed at that comment. Rowdy said, "Shorty, I'm sorry for what I did and I sure deserved what you gave me. Will you let me go back in there and apologize to Mrs. Ryan?" Some of the people there weren't too sure, but Shorty said, "OK, come with me."

As they entered the school, there wasn't a sound from anyone. Shorty and Rowdy walked across the floor to where Dawn stood. "Mrs. Ryan," Rowdy said, "I would like to apologize to you for what I did. As of right now I am a changed man. I am all through with alcohol. You might say I saw the light, in fact, I saw lots of lights, just like those fireworks!" Everyone in the school laughed at what Rowdy had said. Rowdy continued, "Everybody has known me as Rowdy for a long time. My name is Randolph. From now on, I want to be known as Randy. Rowdy is no more." The whole room full of people cheered. "Mrs. Ryan," Randy continued, "I'm not good enough to shine Shorty's boots, but if you would allow it, I would like to help Shorty with the work at your place. It won't cost you anything but a bit of grub, mostly soup for a few days!" This nearly brought the house down with laughter. Randy said,

"Anytime you want me to leave, just say the word and I'm gone. I think Shorty will see to that!" The crowd cheered. Dawn smiled and said, "Randy, we would welcome your help. You can come out tomorrow if you want to." Again the crowd cheered. Somebody said, "I think it's time to get this dance started up again!" The music started and Dawn danced with Randy. The applause nearly drowned out the music! After a happy ending, to what could have been a bad scene, everyone enjoyed themselves even more. Matt and Shorty had brought their bedrolls and had picked out a spot near their horses to sleep. About midnight, Matt said goodnight to those he knew and headed for bed. Shorty hung around until about 2:00 a.m., and then he left the party also. Dawn left to camp with a few other women, including Angela. A few people danced until the sun came up.

Shortly after daylight arrived, Shorty and Matt saddled up and headed for the R-R. There was always plenty to be done there. The work should go faster now that Randy was coming to help out. Dawn was going to bring the hogs Matt had bought, with her when she came home with Angela on the wagon from the Axe. The women would be along later as they planned to stay and help with the clean up. When Matt and Shorty got to the ranch they unsaddled, but left Matt's borrowed horse tied to the fence. When the wagon arrived, the saddle would be put on the back and the horse tied on behind. In this way, Shorty wouldn't have to return the horse, giving him more time to work at the R-R.

Matt thought, since he had two hogs coming, they should build a pen for them. Shorty agreed that was a good plan. Matt gathered up a lot of fence rail ends while Shorty sharpened them with an axe. They drove them in the ground about ten feet apart, marking off a pen about fifty feet square. They then went up the creek to a grove of small pine trees. They cut dozens of these small trees and limbed them to a small top. Since the wagon was still in the hills, Matt got a horse and the scoot sled. He piled a lot of poles on the sled and hauled them down to where the pig fence was going to be. Matt unhooked the load and the horse pulled the sled out from under the load. Back up the creek he went to get a second load. Shorty had enough poles cut to load the sled again. "That should be enough Matt," he said, "If we don't have enough, we can always come back for more." Matt hauled this load down to the pen they were building also.

"Now, Matt," Shorty said, "you go get a couple of hammers and some four-inch spikes, and maybe we will be ready when your hogs get here." When Matt got back, Shorty had some of the poles spread along by the fence posts. Shorty explained to Matt, "Always put the rails on the inside of the fence if you are keeping something in, and on the outside if you want to keep it out! As the animals push on it, they might push it off if it is on the other side of the post. We will have to put one rail right on the ground to keep a pig from getting out. They do a lot of rooting and digging, and if the bottom rail is off the ground, they will have a hole dug and be out in no time. With a big pen like this, they shouldn't bother the fence for a while. When you pull weeds from the garden, toss them in to the pigs. All the table scraps that the hens don't get, your pigs will eat too. They will need some grain, especially in the fall, but you can feed them quite cheaply through the summer. They will eat a lot of grass, too. When we get finished with the fence, we will have to build them a shelter from the rain. Maybe we can use a few boards with some tar paper on the top. We'll put that at the highest corner so it will stay dry. When it starts getting cold, we will have to build them a shed or move them into the barn. They will survive outside, but they won't grow as fast, as they will need a lot more food just to keep warm. You will have lots of pork for yourselves, and you will have some to sell or trade for something you need. We can pickle some of your pork and smoke it so you will have pork that will keep a long time. If you keep one to butcher after it gets cold enough to freeze, you will have fresh pork all winter. I think getting those hogs was a smart move on your part." Matt said, "When I went to see the man about the hogs, it was getting late in the day. He wanted to get rid of them, so he didn't have to take them home again. I got the two of them for a dollar and a half and I still have some money left!"

They were just about finished building the fence when the wagon arrived with the pigs. They decided it wouldn't hurt them to stay in the sacks for a few more minutes. The rails were about six inches apart so it wasn't long until the fence was two feet high. The pigs were turned loose in the pen as they finished the fence to the height they wanted. The pigs were so busy eating and checking out their new home, they had very little interest in the fence. Matt was now the proud owner of two black and white hogs, next winter's ham and bacon!

Chapter 4

D AWN HAD A fire going in the stove in short order, and they knew there would be a meal ready soon. About this time Randy arrived, with his bedroll tied behind his saddle. Shorty smiled and said, "Randy, you probably heard about the fellow who was going to stay with a friend. The friend said, 'I hope you can make your own bed' and the guy said, 'sure I can make my own bed'. His friend says, 'Good, here's the hammer and nails, the boards are over there.' Well Randy, there is the bunkhouse over there in that pile of logs. After we get it built, you will still have to make your own bed!" They all had a good laugh and headed for the house for dinner.

After a good meal, the boys decided to get a start on the bunkhouse. Shorty had figured to build it ten by sixteen inside, so the logs had to be about eighteen feet long. First the tamarack had to be cut to the right length and put into place. They were quite heavy, so it wouldn't be easy to carry an eighteen foot log. They got a horse and the scoot sled and pulled the log into place. With the help of the peavey, it was rolled into place. Shorty suggested the base logs should be dug into the ground a bit to keep them from rolling around. A shallow trench was dug and the log was rolled into place. The same procedure was carried out on the other side. Shorty asked Matt to go to the shed for the adze while he did some measuring and figuring. He decided to halve the base logs together but the end log should go under the side logs. The first wall log would be on the end with half its thickness protruding above the side logs. Each course would be half a log higher than its touching counterpart.

The end base logs were halved together and put into place. These joints would have to be fastened together so they couldn't spread. Matt took on the job of boring holes at each corner and driving in wooden pins, to hold the base logs solidly together. Once the rectangle was formed and secured, the floor joists had to be put into place. Small straight logs were picked out and set in place. Where each joist would go, two saw cuts were made on the inside of the base logs, a bit narrower than the joists. The wood between these cuts was chipped out with the axe and adze. The joist was then shaped to fit the notch and trimmed to a snug fit. When both ends were fitted, the joist was driven into the notch and fastened solidly. Matt went to the barn and got two long straight boards, to be used in making sure all the joists were even on top. After all the joists were in place, they would be flattened on top, so the boards would lay flat and smooth.

By the time they had the floor joists in place, Dawn was calling them for supper. It didn't look as though they had accomplished very much, but it had been a slow process, measuring, cutting, fitting and trimming, so each piece would fit snugly. Now that the floor joists were all in place, the walls wouldn't take very long to put up. After the filling supper, Dawn had ready for them, they sat and talked for a bit with another cup of tea and some of Dawn's prize-winning doughnuts. Randy said, "Shorty, I can see what brings you back here every weekend! It would be worth a days' work just to have some of these doughnuts. I don't think I ever ate better, of course, having a fine lady like this to cook your meals for you helps a lot too!"

After they finished their doughnuts, the boys decided to lay the floor for the bunkhouse. With a solid floor to work on, it would be much easier to get the walls up. Matt started carrying boards from the barn, while Shorty and Randy flattened and leveled the floor joists. Before it was time for bed, the floor was all down and nailed solidly. The bunkhouse was now starting to take shape. The door was positioned three feet from the wall to the right. This would give room for a three-foot bunk behind the door, if one was needed. It also left more room for the window that was to go in the end wall, to the left of the door. Matt had brought some eight inch wide, two inch thick planks up from the barn. These were cut and fitted together to form a frame for the door. It was three feet wide and six and a half feet high. A log had been fitted in the end wall and notched for the door frame to sit in. The frame was squared and plumbed and tacked in place. The next logs could be butted up against it. All this work had brought the time around to bedtime. Dawn had a snack and a cup of tea ready for them and of course there were a few doughnuts also. Working with an axe and saw and handling heavy logs worked up an appetite. It also made a person tired, so the hay was starting to look good.

Dawn had breakfast ready early because she knew the men wouldn't want to waste any daylight. As they ate breakfast, they discussed what they should do for the day. It was decided that another load of logs was in order, as on the previous trip they had brought mostly long logs. The wagon was still in the woods, so the team was harnessed and hitched to the scoot sled. It might not be needed, but if it was, it would be close at hand. Randy and Shorty loaded the bigger logs while Matt loaded the smaller pieces. As they worked, Shorty said to Matt, "You know Matt, if there is enough of these smaller logs left over, we could build a good shelter for your pigs. Maybe we should come back up here and cut and peel a few more logs. I have an idea for another project, but right now we have to get the bunkhouse built. It wouldn't take long to fall and peel a bunch more logs, though. They still peel a lot better than when we first started."

When the wagon was loaded, they headed back to the ranch. The wagon was left close to where the logs would be needed. It wasn't unloaded as they didn't want too many logs in the way until they could be used. They gathered up the tools they needed and went up to the bunkhouse to begin work. A log the same size as the one placed at the doorway was notched into place on the back end wall. Then two long side logs were fitted, one on each wall. The first complete course of logs was now in place!

Matt was busy sorting the logs to get uniform pairs. As each log was placed on the wall, it was alternated, so the big end rested on the small end of the one underneath. This kept the wall generally level as it became higher. If the log didn't lay closely on the one underneath, it was rolled to the inside and shaved down with an axe or adze. As the short logs were fitted on each side of the doorway, Matt drove a spike through the frame into the end of the log. He was also constantly checking the corners to make sure they were all coming up straight and true.

At this time, Dawn called for Matt to come down to the house. He helped her carry a lunch up to where they were working. Dawn had made cold meat, sandwiches, hot biscuits covered with a towel and cold milk and water. The walls were just the right height for a seat, so they ate their first meal in the new bunkhouse. When they were almost finished eating, Matt went back to the house and brought back a pot of tea and a bowl of doughnuts. It was a beautiful day for a picnic. When the food was all gone, it was time to go back to work. With a good meal under their belt, they felt like working again.

With one man at each end of the log, it didn't take very long to get a log notched into place and soon it was time to leave a place for the windows. The window frames were built of two by eight planks also. As before, a series of saw cuts were made into the top of the log and removed with an axe. About two inches of wood was removed to make a flat level surface for the frame to rest on. The frame was placed in the notch and, when square, a strip of wood was nailed from corner to corner. When the frame was plumb, a board was fastened from the top of the frame to the floor. This held the frame solidly in place. This same process was repeated for the window beside the door. The window in the end wall was made a bit narrower, as with the doorway already taking part of the wall, the window would have to be smaller. Now two walls were being formed of short pieces, which were faster to work with. As each log was butted up against the frames, Matt would drive a spike through the frame into the log. A string was stretched from corner to corner to ensure the building was kept square.

By the time supper rolled around, the walls were halfway up the window openings. It felt good to all of them to sit and rest while eating supper. They talked over what they had accomplished and what had to be done. They agreed to spend another half day cutting and peeling logs. They would need more logs to complete the storage area of the bunkhouse and there would be other uses for peeled, dry logs. In the morning, Dawn would pack a lunch and they would all go back to the hills to cut and peel logs. It would be much faster to peel the logs now, because in a few weeks, the trees wouldn't be growing as fast and it would be harder to get the bark off. June to mid July was the ideal time to peel logs while they were growing fast. As they were discussing what was to be done, Shorty tossed this idea in for comments. He said, "I think you are going to have a good garden this year from the looks of it. You should have a place to store the vegetables. I've been thinking we could build an underground root cellar. It would take a lot of digging, but a root cellar doesn't have to be very big to hold a lot of vegetables. We could dig into the hillside right here beside the house. If we made it eight feet by ten feet inside, it would hold more vegetables than you would need in a year. When they are built right, they keep everything cold but they don't freeze. I've heard of vegetables in a good root cellar a year old, looking as fresh as right from the garden. I've seen some dug in flat ground, but it would be easier if we dug into a hillside. There would be good drainage, so water wouldn't be a problem, also Matt, when your hogs are butchered, you could pickle the meat and store it in the root cellar." Everyone thought this would be a good project, but there would be no rush for a bit. Everybody agreed though, that the logs should be cut and peeled, so they would dry. Well-dried logs would last a lot longer, even in the ground. Instead of going back to work on the bunkhouse, they decided to go outside and look for the best site for the root cellar.

The house was set close to the side hill, which came in handy for running the water into the house. The root cellar could be built into this hill also, which would put it close to the house. Matt was looking at the side hill and said, "There is a bit of a low spot right here between these two humps. If we dug in there, it would save moving so much soil. On second thought though, maybe water would run down that hollow and get into the cellar." Shorty said, "That's a good spot Matt, anything that saves us some digging is a help. As for the water, there wouldn't be much, and we will need a lot of dirt to cover the root cellar. If we think water might be a problem, we could dig a shallow trench through the upper edge of that hill and run any water away. I think you picked the best spot."

Randy spoke up then, "If we had a scoop, we could use a horse with a long rope to pull a lot of the soil uphill. It would save a lot of shoveling and the soil would be up on the hill above the root cellar. It would be a lot easier to move it downhill than uphill when we have to fill it in!" "Right Randy," Shorty said, "We won't be able to move it all with a scoop, but every little bit helps. I know they have a scoop at the Axe and the boss said I could borrow anything I wanted. I'll try to bring it the next time I come over. I can flip it upside down and pull it over with my rope. It isn't too heavy so it will pull easily. Now I think we should get some shut-eye, so we can get more building material tomorrow." They all thought that was a very good idea.

In the morning, Dawn was up early, getting a good breakfast ready and packing a lunch to take with them, back to the hills where the trees grew tall and straight. She had no intention of letting them go without her. She felt she should be doing her share of the work since it was her property. Matt was helping with breakfast, while Dawn worked on the lunch. Shorty and Randy fed the horses and made sure everything was shipshape around the barn. With running water at the barn, there was much less work to be done. They soon had the horses harnessed and the tools loaded in the wagon, now it was time to go inside and wrap themselves around a good breakfast. Since Shorty was mainly a tea drinker, as was Dawn, Randy drank tea too. He usually drank coffee, but he said tea was fine with him. Most cowboys drank coffee, strong and black, but there were always a few exceptions to the rule. After a good breakfast, the horses were hitched up and the wagon was on the way to the hills.

When they got to the site where they had cut the pine and stopped, Matt said, "If tamarack will stand the moisture better, why don't we use all tamarack for the root cellar. There might not be enough left where we cut the base logs, but there are still some. At least we would have enough for the bottom where there is the most dampness." Shorty said, "You're right Matt, tamarack is better. We can use all tamarack if there is enough, if not we can use pine for the top of the walls. We don't need big logs, so we will just cut the ones under twelve inches, they won't be too heavy when dry. We can get the wagon a bit closer, and then carry our tools. OK, let's go!"

It wasn't a great distance to the tamarack grove and they could take the wagon most of the way. They tied the horses to a tree and tossed some of the hay they had brought between them. Shouldering their tools, they hiked the short distance to where they were going to work. Shorty notched the first tree with the axe, then he and Randy made short work of putting it on the ground with the crosscut. Using the peavey and a handspike (a short pole used to help lift or roll logs); they lifted the butt off the ground while Matt and Dawn rolled a piece of a dead tree under it. This kept it high enough off the ground for easier peeling, and it would help it to dry faster. Once the bark was started, a sharpened stick was used. The trees peeled so easily now, they were soon up to where Shorty and Randy were chopping the limbs off the top. As before, when they got to where the trunk was too small to be used for logs, the top was left on to draw the moisture from the log. Matt and Dawn stayed well out of the way when a tree was about to fall. This was just in case a tree broke off and fell the wrong way, but that very seldom happened when Shorty notched a tree. He took care to see that a tree went exactly where he wanted it to. When possible, they dropped trees across the logs already down and peeled. These trees didn't have to be lifted off the ground. When it came time to haul the logs home, the upper ones would be topped and moved first. When lunch time rolled around, they thought they had enough logs to build the root cellar, and some for the outer wall of the storage area at the bunkhouse. The thought of a short break and some food cheered the workers.

They carried their tools out to where the horses were waiting. The tools were placed in the wagon, and a comfortable spot was found to sit and eat. Fresh air and exercise always make food taste better and this time was no exception. When the meal was just about over, Dawn came up with a couple of doughnuts for each of them. This was a fine finish to a good meal. Before they got up from where they were sitting, Shorty said, "I think we should cut and peel a few more pine before we head back. A dozen or so should be enough. Very soon they won't peel to easy at all, so it should be done now." The crew agreed with Shorty, so the horses and wagon were moved out the trail to where the pine grew. A couple of hours were all the time needed to drop, limb, and peel a dozen or so pine trees. By the time they were needed, they would be much drier and lighter to handle. It was getting late in the afternoon, so the tools were loaded and the woods crew headed for home. Since this was Sunday, Shorty and Randy would be leaving for their home ranches after Dawn filled them with a good supper. Throughout the week, Matt and Dawn worked at their usual chores and kept the garden looked after. Life on a small ranch wasn't easy, but if they worked hard now, hopefully someday things would get easier. At least they were working for themselves, doing what they enjoyed.

The first of the week, as Matt was doing a few small jobs around the place, he was thinking of the root cellar they planned to build. If the whole thing was buried in the ground, it would be cool but not cold enough to freeze. He thought, 'I have to build something to keep my hogs in before winter. Why couldn't I dig into the bank and build a smaller root cellar for the pigs to live in? It could be buried until just the front was showing. It would need a door big enough for a person to get through but I could make a small door just big enough for a pig to go through. A feed sack over the hole would stop most of the wind, or I could make a wooden door, hinged at the top so it would swing both ways. A small yard outside would be enough for feeding and give them some exercise, but they would probably spend most of the time inside where it's warm. An armload of hay or straw should keep them comfortable. I'll run my idea past Shorty and Randy next time they are here. I guess I could start digging when I have some spare time. When we put running water in the house and to the barn, it sure saved a lot of time and work.'

The next day Matt started digging for his 'hog haven'. He picked a good spot where the pig fence could be extended to allow them to get into the shelter. Matt decided to build it seven feet wide and eight feet long inside. The small size would be warmer in winter and probably wouldn't be needed in summer, but it would be cool in hot weather. He loosened the soil with the pick and tossed it to the side but against the hillside. Matt figured the hole would have to be at least ten feet wide to allow room for the logs forming the walls. He planned to work at digging for a while and then go to a different job. No point in having all the fun at one time. He had heard somewhere 'A change is as good as a rest.' He thought, it's not quite as good but a change of work helps a lot.

When he left the digging, he helped Dawn work in the garden for a while. It was coming along fine since that thunder storm just after planting it. Maybe there was something to that tale about thunder storms making the crops grow. Someone said the lightning releases the nitrogen in the air and it comes down in the rain. Matt realized everything did grow better after a thunder storm. Dawn was talking to Matt and said, "The turnips are too thick to grow well. We will have to thin them out in a week or two. Anyplace there is a spot where something didn't grow, we will transplant turnips. I'll show you how, even though they are a bit small yet. Where they are too thick, you pull some out carefully, trying not to break off too many roots. You then break off most of the tops, being careful not to hurt the crown or it will die. Then you make a hole and plant it and watch it grow. The best time is just before, or just after a rain. If it's dry, you water it after transplanting them. If we have too many for us, the cows, horses, even your pigs will eat turnips. When we start transplanting, the hens and pigs will eat the tops. 'Waste not—want not' as they say. You know, I bet we could get enough turnip tops and pigweeds (lambs quarter), for a meal." As they worked in the garden, they gathered enough greens to make a meal. It had been nearly a year since they had eaten fresh greens, and they were getting hungry just thinking about it.

When they got the root cellar built, they would have a good place to store more vegetables, so maybe next year they could grow a bigger garden. With Matt's two hogs for meat and plenty of vegetables, the winter wouldn't look so long and cold.

Keeping busy helped the time to go by, and soon it was Friday evening and Shorty and Randy arrived. Dawn and Matt looked forward to their coming, especially Shorty. It had been only a couple of months now that he had been helping out, but it seemed a lot longer. They both commented on how well the garden looked and were told of the fresh greens they had eaten; the first meal from the garden.

Matt told them of his idea for a shelter for the pigs, and he showed them where he had already started digging in the hill. Randy told him, "Well, Matt, it seems like you will soon be as good as Shorty at coming up with ideas. In a couple of more years you will be giving him pointers!" Everybody had a good laugh at that but Matt knew that because Shorty always explained how and why he was doing something, he was causing Matt to see and think differently. Some people seemed to get their mind in a rut and couldn't see to the side, only straight ahead.

Shorty had brought the scoop with him, so they decided to work a bit at digging the root cellar. There was no rush for the root cellar, but it would give them something to do until bedtime. A horse was harnessed with collar, hames, and back pad. The full harness wasn't needed as there wasn't anything to be held back. Matt led the horse up on the hillside and a rope was hooked between the scoop and the whiffletree. Shorty would dig for a while and Randy would use the scoop, then they would trade jobs. They got a change and used a different set of muscles. A person didn't get as tired this way. After more than an hour, they called a halt to the work. This was enough for the first evening. When time permitted, or they wanted a change of work, the digging would be waiting for them. Right now, when the horse was looked after, it was time for a cup of tea and some of Dawn's doughnuts. Then, after a good night's sleep, they would be back at work on the bunkhouse.

When the rooster started telling the world it was time to rise and shine, everyone was out of bed and ready to eat. Randy and Shorty made sure everything was OK around the barn and there was plenty of feed and water for the stock. Dawn was working on breakfast, which was pancakes, bacon and eggs, hot biscuits and tea. Randy commented on the meal he was expected to eat. Dawn smiled and said, "I expect you to work and you can't do that on an empty stomach. Eat up and get to work!" Everybody laughed and dug into the good food.

Everyone was soon hard at work. Dawn had her housework to do and then there was a bit more to do in the garden. While she was working, she was thinking of what to have for dinner. With an extra mouth to feed, it took a bit more planning. She didn't mind though, as the extra mouth to feed also did an extra day's work. She didn't have to spend as much time outside now, although she enjoyed being outside. The three men were busy at the bunkhouse. They put a log in place, measured, marked, and notched it, tested the fit, and sometimes adjusted the notch.

When the notched ends fit well, sometimes the middle had to be shaved down a bit. It took time, but the walls were going up one log at a time. Matt was doing whatever he could to help. He held the logs steady while they were being worked on, as well as making sure the corners were square and straight. If something was needed from the house or barn, Matt was the 'Gofer.' There were a lot of things he could do to help, even though he wasn't big enough to do all the jobs. Little by little, log by log, the walls crept higher. By the time Dawn came out to get them for dinner, they had the walls almost to the top of the window openings. She was very impressed with the progress being made. Right now, it was time to put on the nosebag, so they made a beeline to the house to get cleaned up for dinner. As the meal was being eaten, they discussed how they were doing and what they should be doing. Randy thought that, although it wasn't really necessary, they should install ceiling joists. If they were put in similar to the floor joists, they would make the building stronger and keep it from spreading. Shorty agreed that putting in ceiling joists would make the building a lot stronger. They talked about this for a few minutes and decided to put in three joists, four feet apart. The ceiling joists could be smaller than the ones in the floor, as they would carry very little weight.

After a last cup of tea and a donut, they were back at work. A short while later, the sidewalls were as high as they had planned for, now it was time to put in the ceiling joists. They were put in place almost identically to the floor joists. When in place, they were fastened solidly with wooden pins and six-inch spikes. A few boards were tossed up on them to give them something to stand on while working.

Now it was time to decide what they were going to use for rafters. Should they use heavier poles four feet apart or lighter poles closer together? They settled for five-inch poles for rafters, directly over the ceiling joists, this would allow them to build a truss, so the roof couldn't sag. They also planned to put lighter poles in between the main rafters, making a very solid roof. Shorty decided a three-foot peak would be high enough, as the building wasn't very wide. They would put a shallow notch on the underside of the rafter and notch the wall logs a bit deeper. They also wanted a two foot overhang, at the least, to put the water farther away from the building. On the high side of the bunkhouse, the rafters would be longer to cover the storage area. The smaller leftover wall logs would work for that side. They looked through the logs and found enough of the smaller plate logs, of the right size to do. These were moved to the proper position and leaned against the wall. Five pairs of rafters were placed where they could be reached from up above, short on one side, long on the other. They decided to put the rafters over the end walls and fill in the gable ends later. Only the three inside rafters would need to be trussed.

The wall notches were mainly on the outside, so they could be cut with a saw and split out with the axe and adze. All the notches were cut a bit narrow, so the rafters could be shaved down with the axe to fit snugly. The top ends were bevelled before the notches were cut, so everything joined tightly. Where the rafters sat on the wall, Matt bored a hole and drove a wooden pin to join the rafter to the wall securely. When they built something, they built it to last! The long rafters on the uphill side were clear of the ground, so a piece of trimmed log was placed under each to prevent sagging. Soon there would be a wall built under it. Where the paired rafters met, they were spiked solidly. Before they had more than one pair of rafters in place, Dawn came out to tell them supper was ready. She was quite surprised to see how much had been completed.

Supper sounded good to the 'bunkhouse boys' as they were ready for Dawn's food anytime. Again their project was discussed over supper. Dawn asked what they planned to use for the roof. Shorty replied, "We could use boards and tar paper, but tar paper doesn't last very long. I brought along the shake splitter and thought maybe we could split shakes to cover the roof. It would take more work but less money. Tamarack shakes would last a long time if we put tar paper between them. Straight grained tamarack should split easily, but if not we could use pine."

Randy spoke up at this time, "I like the idea of shakes for the roof. My suggestion would be to cut them three feet long. Put them on at twelve inches to the weather. Put half a strip of tar paper at the top of each course. That would make three thicknesses of shakes and the tar paper would be covered, so it would last longer. The tar paper wouldn't really be necessary, but it would guarantee no leaks." This suggestion was thought to be perfect. It would take more work, but the roof would last almost forever. Narrow boards would be strong enough with all the support under them. The first rib would go at the peak and the others centered at two foot intervals on down the roof. When all of the ribs were in place, the shakes could be nailed on. First though, the shakes had to be cut and split. Luckily they still had most of the summer ahead.

When supper was over, it was back to the bunkhouse and work. Before they got underway, Shorty spoke up, "I would like to have an open, roofed porch over the door. We could make a shed roof, but I would prefer extending the roof about eight feet. Anybody have any other suggestions?" Matt and Randy thought this was a good idea. More work than a shed, or lean to roof, but it would look much nicer when finished. Matt thought, with a bench against the wall, maybe a chair or two, a great place to sit in the evening or when it was raining. "OK," Shorty said, "If we're agreed, we have to plan for this porch before we go much farther. We can put a tamarack log down to support the roof and the floor. Next we have to join a plate log to the top wall log. I guess we could halve them together."

They thought about this for a minute then Matt suggested, "Couldn't we cut the top logs back two feet and then halve them together for twelve inches? With a twelve foot log, it would give us an eight foot overhang with some to trim. The plate would have to be notched in, but it would be stronger wouldn't it?" "Good plan Matt," Shorty said, "I should have been thinking of this before we put the top log on, we could have used a longer log on this end and just butted them together. If we do that now, we have to notch in that joist too. As far as I can see Matt, your plan is what we'll use."

Randy agreed it was easier to cut one notch than two. The top logs were cut back two feet, and the top half was split off for twelve inches. Next a twelve-foot log was halved for twelve inches and joined to the top wall log. A prop was placed under the outside end to support it. Matt bored two holes through the logs where they joined and one near the end of the wall. He then drove wooden pins solidly into the holes. The holes were about five inches apart and staggered, one each side of center to avoid splitting, since they were close to the ends. When the two plate logs were in place, the tamarack was dug into the ground a few inches. Two upright logs about six inches in diameter were trimmed for length. Each end of the base log had been flattened on top for the uprights to sit on. Matt suggested boring a hole in the base log for a wooden pin. A slightly bigger hole in the butt would fit over the pin, making a sturdy joint. Randy thought this was a good idea, so Matt started boring holes while Shorty and Randy looked for a top log to tie them together. The bottom side of this log was flattened a bit where it rested on the uprights. Matt got his plumb line and the uprights were held straight, while a board was tacked from the wall to the upright and from the upright to the base log, with these stays in place the upright posts were held solidly in place. The top log was then hoisted into place, bringing the top logs up level. When everything was in place, Matt went up and bored through the plate log, the top log, and into the upright. With wooden pins driven solidly in place, the framework was secure. They were ready to install the other rafters, but it was sack time for everyone now.

It seemed like they had hardly closed their eyes when the rooster told them it was time to get up. By the time the few chores were done and everyone was washed up, Dawn had breakfast ready. Since today was Sunday, they didn't plan to work as hard as usual. If there hadn't been so much to get done, they probably wouldn't have done much at all. As it was, they only had two days of the week and there was much work to get done. As they ate breakfast, they talked over the coming day's activities. Randy thought they should start getting some wood cut for shakes. A little more effort at the bunkhouse and they would be ready for the shakes. It was a unanimous decision that getting some shakes on hand was the next order of business. When the meal was inside them, the horses would be hitched up and they would go up to the hills where the tamarack was drying. It would be cut to three foot lengths and loaded on the wagon, to be hauled back to the ranch. While the men were getting the team harnessed and hitched up, Dawn was getting a lunch ready for them. She didn't plan to be left behind.

When they got to where the pine logs had been cut, the horses were unhitched. The team was then hitched to the scoot sled to go back to the tamarack grove. At the end of the trail, the scoot sled was maneuvered close to the butt of the nearest tree. With peavey and poles, the butt was placed on the bunk of the sled. Matt secured it with the chain as Shorty and Randy limbed out the top, until it was too small for firewood. Since it was a heavy tree and it wasn't very far, one tree at a time was taken out. One three-foot piece was cut off the butt while it was still on the sled. As the tree was pried up, Dawn and Matt rolled the block up the tree as far as it would go. Dawn and Shorty would cut this tree into blocks, while Randy and Matt went back for more. Dawn and Shorty made a good team on the crosscut, so when another log arrived, the first was almost completely made into shake wood. With these long logs, without much taper, three would make a load for the wagon. When the log was down to six inches, or they reached the area where the limbs had been, the log was moved to the side and left long. The small top logs might come in handy for Matt's pig shelter or other uses. They wanted only knot-free wood to be split into shakes. When they had a load of shake wood on the wagon, Shorty went back to help get the rest of the trees out. They decided to pull the last of the trees out with the limbs on so they could continue drying. When lunchtime rolled around, they were ready to eat. They decided to go back to the ranch and start splitting shakes. They wanted to find out how the wood was going to split. The split shakes would be loosely stacked to allow them to keep drying. Matt could split some shakes through the week if they split easy enough.

Back at the ranch, the load of wood was dropped off near the bunkhouse. It was much easier to have the building material close at hand than to move it later. A test run of the shake splitter turned out well, so they decided to do some more work on the bunkhouse, to get ready for the shakes. They had started putting the rafters in place, so they continued on where they had left off. The top ends were cut to the proper angle, and then Matt held them in place while they were marked for the notches. When marked, Matt held the rafters while Shorty notched it. Randy was working on the wall notch at this time. When one rafter was finished, Shorty would cut the wall notch on his side while Matt held the rafter for Randy. This arrangement kept everyone busy and productive and the work was progressing well.

When the notches were completed, Matt held the rafters in place while they were test fitted in the notches. The sides were shaved down to allow them to fit snugly. When everything fitted correctly, the top was fastened together, and then one of the men held it in place while Matt bored and pinned the bottom ends. He had cut a good supply of small saplings for this purpose, so there was always plenty on hand. When one man was busy holding rafters for Matt, the other would be shaping more pegs for future use. The pegs didn't have to be perfectly round, as long as they would drive into the holes snugly. Some were more square than round when shaped with an axe, but the wood would compress as it was being driven and fill the hole solidly. Sometimes only the end was whittled down enough to allow it to be started into the hole. They had the next pair of rafters almost completed when Dawn came out to announce that supper was ready. They were so near to finishing that pair, she told them to complete it before stopping, as supper would wait a few minutes. The work was finished and a board was tacked on diagonally to hold everything in place. This would prevent anything from shifting, even though they were securely fastened. With everything secured, the tools were gathered up and put away, before they all washed up to enjoy another of Dawn's delicious meals. This was Sunday, so after the meal Shorty and Randy would be on the way back to their home ranch and another week of work.

Chapter 5

THERE WAS ALWAYS plenty of work to be done on the ranch. Matt and Dawn were busy with the everyday chores, the garden and splitting shakes when time allowed. The time passed quickly until the weekend was almost here. Meanwhile, back at the ranch, Shorty was working hard at whatever he was doing. He was talking to the foreman, Chuck, one day and mentioned that he must have missed his weekend to work. The foreman told Shorty, "You don't have to work weekends now. It isn't too important anyway, just keeping an eye on things and spot trouble before it gets out of hand. The boys all know you are helping the widow Ryan and her son. They feel they are helping a bit by leaving your weekends free to help them. The crew decided to do this on their own. In fact, I rode the range in your place last time. We have a good bunch of men here and this is their way of helping the Ryan's."

Shorty spoke up, "But that isn't fair. I'm just trying to help Mrs. Ryan and Matt get back on their feet. I don't plan to neglect my duty to the ranch!" The foreman replied, "Shorty, you couldn't change it now if you tried. The men refuse to let you work weekends, so you might as well forget it. I agree with them one hundred percent. You just keep helping the Ryan's and let us do your job here on the weekends."

That night Shorty spoke to the men in the bunkhouse. "I appreciate what you boys are doing," he said, "but it's not right. I feel I am not pulling my share of the load around here. I don't expect anyone to do my job for me." Now, it was time for Gus to have his say, "Shorty, we know we are as good as most cowhands and better than some. Then you showed up and did so much more, it made us look like a bunch of schoolboys. You do more than your share every day. If we could do half the things you do, we would be over there helping out too. We can do a little bit by keeping you free to help the Ryan's. Now, if you don't want to tackle each and every one of us, you just get on over there every weekend and leave this ranch to us! Case closed!"

The boys all agreed that was the way it was going to be, so Shorty had to admit defeat. He told them, "I don't think I ever worked with a better bunch of men. I'm real proud to call you all my friends." They all cheered and shook hands with Shorty, and he thanked each individually.

Later in the week, Shorty met up with the boss in the yard. He asked Shorty, "How is the work coming along over at the Ryan's? I hear you have another helper now. Seems like you put Rowdy, er, Randy Ripley's life back on track. People tell me he's a new man now." Shorty answered, "Well, boss, we got a lot accomplished in the last few months. There is still a lot to be done though. The place was falling behind, but it wasn't their fault. They just needed a few pointers and some help with the heavy work. Matt and his ma sure are hard workers. We can hardly do anything unless she is right there doing her share. Young Matt is going to be a fine man in a few years. As for Randy, he would have regretted insulting a lady. Any man would have done the same thing. I just happened to be the closest. Once Randy found out alcohol was causing his problems, everything improved. He's a good man once he was shown the error of his ways!"

The boss said, "You are right about Dawn being a good worker. If her husband had been half the man you are, they would be doing good now. He got himself in trouble with the law a few times, nothing serious, but he was wasting his energy in the wrong places. The last time was more serious. He could have gone to prison for a year or two. I helped them get the ranch and came up with enough money to keep him out of jail. We thought, maybe, if he got away from his 'friends', he might be better off. It was working, but he wasn't much of a man to work with his hands like you. I gave him a job on the ranch, not that he was a hand, but it gave them a little money. Then last spring his horse went over backwards on him. He lived about an hour before he died. Dawn and Matt heard that he died instantly."

Shorty said, "All I heard was that he died. It won't help Mrs. Ryan and Matt to hear anything but that he died quick. That's the story I got from you!" "Thanks, Shorty," the boss said, "I knew you would understand. We try to help out, but they don't want charity. They have a good spot to cut hay, so we cut the hay on shares to help out. I think she knows the Axe takes a very small share, but that is one way we can help out a bit. We do what we can to help out because, after all, she *is* my sister-in-law."

Shorty was shocked. "You . . . you mean," Shorty stammered, "Dawn is your wife's sister? I didn't know that. I guess it would be better if I didn't go over there so much." Shorty didn't realize that the boss's wife had come up behind them and had heard most of what they had been talking about. When she spoke, Shorty almost jumped out of his boots. "Shorty Aloysius Stout, if I thought for a minute you were serious about what you said, you would be in big trouble!" she almost shouted. "Is there a good reason why you shouldn't be working for my sister?" "Oh no, ma'am, it's not that," Shorty said. "I was just trying to help them out a bit. Your sister shouldn't have to work as hard as she does, and Matt does a man's work even though he shouldn't have to. They are fine people, two of the finest people I have ever met. The trouble is I'm not really good enough to be working for them. I'm just a two-bit saddle tramp, and they own that ranch. I don't think I should even be helping like I am!"

"Shorty Stout," Angela said loudly, "you are the best thing that ever happened to that ranch, Dawn, and Matt. If you run out on them, I'll get a shotgun and hunt you down like a rabid coyote. Dawn probably wouldn't have been able to hold on to the ranch much longer when you showed up. The ranch is in better shape now than it ever was. You think you aren't good enough? You are three times the man that jailbird husband of hers was. Dawn realized she had made a mistake, but she was married to him and had a son to think of. Now, if you plan to keep working here, you just better plan to keep working for my sister too! From now on you work here four days a week, take your pick, Monday or Friday. By the way, your pay stays the same! You always do more than your share of the work anyway! Do you understand what I just said?"

"Yes, ma'am, I understand," Shorty stammered, "but I don't feel right getting paid when I'm not working. I have always worked for my money!"

"You will earn your money, Shorty," Angela stated. "It's just that you will be working for my sister. I heard what the other hands have done, so you have more time to help Dawn and Matt. She won't accept charity, so this is one way we can help out a bit. We know how hard you have been working over there for them." Also, very soon I'm going to ride over there, and Matt and I are going to town and get another wagon load of lumber. You will have to explain it to her somehow!" The boss spoke up then and said, "You heard the lady, Shorty. When she speaks, you better listen! I won't go against what she says, and if you are smart, you won't either." Shorty said, "But, boss" . . . "No buts, Shorty," the boss said. "The 'Boss' has spoken. Do what she says, or there will be no peace for anyone," he said with a smile. "Now the best thing you can do is vamoose!"

Shorty headed for the barn. There was a smile on his face, but he was still in shock after learning Dawn and Angela were sisters. 'Well,' Shorty thought, 'it's too late to worry about that now. I guess I'll just have to keep going the way I have been. It seems like Angela made it plain she wants me to continue helping them.' Shorty decided the best way to keep peace in the family was to pretend this meeting never happened. He was going to give it his best shot.

Shorty now had a three-day weekend, so his plan was to go over to the R-R on Fridays. This way he could dig in on Friday and Saturday and take it a bit easier on Sunday. He wasn't what you would call a religious man, but he was raised believing a person didn't work on Sunday unless it was necessary.

On Thursday evening, he set out for the R-R. Dawn and Matt were surprised to see him a full day ahead of when they expected him. They were curious as to why he was here so early, and Dawn asked him to explain. "Well, ma'am, Dawn," he said, "I sort of got fired." They looked shocked as Shorty went on, "It's not permanent. It's just that the boss's wife thought I should have more time to help out here. I explained to her that we were getting a lot done here, but she insisted. So to keep the ranch in one piece, I now have Fridays to help out here." Dawn and Matt both seemed pleased to have him here for an extra day, as they both had grins from ear to ear!

"Uh, m . . . Dawn," Shorty began, "why didn't someone tell me before that you and Angela were sisters. I just found out yesterday!" Dawn smiled and said, "Would it have made any difference?" "Well," Shorty said, "It might have if I had known earlier. I don't think I would have come here so much if I had known you were the boss's sister-in-law. It doesn't seem right somehow."

"I see nothing wrong with you helping us, Shorty," Dawn said. "If you hadn't met up with us in the woods that day, we probably would have lost this place eventually. We were trying, but Matt and I just didn't have the know-how, or the strength, to do what needed to be done. Do you have a problem with being here?"

"Oh no, ma'am, uh, Dawn," Shorty stammered, "I have no problem with being here. It's just that some folks might think I was trying to take your ranch!" Dawn said, "Well, Shorty, Matt and

I know you aren't trying to take anything from us. You have given us far more than we can ever repay you for. You have given us your time, the knowledge to do so much we couldn't do before, and friendship. Even if we had money, no one could ever pay for that. As for what other people think, we don't really care. If some people think that way, their opinion isn't worth much! Now, let's have a cup of tea and some stale doughnuts before bed. You sneaked in here and caught me without fresh ones, and we have work to do tomorrow!" They enjoyed a bedtime snack and caught up on a bit of news before heading for bed.

All three rolled out of bed as the rooster began his early morning serenading. Shorty made sure the stock was looked after while Matt milked the cow. They washed up in the sluice running by the barn and then headed for the house where the cook had mouthwatering smells coming from the kitchen. Matt took the pail of milk to the sink and placed it inside. He took a plug off the shelf, pushed it into the drain hole, and opened the pipe to let water run into the sink. When the water was up to the top of the plug, he slowed the water down to a small trickle. Shorty could see the plug was hollow and the water ran down the center, keeping the water level constant. As they ate breakfast, the milk would cool.

Shorty looked at Matt and said, "That's pretty good Matt, is that your idea?" Matt said, "Well, I guess it was Ma's idea. She was trying to cool the milk, but would have to drain the water now and then to keep it cold. If the water was left running it might overflow. I tried to think of what you would do. I tried to bore a hole through a small stick, but that didn't work so I went looking for one of those bushes with the brown center. I worked at it until I got the hole big enough. It works, now we don't have to carry the milk to the creek to cool it."

Shorty smiled and said, "I knew you had a good head on your shoulders Matt. I've been trying to help you think differently and I guess you do. I bet your ma is real proud of you." Dawn said, "Yes, I am very proud of Matt, but you are the one always explaining how and why you do something. You also tell us to stop and think; that there is usually some way around a problem. You have helped us in so many ways, Shorty. I don't know how we got by before you came along!" Shorty said, "I'm just trying to help out Dawn, my pa always explained how and why he was doing something. I just try to do the same. Now, we better finish this meal before it gets cold"

They dug in while the food was still hot, and a short time later, they were out working at the bunkhouse. Since Randy wasn't there, Dawn insisted she was going to work in his place. When the necessary housework was finished, she was out there working alongside her 'men.' She helped Matt hold the rafters while Shorty beveled the top ends. When the notches were marked, she made the saw cuts for the notches. While Shorty chopped out the notches, she made the cuts on the other side. It wasn't long before the pair of rafters was solidly in place. A board was tacked from this pair of rafters to the ones already secured. Matt bored and pinned the bottom ends while Dawn held the next ones for Shorty to work on. When the last rafters for the main roof were in place, they began working on the two pair for the porch roof. Dawn went to the house to put wood in the stove while Matt and Shorty built a temporary floor to work on. Matt went to the barn and got an eight inch wide plank. This was placed on edge on the log holding up the plate logs and nailed to a fence rail, which was stood against the end wall. When boards were laid across the plate logs and this plank, it made a sturdy floor to work on. Before they could begin on the rafters, a ceiling joist had to be notched into the plate logs. Matt got a small log while Shorty started cutting the notches. When Matt came back with the log for a joist, it was trimmed for length, the sides shaved down and it was fitted in place. The joist was fastened in place when Dawn called them for dinner. As the meal was being eaten, the work was discussed a bit. The gable end over the porch would be left open, unless the rain blew in, which was unlikely.

With three of them working steadily, the rafters were in place with time to spare before dinner. Dawn left to get a meal ready, while Shorty and Matt started trussing the rafters. Matt gathered up some small poles for this purpose. Shorty cut a four-inch log, so when flush on the bottom, it protruded slightly at the top. When held in place, it was marked at the top of the joist and the bottom of the rafters. This small log was sawed halfway through at these marks. The upright was held in place and the rafters and joist were marked. These cuts were made just inside the marks, and the wood was split off. Shorty used the axe to shave the sides of the upright until it fit snugly in the slot, the surface being flush with the rafters and joist. Matt got a smaller pole and held it in place, just touching the top of the upright and contacting the joist about two feet from the center. The notching process was repeated, so this piece also fit flush. Another small piece was fitted on the other side and the truss was completed.

Shorty said to Matt, "By putting the truss on the back, you don't see the notches when you come in the door. Even from the back, they look good. We could have just notched the small pieces and nailed them on the back but I think this looks better." Matt agreed this way wasn't much more work but when finished made a nicer-looking job. Dawn called them for dinner just as the first truss was finished. Work was halted as it would be there later, dinner might not be.

As they ate, Shorty told Dawn her help wasn't really needed for a while. They would be working on the trusses and it was a slow process and only two people could work at a time. Dawn had enough to do in the house to keep her occupied for a few hours. After the meal, now that Matt knew what to do, he could cut the pieces to the proper length, and make some of the saw cuts, which speeded up the process considerably. It didn't take long to get the three inside trusses in place, and they started on the porch trusses. Shorty said to Matt, "I think we will put the end truss on the inside of the rafters, I was going to fill it in with logs but I think it will look better with the open truss. If the storm blows in and it has to be filled in later, the notches will be on the inside." With the temporary floor in place and knowing what to do, both trusses were in place shortly.

Matt looked around and then said, "We will have to fill in the gable ends before we put the roof on, won't we? There isn't going to be enough room to work and it will be hard to fit the logs in." Shorty looked around and said, "I'm glad you noticed that Matt. I was going to start putting the ribs on, but it will be much easier and faster to fill the ends in with nothing in the way. I always heard that two heads were better than one and you have proved that lots of times, lately. Let's get those ends filled in before I forget them again!"

They went down below and picked out the logs they wanted. They carried them over and stood them against the wall. Matt climbed up and pulled as Shorty pushed and the logs were up on the temporary floor. They only needed short logs as each tier got shorter quickly. Matt used a straight board to check that they were straight and smooth. If not Shorty trued them with the axe and adze. The first log was held in place, one end marked and cut and that end was slid into place. The second end was marked and cut also. The log was now pushed and tapped into place and fitted snugly. To fasten the log in place, Matt bored through the rafter, through the angled end of the fitted log and into the log underneath. A wooden pin was driven solidly in place and the log was secured. When the other end was bored and pinned, it made a solid job. The process was repeated, with each log becoming much shorter. With only three feet of height to start with, the end wall was soon completed. Dawn came out to get them for supper and praised their work. She thought they had done a beautiful job on the trusses and they really made the cabin look good. The boys tried not to let their swelled heads get too big.

Shorty said to Matt, "Let's go in and praise your mother's cooking!" After a good meal, and a few words of praise to the cook, Matt and Shorty were ready to go back to work. They were anxious to get it completed, now that it was starting to look like a building. The second end of the cabin was tackled. Repeat jobs always went faster, as they learned the right and wrong ways on the first one. Only half the time was needed to finish the second end. The next job was to put the small poles between the main rafters. They picked out some of the fence rails of a uniform size and carried them to the bunkhouse where they were leaned against the wall. These poles were much lighter and easier to work with. With a board laid on the rafters and the pole held tightly to it, the proper angle could be cut. Where the rafters were notched in, these smaller poles were nearly level, on top of the wall. One or two had to be shaved down a bit to make them even. Before darkness called a halt to the work, all of the smaller poles were in place. Matt got a long straight board and laid it on edge on the rafters to see if they were all of a uniform height. Shorty shaved the high spots with the adze. When darkness finally drove them out, one side of the main roof was leveled. Low areas were marked and a thin shim would bring it up level as the ribs were put on. Matt got some tar paper from the shed, while Shorty put all the tools in one place. Covered with tar paper, they would be dry in case of a shower and handy to start work with in the morning. As they headed for the house and a bedtime snack, they heard Randy coming in the dusk.

Shorty laughed and said, "A fine time you picked to appear! It's too dark to work and there's food on the table. Well, I guess we'll have to make you pay for that tomorrow!" Randy snickered and said, "First I have to sample the food, if it's not up to my standards, I might have to leave." Matt grinned and said, "Fat chance of that Randy, once you get another of ma's doughnuts, you won't be going anyplace!" All three were laughing as they went through the door. Dawn looked up from what she was doing and asked what was so funny. Shorty chuckled and said, "We were just talking about this lazy freeloader who just wandered in looking for food. You might have to run him off with the shotgun!" They talked and joked for a bit as they had a bite to eat with a cup of tea. Then they were off to their beds to get some sleep, before the rooster started to raise a ruckus. Everybody was up and about before the sun cleared the hills.

Randy and Shorty checked over the barn and stock to make sure everything was OK. They washed up at the sluice and then they headed for the house and a good breakfast. Randy was quite impressed with the progress made on the bunkhouse and pressed Shorty for details of how he got so much done in one evening. Shorty grinned and said, "We didn't have you getting in the way, so we got some work done. You should know by now it doesn't take me all day to do a day's work!"

Randy snorted and went in the kitchen for breakfast. A few minutes later, Matt came in with the pail of milk. Shorty told Randy, "Now, if you were as sharp as this young man here, you might go places. Do you see what he came up with?" Randy was visibly impressed and told Matt so.

Breakfast was soon eaten and all three headed out to the bunkhouse and their day's work. They had just gotten started leveling the rafters when they heard riders coming. They stopped work for a minute to watch three riders coming up the trail. Shorty was surprised to see Gus, Slim, and Rusty, the three Axe hands. Shorty called out to Gus, "What are you guys doing here, looking for strays?" "Yep," Gus replied, "We were following strays until we lost their trail. For the last two miles, we've been following our noses. We picked up fresh 'bearsign' back that far. We also heard rumors that you were getting fat eating doughnuts and laying around. These guys thought we should help eat them, so you wouldn't get sick!" Dawn had come to the door and heard the exchange of words and said, "If you came all this way for them, I might be able to find a couple for each. There is still some hot tea if you drink it."

The cowboys hitched their horses to the corral fence and trudged over to the house. They sat on the woodpile and Dawn passed them the doughnuts that were left in the dish. She then brought out three cups and a pot of tea. The cowboys thought the doughnuts were mighty fine, even though Dawn explained they weren't fresh. The boys had two each and there was still some left in the dish. Gus told Dawn, "Ma'am, we heard Shorty was having himself a high old time here while we slaved at doing his job on the ranch. We decided we were coming over here to have some fun too. Now, you just point us in the direction of something you want done and we'll get started."

By this time Shorty had climbed down off the bunkhouse roof and arrived at the house. He asked Gus, "What are you doing here with this lazy bunch? I already have one freeloader that I'm trying to get a little work out of!" Gus snorted, "You just point us to something that needs done and stand aside. We'll show you who's lazy!" Shorty said, "Well, if you came here to work, we have some here for you. One of you throw some harness on one of those horses and I'll explain what to do. Might as well unsaddle your nags too and put them in the corral." One man went to harness a horse and the other unsaddled their mounts. Shorty and Gus went over to where they had started to dig the root cellar and Shorty explained what they were doing. They agreed it was more work to move the soil uphill, but a lot less work when it came time to backfill. A few minutes later, they were busy digging with the pick and hauling the soil up the hill with the scoop.

Shorty went back to the bunkhouse and continued work on the roof. With Matt holding the straight edge and Randy and Shorty wielding the axe and adze, they soon had the main roof rafters leveled up. They moved over to the porch roof and before the morning was half over, the roof was ready to nail on the ribs. Matt suggested, "If I went over there and led the horse for Gus, there would be a spare man for other work. Maybe one of them could split some shakes for the roof. It won't be very long before we will need them." Shorty agreed and said, "That's a good idea Matt, you can lead the horse as well as anyone and you're right, it will give us another man for the heavy work. You do a good day's work, but there are some things you aren't quite big and strong enough for. Let's go have a talk with Gus."

Shorty and Matt went over to where Gus was working. They explained what they were thinking and Gus agreed. Matt took over leading the horse and Slim took over the pick from Rusty. Shorty took Gus over to the pile of shake wood and explained what they wanted. Gus started splitting shakes while Shorty returned to the bunkhouse to help Randy. Dawn was inside working at getting a meal ready for this big crew that was now working for her and Matt. She had cut up and fried several pounds of meat. It was now in a large pot on the stove as she cut up potatoes, carrots, and turnips to go into the pot. When it came time to eat, she would have a big pot of beef stew ready for the men. She had a small pot to one side with about two cups of barley in it boiling. This would go into the pot just before time to eat. By adding the barley later, there was less chance of it scorching on the bottom. She might even whip up a batch of dumplings to put on top of the stew. With the vegetables in the pot and bubbling away, she had a few minutes to think. She had bread and butter and a few doughnuts. After the dumplings were in the pot, she would make a big batch of biscuits. There was some coffee in a can on the shelf, so she would make coffee as well as tea. Most cowhands drank coffee, strong and black. There was also lots of cold milk and water. Milk was something most cowhands wouldn't even look at, let alone drink it! Next thing, she wondered where will everybody eat, there wasn't enough room at the kitchen table and not enough chairs either.

Suddenly, Dawn thought about the sawhorses Shorty and Matt had built in the barn. If she had those with some boards laid on them, she could toss a sheet on them for a tablecloth. She didn't have enough chairs, but she could get Randy or Shorty to cut some blocks off a log. A wide board on top would make a bench. Now, there isn't room enough in here, so we will have to eat outside. No, she thought, we will take everything up to the bunkhouse; at least there will be a floor under our feet. Now that she had figured out what to do, she had to get it done. When she went up to the bunkhouse, Randy was down below getting lumber. She asked, "Randy, can I get you to help me for a few minutes? I need some help to bring a few things up here." Randy answered, "Well, ma'am, I will if that slave driver up there can spare me for a minute!" Shorty snorted and said, "Well Dawn, if you can get any work out of him, you must be better than me. Take him if he's any good to you!"

Randy went with Dawn and she explained what she wanted. First he carried the sawhorses up to the bunkhouse. He got two short boards and nailed one on each bench. He got some seven or eight foot boards to put on top to form a table. The outside boards, he nailed in place to hold them steady. Then he got a short log and cut six pieces off it, sixteen inches long. He placed two on each side of the 'table', and put a wide board on top. He went to the house and got a box of dishes and eating utensils which Dawn had already packed. When he returned to the house, he rang the dinner triangle and then carried the pot of stew up to the bunkhouse wrapped in a blanket to keep it hot. Back at the house he got a large, hot, Dutch oven, with a pot of tea and coffee in it. The hot iron would keep both hot.

Gus had put the horse in the barn and washed up at the sluice. As he went by the house, Dawn gave him a jug of milk and one of water. Slim took a big pan of hot biscuits, covered with a towel. Rusty took a chair from Dawn's hand, as well as a basket of sliced bread. All that was left for Dawn to carry was a dish of butter and a soup ladle. The men were lined up ready to heap their plates with the delicious smelling stew. Slim said, "Ma'am, we didn't expect to get a meal like this. A piece of bread and some cold water would have been fine." Dawn smiled and said, "If you don't want to eat, you can always go back to work." Slim replied, "Well, ma'am, I wouldn't want you to think I was too good to eat with you. Maybe I better stay here and eat beside you!" They all laughed at the exchange of words and then they dug into the food.

Half of the big pot of stew had disappeared, all of the biscuits, and most of the bread was gone. The few surviving doughnuts had vanished, along with most of the tea and coffee. Surprisingly, two of the men had a cup of cold milk, before starting on the coffee. No one was hungry anymore and they all complimented Dawn on the excellent meal. They were ready to go back to work, but as each man left the almost completed bunkhouse, he picked up something to take back to the house. There was only a few things left, so Matt and Randy took these items. This was the second meal they had shared in the new bunkhouse. Soon everyone was back at the job they had left.

Gus and his crew would work for about half an hour, then change jobs. Whoever was splitting shakes would take over on the pick. The man on the pick moved to the handles of the scoop and the man on the scoop would split shakes for a while. Changing jobs frequently made for a much easier workday than working at one job continuously. The new hands were making good progress at digging the root cellar. Already they had a small mountain of dirt piled up on the side hill. With three men working steadily at digging and moving soil, a lot could be accomplished in a day. When the men had stopped for dinner, the horse they had been using was traded for the second one. The work wasn't very strenuous, as the scoop would hold less than three hundred pounds of soil. Like the men though, it was easier on both animals to spread the work around.

Shorty and Randy, with the rafters all leveled, had gotten all the ribs all on the short side of the roof. Now they decided it was time to get the last wall up for the storage area. First they dug a tamarack base log into the ground, front and back, butting against the base logs of the cabin. Both agreed that the logs didn't have to fit as closely as the cabin walls. A flat notch pinned together should be OK. The first log was put into place, marked, cut, and one-third of its thickness split off. This was repeated at both ends of the wall log and both base logs. The wall log was nudged into position and bored and pinned. The boys decided to dig a narrow trench into the bank at each end and in the middle. Short logs would be buried in the bank to hold the wall from pushing in with the weight of the soil. One quarter of the thickness was cut and split off and a notch cut into the wall log, to one quarter of its thickness. The next wall log was notched to fit on these short logs. When in place, a hole was bored into all three logs and they were pinned together solidly. Since these notches were simply a matter of sawing to the proper depth and splitting the piece off, the work went ahead much faster than the cabin walls. When the wall was as high as was needed, a small log was placed from the top of the wall to join onto the cabin wall at each end. This made a solid support for the wall they had just built. The wall was now supporting the ends of the long rafters, which had been resting on blocks of wood. A shallow notch had been made in the top of the log and the bottom of the rafters. This provided extra support for the mainly, free standing wall. These joints, as with the others, were securely pinned. The rafters over the storage area still had to be leveled and then the ribs could go on.

It wouldn't be long now until there would be a roof on the bunkhouse and except for the windows and door, the cabin would be dry. Just at that time, Dawn rang the supper triangle. Shorty and Randy gathered up the tools, placed them in a corner, and covered them with tar paper. The digging crew unhitched the horse, led it to the barn, and unharnessed it. After washing at the sluice, all the men headed for the house. They each carried a load of food or other items up to the bunkhouse-dining room. Dawn had been busy in the house all afternoon. She had a roast of beef, cooked to a golden brown, dishes of vegetables, and a pot of gravy. The leftover stew had been reheated and another large pan of biscuits was fresh from the oven. The tea, coffee, and milk were ready to go. While the meal had been cooking, Dawn had been busy making doughnuts. She had two big dishes full of warm doughnuts. The comments on the wonderful food smells were as plentiful as the doughnuts. The men soon were lined up to heap their plates. With a full plate in front of everyone, there was very little conversation taking place. When the sharp edge had been taken off their appetite, they began to talk of the day's work. Gus thought they had almost enough soil removed for the root cellar. He suggested the rest of the soil could be dug loose and shoveled to the side. Mostly it was just a matter of squaring up the sides to make enough room to fit the logs together.

Dawn commented on the amount of work everyone had done today. She said, "I don't know how I will ever thank you boys for everything you have done for Matt and me. I don't have the words to tell you how much we appreciate your help." Gus spoke up then, "Well, ma'am, if you keep a few of those doughnuts on hand, we just might be in the area after strays now and then and we could stop in and visit. We wouldn't want those tasty little critters to get old and stale!" When the laughter died away, everyone reached for another doughnut.

With the meal out of the way, the men helped to carry everything back to the house. Good-byes were said all around, but before Gus, Slim, and Rusty left, Dawn gave them each a package of a dozen doughnuts. With a last farewell and a wave, the boys rode away to the home ranch.

The remainder of the crew walked over to inspect the job the new crew had done at the root cellar site. As Gus had suggested, all that remained to be done was to pick and shovel the hole into the proper shape for building. All four then went up to the bunkhouse to see what had been accomplished there. Dawn and Matt were impressed by the progress being made. Shorty and Randy explained that, with the rafters being leveled and most of the ribs already on, the roof could be closed in quite quickly. Shorty decided to split more shakes until dark as lot more shakes would be needed before the roof was completed. The roof, when finished, would be thirty feet long, with the overhang at the ends. There was a substantial pile of shakes already split and waiting, thanks to the generosity of the boys from the Axe. When completed, the bunkhouse would be a well-built, solid, tight building that would need very little upkeep for many years.

Shorty and Randy were splitting and stacking shakes, so Matt asked what else needed to be done for the bunkhouse. Shorty answered, "Well, Matt, we should have a lot of moss to fill in the cracks. The joint will be filled with moss and some of them will have a small stick nailed over that. Then we cover everything with clay. We could use all clay, but solid clay isn't as warm as having the moss in first. You have seen how the nails inside the barn are all frosted up in winter. The cold follows the nail through the wall. With a space filled with moss between the two layers of clay, the cold doesn't go through as easily. It makes more work, but you have a lot warmer building if it's going to be used in the winter. When you want a break from a job you are doing, you can gather a lot of moss. It will take a lot too. Two or three feed sacks full should give us a good start. Also, if you could find a spot where there is a lot of small saplings growing, you could cut some and have them drying. Like the logs, cut them down and leave the twigs and leaves on. If it's not too far, you could drag them out, or we could use the scoot sled later. You could start putting the moss in anytime, but the saplings should dry first. Now, I better get back to work before this 'no-good' here with me starts crying that I'm not doing my share!" Matt was laughing as he headed for the barn to get a feed sack.

Shorty and Randy worked for another hour or so, and then they each took an armful of shakes and went up to the bunkhouse. A few at a time, they were pushed up onto the boards laid on the ceiling joists. They climbed up above and began laying shakes to see how everything was going to work. They laid about six shakes side by side on the ribs. The following course was placed directly on top of the first, but staggered to cover the cracks. The third course was laid so one foot of the second layer showed, but again covering the cracks. A few more courses were laid, always covering the joints underneath.

Randy thought if the first rib at the eave was doubled and the top of the shake placed just below the top rib, the shakes would lie flat on the ones underneath. They tried this and decided to follow this plan. When the first course of shakes was put on, a full sheet of tar paper would go on top of it. The next course would go directly on top, but staggered to cover the joints. From this point on, the tar paper would be split length wise and placed at the top of the shakes, thus being covered by the following course. The tar paper wasn't really necessary, but was cheap insurance that this roof was not going to leak!

It was just about too late in the day to start putting on shakes, so they went back to splitting more. They would need a lot of shakes split ahead and someone to carry them, when they started nailing on the roof. Darkness was moving in, so they put away their tools and went to the house for a cup of tea. As they had their tea and a snack, they talked over what had been done and what was still to be done. Some good ideas came out of these chats because, as they say, four heads are better than one. Each person saw things from a different angle, so two or three different ideas sometimes formed a completely different and better idea altogether. After a short discussion and a few doughnuts, they decided to start putting the roof on tomorrow morning. Right now though, it was time to say goodnight and hit the sack for some rest. That pesky rooster would see that all would be awake come first light.

Chapter 6

WHEN THE COCK crowed the next morning, he caught no one in bed. It was just getting light enough to see and Shorty was checking the livestock. Matt was going to milk the cow, so Shorty fed the hogs and turned the chickens loose. Dawn had a fire going in the stove, water heating for tea and she was mixing batter for pancakes. It was only a short time until the chores were done and breakfast was on the table. Randy had been busy carrying tar paper and nails up to the bunkhouse, so everything was in readiness to start work after breakfast. A good meal of pancakes and cold beef, hot biscuits and tea, topped off with a couple of doughnuts each, and everyone felt ready to tackle a new day's work. As they headed for the bunkhouse, they each took a big armload of shakes with them. These were stacked on the makeshift table, until they could be pushed up to the temporary floor above. Matt was going to cut the tar paper to the proper length for the first strip, then split the sheet lengthwise for the following courses. It would take a lot of room to lay the tar paper out for cutting and splitting. Well, there was a slight problem, so he stopped to think about it. He rolled the problem around in his head for a bit until suddenly he came up with the solution. He took three-long boards and placed them from the doorway out over the porch support log. These were fastened with one nail in each end, driven flush, as the tar paper would be laid on them. Next he took an axe and went looking for two small crotched saplings. He found two and cut them about three feet long and six inches above the crotch. He also cut a small straight sapling one inch in diameter and four feet long. The crotched sticks were sharpened and pushed into the ground about three and a half feet apart and just outside the line of the doorway. He slid the straight sapling through the roll and placed it in the crotches. He then pushed a board up to Shorty and told him to measure how long the roof was. The board was passed back down and Shorty told Matt it was three lengths of the board plus to the pencil mark. Matt measured the three lengths plus the extra and marked a line on the boards. He nailed a short board to the long ones just past the pencil marks. He pulled the end of the tar paper into the bunkhouse, as it unrolled easily. He went back outside and cut the tar paper to the correct length with his pocketknife. He rolled the paper loosely, took it to where Shorty and Randy were nailing on shakes and passed it up to them. He then went back to his improvised reel and unrolled another strip. This was cut off and folded and creased exactly in the middle. Matt opened up the sheet and cut it into two equal pieces, following the crease. These he rolled loosely also and passed them up above.

Matt could now concentrate on carrying shakes into the cabin. As the shakes were nailed in place and the supply dwindled, Matt would pass more up to Shorty or Randy, whoever was handy. When Matt had the table covered with stacks of shakes, he started filling the cracks with moss. When Dawn got her housework completed, she came out to help Matt carry shakes to the roofers. She was surprised to find Matt had a supply of shakes and tar paper ready, and was starting to fill the cracks in the wall. Matt took a few minutes to make a couple of sticks to make the job easier. The sticks were like small paddles, about four inches wide and one quarter inch thick. The wide end was left blunt and the other was whittled to a good handle for holding. A handful of moss was held up to the crack and pushed in with the paddle. It was much faster and easier than using the fingers. They wanted the cracks filled with moss, but not packed too tightly. As the boys above needed more shakes, Matt or Dawn would pass more up to them. When the supply got low, both would go out to the pile and carry more inside. In this way, they could keep the roofing crew working steadily while they were getting a lot of the cracks filled. No one was working too hard, but a lot of work was being done.

Randy and Shorty had completed the first course of shakes, the wide strip of tar paper, and the second course of shakes on that. The third course was going on quickly and the roof would soon begin closing in. Matt and Dawn were busily pushing moss loosely into the cracks and carrying shakes to the men working upstairs. Matt decided it was time to get more tar paper ready before it was needed. He went outside and pulled the end of the sheet over to the doorway, and asked Dawn to pull it to the back wall. He cut it and Dawn helped him fold it evenly up the center. When split, he and Dawn each rolled a strip and set it aside until it was needed.

Dawn thought it was time to get something for this crew to eat. She told the boys, "You might have to settle for bread and tea for dinner, I've been doing your work and haven't had time to get something ready." Randy looked down and said, "That's OK with me, ma'am, as long as there are a few doughnuts to top it off. You shouldn't have given so many to the other crew, there would have been more left for us." Dawn laughed and said, "Randy, if you eat any more doughnuts you won't fit between those boards to get up on the roof. But don't worry, I still have a few left!" With that remark, she headed for the house to get something for this starving bunch to eat. About twenty minutes later, the triangle called them to dinner.

As the boys went past the house to wash up, they could smell something a lot better than bread and tea. They washed in a hurry and almost ran to the house. Dawn had chopped up a big pan full of roast beef and leftover potatoes. She had fried this to a golden brown and even had some gravy to pour over top. There was also a bit of twice reheated stew which smelled wonderful. She had put a few leftover biscuits in a covered dish with a few drops of water and heated them until they were like fresh ones. There was milk and tea, but on Randy's plate there was a slice of dry bread and a donut. This provided a laugh for everyone, even Randy. He took the dry bread and with a fork held it over the coals in the stove, toasting it to a golden brown. He put it on his plate spooned gravy over it and began to eat. It looked and smelled so good, everyone tried it. It was good! Even a joke had a good ending. From a threatened meal of bread and tea, to a meal of leftovers fit for a king, everyone enjoyed it. All agreed that, although the meals the day before were very good, the reheated meal had a much better flavor. After a couple of doughnuts and a last cup of tea, everyone was ready to go back to work.

Shorty and Randy were at work covering the second narrow strip of tar paper. Three more courses of shakes and this side of the roof would be done except for a cap on top after the other side was completed. Before suppertime rolled around, they would be starting on the long side of the roof.

As they worked, Shorty was thinking ahead to what still had to be done on the bunkhouse. He thought of the windows and said to Matt, "Matt, you get that carpenter's rule and measure those window openings for us. Write down the exact measurements on a piece of board or something. If someone is in town next week, stop at the hardware store and ask to have those windows made. I could do it, but it takes a lot of time. I can build a door easy enough. I'll pick out a few boards for you to plane down smooth next week. We'll build the door next weekend." Back at work driving nails, Randy spoke up, "I think we will need more tar paper before we get the roof finished, maybe you should put that on your list too, Matt." Shorty said, "That's right Randy, this long roof takes quite a bit of tar paper, but it makes a much better roof. OK Matt put two pair of hinges on that list too, one pair with a loose pin if they have them. If not I'll fix the regular ones the way I want. Can anyone think of anything else we need?" Dawn said, "We have the stove pipe and I think there is a heating stove in the barn. We had it in the house until I got the cook stove. What about something to take the pipe out through the roof?" "A roof jack," Shorty said, "That's right, we need a three in five roof jack, Matt. Add that to your list. I think that just about covers everything we need to close this building in. Can you think of anything else Randy?" Randy scratched his head and thought for a few seconds. He said, "As near as I can see, everything we need is on that list. If we missed something, it will just have to wait for another trip to town. We'll have the most important things anyway."

Shorty said, "Dawn, when you go in the house you can write that list on a piece of paper. The first time anyone is in town, the windows can be ordered and the other things brought out. Except for the windows, we should have this bunkhouse ready to live in next weekend!" Dawn said she would take the list in the house as it was about time to start getting a meal ready. Upstairs the men were nailing shakes in place, while Matt stuffed moss between the logs and carried more shakes to keep the other two busy driving nails. By the time Dawn called them to supper, the pile of shakes was very small. More would have to be split before much more roofing could be done. At least there was enough roof on the bunkhouse to keep the tools dry.

After a good supper, Shorty and Randy split shakes for a bit before heading for their home ranches and a week's work. With the crew from the Axe helping, a lot of work had been done in a short time. Next weekend should see the bunkhouse very nearly completed. In the meantime, Dawn and Matt had plenty of work to be done. Matt had plans to gather at least one more sack of moss to stuff in the cracks at the bunkhouse. He also had to find a grove of small saplings, to cut and have drying. He would look for a place where a big tree had fallen down. In these places, there were always a lot of small saplings, growing straight and tall trying to get ahead of its companions to get the light necessary for growth. Matt would cut most of these, leaving just enough to grow and fill in the hole in the forest. In this way, he was helping the trees by taking out the competition and giving the remaining saplings the room and light to grow much faster.

After Shorty and Randy left, the ranch felt empty. From having seven people working on Saturday down to two people Sunday evening, made the ranch feel big and empty to Dawn and Matt. They planned to keep busy; this would help the time pass quickly and get more work done also. Matt went to the pile of wood to be split for shakes. He wasn't strong enough to do as much as the men, but he worked steadily and still got at lot accomplished. He worked away at the pile until darkness began settling in and he had a good beginning on the necessary pile of shakes. Working a few hours each day would make the pile grow considerably.

Before going to the house, Matt made sure the chickens were closed up and everything else was looked after for the night. Matt and Dawn sat and talked for a few minutes over a glass of milk and a doughnut. Dawn's doughnuts were a popular item with everybody, it seemed. Dawn told Matt she would help him split shakes throughout the coming week. They hoped to have enough to finish the bunkhouse roof by next weekend. Someway they had to get to town and get the items on their list for the bunkhouse. That could wait until later in the week, as they might think of something else before then.

When the sun came up, they were busy as usual. Matt turned the chickens loose and looked after the other animals, along with milking the cow. After breakfast, Matt went to the woodpile and began splitting shakes. He planned to work here for a while then gather more moss. He would switch back and forth from heavy jobs to lighter, but equally important ones. He also had to find and cut a lot of small saplings and have them drying.

When Dawn finished her housework, she went outside and took over splitting shakes for Matt. Now that she didn't have so many workers to cook for, she could spend more time outside. She didn't mind housework, but she always liked to get outside in the fresh air. Dawn and Matt had been doing everything on the ranch for more than a year now, so she was almost as strong as most men!

Matt decided to take a hand ax and go looking for some saplings for the bunkhouse. He went up the hill and soon found what he was looking for. In a spot where a big tree had fallen down, there were dozens of small trees, growing close together like a crop of grain. Most had only a few limbs on the top and very straight. The biggest trees in the bunch were only two inches at the stump. Matt cut the smallest, nothing over one and one half inches in diameter. He cut a lot of trees, gathered up an armful, and dragged them to an old fallen tree where he dropped them with the butts clear of the ground. He kept cutting and moving the trees until he had all the ones of the size he wanted. He had thinned the grove considerably and the trees that were left had room to grow. He found another thicket of small trees and began cutting again. When this place was thinned out, he had another large pile of skinny poles.

He stopped for a minute and did some figuring. 'I have about sixty poles in each pile. All of them are at least ten feet long or more. That makes about six hundred feet of poles. The cabin is eight logs high and about fifty feet around outside. The ends are a bit higher, but the door and windows take some away. If I figure five hundred feet of joints to cover, inside and out, I should have enough poles. I'll get about twenty-five more, as a few of these probably won't be useable and it's better to have a few extra.' He found another place to cut some poles and soon had his twenty-five more. When he got back to the house, Dawn was getting dinner ready. He told her he was going to get the poles out of the woods and would be finished in time for dinner.

He harnessed the horse and got a chain and whiffletree and was ready to go. He hooked up one trace and let the whiffletree drag, so it wouldn't catch anything or bang the horse's heels. With the chain on his shoulder, he set out up the hill. At the first pile the second trace was hooked up and the chain, with a ring on one end, was pushed under the pile. He slid the ring to the bottom of the pile and hooked up to the horse as close as possible. When the horse pulled, the chain tightened and the butts of the poles lifted a bit so they dragged easier. A few minutes later, he had the load beside the bunkhouse. He put a small stick on the ground and pulled the poles onto it. The chain was unhooked and he and the horse went back for the second load. Dinner was ready when the second load was at the bunkhouse. Matt unharnessed the horse, put it in the barn, and went to get his waiting dinner.

After dinner, Matt split shakes until his mother came out and took over for him. He went to the bunkhouse and filled some more cracks until he had almost finished the supply of moss he had on hand. He took the feed sack and went up on the hill to gather more. If he had the moss on hand, he could work at it even if it rained. It was about an hour later when he had the sack stuffed full; even full it weighed very little. He carried it back to the bunkhouse and left it sitting on the roofed inside of the building. The crack filling could be done at any time, so he went to work on the root cellar for an hour. He would dig with the pick to loosen the soil and then shovel it to the side. When Dawn went inside to get supper ready, Matt split shakes until he was called to supper, he couldn't split them as fast as his mother, but he kept at it and the pile of shakes grew.

Meanwhile, back at the ranch, about the middle of the afternoon, Shorty was crossing the yard and met up with the boss's wife, Angela. She stopped Shorty and said, "I'm going to take Matt to town tomorrow to get a load of lumber. Is there anything else you need to work with over there?" Shorty answered, "Dawn has a list of things we need to be picked up. I know they are short on cash, so I was wondering if you could pay for the lumber and the other things from the money I have coming. I'll worry about getting paid back later. Right now, we are trying to get the ranch back on its feet, and with the crew we had on the weekend, it must be cutting into the food supply."

"Oh no, you don't!," Angela stated, "I told you I was going to get the lumber and that's final! I can use your money for the other things if you want me to. I'll get Dawn to make a list of anything else she needs. I'll make sure we get a bag of flour and one of potatoes, to keep things going until the garden starts producing. She will insist on paying for everything. Well, we can take her money, but use yours, especially for the stuff she doesn't know we're getting. It will be left for you to explain it to her when you get there. I'm taking the light wagon over there and I'll get Matt to hitch our horses to theirs, that way the lumber can stay on the wagon. If you think of anything else, let me know before I leave in the morning."

Shorty said, "I sure appreciate what you are doing to help out and I'm sure Dawn and Matt will, too. Well, I better get back to work and if I think of anything else, I'll let you know in the morning!" Angela said, "This is my sister and my nephew we are talking about Shorty, we've tried to help them but Dawn doesn't want handouts. There are times though, that even if a person doesn't want to, they have to accept a hand up, to get back on their feet. Like I said before, if her husband had been half the man you are, they wouldn't be so badly off now. Maybe together we can all help a bit until they get the ranch up and running and can help themselves. Let's hope so, especially now that they will let us help them!"

Shorty agreed and figured he had better get back to work. He didn't really look forward to trying to explain to Dawn what they were doing, but in a few days he would have to face the music. Shorty kept busy for the next three days and the time went fast. Soon it was time to head for the Ryan ranch.

Meanwhile, Angela arrived at Dawn's place about nine thirty Tuesday morning. Dawn was surprised to find her here at that time of day. Angela asked Dawn if she could use her wagon and take Matt to town with her. Dawn tried to find out why, but Angela avoided her questions. She asked if there was anything they needed while they were in town. Dawn said, "Yes, we have a list of things we need for the bunkhouse. With all of us contributing, we made the list the other day. I don't have much money left but there might be enough for what we need. We need more groceries, but the garden will be producing soon so I guess we'll get along."

Angela told her, "You write down what you need and I'll get it. If you don't have enough money, we'll work something out later. While you have some help, you might as well have the things to work with to get everything in shape. Shorty likes to keep busy, so we should have something for him to work with. I can see just coming in the yard that he's been busy lately. By the way," Angela grinned, "How are you and Shorty getting along?"

"We get along just fine." Dawn said, "Shorty has done so much for us, and showed us how to do so many things the right way. Shorty explains to Matt how and why to do everything. Matt is starting to come up with his own good ideas. We would both miss him if he ever stopped coming and he is always a gentleman." Angela said, "I know Shorty is always a gentleman around women. I wanted to know you are getting along as a man and woman! There is a difference you know!"

Dawn's face got red as she said, "I don't think Shorty is interested in me as a woman. I think he is more interested in helping Matt with the work and teaching him to do things. It would be nice if he was interested in me, but I don't think that is going to happen. He probably likes my doughnuts more than me!" Angela said, "Well, keep feeding him your doughnuts anyway, as long as he is around here, who knows what might happen! You might trip over something and fall into his arms or some such thing." Dawn was shocked and said, "I am not going to throw myself at a man! If he's interested, he will tell me when he's ready." "Dawn," Angela said, "Sometimes a man has to be hit with a fence post to get his attention, before they realize there is a woman around. If you are interested, maybe you should let him know that you are. He might not even realize you are a woman, the way you are always dressed in men's clothes all the time. Maybe you should grab the bull by the horns and give his head a good shake, to let him know you are a woman. You know yourself there probably isn't a better man within five hundred miles."

"Angela," Dawn said, "I am not going to throw myself at Shorty. I know there aren't many men like Shorty Stout in the country. I don't want to scare him off because he has been such a good friend and a big help. We will just have to wait and see what happens." Angela said, "Well, I guess it's up to you. Right now we have to leave as I see Matt has the team ready. I'll be in for a minute on the way back." With that Angela went out the door with the list and Dawn's money, which she had no intention of spending. She would use Shorty's money and let him try explaining it to Dawn. That might get them close together for a few minutes anyway.

On the way to town, Angela told Matt what she was going to do. She was buying a load of lumber and Shorty was using his money to buy the other things plus a bag of flour and potatoes. Maybe later, when they got the ranch up and running, they could pay it back. Angela said to Matt, "If there is anything you need at the ranch, you write it down. While you can get help you need something to work with. It must have made quite a hole in the groceries to feed that crew last weekend. Your garden is doing good, but it will be a while before there is much to eat from it. The flour and potatoes will help keep you going until then."

When they got to town, Matt thought they should order the windows first. They could then look around town and get a few of the smaller things. Just before leaving, they could load the lumber, pick up the flour and potatoes, and then pick up the things at the hardware store. Angela agreed that was what they would do, so the hardware store was the first stop.

Matt told the owner the size of the two windows they needed. He also asked if they had the roof jack readymade, or if they would have to get it another time. He said, "We have a lot of different roof jacks in stock. We will have the one you want. When are you leaving town? We aren't too busy right now, so we might be able to get those windows made for you by two thirty or three o'clock."

Angela spoke up then and said, "If you can have them ready before we leave, we would really appreciate it. We will be in town for a while, and we have to stop here before leaving anyway. Matt, you tell him what else you need and it will be ready when we get here." Matt said, "I think we better have two rolls of tar paper, two pair of hinges, one pair with loose pins if you have them and I think we better have twenty-five pounds of two and a half inch nails and ten pounds of four inch. With the windows and roof jack, that should be all."

The owner said, "OK, we'll have that ready, and we'll try to have the windows ready by then too. See you later." Matt and his aunt Angela looked around some of the stores. Angela asked Matt if he thought it wasn't time to have a bite to eat, as it was near noon. Matt followed Angela to a small restaurant where they could get some dinner. Angela ordered steak with all the vegetables plus a glass of milk for each. It was going to cost seventy five cents. Matt still had a bit more than a dollar from his first of July winnings in his pocket.

He said to his aunt, "Aunt Angela, you have been helping ma and me a lot. Can I pay for our meal please? I still have some money left that I won on the first of July." There must have been some dust in the air, because Angela had to wipe her eyes and blow her nose. "Well, Matt," she said, "you are a real gentleman just like Shorty. OK, you can buy our dinner, but I'm going to pay for desert. Pie and ice cream, any kind you want that they have. Is it a deal?" Matt replied, "It's a deal! Shake?" He reached across the table and shook hands and then laughed. They finished the meal and decided to look around town for a while before getting ready to head for home; this would also give more time to have the windows made. Matt and his aunt Angela looked in most of the stores in town, which weren't many, considering it was a small town. Matt said to his aunt, "I'd like to get something for my mother, something not too expensive because I don't have much money. What do you think she would like? "Well, Matt," she answered, "most women like pretty things, or something that makes them look or smell pretty. There is a ladies wear store at the end of town, let's go see what we can find!"

It wasn't very far from where they were and a couple of minutes later, they were on the boardwalk in front of the store. "Now Matt," Angela said, "this store has only ladies things and most men wouldn't be caught dead inside. Do you want to come

in with me, or do you want me to look for something for you."
Matt said, "I'm going to get something for my mother. I want you
to come with me, but I'm going to pick it out myself!" "Good man,
Matt," Angela said, "let's go!"

First they looked at jewelry but Matt didn't think that was
what he wanted. Shoes and hats were too expensive and he wasn't
too interested. As they walked past the perfume counter, there
were lots of beautiful smells. He was looking them over when
the lady behind the counter asked if she could help him. "I want
something special for my mother," he said. The lady opened tiny
bottles and passed them to him. He smelled roses, lavender,
spices, and many other wonderful smells. Nothing seemed to
be just right for his mother. The lady passed him another bottle
and his face lit up. "What is that?" Matt asked, "I like that!" The
lady said it was mayflower. She passed him another bottle and
he smiled and said, "That's nice too, what is that." She told him it
was white violet. Matt couldn't decide which one he liked best.

Angela took one bottle and put a dab on her wrist. She took
the other bottle and put a dab on the other wrist. She said, "Now
Matt, you just wait a minute or two and then see which one you
prefer!" Matt sniffed both wrists a time or two and said, "That's
the one I want!" When Angela told him it was mayflower, he
asked the lady how much it was. She said it was twenty cents.
She also told him, "We also have some pretty hankies. They are
two for fifteen cents. I'll tell you what I'll do Matt, since it's for
your mother, you can have the hankies and the perfume for thirty
cents. Matt picked out two pretty lace hankies and said, "Can you
wrap them up for me? I want it to be a surprise!"

They were soon on their way back to where they had left
the horses. The wagon was at the lumberyard where it had been
left to be loaded. When hitched up, the wagon was moved to the
general store where the flour and potatoes were loaded. The next
stop was the hardware store for the building materials and the
windows, if they were ready. At the hardware store, the owner,
George Connors said, "While you get these things loaded up, we'll
get the last window finished. There are only two more panes to

be put in and it will be completed." Matt shifted some lumber to leave a narrow slot between the boards for the windows to slide into, one behind the other. He knew windows should always be carried on edge to avoid breakage. When everything was loaded up and secured, Matt and Angela headed for home. They let the horses walk along slowly to avoid breaking the windows.

When they got to the ranch, Matt stopped the team close to the barn. The lumber would go in the barn, so he wanted it as close as possible. He wondered how he was going to get the hundred pound bag of flour to the house. He soon came up with what he thought was a good idea. Angela's light wagon wasn't far away. He pushed it back against the big wagon. He carefully rolled the bag of flour and the potatoes into the light wagon. He unhitched the team and hitched them to Angela's wagon. With this accomplished, he drove over to the house and backed up to the door. With the help of his mother and Angela, the flour and potatoes were soon in the house.

Dawn wanted to know how they got the lumber, hardware, and the flour and potatoes with the little bit of money she had given her. Angela told her she would have to take that up with Shorty when he arrived next time. Dawn had tea ready, so they visited over a cup, but Angela said very little about the supplies they had bought. Shortly it was time for Angela to be on her way. The things she had bought in town had been loaded on her wagon when Matt had loaded the flour and potatoes. There were hugs all around, and then waves as Angela left the yard. Matt went out and carried everything from the wagon to the bunkhouse, except the lumber, which would go in the barn. The windows were carefully carried to the bunkhouse and stood in a corner. Matt made sure the animals were looked after before he went to the house for supper.

After supper Matt took a few new boards up to the bunkhouse. The temporary table was in the corner, so he put the boards on it and got the plane to make the boards smooth. This weekend, he would help Shorty build a door for the bunkhouse. As he worked, he was thinking of how nice the bunkhouse was going to be when it was finished. There was plenty of tar paper for the roof now! Matt had gotten more nails, as it took a lot of nails for the roof. With the roof jack and hinges, they might be able to finish the bunkhouse this weekend. Matt decided he was going to sleep in this new bunkhouse as soon as they had some bunks built. When he finished with the lumber, he thought he should split more shakes. He hoped to have enough ready to finish the roof by the time Shorty arrived.

When darkness approached, Matt went to the house. He still had the surprise for his mother. He had thought of waiting until Shorty arrived, but there would be too many things happening then. He was going to give it to her just before bedtime. He made sure the chickens were closed up before going inside. He went to the house and washed up and ate a doughnut.

He got the package for his mother and placed it on the table in front of her. She had a surprised look on her face and then she asked what it was. Matt said, "It's something I got for you today in town. I bought it with the money I got on the first of July." Dawn unwrapped the package slowly. She looked at the hankies and held them to her face. She then opened the bottle of perfume and dabbed a bit on her wrist. Her eyes got bright as she sniffed the perfume. "Oh Matt," she said, "it smells just wonderful, and the hankies are much too nice to use. You didn't have to use your money for me!"

Matt said, "I wanted to get you something like this for your birthday, but I had no money. Maybe I should have got something we needed, but I thought getting something nice for you was more important." Dawn got up and walked around the table. She wrapped her arms around Matt and started to cry. "Matt, this is the nicest thing anyone has ever done for me. I should save this perfume for special occasions, but I'm going to use it almost every day. It will remind me of the wonderful man I have for a son!" Matt thought he had made his mother very happy. A short time later, it was bedtime for two happy people.

Morning usually came early on the R-R. After the morning chores were taken care of and breakfast finished, Matt went out to split more shakes. There was a good pile waiting now, but Matt knew it wasn't enough to finish the roof. When Dawn finished her housework, she went out to the garden. As she worked at pulling weeds, she had a pail and a bowl alongside her. She put the best weeds in the bowl and all the others in the pail. When the pail was full, she gave some to the chickens and the rest to the pigs. Matt's two pigs were growing fast. The weeds in the bowl were for dinner. Pigweeds (lambs quarter) and turnip greens would make a good meal of greens. When the bowl was full, she took it to the house and put them in the sink. She then ran an inch of water into the sink to keep the greens fresh. Back in the garden, all the weeds went into the pail for the pigs. She thought there should be a few small potatoes by now, so she reached into the soil under the plants and picked one or two from each plant. She looked under the bean leaves and found a few beans almost big enough to eat. She thought to herself, 'Potatoes and greens will make a meal for Matt and I. Friday I will get a few more new potatoes, greens, and a few beans for a good meal, when Shorty is here.' Nothing would beat a meal of fresh vegetables straight from the garden! She decided to leave some of the garden unweeded, so she could get more greens later in the week.

She went over to where Matt was working and took over splitting shakes until it was time to get dinner ready. Matt would be surprised to have fresh greens and new potatoes. After a tasty meal of fresh vegetables, Dawn and Matt traded off at splitting shakes, putting moss in the cracks, and other small jobs around the buildings. Matt took a few minutes and went up on the bunkhouse roof. He counted how many shakes were in one row on the roof. Back at the pile, he put the shakes in stacks of ten. He had a lot of stacks, side by side and cross piled on top. They could keep track of how many they had ready and approximately how many more were needed. Shorty would be here tomorrow evening, and if they didn't have enough, he would remedy that situation in short order.

Matt looked forward to working with Shorty. They got along well together, and Shorty treated Matt like he was a man, even though he was only seven, well, almost eight years old. Matt would have a birthday in the fall. He hoped that someday Shorty and his mother would get married, but so far, though they were good friends, they didn't seem interested in each other. He wished there was something he could do about that. Well, Shorty had taught him to think, and he would keep thinking about this; maybe, someday he could come up with a solution to this problem! Right now, it was time for Matt to quit daydreaming and get some work done; after all, he was the man on this ranch!

He decided to do a bit more digging at the root cellar. A couple of more hours should have it ready to start building. Matt worked steadily at digging the soil loose and tossing it to the side. He was about to go to another job when Dawn called him to dinner. With a meal inside him and a short break, he would feel like going back to work. They talked as they ate, and Dawn asked Matt, "Where did the money come from to buy the potatoes and flour? I hardly had enough to pay for the things we needed for the bunkhouse, so Angela must have paid for it." Matt replied, "I think she said she was using Shorty's money for some of it, but I think she paid for the lumber. Maybe Shorty thought we wouldn't have enough food to last until the garden was ready." "Well," Dawn said, "I guess we'll find out when Shorty gets here. We have some cattle out there on the range someplace, and we could always sell a few if we have to. I don't want people to think we can't look after ourselves!"

Chapter 7

MEANWHILE, BACK AT the ranch, Gus and Shorty were out looking for strays, along the edges of the hills. They were pushing the cattle from the hills out onto the open range, where the grass was still good. Later when the weather got drier, the cattle would drift back into the hills and brush, where the grass didn't dry out as soon. Shorty had never been on this part of the range before. They were still finding a few R-R cattle, but they were few and far between. They came across a narrow gully with a few cattle tracks leading up it into the hills. They decided to follow the tracks and see if they could chase these cattle back out on the range. They followed the gully for half a mile or more, when suddenly it opened up into a wide valley! The valley was as flat as a floor and covered with knee-high grass. Near the middle was a small pond or lake, with a small stream coming from the hills keeping it full. As far as they could see, there were cattle. There was a lot of big cattle that should have been shipped a year or two ago. They rode slowly around the valley, checking brands. The only brand they saw was the R-R and two bulls wearing the

Axe brand. Shorty and Gus estimated there must have been three-hundred acres in this valley. The sides were too steep for cattle to climb, except in one or two places. These climbable areas led back into the rough, brushy hills, and there was no reason for cattle to go back there, with all the grass available in this valley. Only the biggest cattle had brands on them. The boys decided these cattle had been here for years, breeding and multiplying. Apparently, a few of these cattle had found this place years back, and there was no reason for leaving. All the cattle they could see a brand on belonged to the R-R. All of these cattle, young and old, belonged to Dawn and Matt Ryan!

A quick tally put the number of cattle at more than two hundred head, probably closer to two hundred and fifty! These cattle could be rounded up in the fall and the older ones sent to market. They were all fat and glossy and could be sold at anytime. As Gus and Shorty rode around the cattle, they were looking and thinking. Shorty said to Gus, "You know, Gus, my idea is that at one time in the past this valley was a lake!" Gus looked around a bit and replied, "I think you're right. This valley was the bottom of a lake. That's the reason the ground is so flat. The steep sides were the lake bank. The gully was the stream that drained it. Yep, you hit the nail on the head that time. What are we going to do? We can't take them out of here by ourselves, so I guess they will have to stay here!"

"For now anyway," Shorty said, "they will stay here. There is no reason to move them as they have the best of everything here, plenty of grass and water, a few patches of trees for shade and shelter. I bet this place is warmer in winter than the open range and the wind wouldn't be too bad with the hills all around. That's probably why the first ones stayed when they found it; the best grass in the country, water, and a sheltered spot in the winter. We'll tell the boss, but my guess is that the cattle will stay here. In the fall we can separate them and drive the older ones to market, the rest can be branded and left here. This is the best place I ever saw to raise cattle and I've rode a fair bit of range in my day. Did you notice how quiet they are, Gus? I bet most of these cattle have never seen a man or a horse before in their life, yet they are as quiet as a newborn kitten! They seem to have no reason to fear us. There can't be many varmints around here, as I haven't seen any bones or dead animals."

Gus agreed that this seemed like cow heaven, if there was such a place. With the rich lake bottom soil and plenty of water and grass, this valley would easily support this many cattle and probably a lot more. The snow probably wouldn't drift in this sheltered valley, so the cattle could feed easily all winter. It was getting late in the afternoon, so the boys decided to make tracks for home. They would tell the boss and get his idea on what was to be done. By the time they got back to the ranch, it was past supper time. But they knew when someone was late, the cook always kept something hot for them. The boss and the foreman were talking in the yard, so after unsaddling and putting their mounts in the corral; they walked over to tell them what they had found.

The boss and foreman could hardly believe what Gus and Shorty had to say. Neither of them had ever seen or heard of any place like this. The boss asked, "You say they are all R-R cattle?" Shorty said. "The only brands we saw were R-R. There were a couple of bulls with the Axe brand. Most of the cattle in there never saw a branding iron or a man in their life! We think the R-R cattle wandered in there and made themselves at home. With grass, water, and shelter like they have, why would even one want to leave?" Gus added, "That's a real cow heaven if I ever saw one. We figured, at one time, long ago, that valley was a lake and the water drained out through that cut we followed in. That valley is flat as a floor, with knee-high grass. No critter would ever leave there on its own!"

The boss and the foreman both agreed they were going to see this 'cow heaven,' at the earliest opportunity. It looked like the first chance they would have would be next week. "Well," the boss said, "it looks like Dawn and Matt will have some money to work with, when we can get some of those cattle out and sold for them. I've been wondering where all the R-R cattle went to. When they first came here, I sold them fifty head of young heifers for breeding stock. There is a few here and there, but by now there should have been a lot more. Now we know why they aren't on the range. I'll bet Dawn will be pleased to hear about this!"

The boss went in the house to tell his wife, and Shorty and Gus went to the cook shack to get a late supper. It was late, so very soon it would be time to hit the bunk and rest up for another day. When busy, time passes quickly and the following day was no exception at the Axe. Shorty wasn't one to let the grass grow under his feet, so the day fairly flew by. After eating supper, he was on the trail to the Ryan ranch. He had a wonderful surprise for Dawn and Matt. As he rode along, he was wondering how they would react to being the owners of so many cattle. They would now have some money to buy some of the things they needed so it wouldn't be necessary for them to work so hard. The money might not be available until the fall roundup, but it was like having money in the bank.

The sun was still above the horizon when Shorty rode into the yard at the R-R. He could see that Dawn and Matt had been busy. The garden was looked after, there was a pile of shakes ready to go on the bunkhouse roof, and there had been fresh digging at the root cellar site. No one could say the Ryans' were lazy, as they worked just about all day, every day. Shorty rode his horse up to the barn, unsaddled, turned his horse into the corral, and put his saddle in the shed. He could see Dawn and Matt were waiting at the door for him. He felt like he was coming home. As he crossed the yard, he could smell fresh doughnuts and hot tea. Dawn handed him a cup and waved him to a chair. She got her own cup of tea and sat down opposite him.

Dawn looked at Shorty and said, "I think we have to have a talk!" Shorty said, "OK, it's kind of late in the day to start working. What do you want to talk about?" Dawn said, "Well, I want to know who paid for everything Matt and Angela brought home from town. There is the load of lumber, all the things for the bunkhouse, and the flour and potatoes. I gave my sister what money I had, but I don't think there was enough to buy what we needed for the bunkhouse!"

Shorty answered, "Your sister told me last week she was going to take Matt to town and get a load of lumber. She saw we were getting a lot done here, and she wanted to make sure we didn't run out of material to work with. I had nothing to do with that, but she said I would have to explain it to you some way. I told her to use some of the money I had coming to get some flour and potatoes. Feeding that crew last weekend must have made a big dent in the food supply. I also told her if you didn't have enough money, to use mine and get the things we needed. We should be able to finish the bunkhouse this weekend, but not if we have nothing to work with."

Dawn said, "Does everyone think we can't look after ourselves? We don't want charity!" Shorty answered, "I wouldn't call it charity. Let's call it a loan. You can pay me back when you get the ranch on its feet. I know it's been hard for you and Matt to keep this place going. Your sister and I just want to help you get going again." Dawn looked at Shorty and said, "It might be years before we have enough money to pay anyone back. We will probably have to gather up the few cattle of ours that are out there on the range and sell them just to live on!"

Shorty smiled and said, "By fall, you can pay off what you owe and have a little left to live on, I can guarantee that!" Dawn asked, "How are we going to do that? Rob a bank?"

"Nope," Shorty answered, "you have a lot more cattle than you think. Gus and I found a small herd of your cattle back in the hills. Some big ones that should have gone to market before now! We can round them up in the fall, brand them, and sell the older ones. You won't be rich, but you will have some money to work with. The rest of the cattle can stay there. It's just like having money in the bank!"

Dawn got up, went around the table, sat on Shorty's lap, put her arms around him, and kissed him. She began to cry and said, "Oh Shorty, I don't know what we are going to do with you. Every time things look bad, you show up and fix it for us. How do you

manage to do everything right and always just at the right time?"
Shorty felt a bit embarrassed, but he liked the feel of Dawn's arms
around him. He wouldn't mind feeling like this more often!

Matt was sitting at the table, watching with a big smile on his
face. He was thinking that things were finally starting to go the
way he was hoping for. He hardly dared to breathe because he
didn't want to disturb anyone. After a few minutes, Dawn got up
and went back to her chair. She had a big smile on her face too.
Shorty said, "The boss and foreman are going with us next week
to look at the cattle and the valley. I'm sure they wouldn't mind
if you and Matt went along, after all, they are your cattle. We can
probably find a horse and saddle at the ranch you could use for
the trip. There is no way to get a wagon in there, so it's either by
horseback or on foot." Dawn and Matt were both anxious to see
this hidden valley, full of their cows. It was an answer to their
prayers, moneywise at least. They talked a bit more about the
cows and then decided it was time to get some shut-eye and rest
up to get ready for work tomorrow.

Early the next morning, all three were up and busy. Shorty
looked after the stock, while Matt milked the cow, and Dawn was
getting breakfast ready. When Dawn called them to breakfast,
it only took a minute to wash up and head for the house. A hot
meal went down quite easily and then it was outside to work.
Matt and Shorty stopped at the pile of shakes and studied it a
bit. Matt told Shorty he had counted the shakes in one course on
the roof and then piled them in neat stacks for easier counting.
They thought it looked like almost enough, but they would put
some on the roof before splitting more. They each took a stack of
shakes and headed to the bunkhouse. They made several more
trips, carrying stacks of shakes, before gathering up their tools
and starting work.

Shorty tacked a long, narrow board onto the roof at the exact
level for the butts of the next course of shakes. The shakes were
laid in place, making sure the joints in the underneath course
were covered. It was a simple matter to drive two or three
nails in each shake, being sure to have them high enough to be

covered by the next course. As each course was finished, a strip of tar paper was laid in place and the job continued. With a good supply of shakes handy, the roof was being closed in quickly. Before the boys got too far advanced, Dawn came out to give them a hand. Matt suggested she help Shorty nail shakes and he would carry them and have the tar paper cut and ready. He was secretly thinking that this was another time to get Shorty and Dawn close together. Since the roof came almost to the ground on the upper side, Matt could carry a load of shakes right up on the roof. When the job had started, there was a good supply of shakes on the roof waiting. Now Matt was kept busy as this supply was almost gone, and occasionally he had to split more tar paper so the roofers didn't have to wait.

Matt took a few minutes to run to the house and make some tea. He carried a couple stacks of shakes before going back to the house for the tea. He put a small bottle of milk, three cups, the pot of tea, and six doughnuts in a box and carried it up to the bunkhouse and up on the roof. Once there, he called, "Teatime!" and all three sat on the roof and enjoyed a short break and a cup of tea. Matt didn't drink tea all the time, but now and then he would have a cup.

Shorty asked Matt, "Well, Matt, what have you done all week? I can see you have most of the joints filled with moss and a lot more gathered along with getting the saplings cut and drying. You and your mother had a lot of shakes split and you have been digging at the root cellar. What do you do with all your spare time?" All three laughed at that and Matt answered, "Well, sometimes I go to town and just look around!" Shorty got a chuckle from Matt's answer.

When the tea and doughnuts were gone, it was time to go back to work. Matt took everything back to the house as Shorty and Dawn started driving nails again. Before dinner time rolled around, they were over halfway up the roof. At the rate they were going, they should finish the roof before night, if they didn't run out of shakes. Later, Dawn went into the house to get a quick lunch. She was going to make some roast beef sandwiches, as all three were anxious to get the roof done. She planned to take the time to get a good meal for their supper. After a quick lunch, they were all back at work on the roof. Matt always had a couple of stacks of shakes on the roof so the hammers seldom stopped. The only time there was silence was the time it took to roll out another strip of tar paper. With two hammers driving nails, the shakes disappeared almost as fast as Matt could carry them, but he could gain on them when the tar paper was being spread out. All three seemed to be working as fast as they could, and they got more excited as the hole in the roof got smaller.

Suddenly Dawn stopped and said, "What about the stove pipe?" Shorty laughed and said, "It's a good thing we weren't all sleeping on the job! We would have had the roof finished and no place for the smoke to come out! Now, we better get the stove out of the barn and decide where the smoke hole is going to be."

They got the stove out of the barn and brushed it off. It wasn't very heavy, so it was carried up to the bunkhouse. They had planned to have the stove in the middle of the building so it would heat it all evenly. The stove was placed in its approximate position, and the stove pipe set in place. Shorty went up on the roof, looked down, and made some marks on the roof. He wanted some support under the roof jack, but he also wanted the wood as far away from the pipe as possible. They had found a short piece of larger pipe in the barn and this would come in handy. It would go into the roof jack with the smaller pipe inside it. This would make a heat shield, to keep the heat from the pipe away from the wood.

With Shorty's measurements and pencil marks to go by, they could keep nailing the shakes in place. It only took a few minutes to trim a few shakes to fit around the hole for the roof jack. When the hole was closed in on three sides, the roof jack was put in place, and the upper shakes went over the base of the roof jack to carry the water over top of it. When the shakes reached the peak, the next course had one foot trimmed off them. With this row in place, a double layer of tar paper was placed over the peak and the twelve-inch shakes were put in place. The shakes were now all on the roof! Another narrow strip of tar paper was placed on the peak and a four and a five-inch board were nailed together to form a trough, which was placed upside down on the peak When the peak cap was nailed in place, the roof was finished!

Completing the roof called for a celebration. Dawn was thinking she had some fresh greens, potatoes, and string beans ready for the pot. This would be their celebration supper. She told Shorty and Matt, "You boys keep busy for half an hour or so while I get some supper ready." The vegetables were all ready, so all she had to do was get the water hot to boil them. Occasionally through the day she or Matt had put wood in the stove so supper would be ready soon.

At the bunkhouse, Shorty and Matt were preparing to put the windows in place. First a board was tacked to one side of the sawhorses. A three-inch board was tacked to this, with one edge hanging over. A line was marked one inch from the edge and this piece was cut off with a ripsaw. Two three-inch boards were split into one-inch strips, and then planed smooth. Two strips were trimmed and nailed, one on each side of the window opening. The window was placed against these strips and another nailed against the window to hold it in securely. The same process was used to put the second window in place. Later, strips would be placed all around the windows to seal all the cracks. The bunkhouse now boasted two glass windows!

Now it was time for a door. Shorty brought a rabbet plane from the ranch with him. This would cut one half of the edge off a board. Several boards were planed this way, and then trimmed to the right length. These boards were laid on the benches, and a narrow board placed one foot from each end and nailed in place. Another narrow board was placed diagonally between the cross boards for a brace so the door wouldn't sag. The hinges were nailed to the door directly over the cross boards. The door was held in place, pushed to the top of the hole, and the hinges nailed to the door frame. A wooden handle was made and fastened to the door and a narrow strip of lumber nailed inside the frame for the door to close against. Later, these strips would go all around the frame to seal it tightly. The door needed a latch to hold it closed but this would come later. When Dawn came to get them for supper, she was surprised to see how much they had done in such a short time. The bunkhouse was really taking shape now!

Dawn had a special supper ready to celebrate the completion of the bunk house. Shorty was surprised to see the fresh vegetables Dawn had prepared for the meal. He hadn't expected the garden to be this far along so soon. With the new potatoes, beans, and fresh greens, he felt he was eating like a king. Nothing, absolutely nothing, is better than fresh vegetables right from the garden! This was two celebrations: a wonderful meal to celebrate the completion of the bunk house and the meal of fresh vegetables was a celebration itself! All three felt the meal was a fitting tribute to their hard work, the completion of the bunk house, and the work involved in having a garden producing fresh vegetables. As they ate, they all decided to celebrate further, by taking the evening to relax. They had all been working without a break for a long time it seemed.

Shorty thought he would put a couple of joists in place for the floor of the porch at the bunkhouse. He said it wouldn't be much work, and with the bunkhouse mainly completed, they should have an easier way to get in and out. After supper, he and Matt went out to do the porch floor. Shorty told Matt, "You go find a half dozen of those small poles like you cut for the chinking, but just a bit bigger. I have an idea for something we can do when we get this floor done. I'll keep working on it while you are getting the poles."

Matt took the axe and went up the hill, while Shorty began work on the floor. He looked the project over and decided to use sawn lumber for the joists as it would be faster than logs. He cut small notches in the base log of the cabin, but since the outside support log was smaller, the joists would set on top of it. He went to the barn and got five, eight foot two by six planks. He trimmed the ends to fit the notches and shaved the outer ends until they sat level. All were then nailed securely in place. The boards that had been used for a temporary floor for the roof work were nailed on the porch floor. Since this floor would get wet occasionally, narrow cracks were left to allow water to drain through and so the floor would dry.

By the time Matt returned, Shorty had half of the floor done. Matt picked up a hammer and began driving nails too. They soon had the floor finished, as it was only about eight by twelve feet. The thickness of the log walls left only ten feet of width inside. Shorty told Matt, "You get two more planks for us, I have another idea!" Shorty measured thirty inches from the floor and marked the upright post. On the wall of the bunkhouse, thirty inches was at a joint between two logs. A two-inch notch was cut in the upright and a plank trimmed to fit the joint in the wall and the notch in the upright. The plank was tapped into place and nailed securely. When the same operation was done on the other side, they had two railing-seats for the porch. Matt trimmed two short pieces to be fastened upright under the middle of each railing for extra support.

By this time, Dawn had her housework finished and had arrived at the bunkhouse. The floor was nailed down, and the two railing seats were in place and supported. Dawn asked, "How did you get all this done in such a short time? I was hardly away half an hour and look at what you two have done in that time. I love these railings. They are just the right height for sitting on, but I thought this was going to be an evening to relax." Shorty said, "Well, if we are going to take it easy, we need a place to relax. This wasn't very hard work and now we have a place to sit and enjoy the evenings, even if it rains."

Dawn asked them, "What are you two up to now?" Matt told her, "You just sit there and watch. You will find out soon enough!" Shorty was cutting and measuring and marking spots for Matt to bore holes in the sticks he had brought down from the hill. They had two matching pieces about three feet long and two matching pieces about eighteen inches long. Shorty started whittling some smaller sticks to fit in the holes Matt had bored, and asked Matt, "Can you find us a short piece of small rope? Five or six feet will do, but we can cut a bit off a longer rope if

SHORTY'S STORY | 125

necessary." Matt went to the barn to look for some rope while Shorty continued whittling.

Dawn said, "I can see you are making a chair, but what do you need the rope for?" Shorty smiled and said, "Don't be impatient! Like Matt said, you will find out soon." Shorty had four sticks the same length with the ends whittled down to fit the holes. He laid the long pieces on the floor and drove two small sticks in each one. He then took the shorter pieces and drove them onto the small sticks or rungs. He now had two chair halves. Matt was back with some rope by this time and he helped Shorty whittle ends on more chair rungs. Four of these small sticks were driven into holes to form a chair back. The other chair half was placed over these ends and tapped lightly together. A rung was placed in a hole near the bottom, and the chair was driven together solidly. Two slightly longer sticks were driven into holes in the front of the chair. They now had a complete chair without a seat. Shorty measured and marked a small stick and told Matt to cut about ten more and bore holes about one inch from each end. Shorty checked each stick to be sure they were smooth and if not whittled them until they were. He then bored a hole in the front and back seat pieces the same spacing as Matt had bored the small sticks. He pushed an end of the rope through the front hole as Matt did the same. The small sticks were threaded on the rope until the seat was full. A knot was tied in the rope behind the back piece and pulled tight, and with about a foot of spare rope in front, one at a time the ropes were pulled as tight as possible and tied. The chair was finished! Both Shorty and Matt insisted Dawn had to try it out first. Dawn carefully sat in the chair; a big smile crossed her face. "This is the most comfortable chair I have ever sat in!" she said. "It feels like there is padding on it!" Both of the boys had big grins on their face. Shorty said, "That's because the rope allows the chair seat to mold to your body. The pressure is the same all over, so it is more comfortable. On a hard seat, your hip bones take most of the weight, so after a while you feel the pressure. Now, do you still think we are working too hard?" Dawn said, "*Yes*, I do, but I love this chair!" Both Shorty and Matt tried the chair and agreed that it was very comfortable, but they insisted Dawn had to sit in the chair.

Shorty told Matt, "You go hunt up the widest board you can find, ten or twelve inches if possible. It doesn't have to be very long, but we can cut what we need from a long one." Matt went to look for a board, and Shorty started cutting and whittling again. He cut four sticks about two inches through and sixteen inches long, these he whittled down on one end. He got Dawn to hold them with one end on a board while he bored a hole straight down. This put the hole at a slight angle. He then cut two pieces of two by four, ten inches long. A hole was bored near the ends at a slight angle, on both pieces. Two of the round sticks were driven into the holes and a small stick driven into the angled hole for a rung. All the joints were driven solidly together. Matt was back with the wide board and a piece was cut off for their purpose. The short two-inch pieces were nailed to the wide board, and the boys had another good place to sit. With a good place for everyone to sit, that was what they did! They sat and talked and enjoyed the evening until time for bed. They all agreed that other evenings would be spent here!

They figured Randy would arrive in the morning, and they would probably have to get more logs before starting on the root cellar. They would go back up in the hills and get what tamarack was left and get some of the pine that was drying also. The root cellar wouldn't have to be as tight as the bunkhouse, so it could be built with square notches. This would save time and work. First thing in the morning, they would get the tamarack logs, and if there was more digging to be done, it would be done after the logs were on site. Just before darkness settled in, Dawn went to the house and brought up tea and doughnuts for a bedtime snack on their new, open porch. It was such a nice spot that no one was anxious to leave, but sleep was calling them, so off to bed they went.

As the sun was coming up the next morning, the usual chores were being done. Most mornings on the ranch promised to be busy ones, and this morning was no different. Shorty made sure the horses had a bit of grain as they would be working today, unlike some of the days the team had spent recently. Dawn had a lunch ready, and the horses were hitched up ready to go. Matt thought they should leave a note for Randy in case he arrived. This was done and left on the bunkhouse door. If Randy came, he could dig at the root cellar or walk back to the hills, whichever he preferred. With the tools and people loaded, the wagon was on the way back to the hills. Since the scoot sled was still in the woods, they stopped where the pine logs were and unhitched the horses. The team was hitched to the sled, and they continued on to where the tamarack was located. There wasn't many left as they had used a lot of them to make shakes. Shorty decided the six logs that were left could be taken out in one trip with the team. Shorty started limbing the top that had been left on for drying. When one log was ready, Matt would hook the horses to it and pull it ahead to a wider spot. With half the logs out, all three joined forces and pulled the sled alongside. With poles and peavey, the butts were loaded on the sled. The other three were treated in a similar manner and soon all six were on the sled. The chain was given a double wrap around the logs to prevent them sliding off. When they reached the wagon, Matt suggested, "Why not take them all the way to the ranch on the sled? It doesn't matter if they get dirty or scraped up, as they are going in the ground anyway. We can cut them up out there and this way we won't have to load them." Shorty and Dawn thought Matt's idea was a good one. It was the easiest way to get the logs out to the job. Matt would take the logs out while Dawn and Shorty limbed some of the pine and cut them up.

The root cellar was to be eight by ten inside, so the logs would be cut ten and twelve feet long. Shorty tried to cut both long and short logs from the butts so they would be basically the same size. The bigger ones would go on the bottom and the smaller ones on top. Dawn reminded Shorty that they had six-long trees on the way out that were for the root cellar. Shorty said, "That's right, maybe we shouldn't cut too many until we need them. No point in having them cut to the wrong length. We can limb the rest and leave them long."

Dawn and Shorty worked at limbing the pine, leaving them tree length. Now and then, they would take a short break and sit and talk. This hadn't been happening much as, in the last few months, they had been busy working. They were just finishing the last of the logs when they heard the horses and sled coming, with Matt and Randy walking along behind it. Randy had been digging at the root cellar when Matt had arrived with the logs. He decided a change of scenery was in order, so he came back with Matt. Here was some extra manpower to help load the logs that Shorty and Dawn had cut up. The logs were loaded in short order and the smaller logs and firewood were tossed on top. Since Dawn had packed the lunch and it had come along, it was only right that they stop for a bit and sample it. Besides that, it was starting to feel like eating time.

They found a nice mossy spot among the trees and had an old fashioned picnic. There was no hot tea but there was plenty of cold water. Randy thought they had made great progress on the bunkhouse. He still hadn't heard that Shorty had a three-day weekend. When they finally told him, he said, "I've been wondering how you could get so much work done in one evening. Nobody told me you were working all day Friday and pretending you weren't. Just for that, I'm not coming to help you next weekend. You will have to do all the work yourself!" Randy didn't seem upset but he wasn't smiling, so they thought he might be serious.

Dawn asked him, "Would it help if I promised to make lots of fresh doughnuts for you?" Randy said, "Nope, not even if you . . . hey, that's not fair. You know nobody can resist your doughnuts! Especially me! I shouldn't tell you this, but something has come up that's going to keep me busy next weekend. I should have let you think I was upset with you. I will probably be here the weekend after, though. Now, if we are going to get something done on that root cellar, we better get moving. Next weekend you won't have my expert help." Everybody had a good laugh and agreed they should get moving before bedtime caught them. When they got to the ranch, the wagon was left as close as possible to the job and the team was unhitched. There wasn't much digging to be done, so the logs were pried up and sticks placed under them so they could be cut off. The length was marked on some and Randy and Shorty made short work of cutting them off. They decided to start with the end logs first. They would dig them into the ground so it would be easier to step over going into the root cellar.

One-third of the top of the log would be sawed into and split off. The front log could be sawed in place but the back one had to be notched before going into place. The side logs could be rolled into the middle to be notched. Since the front wall wasn't going to be put in place, at least right now, they decided to put a vertical log just inside the wall at the front. It would be notched into the bottom log with a cross log on top. All three would be fastened together and a corner brace put in each top corner. To help hold the front wall also, short logs would be notched in, but extend outwards into the bank. With square notches, the walls would go up quickly. Once work got underway, they found it was easier to notch the logs in the open and then slide them into place. One quarter of the thickness of the log was taken off, top and bottom. The ground would be pushing inwards, so the logs didn't actually have to lock together, as long as they couldn't collapse inwards.

Before Dawn called them for supper, they had the walls about four feet high. Supper was a hurried affair with very little talk, as all were anxious to get back to work on the root cellar. Dawn promised to have a good lunch at bedtime. In a short time, they were back at the root cellar. They had two more courses of logs on it before deciding to call it a day. Dawn had kept her promise and had a good lunch ready, which they enjoyed sitting on the porch at the bunkhouse. Randy too, was impressed with the new porch. He thought it was a great spot to eat lunch and finish the day.

The next morning the boys were doing the chores, and Dawn was cooking breakfast when the sun appeared. Then, with a quick but good meal inside them, they headed for the root cellar and work. The walls of the root cellar had to be over six feet high so a person could stand inside. After the walls were completed, they would notch in five logs across the top to keep the walls from pushing in. The logs would also serve as roof supports.

Finally, the boys decided to put one upright log in the center at the front and one upright in the center of the root cellar. The back wall would be logged up higher and a log would rest on the two uprights and the back wall. Smaller, shorter uprights would support the main roof beam and set on the logs across the cellar. They were tossing around the idea of splitting logs for the roof. The first course would be laid flat side up, the next one flat side down. It would make a tighter, more waterproof roof but it was more work. The walls had to be built to the right height before any roof could go on. In a couple of hours, they were ready to start on the roof. Though it was more work, they decided to go with the split logs. Shorty and Randy sawed a lot of logs into six foot lengths. Matt got a couple of wedges and a maul and began splitting logs while the two men got the roof supports in place. First the five logs were notched and put on top of the walls. Next in line were the small upright support logs, at this time they decided to put one at the back too. With the uprights in place and the long log on top, the short uprights were placed under the main log on the cross logs. Holes were bored through the top log into the long uprights and wooden pins driven in solidly. Now, they were ready to start on the roof logs.

Shorty and Randy helped Matt split more roof logs. One man would drive an axe into the center of the log at one end; Matt would then drive a wedge into the crack, making it wider. The man with the other axe would follow the crack, finishing the job. With three men working on a log, it was split in no time. A short time later, there were enough logs split to cover the roof. Shorty climbed up on top and Randy passed the split logs up to him as he laid them in place. Randy asked Matt to go up to the bunkhouse and bring the tar paper down for them. It would be laid on the flat upper surface and covered with the second layer.

This would be another roof that shouldn't leak. These logs didn't have to be fastened too solidly, as once they were covered with soil, nothing could move.

Before they had much roof on, Dawn came out to tell them dinner was ready. She was surprised at the progress they had made on the root cellar. Yesterday morning it was a hole in the ground, now it was an underground house, once it was covered over. Everyone was pleased with how the root cellar was taking shape. They were also pleased with the meal Dawn had waiting for them.

After a good meal and a short break, they were back at work. They thought it would be easier working if the hole was filled in around the walls. With three shovels moving loose dirt downhill, the job was history in no time. Matt cut the tar paper and this too was put in place. A few more logs had to be split, but the roof was soon completed. Shorty stopped suddenly, "Matt," he said, "see if you can find a couple of lengths of stove pipe in the barn. We forgot to put a vent in the roof to let the moisture out. Without a vent, the moisture builds up and the vegetables won't keep as well. We will get a place ready for it while you get the pipe." Randy and Shorty removed a couple of split logs and chopped a hole in the underneath logs. When Matt came back with the two lengths of pipe, the hole was ready for it. Randy suggested wrapping the pipe with tar paper so the soil wouldn't rust it too quickly. The pipe was soon in place and the roof was ready to be covered over.

They knew they had some time before supper, so they decided to use a horse and the scoop. It wouldn't take long to move a lot of soil with some horsepower. Matt led the horse, and Randy and Shorty took turns with the scoop and shovel. Before Dawn called them to supper, the root cellar was completely covered to a depth of three feet or more. No matter how cold it got, the vegetables wouldn't freeze inside. This left only the front of the root cellar to be finished and that would be done at a later date. Randy wouldn't be here next weekend, so it wouldn't be too big a job for Shorty and Matt to finish the front, now that the heaviest work was done. The horse was unharnessed, and all three got washed up, ready for supper.

Usually, after everyone had their appetite partly satisfied, they discussed their days labour and the next day's also. Shorty thought, instead of closing in the front with logs on their flat, he would stand them upright. It would be faster and probably stronger. As at the bunkhouse, the joints would be filled with moss then sealed with clay. A wide doorway would make it easier to carry vegetables through.

Matt asked, "Won't the cold go through the door? If the wall is thick logs, it will be warmer than the thin boards in the door." Shorty answered, "Well, Matt, when we get through building, the door will be warm too. I plan to have a tight fitting door on the outside and another door on the inside at least four inches thick. It will be filled with moss, leaves, straw, or something to help keep the cold out. If it gets really cold, the vent can be plugged until it warms up a bit. The front is the only place the cold can get through, with the rest of it buried in the ground like it is. Maybe later, we could dig a small pit under the house, with a box that can be pulled up with a rope. Enough vegetables could be stored down there to last for a few weeks. When the weather warms up a bit, you open up the root cellar and bring in enough to last for another few weeks. Most vegetables in this root cellar will keep the year round."

Chapter 8

THIS WAS SUNDAY evening, so Shorty and Randy would be leaving for their respective ranches soon after supper. They explained to Randy about finding the hidden valley and the R-R cattle. When the older cattle were separated and sold, Dawn and Matt would have some money to work with. Shorty told Dawn, "I'll see if I can get word to you before we leave for the valley. Maybe Angela could bring the wagon over to get you or even ride over with a couple of saddle horses. We'll work something out."

Dawn and Matt would be on their own for a week, or at least until word came from the Axe about the trip to the valley to see their 'found' cattle. They were both looking forward to this break in their normal routine. Dawn was wishing they could afford a couple of riding horses. Matt should be going back to school in the fall, and it was either ride a work horse or walk. Maybe when they sold some of these new found cattle, they could each get a horse. Well, she thought, enough daydreaming, time to get on her feet and get to work.

Matt went outside and looked around. He decided to finish stuffing the cracks with moss, as there wasn't much left to do. When he went inside, he was thinking what a nice bunkhouse they now had. It was clean and smelled of fresh wood. He decided, when the bunks were built, he was going to spend a few nights sleeping here. It seemed like an awful big place with just the stove, sawhorses, and a bit of lumber. He knew, when they got the bunks built, a table, and a couple of chairs, there wouldn't be as much room, but it would still be a cozy spot. He was pushing moss into the cracks while he was doing his thinking. He soon had all the cracks filled on the inside, so he went outside to stuff a bit more in a few spots. When he finished filling the cracks, he thought about putting the saplings in the cracks. He should have asked Shorty how he wanted it done. Well, he thought, 'Shorty showed me how to think, so that's what I'll do.' He trimmed a few more branches off a sapling until it was no bigger than his finger and then chopped the top off. He kept this up until he had about twenty long, slim poles. He decided to start in the storage area. This way if it wasn't done right, it wouldn't show very much. He held the pole in the joint and drove a few nails to hold it. He knew the joints would be filled with clay, and the sapling was mainly to give the clay something extra to grip. The sapling looked like he thought it should, so he put another one in place. He put the big ends at the corners and joined the tops in the middle. In half an hour, he had the wall in the storage area completed. It was about bedtime, so he went to check the stock, close up the chickens, and head for the house.

Dawn and Matt ate a snack while sitting at the table and talked about the cattle Shorty and Gus had found. This meant that when the cattle were sold, there would be some money to buy a few things they needed. It might not be a lot of money, but it would be more than they had now. As Shorty had said, 'cattle on the hoof were just like having money in the bank.' It was also going to be exciting to go someplace that very few people had ever seen. Maybe Gus and Shorty were the first people to ever see this hidden valley! Well, here it was bedtime again, and maybe tomorrow they would be going to see their cattle!

Meanwhile, back at the ranch, Shorty was talking to the boss's wife, Angela. He mentioned telling Matt and Dawn about finding the valley full of their cattle, and that they were interested in seeing them. Angela thought that was a good idea. After all," she said, "they are their cattle. I'll find out when everyone is going and I'll go over and get Dawn and Matt. You said it was too rough for a wagon, so I'll have a couple of horses saddled to take to them, and we can ride together. We have a small horse and saddle that would be good for Matt, and there are lots of quiet horses that Dawn and I can ride. Shorty, you have helped Dawn and Matt a lot in the last few months. Finding those cattle have helped them even more, now they will have a little money to work with."

"Well, ma'am," Shorty said. "We didn't set out to do that. We were just following strays, we thought, and we ran across them. I know it's going to help them a lot to have some cash money. I also think it's going to be good for them to get away from work for a few hours." Angela said, "You're right, Shorty, they work too hard, but what can we do? They don't seem to want others to think they need help. We do what we can, but you know what it's like to try to help them. I don't know how you managed to get them to allow you help. I still don't know how they could have kept going without your help. It sure was lucky for all of us that you came along!" Angela went to talk to her husband, Xavier, X to most people, to find out when they were going to see the hidden valley and the R-R cattle. He said they were going to take a lunch and leave about nine o'clock the next morning. Angela told him about Dawn and Matt wanting to go, too. He also thought that was a great idea.

Angela told him, "I'm going to have a couple of horses saddled and take them over for Dawn and Matt. We can meet you someplace over that way so we don't have to come all the way back here." The boss said, "Instead of you doing all that riding, why don't you send Shorty to take the horses over? You can go with us when we leave later. You have been trying to get Dawn and Shorty together. Here is a good time to do that." Angela asked, "What gives you the idea that I'm trying to get them together? They spend every weekend together, don't they?"

"Angela, you have been trying to play matchmaker for months now," the boss said. "I've been around you long enough to read you like a book. I agree with you on this point, though, Dawn will never find another man as decent, hardworking, honest, and smart if she looked the rest of her life. I think they were made for each other, even if they don't realize it yet. There isn't much we can do about it though, except to put them in each other's way as much as possible. Here is one time we can do that."

"You are right," Angela admitted. "I'm sure Shorty won't object to taking the horses over and riding with them. As you said, we can put them in each other's way for a few hours. That's what we will do then! Maybe you can ask Shorty, he probably won't suspect you of playing matchmaker!" Angela was laughing as she went into the house.

The boss talked to Shorty and he agreed to take the horses over to Dawn and Matt. He would leave early so Dawn would have time to get a lunch ready. He explained to the boss where they would meet up with the others. With this all settled Shorty headed for his bunk, as he would be on the trail early.

When the sun came up, Shorty was on the way to get Dawn and Matt, leading two saddled horses. It was a beautiful day to be out, and even better because he was going riding with a beautiful lady. Things were looking up for Dawn and Matt, now that the missing cattle had been located. He soon crossed onto R-R land, and a short time later, the ranch buildings came in sight. As he rode into the yard, Dawn came to the door with a smile, and Matt came from the bunkhouse. Shorty told them several people were going to see the valley and cattle and asked Dawn if she could make a lunch for her and Matt. As she went into the house to get a lunch ready, Matt said to Shorty, "Shorty, I would like you to see what I'm doing at the bunkhouse, and tell me if I'm doing it right." Shorty tied the horses and walked up to the bunkhouse with Matt. "I finished putting the moss in the joints and started to put the saplings in too. You take a look at it and tell me if it's right or wrong. I forgot to ask you before you left on Sunday."

Shorty looked at the job Matt had done and told him, "You couldn't do much better than that Matt. We just want to hold the moss in and give the clay something to grab hold of. I would use the smaller saplings on the porch end and the house side so the clay won't cover up too much of the log. Use smaller ones on the inside too, and the bigger ones on the back. You see, Matt, you stop to think before you do something. Sometimes a little headwork saves a lot of legwork. Now let's go see if your mother has your dinner ready."

Dawn had the lunch all ready and packed in a small knapsack. She asked Shorty, "We can take a minute to have a cup of tea and a doughnut, can't we? The tea is ready and so are the doughnuts!" Shorty smiled and said, "There is always time for one of your doughnuts. We will have plenty of time to get to our meeting spot."

When they had finished their tea and a couple of doughnuts, they mounted up and headed for the Axe. Most of this was open country, except for the hills which were covered with brush and in some places, good-sized trees. Shorty rode along with Dawn on one side and Matt on the other, both excited with the prospect of seeing this lost valley and their equally lost cattle. It was only a short time later when they got to their proposed meeting spot, and they could see the others coming about a mile off.

Soon everyone was together with much helloing and greetings, as if it had been months since their last meeting. Finally Dawn said, "I want to go see our cattle! Can we go now? I feel like a little girl on Christmas morning!" There was much laughter at this remark, but they all agreed it was time to get moving. Shorty started the procession, but Dawn soon caught up to him and rode alongside. Angela was pleased to see this, and her smile told everyone else how she felt. Next in line was Gus, with Matt riding alongside him. The others strung out along the trail, but it was quite obvious to all, that Gus and Matt left a longer gap between them and the leaders than there were between the followers.

About twenty minutes brought them to the gully, where Gus and Shorty had followed the tracks and discovered the lost valley. Here it was single file only, so Dawn dropped back a bit to let Shorty lead. There was a line of people on horseback, winding their way up this twisting, rocky gully. About ten minutes after they entered the bottom end of the gully, they came out into this beautiful flat valley.

Shorty and Dawn rode a short distance and stopped. The others rode up and stopped beside them. There was a chorus of "Oohs" and "Ahhs" and "Wow." Most of the riders sat speechless for a few minutes. Finally the boss spoke, "Well, Shorty, you and Gus really outdid yourselves this time. I had no idea there was a spot like this in these hills. You two were probably the first white men to lay eyes on it, maybe the first men of any colour. If I had found this years ago, I think I might have moved in and lived here!" Everyone felt the same; that this valley was the most beautiful spot they had ever seen. Angela moved up alongside Dawn and said, "Well, little sister, the lost is found! Thanks to Shorty and Gus, this lost valley, and your cows are now found. For once my husband is right. If we had found this, years ago, we would probably be living here now" The boss looked at his wife and smiled, "Well, once in a while, I get a little credit for something I do or say. Not too often, though!"

They all laughed so loud the horses started to fidget. Somebody said, "Well, we came here to look around, so let's look!" They separated into several small groups and spread out over the valley. Dawn, Shorty, and Matt set out to do their own bit of exploring. Dawn's eyes were so big and her smile was so wide, she looked like a little girl in a candy store! Shorty didn't think of her as a little girl, though.

They swung to the right and followed along a short distance from the bank of the former lake. There were several groves of trees in this huge meadow, mostly poplar, with some lodgepole pine. Riding slow as they were, it took quite some time to reach the far end of the valley, where the small stream came from. They explored up the stream, which came from a narrow cut in the hills. About a hundred yards up this narrow valley, it widened out to form a tiny valley of several acres. The small stream dropped a distance of twenty or twenty-five feet as a beautiful waterfall, into a small pool at the bottom. There were some trees around the edge of this tiny valley, which was more like a park than wilderness.

All three were speechless as they looked around at what to them seemed to be a small part of Heaven. Not one of them could believe there could be a spot so beautiful. They were afraid if they spoke, all this beauty would disappear. They sat and looked for a few more minutes, then started back the way they had come. When they were back out in the main valley, they found their voice. Shorty said to Dawn, "Did we really see that or was I dreaming? What I think I saw is almost too beautiful to believe!"

Dawn almost whispered, "If you were dreaming, then we all had the same dream. If someone had told me there was a spot that beautiful, I wouldn't believe them. I want to come back here sometime and camp overnight in that beautiful spot. I'm sure I could feel God's presence in there. Do you suppose Heaven could be that beautiful?" Shorty spoke softly, "I think you were right with everything you said. I don't think Heaven could be a bit more beautiful than that little valley. You are right, though. You could never tell anyone how beautiful that place is and have them believe you. Now, should we try to tell the others how beautiful this little corner of Heaven is, or do we keep it to ourselves?"

Matt spoke up at last, "I think we should keep quiet and not tell anyone. It seems wrong for people to go in there and disturb anything. I feel that a person shouldn't even talk while you're in there. I guess we will have to tell them, though, because somebody will find it sometime. I just hope everybody feels the same as us when they are in there. Maybe we can ask everybody here, not to tell anyone else about it."

Shorty said, "I think you are right, Matt, I wouldn't want a lot of people going in there and messing it up and maybe destroying it. Hopefully, everybody that goes in there will feel the same as we do and want to leave it just as it is. A little bit of Heaven!"

They rode slowly along the way they were until they met up with the boss, Angela, and Gus. All three were talking about this beautiful lost valley. Angela noticed that all three: Dawn, Matt, and Shorty were very quiet and had a solemn look on their face. She said to Shorty, "What's the matter, Shorty, did you see something that scared you?" "No, ma'am," Shorty answered, "this place is almost too beautiful to put into words. We found a little corner of Heaven back there that 'is' too beautiful to put into words. I can't think of words that would do justice to that place. Maybe Dawn could explain it better than I can." Dawn said softly, "Shorty is right. I don't think there are words to describe the beauty of that place. It has to be a little bit of Heaven, dropped down here on earth. While we were in there, not one of us could say a word. It's a quiet, peaceful, beautiful, Heavenly place. That doesn't even come close to what you see and feel in there. Let's go over to where that stream runs into the lake. We'll have dinner and then take you for a short walk into Heaven and back again."

They rode slowly over to the spot Dawn had indicated. The horses were tied to a rope stretched between two bushes. They had been watered and now they could eat the rich grass while their owners ate also. After eating, they were going to make a short, return trip to Heaven. The little talking that was done was done in hushed tones. Everyone could feel that there was something different about this valley and especially in this area. After the meal, Shorty, Dawn, and Matt led the others on a guided tour of Heaven.

As they entered this little inner valley, everyone stood with eyes and mouth wide open. No one made a sound. They walked on slowly, looking around as they went. The beautiful waterfall tumbling into the pool was the only sound to be heard, and even the waterfall seemed to be a lot quieter than it should have been. They all stood and looked for a few more minutes, then turned, and slowly walked back out of this spot that they all felt was a corner of Heaven. No one spoke a single word until they were back at the horses.

Dawn put her arm around her sister's shoulder and asked softly, "Now, can you tell us what you just saw?" Angela whispered, "I can't. I think I've been dreaming and I'm not awake yet. You are right, there is no way to put into words what you see and feel in there. Especially what you feel, it's indescribable. The feeling, it's not eerie, scary, or bad. It's peaceful, beautiful. I guess I'm not doing very well, am I?" Everyone there agreed that it was impossible to describe what a person felt while in the inner valley. Mere words cannot describe peace and beauty.

Now, hardly talking above a whisper, everyone felt it was time to leave. Not until they were out of the rocky gully, were people able to talk freely. What they saw back there seemed like an almost forgotten dream. After a while, everyone got their voice back and began talking, still quietly, barely above a whisper. They were still affected by the feeling of that inner valley. They rode on for a couple of miles talking quietly and then the boss stopped. "Dawn," he said, "You and Matt might as well keep those horses at your place. Matt's horse is too small for anyone at the ranch and the saddle is too small for the other horses. We have more than enough horses for the ranch work, and with a saddle horse it will be easier for you to get around, instead of using the wagon. Besides, we might need you and Matt to help us soon. I think the best plan right now is to separate those cattle and ship the older ones. Your cattle are in perfect shape for this time of year, due to a good wintering area and that rich grass. It's too early for rounding up and shipping, so I bet the price right now, for premium beef will be higher than later on when the market will be oversupplied. I'll get hold of my buyers and see what they have to say. Is that OK with you?"

With everything that had been happening lately, Dawn seemed to be in shock! She looked around for a few seconds before she said anything. Finally she spoke, "You mean we can sell some of our cattle now? I thought we would have to wait until fall!" The boss continued, "Dawn, for the time of year, you probably have some of the best beef in the area, due to the amount of grass in that valley. You will probably get a far better price right now than you would later on. With some money to help out, you will probably find other projects to keep Shorty occupied!"

Everyone laughed at this remark and Dawn got a bit of colour in her cheeks, but she smiled broadly. She said, "Well, we can sure use some money right now, what do we have to do?" The boss answered, "Right now, all you and Matt have to do is a bit of riding, to get you used to the saddle again. I'll get hold of my buyers and if the price is good, which I expect it will be, I'll tell them to go ahead and make the arrangements on their end. I should know something by the weekend. I'll send word with Shorty when he goes over Thursday evening. We should be able to start separating them the first of next week. We will need you and Matt to give us a hand. Do either of you have any other questions?"

Dawn decided she had enough information for the present and she would find out more later. Right now, she and Matt had to get home and get some work done, as it looked as though they wouldn't have much time at home next week. Good-byes were said and Matt and Dawn headed for home.

The others continued on to the ranch where the boss would begin making arrangements for an early roundup. He would have to go to town to contact the buyer's local representative: he in turn might have to ride farther to telegraph the higher ups. If all went as planned, they should begin to separate the older cattle from Dawn's new found herd, sometime early next week. This would give some of the hands a break from the usual routine, but it might not be any easier. Sometimes roundups were very strenuous affairs.

When Dawn and Matt arrived at the ranch, the horses were unsaddled and turned into the corral. They wanted them handy as they would probably go riding every evening for a bit. They hadn't been doing much riding lately, and it would be better to start out slow and gradually work up to longer periods in the saddle. Neither Dawn nor Matt was strangers to the saddle, so even though they might be a bit sore later, they would be able to help with their roundup. 'Their' roundup; that sounded good!

Matt decided to work on the bunkhouse for a while. He would only have until suppertime, as he and his mother would probably go riding in the evening for a bit. They both wanted to be in shape to do their share at the roundup. Matt decided to start putting the saplings in the wall of the bunkhouse nearest the house. He would leave the porch and inside for later as he could work there even if it was wet.

The saplings were long enough that two would do one joint. After he had trimmed an armful, he began nailing them in place. In a short time, he was at the point where he couldn't reach any more. He brought out the sawhorses and put a couple of boards on them to complete the wall. He moved everything around to the back end, where he continued working. He used the bigger saplings, but even they fit well into the joint. Soon he was above reaching from the sawhorses. It would be quicker to use a ladder for the small amount left to do, than to build a staging. That would be necessary when it came time to fill the joints with clay, however. The ladder would have to wait until tomorrow, as Dawn was calling him for supper.

As they ate supper, Matt and Dawn talked about the roundup and what they would use some of the money for. They both agreed that it would be used sparingly, as it might be some time before any more came their way. There were a few necessities they would be able to get to make their work easier. When supper was over, Dawn washed the dishes and swept the floor, while Matt went out to saddle the horses. There were only a couple of hours before dark, so they planned to use the whole evening riding. They knew they might spend days in the saddle at the roundup, so it was better to get in shape now.

Next morning Matt was working on his 'Pig cellar' soon after breakfast. He would do some digging while it was still cool, and then work at the bunkhouse when it warmed up. By the time Shorty arrived, he would have the bunkhouse all ready to be plastered with clay and maybe he would have the hole dug for the pig shelter, only time would tell. Dawn and Matt kept busy all week, doing every day chores, working in the garden, and many other things. They usually spent a couple of hours each evening riding to get in shape for the upcoming roundup.

Shorty arrived on Thursday evening as usual. He brought the news that the roundup was to start on Tuesday morning. If the cattle cooperated, they might get it done in one day but it might take two or three. Matt and Dawn would take enough supplies to do for a three-day stay. A canvas tarp would make a roof to sleep under if it rained. A bedroll would be made up for each of them. Gloves, spare clothes, a few cooking utensils, and other items would be taken along. Spud, the cook from the Axe, would be there with a couple of packhorses and more supplies for the crew. Dawn planned to take along some food just in case; better to be safe than hungry! They spent most of the evening trying to decide what to take along while they ate their lunch of tea and doughnuts. Matt was excited as this would be the first time he had helped out at a roundup. He wasn't a real cowboy yet, but he could ride and help herd cattle. Soon it was time for bed as they had a busy weekend planned and probably a busy week next week at the hidden valley.

When the rooster started yodeling the next morning, all three were busy with before-breakfast chores. With a good meal inside them, Matt and Shorty went up to the bunkhouse to see the work that had been done the previous week. Matt received good marks from Shorty's inspection, so it was off to the root cellar and another day's work. The logs were all handy, so it was just a matter of cutting and fitting them into place. With the roof support upright in the middle, it was just a matter of filling in the space on one side with upright logs. The logs were trimmed and fitted and the sides shaved down until they fitted snugly together. One by one, the logs were put in place and secured until there was room for only one more. Shorty shaved both sides down until it could be tapped into place. The opening on the other side was just under four feet, so the door would be made as wide as possible, to make easy access while bringing in vegetables.

Matt went to the barn for a couple of planks to make a door frame. He came back with two eight inch wide, two inch thick planks. This would give them more room for a thick inner door. The planks were cut and fitted on each side of the doorway. The end pieces were trimmed to fit top and bottom. This made a solid frame for the door to close tightly against. Shorty measured the height and width, and they went to the bunkhouse to build a door. This door didn't have to be of planed lumber like the bunkhouse door, even though it was to be tight. The boards were trimmed and laid side by side on the sawhorses. A strip of tar paper was placed on top before the cross boards went on. These were nailed in place but the nails were driven only partway, they then turned it over and nailed it securely from the front before removing the first nails. A brace was fitted between the cross boards and nailed in place from the front again. Matt got the spare pair of hinges and these were secured over the cross pieces. The door was ready to be hung in place at the root cellar. Matt tacked some narrow strips of wood over the tar paper to hold it tight and make it windproof. He also sawed out and whittled down a handle for the door, with this in place, the door was carried to the root cellar. All it needed was a latch to hold it closed and the cellar was ready to be used.

Shorty told Matt, "When you get some spare time, you can fill the cracks with moss and saplings over the moss. We will seal it with clay after we do the bunkhouse. Before winter, we will build an inside door, four or five inches thick, filled with moss, leaves or hay to help keep the cold out. After we get the clay plastered on inside, we might build a frame on the other side of the door and fill it, too. This will make a fine place to store your vegetables." Dawn arrived to tell them dinner was ready. She commented on the progress being made on the root cellar. They showed her the inside and explained about the double, insulated door and possibly a filled section beside the door. Shorty said, "We will build bins across the back and on the left side. We have to leave room for the door to swing back out of the way. We'll build shelves at the back above the bins to put jam, pickles, and preserves or whatever on. This place will hold a lot of food for the winter."

It was dinner time so all three went to the house to eat. As usual, Dawn had a good meal ready and not much time was wasted before digging in. Dawn could take a simple meal and make it taste wonderful. With a good meal inside them, Matt and Shorty headed outside to see what other jobs waited for them. The bunkhouse and root cellar were close enough to being finished to wait for a while. Most of what had to be done was inside and could be finished up on wet days.

Shorty thought maybe they should do some work on Matt's pig cellar. They did some measuring and decided a bit more digging was called for. Shorty started digging with the pick and Matt shoveled it to the side. They worked away for half an hour or so and then stopped to measure again. They figured another twenty minutes would be enough for their purpose, so the dirt flew for a while longer before they began working with the logs.

Matt told Shorty that he planned to have it six feet wide and eight feet long inside. Shorty said, "That's a good size Matt, lots of room for two pigs, but if necessary it would hold half a dozen good-sized hogs. It would also be big enough for a sow with a litter. It's always better to build a bit bigger than to start too small. Very little extra work will give you extra room you might want in the future. You have a good head on your shoulders, Matt!"

Matt was always pleased when Shorty praised his work. Praise from Shorty meant a lot more to Matt than it would from anyone else. They thought it would be faster and easier to pull some logs closer to the job with a horse than to carry them. Half a dozen trips with a horse gave them enough logs to possibly complete the shelter. In a short time, they were starting to put logs in place. This building would be built almost the same as the root cellar. The front and back logs would be put in first. These were notched and rolled into place. The side logs were notched top and bottom, and then they were slid into place. If there was a wide space between the logs, Matt put a small pole on the outside to keep the soil from falling through. They were working on the third course when Dawn called them to supper.

After another of Dawn's good meals, they sat and talked a few minutes over another cup of tea and a doughnut. Dawn and Matt were planning to go for another ride and asked if Shorty was coming along. He told them he spends half his life in a saddle and didn't think he needed to get in shape. He thought he would go up to the bunkhouse and start building a bunk.

Dawn frowned for a bit, then she said, "I was thinking of having a small dance before we got too much in there taking up room. I thought just the hands at the ranch and a couple of neighbours, to show our appreciation for all the help everyone has given us. We were going to surprise you with it, too. Do many of the hands play music?" Shorty said a couple of the boys played guitars, but she might have to get a few outsiders to help provide the music. Dawn thought they should invite a few more women so the boys would have someone to dance with.

Shorty asked Dawn, "When did you plan to have this dance?" Dawn answered, "I was just thinking of when the bunkhouse was finished, before the bunks and things were in the way. We probably couldn't have it next weekend as we are going to be busy with the cattle, so the earliest would be the following weekend. I guess you want to get a bunk built so you don't have to sleep in the barn. I'd like your opinion on it, Shorty. Do you think we should try to have a dance or just keep working on the bunkhouse?"

"Well," Shorty said. "I think it's a good idea to have a dance for the Axe hands. Some of them have helped here, and the others are doing my work at the ranch so I have more time to work here. That's a good way to thank them, as all cowhands like a good shindig. I've been thinking of building a table that folds up against the wall. I could work on that because it wouldn't be in the way. I could also start sealing the joints with clay and leave the bunkhouse open for the dance. We can put the stove out in the storage area until later. There isn't a lot of room up there, but then you weren't planning on a big crowd anyway. Also, a dance will show off your new bunkhouse!"

"Shorty, you always agree with everything I say," Dawn said. "Is that your honest opinion or are you just trying to humour me?" Shorty stated. "No, I don't always agree with everything you say. You asked my opinion and I gave it. I'm not going to lie just to please someone. I think a dance is the best way to show how much you appreciate all the boys have done to help out. Two weeks from now would be a good time for it. Now, if you are going riding, you better vamoose so I can get a start on that table. I'll give Matt a hand to saddle up, and then I'm going up to the bunkhouse!"

Dawn and Matt rode away on another evening ride. They were learning a lot about the horses, and the horses were learning a lot about them. Every rider handles a horse a bit different, and the horses were learning what the riders wanted them to do and when they were supposed to do it. Sometimes it looks like the horse is doing all the thinking and the work, and the cowboy is just along for the ride. This comes about from the cowboy and the horse working together, day after day, year after year, until the horse and cowboy seem almost like one animal. Dawn and Matt weren't going to be that good in just a few days, but they were getting better. They were learning a lot about their mounts and how to handle them. Some working horses need only a light touch on the reins and just leaning in the saddle would turn them the way a rider wanted.

Tonight, the cowpokes-in-training cut their ride a bit short and turned the horses for home. Dawn enjoyed having Shorty's company, and she didn't want to be away while he was on the ranch. Meanwhile, back at the ranch, Shorty was keeping himself busy. He had placed the sawhorses close to one wall and had put several boards on them, with their ends against the wall. He took the plane and made a smooth surface on both sides. He figured a bunkhouse didn't require a large table, so he planned for one four feet long and thirty inches wide. He planed a narrow board on three sides, cut two pieces twenty inches long, and put them rough side up under his planed four-foot boards, on the sawhorses. He nailed them securely with small nails, eight inches from each end of the tabletop. He nailed a narrow board to the wall, thirty inches off the floor. The table would rest on this board and be hinged to the wall. He planed another narrow board and placed it between the crosspieces at the front of the table. He put the tabletop on the support board, with the front resting on a sawhorse, and drove two nails part way at the back. He planed and trimmed two boards to reach from the front underside, to the floor at the wall. He was beveling the three edges of the table when he heard Dawn and Matt riding by. As they were unsaddling, he brought in the chair he and Matt had built for Dawn. When they walked through the door, he was sitting in the chair at the table. Shorty said, "I thought you must have gotten lost. I've been sitting here for hours!"

Dawn and Matt both laughed, as they had seen the chair sitting on the porch when they rode by. They both admired the beautiful job he had done on the table. He pulled the two nails holding the table to the wall to demonstrate how it worked. Matt took one end and Shorty took the other. Holding the supports with one hand, they swung the tabletop up against the wall. No part of the table protruded more than two inches. When the hinges were put on, he would make a simple wooden button to hold it flush against the wall.

Dawn thought it was time for another small celebration, so she went to the house for a snack while the boys put the table back in the proper position. Dawn's chair was placed at the center on the long side, and blocks of wood were placed at the ends. Dawn arrived with a light lunch and a cup of tea, and a bedtime snack was eaten at the new table. With the supports placed the way they were, there was plenty of legroom under the table. A fine finish to another day of work on the ranch! The few dishes were carried back to the house as everyone was on the way to their bed.

Chapter 9

A S USUAL, DAWN had a good breakfast waiting when the chores were done the next morning. After eating their first meal of the day, the boys decided to work on Matt's 'pig cellar' for the day. They began cutting, notching, and stacking the logs in place on the walls. As in the root cellar, they placed an upright on each side at the front, notched into the base log with a cap piece on the top. This took only a short time, and they were soon back at raising the walls. When the walls topped six feet, building was halted.

Shorty told Matt, "You see, Matt, most pigs are very clean animals. You probably noticed one corner of your pig's yard is wet; the rest is clean and dry. All their mess is in one spot. If they can get outside, even in winter, they will keep their bed clean and dry. I like your idea of a door that swings both ways. If they can get outside, you won't have to go inside very often, only to give them more bedding once in a while. We will build a door at least three feet wide with a section in the bottom that swings both ways. You might have to go in there a few times in the winter and very seldom in summer. With a trough outside to feed them in, they won't be much work. The biggest job will be to keep them supplied with water when it gets cold. Maybe later on, we can run water from the house spring to keep them supplied. We can think about that anyway."

Since the pig shelter wasn't very wide, they settled on a flat roof for it. The logs were notched and laid across the walls. Small poles were laid in the cracks to keep the soil from falling through. There was lots of soil to cover it deeply, and when rounded up, there should be no water leak through. When Dawn called them for dinner, they felt they had done a good morning's work. They washed up by the barn and followed their nose to the house.

Dawn had a pot of beef stew with fresh vegetables, barley, and dumplings. To finish the meal, there were hot biscuits, tea, and, of course, a couple of doughnuts, a meal probably a lot better than most kings ate. As usual, past, present, and future work was discussed. Dawn thought they had made good progress with the pig shelter. Shorty said, "I don't see why we can't let the pigs use it now. We have to build a door but that won't be necessary for a while yet. We can drive a few small stakes on each side so they can't dig in the fresh dirt, and after we fill in the sides, they can use it. We can build a fence from their yard to the shelter and it's theirs!" Matt thought that was a great idea, and he could keep working at filling in around it through the week.

After the filling meal, Shorty and Matt shoveled the loose dirt in around the logs. When they had a foot of soil in, one or the other would jump in and tramp it solidly, another foot and another tramping job. The soil would settle by itself in time, but it would have to be refilled if not compacted. It was much faster to fill in around the logs than it was to dig it out.

The pig yard was only about forty feet away from the shelter, so it wasn't too big a job to build a fence to allow access to their new home. They drove stakes in line with two posts of the pig yard. Some of the small rails that were left over were used on this fence. When they were almost to the shelter, the fence was narrowed in until the rails would join onto the logs. When the fence was completed and checked over, they removed the rails from the original fence and the pigs started inspecting the new area. It took at least ten minutes of sniffing and tasting before the pigs finally got to the shelter. More time was spent stretching necks to see into the shelter before venturing inside, where there was more sniffing and snorting as they looked over the inside. They seemed quite interested, even though they probably wouldn't spend much time inside unless it was a very hot day. The boys decided to start shoveling soil onto the roof of the shelter until suppertime, which they knew wasn't very far away.

As they worked, Matt asked about the roundup that would be taking place next week. Shorty explained, "Well, we'll be trying to separate the older ones from the cows and calves. The ones that are big enough for market will be driven or roped and pushed to the bottom of the valley. Your job, with Dawn and a few others, will be to hold them from getting back into the herd. Those cattle seem quiet so it might not be too hard to do. There will probably be sixty or seventy head to come out of there. When we have them separated, we will probably drive them to one of the Axe holding pens. If they are to be branded, it will be done there. The buyers just might decide to take them unbranded, since they are full grown now. We will probably find out Tuesday if we will drive them to the railroad or if the buyers will. If we drive them, you could probably go along to help. That would save paying another hand, since they are your cattle." At this time, the conversation was interrupted by a call to supper. The shovels were laid aside as they were about to start looking for something to eat.

As supper was being eaten, the talk drifted to the roundup. Shorty told Dawn very much the same he had told Matt. They, with a few others would help to hold the separated cattle in one place. The most experienced hands, who were good ropers, would separate the cattle. Most would be easy to separate, while there would be a few that would probably have to be roped and led to the holding area. These cattle seemed to be gentle and unafraid so the job might not be too hard though a few balky cattle could slow the process considerably. Shorty told Dawn and Matt if the cattle were to be branded, they probably wouldn't be needed.

With the meal over and the conversation ended for the present, Shorty helped saddle the horses for the evening ride. He went up to the bunkhouse to start work on the bunks, even though they wouldn't be put in place until after the dance. He could start figuring, cutting, and planing the lumber that would be used later. Shorty was over six feet, so at least one bunk would have to be built to accommodate him. He began by measuring the length and width of the bunk-to-be. He measured and marked the position on the floor and walls. He planned to fasten the bunks solidly to the wall so only one upright would be needed for the outside corner. First, he trimmed a two by four to reach to just above the ceiling joists from the floor and two six-inch boards were trimmed to six feet six inches in length. He then cut two six-inch boards, three feet long and all were set aside to be planed smooth. He got a four-inch board and split it into two equal pieces. He fastened these together and cut small notches every four inches. After the wide boards were planed, the narrow strips would be fastened to them, with the notches against the board. When everything was securely fastened, thin rope would be wound through the notches from side to side, making a flexible support for the bunk. With a straw filled mattress on top, a person would sleep comfortably. When all the lumber was ready, Shorty began planning the boards to have it ready to build the bunk.

The two by four was planed smooth and all four corners were rounded. The long and short boards were planed all around and the corners rounded also. The narrow notched strips wouldn't need to be planed, as they would be under the mattress. Shorty nailed the strips to the wide boards, an inch and a half from bottom edge. He measured and used a plumb line to mark where the upright would be placed. A two by four was nailed to the top of the ceiling joists to secure the upright to. He put the upright in place and nailed it temporarily. He marked a line at twenty inches off the floor on the upright and several places on the wall. This would leave enough headroom for a person to sit upright on the lower bunk. He used an adze to flatten the log surface so the boards could be fastened securely and the end wall was treated in the same manner. Shorty nailed a long board to the side wall following his pencil marks, and did the same with a short board on the end wall. He then tacked the other long board to the upright and the short end board. The end board was tacked into place and the frame of the lower bunk was completed. As he was putting the final board in place, he heard Dawn and Matt going past the bunkhouse. It took only a few minutes to unsaddle and then he heard them approaching the bunkhouse. They came in to inspect his handiwork and he explained that the boards on the wall were solid, but the others were just tacked in place. The ones on the wall wouldn't be in the way and the others could be laid up on the ceiling joists out of the way. Two minutes work would have a wide open bunkhouse again.

Dawn went to the house to make a cup of tea while Matt and Shorty dismantled the bunk and stowed it on the ceiling joists. After a light lunch and a cup of tea, with the ever present doughnuts, it was time to hit the sack. Shorty said, "Tomorrow, we will get the things ready for you to take on the roundup. If we start early, we will probably think of some other things you want before you leave. Dawn, are you going on the drive if we take it to the railroad? It won't be all that hard, just riding along to make sure none of the cattle stray from the herd." It didn't take Dawn long to answer as she said, "Yes, if we take them, I'm going along. As you say, it will save paying another rider, and they are our cattle. I'm not a cowhand, but I can ride and I should be able to help keep the cattle in line. We will have to take a few more things along if we go on the drive." Shorty said, "We can figure that out tomorrow. A lot of your gear can be stowed on the chuck wagon if we make the drive. It's about time to get some shut-eye. We can get everything sorted out tomorrow." Shortly everyone was in bed and asleep.

The next morning, Dawn and Matt were more excited than ever, as this was to be their first roundup and possibly the first cattle drive they had ever helped with. Over breakfast they began to plan what they would need. Dawn got a pencil and paper and began a list of things they would take along. Shorty said, "If you have rain gear you should take it with you. There is a big pack out in the barn. Put all the things in it that you can't carry on your saddle. A change of clothes might come in handy too. Maybe you should take along a little food just in case. There will be a couple of packhorses from the ranch, to carry food and supplies, but a bit extra won't hurt, better to be safe than hungry. There is some canvas in the barn, so we will make up a bedroll for each of you."

Matt asked Shorty, "How long will it take to drive the cattle to the railroad? A week?" Shorty answered, "No, Matt, it might take three or four days. We will probably put them in a holding pen overnight and leave the next morning. I guess it will depend on what time of day we get them separated and out on the range. Dawn, did your husband have a handgun around here?"

Dawn answered, "Yes, he did. It's in a drawer in my bedroom. Why, do you want to borrow it?" Shorty said, "No, I have my own. Maybe you should put it in your saddle bag, with a handfull of shells. You never know when you might need it. Can you use it?" Dawn answered, "Well, I've fired it a few times but I'm not very good with it!" "You don't have to be good with it," Shorty said, "but take it along anyway. Now, we better get outside and get a little bit accomplished, we can be thinking and writing things on your list as we work."

They decided not to work too hard, as Matt and Dawn might have a hard week ahead of them; just being in the saddle all day was work enough. Shorty thought maybe they should check out the creek to see if there was any clay, suitable for their purpose in the banks. They each took a shovel and went up the creek. They found there was a lot of clay on the stream banks. They got a bucket, shoveled it full, and carried it back to the bunkhouse. Shorty and Matt each whittled out a small paddle to use for scooping the clay and smoothing it into the joints. Shorty explained to Matt as they went along, how and why something was done. He said, "You see Matt, the most important thing is to push it in around the sapling so it will stay there. Some people don't use anything like that, but I find it does a better job. Sometimes you have to use your hands to get it in good. We just want to seal the crack and cover the sticks. I think a narrow chinking looks better than a wide one, as I like to see the logs."

They worked at filling the cracks on the back wall first. Better to learn on a spot that doesn't show too much. Shortly they were out of clay. Shorty asked Matt, "Do we have anything bigger to put some clay in Matt?" He thought for a bit then he said, "There is a cut off barrel in the shed, but if we fill it, we wouldn't be able to carry it. Maybe we could use the horses and wagon."

"Tell you what, Matt," Shorty said, "You go get that barrel and I'll start making a handbarrow to carry the clay in. Maybe you should soak it with water before you bring it up. Fill it with water by the barn and let it set until we're ready for it." Shorty got two slim poles about six feet long. He then got a five-inch board and a short six-inch board. He cut two pieces off the five-inch board about thirty inches long and two pieces sixteen inches long. He nailed the two long pieces onto the ends of the shorter ones, making a rectangle, about sixteen by twenty eight inches inside. He cut three pieces off the wide board, the length of the rectangle and nailed them onto the frame, forming a shallow box. The poles were nailed on the outside of the box, on the long sides, with an equal amount on each end. They now had a handbarrow to work with.

Shorty carried it down to the barn where Matt was waiting. They took it up the creek to where they had been digging the clay. The box was shoveled full and carried up to the bunkhouse. "Now Matt," Shorty said, "You go bring up that tub and we'll put this clay in it, and go for another load. I think we should put it in the woodshed so it won't dry out too fast." Matt brought up the tub and put it in the woodshed, where the load of clay was emptied into it and second load was brought up and emptied too.

Shorty said, "I was thinking we could bring up a lot of clay for you to work with next week but I guess you won't be here very much either. We might as well use this up before it gets too dry."

They continued pushing the clay into the cracks and getting it as smooth as possible. Shorty told Matt, "Before the clay gets too dry, we'll get a piece of feed sack or a rag to smooth it out better. You get the rag wet and rub the clay until it's wet and shiny. Try not to smear too much on the logs. We'll leave the woodshed and the porch until later as that can always be done even if it's wet. It's good to have something under cover to work at when it's too wet to work outside." They talked as they worked at sealing the joints with clay, when this bunkhouse was finished; it was going to be a tight, warm building! They were still pushing clay into the joints when Dawn called them to dinner. This was one time they really needed to wash as they were both smeared with clay! They washed off as much as they could, before going inside to eat. There was more talk of the roundup as they ate the meal. Shorty said, "Maybe after we eat we should get your bedrolls ready and everything else we think you might need. I'll be heading back tonight, and you will have to leave early Tuesday morning or tomorrow evening and campout." Dawn and Matt thought it would be better to campout and be there ready to go when everyone else was.

Shorty said to Matt, "Before you go, make sure all the stock is in the pasture. There is grass and water so they will be fine. You can leave lots of water for the chickens or they can get water at the creek. Matt, just before you leave, put some of your clothes by the chicken pen. Something you have just worn, as the smell of a person should keep the critters away. If you go on the drive, it will be too long to leave them closed in. Hopefully the deer won't find the garden. A couple of shirts or other clothes on a stick might keep them out, also. Now, maybe we should get some of your things packed so you won't have to do it later."

Matt got the canvas from the barn and they made up two bedrolls to be tied behind the saddles. There was an extra piece of canvas which could be used as a shelter if it rained. They each had a raincoat to go in the big pack, which would go in the chuck wagon on the drive, if it was made. Dawn planned to make a big batch of biscuits to take with them and some smoked bacon.

She might even take some doughnuts if there were any left. A change of clothes would go in the pack and gloves would go in the saddlebags. When they had everything they could think of ready, they had a bedroll, saddlebags, and the big pack, not too much of a load, but it should cover the necessities. They decided a cup, fork, and a small plate should be enough for meals.

When everything was packed and ready, Shorty and Matt went back to the bunkhouse to work. As they worked, they talked of the upcoming roundup and trail drive. Shorty told Matt the best place for him and Dawn was on the flanks. This was almost at the back and off to the side. This was probably the easiest place but it was also the spot where extra help was often needed. They would be doing their share, but letting the experienced hands handle the important and most dangerous positions. He also told Matt, that in the event the cattle did start running, he and Dawn should drop back and if there were any stragglers, to keep them moving after the herd. Shorty didn't think this would happen as these cattle seemed very quiet and not likely to run. He would make sure to be around to explain things better when they got the cattle moving.

They had busily filling the joints as they had been talking until it was getting hard to reach. Shorty told Matt to get three small poles about six or eight feet long, while he got a few short boards. Matt held the poles upright as Shorty hit then a few good thumps to drive them into the ground a bit. He then nailed a board from the end of a log to the pole, about shoulder high. In the center a board was nailed upright on the logs to fasten the short board to. A few boards were laid on these to make a platform to work on. Since the building wasn't very high, Shorty could reach the top easily while Matt did the lower joints. This was much faster than climbing up and down a ladder and an easier place to work. It didn't take long to finish the end wall, as Shorty had been reaching seven feet from the ground. From the ground up, the building was only about twelve feet high. They were about to call it a day when the cook announced it was supper time. Shorty would be returning to the Axe, so Dawn had picked more fresh vegetables for a special meal. There were new potatoes, string beans and fresh greens. It seemed like Dawn wanted Shorty to remember the meals he ate here! Again, as they ate, the conversation drifted to the roundup. Shorty told them, "If I get there before you I'll try to find a camping site for you. It should be just past where the valley spreads out. We will probably try to hold the older cattle at the bottom end. If you camp there, you will be close to your work. Your campsite should be close to the bank out of the way, but I'm sure you can find a good place without my help. By the way Matt, take a long rope to tie your horses to, that way they can graze easily and you won't have to keep moving them. One end can be tied to a bush and the other tied to a stake driven into the ground. Well, as soon as I finish eating I better get back to the ranch and get my own gear ready. I'll see you two at the valley tomorrow evening."

After finishing the good meal Dawn had made, Shorty saddled up and turned his horse toward the Axe. As he left, he called out, "I'll see you two cowhands Tuesday morning for sure!" Dawn decided, since the stove was hot she was going to make a big batch of 'bearsign' to take along. She thought that would be a nice surprise for the hands at the roundup. The oven would be hot also, so she asked Matt to make some biscuits. Soon the kitchen was full of the aroma of biscuits and 'bearsign.'

When the biscuits were done and cooling, Matt got a piece of feed sack and some water and went up to the bunkhouse to smooth the clay chinking. The rough sacking smoothed out the clay better than a rag. When the wall was done, he moved around to the side and smoothed the chinking on that side too. He was very pleased with the results of his labour and proud too. He was about to start filling the joints in the woodshed, but it was getting late so he went to check on the stock, close up the chickens and go inside. On the way he got the two pair of saddle bags from the barn and took them along. They would be packed full either tonight or tomorrow morning.

Matt and Dawn packed their saddlebags and checked the list to see if there was anything they had forgotten. They racked their brain to try and think of anything else they might need. The pack was emptied and repacked until finally they were satisfied they were all ready. They were in bed earlier than usual because tomorrow was going to be busy and also the start of a big adventure for them.

Early the next morning, Matt was outside doing the chores and checking all around the buildings. There was plenty of grass in the pasture, and the small stream ran through it so there was a good supply of water. The calf would keep the cow milked until they got back. The pigs had lots of grass to keep them occupied until they returned and Matt would make sure they had plenty of water. Matt and Dawn were going to go through the garden and pull all the weeds that were starting to grow. The pigs and chickens would enjoy the fresh greens. The chickens would have to be left to run loose in the daytime, as they would return to the pen before dark. Matt was going to change his clothes just before leaving and hang his used clothing beside the small door of the pen. He hoped Shorty was right about animals not liking the smell of people. As far as Matt could see, everything else was in good shape to be left alone for a few days or a week. Later they would get the garden ready to be left alone also. He knew breakfast was ready for him and he was ready for it!

Dawn had a good hot breakfast ready as it might possibly be the last one for a while. If Spud, the ranch cook, got his supplies into the valley there should be plenty of good food. Just in case Dawn sliced the last of her bread and Matt buttered it. It was wrapped in paper and put in a can with a tight lid. The bread, with the biscuits Matt had made, should keep them going until the cook got there with more supplies. As Shorty said; 'Better to be safe than hungry.'

With everything packed and ready, including the food, they went to the garden to look after the weeds. It was easier to keep the weeds from getting out of control, than to try to take the garden back from the weeds. They kept the garden well looked after, so it wasn't a big job to uproot the few that had a foothold.

The pigs and chickens made short work of these young, tender greens.

Matt got the saddles out and checked over all the straps and ties. He got a piece of rope and tied it to his saddle. He wouldn't be doing any roping, but as Shorty had suggested, it would be good to tie the horses to at night. It wouldn't be a good feeling to wake up and find your horse had gone home without you! Matt got a narrow coil of leather that was hanging in the barn and put it in his saddle bag. He thought it might come in handy if something on their gear broke. He knew it was getting close to eating time so he decided to go and see. Dawn had a meal of leftovers ready, trying to use up whatever would spoil while they were away. If anything was left from this meal it would go to the chickens as nothing was wasted on this ranch. Dawn had a small can filled with tea to take with them. If necessary, water could be boiled in the can holding the bread, and they would have tea to drink.

There wasn't much more to be done around the ranch without starting a new project. When dinner was over and everything cleaned up and shipshape, they decided to saddle up and load up their supplies. Matt changed his clothes and took the ones he had worn out to the chicken pen. While he was there, he noticed his mother in the garden. She had changed her clothes and with a small cross made of poles, she had hung her shirt in the garden. Maybe the human scent and the flapping shirt would keep the deer out of the garden; anyway, it was worth a try.

When the horses were saddled up and everything checked over they tied on their saddlebags and bedrolls. Dawn put the pack on her back and they were ready to leave. One last look around, at the home they might not see for a week, and they were on the trail to Lost Valley. They rode slowly, looking around as they went. Home was a comfortable spot, but sometimes it was good to get away and see different places. Both were excited to be going on a roundup and probably a trail drive for the first time! They knew it wasn't going to be all pleasure, as most roundups were hard work, hot and dusty, but this roundup shouldn't be dusty with all the lush, green grass in the valley.

They were in no rush, but because of the excitement they shared, it seemed like no time until they were at the entrance to the valley. They saw no one and all the tracks were old and coming out of the gully. They turned their horses into the outlet to the valley and rode the short distance to where the valley began. It seemed like more than the half mile Shorty had estimated, but the gully was crooked and rough which made for slow going. As on the first time they had come here, Dawn and Matt sat on their horses and looked across the valley. It was still hard to believe that all these cattle belonged to them! They rode the same way they had the first time they were in the valley. Just at the point where the valley really spread out, they found what they thought was a good spot to camp. They knew the separated cattle would be held at the bottom of the valley where it was narrower. They wanted to be close to where they would be needed, but far enough back that their camp wouldn't be trampled. There were bushes growing along the bank and a few small trees. They picked a smooth, level spot near the bushes, but where there was still plenty of grass for the horses. They tied the horses to a bush and Matt climbed the bank to get a stick to tie the horse rope to and a slim pole to make a shelter. He found a pole that suited and a couple of chokecherry bushes with crotches eight or ten feet off the ground. These were cut down with his pocketknife and the branches trimmed off. He tossed the poles down the bank, with a couple of saplings to make pegs.

He carried these to where the shelter would be and began to put it together. He pushed the crotched poles into the ground, until fairly solid. The slim pole was laid in the crotches for a ridge pole to hold up the canvas. The saplings were cut into three pieces and sharpened a bit. Next he draped the canvas over the pole until it hung evenly. He pushed the pegs into the ground about six feet past the end of the tarp, one in the middle and the others a couple of feet past the sides of the tarp. He got the leather strap and tied the tarp to the pegs with it. When he stretched the tarp tight from the other side, it was held almost three feet off the ground. This made a shelter from any possible rain, plus a shade if it was warm. With the canvas held up in the air this way, they could sit or lie underneath and still see out in three directions.

They moved their bedrolls under the shelter, as well as the big pack. Matt and Dawn both climbed the bank and came back with a bunch of stones, five or six inches in diameter. These were placed in a circle about six feet in front of the shelter. This would make a place for a fire and to cook on if necessary. It would be nice to lie under the tarp in the evening, with a small fire out front. Matt went up the bank again and got some small dead trees for firewood. He got a couple of armloads and brought them close to the fire pit. He broke up some, but decided it was too early to start a fire yet.

Dawn thought maybe they could do a bit of exploring to pass the time until the others arrived. They mounted up and rode slowly up the valley looking around and trying to estimate how many cattle were here and how many were old enough to be separated and sold. The cattle didn't appear alarmed and most just looked at them as they rode by. They could ride right through them and they just moved far enough to let them through. These were Whiteface or Herford cattle. They were much more docile than some of the older breeds that had been on most ranches in the past. Some of these younger cattle had never seen a person until a week ago, but they didn't appear to be the least bit alarmed. They tried to count them, but with them in a bunch and moving slowly, it was almost impossible to get an accurate count. They did estimate that about twenty percent were big enough to be shipped. That number could go as high as twenty five percent. If the price was good, it would give them more money than they ever had before. Even a few hundred dollars would make life a lot easier for them.

As they rode along the lake, they could see the occasional ripple on the surface. They watched for a few minutes before they decided there were fish in the lake. Matt thought if he had some line he would try to catch a couple for their supper. They didn't have a frying pan, but they had cooked fish before without using one.

He looked in his saddlebag and found a coil of small, strong linen thread for fixing saddles and harness. Now, if he only had a fish hook he would be in business. He found a short piece of wire used to repair a break in the halter, which was still on the horse under the bridle. The halter was left on so when the bridle was removed to allow the horse to eat, it could still be tied. Matt gave his mother his knife and asked her to find a slim sapling, as long as she could get. He got the wire unwrapped and began to form it into a hook. Using the bends already in the wire, he shaped it into a double hook. He found that he could squeeze the two hooks together and a sharp kink in the wire would hold them together, but a slight pressure would allow them to spring apart. When a fish took the bait, the spring-loaded hook would hold it securely. He pulled up a couple of clumps of reeds growing near the water and was rewarded with several large earthworms, as in this rich soil, the worms grew big too. Dawn was back with a long, slim pole about ten feet long. Matt got his fishing tackle ready, baited the hook and swung it as far out into the lake as he could. He waited a few minutes until the hook settled to the bottom. He pulled it in and tried again, with the same results. He was beginning to think they were mistaken about there being fish in the lake, or if there were any fish, they didn't seem to be hungry.

He tried a third time and almost as soon as the hook touched the water, something grabbed it! It hit so hard and unexpectedly, Matt almost lost his rod. He didn't know how well his improvised gear would hold up, so he lifted the pole as high as he could and backed away from the water. Seconds later a huge fish was flopping on the grass. He grabbed hold of it and with his knife he severed the spine just behind the head. He had learned that, if you have to kill something, do it quickly so it won't suffer. He had caught a big rainbow trout of at least five pounds! This was far more than the two of them could eat in one meal! There was lots of clay at the edge of the lake, so Matt pulled a couple of handfuls of grass and laid it beside him, he then scooped some clay onto the grass. He mounted his horse and Dawn passed the grass and clay up to him, then she mounted up and carried the fish. Back at the campsite, Matt cleaned the fish, but left the head on, while Dawn got a fire started. He wrapped the fish in clean grass, and then plastered clay over everything, at least an inch or two thick. When the fire was burning good, Matt placed the fish inside the fire pit. As a bed of coals formed, they were raked around the clay covered fish. They figured an hour should bake the fish into a mouthwatering meal. Dawn took the bread from the can and Matt went to the lake for some water. The water was placed beside the fire to heat for tea. When it boiled, Dawn moved it back and put in some tea.

Just at that time, they saw two riders come into view at the lower end of the valley. A few minutes later they could see it was Shorty and Gus. They rode up to the shelter and tied their horses with the other two. Dawn said;" You're just in time for supper, pull up a stump and sit down." About all they could see was a can of tea, but they got their plate fork and cup and sat down beside Matt and Dawn. Matt got a stick and rolled the lump of clay out of the fire. Gus chuckled and asked, "What do we have here, Matt,' Roast Rock'?" Matt picked up a stone and hit the hard clay a few good whacks before it finally broke open. Immediately the air was filled with the aroma of baked trout! Shorty grinned and said, "Well, Gus, I've never met up with a 'roast rock' yet that smelled that good! Not even boiled or fried!"

Dawn pulled a corner of the paper loose and set the buttered bread within reach of everyone. They took turns filing their plates with the moist, tender fish. Then with a cup of tea and a slice of bread, they began to eat Matt's 'roast rock.' After a few minutes Gus had an empty plate in his hand and started to fill it again. He said, "I wouldn't mind having this kind of roast rock a couple of times a week. Sure beats having rocks in the beans when on the trail. Where did you get the fish, Matt? There ain't any stores handy for you to buy it, so you must have brought it with you." Matt and Dawn explained about seeing the ripples in the pond and Matt making his fishing gear. He reached behind him and picked up the rod to show Shorty and Gus. Both agreed it was rough but apparently serviceable fishing tackle. Matt explained how the kink in the wire held the hook closed until the fish pulled on it. Shorty said, "Lots of good ideas came from accidents just like this." When everyone had eaten their fill, there was still some fish left. With the bread and tea it made a good meal. All agreed they would let Matt roast more rocks another time.

As they were finishing their tea, they could see another rider coming up the valley. With the two loaded packhorses following behind, they knew it had to be Spud, the ranch cook. He rode up to where Dawn and the boys were sitting and asked, "Is this private property, or can I set up camp here too? I have to try to feed a bunch of useless cowhands and I don't even have a chuck wagon to work from!" The cook was smiling as he spoke, as was everyone else.

Dawn said, "Yes, this is private property, but I might be persuaded to rent a bit of it to you, how about twenty dollars for the next three days?" The cook grinned and said, "Sounds fine to me, but you will have to try to get it out of the boss, I'm not!"

Everybody laughed and got up to help the cook get his equipment laid out the way he wanted it. Dawn offered him the last of the trout which was still warm by the fire. Spud tried the fish and said; "I think you should have my job if you can cook like this. I don't think I have ever eaten better trout!" Dawn laughed and said, "You will have to talk to Matt, then. He caught the fish and cooked it, I just made the tea!"

By the time they had the cook's kitchen area laid out to his specifications, a couple of other riders appeared. When they got closer, Dawn could identify them as Slim and Rusty. Rusty stated: "Well, leave it to Shorty to have all the comforts of home. I guess he doesn't like to rough it with the rest of us." Shorty laughed and said, "You boys got it all wrong! When Gus and I got here, the hotel was open for business and a meal on the table. Why, even Spud doesn't feed us as good back at the ranch!"

Spud who had been listening now spoke up, "Shorty's right, I don't think I ever ate better fish than I just had. You all know I'm the best cook within five hundred miles, but young Matt here, just may be a bit better. Maybe if you lazy cow chasers did his share of the work, you might talk him into cooking something for you!" The boys looked at each other but no one said a word. They knew the cook very seldom blew his own horn; he let his actions speak for him. Anyone who ever ate his grub would agree he was one of the best, if not *the* best cook in the area. If he praised someone else's cooking; it had to be good! By this time the cook had a pot of coffee on Dawn's fire and Dawn had more tea on the go, too. Dawn then brought out her doughnuts and everyone had a doughnut and a cup of tea or coffee.

Chapter 10

THE BOSS WOULD be here shortly and Angela was coming with him. That would be the extent of the crew. All agreed that should be enough to separate the cattle, as they seemed so quiet. Someone suggested starting to push a few down this way this evening. They thought this was a good plan and if successful, they would camp in small groups across the valley, to keep them from rejoining the main herd. They split into three groups and rode slowly up the valley. Two riders would come up behind a critter that was to go and gradually crowd it away from the rest. Two other riders would take over and push it a bit farther. This system seemed to be working fine so it was continued. With four riders working in pairs, it didn't take long to have eight or ten animals separated. These were slowly drifted down the valley to where they were to be held. Before the boss and his wife arrived just before dark, they had about fifteen head at the lower end of the valley. They stayed in a loose group and none seemed inclined to try and join the main herd. Spud had resaddled his horse and rode slowly across the valley and back above the cattle. It seemed they were more interested in eating than going anywhere.

Just before it got too dark to see, they pushed six more head to the low end of the valley. The boss was quite impressed with how things were going and how easily the cattle were separated. The boys would probably be out at daylight and crowd a few more head out of the main herd, while the cooks were getting breakfast ready. Right now though, it was time to hit the hay. All agreed, if they all spread across the valley to sleep, it should keep the cattle separated. So far it didn't seem like it was going to be much of a problem.

The two women slept under the tarp, while Matt joined the men sleeping in a line across the valley. Since the men had separated, this meant there were people sleeping in eight different places, blocking the cattle should they decide to stray. Although it didn't seem necessary, the cattle were separated and it was easier to keep them that way than to do it all over again. When morning came to the valley, it had been a quiet night on the western front and all the cattle were still in their proper places. Dawn was up and had a fire going before all the stars had gone to bed. She had water on to heat and a fire going at the kitchen area a few minutes later. Water for coffee was on heating there shortly, too.

When Matt brought his bedroll back to the shelter, he decided to try for a couple of trout for dinner. He borrowed a pail from the cook to bring back a load of clay in case he got anything. He went to the same spot he had been the previous day. The fish must have been waiting for breakfast because he had two trout in just over two minutes. He filled the pail with clay and headed back to the shelter where he cleaned the fish and put them in a pan he borrowed from Spud. He got a piece of cloth, wet it and laid it over the pan. As the water evaporated it would help to keep the fish cool. A quick breakfast and it was time to get back on the range with his horse.

Shortly, everyone was out in the valley easing the older cattle from the herd and slowly drifting them down the valley. They worked slowly but steadily so as not to alarm the herd. About ten thirty Matt went to camp and put more wood on the fires. The next time he went past, he stopped, wrapped the fish in grass and clay and put them in the coals to bake. He had borrowed salt and pepper and four strips of smoked bacon from the cook before preparing the fish as he thought the smoked bacon would add flavor to the trout. Each time he passed the camp, he would add more wood to the fire, and pull more coals over the baking trout. When dinnertime rolled around, the fish should be cooked to perfection. Spud, the cook, had left the crew early also and was getting something ready for dinner. When he signaled to someone the word was passed quietly to all the others, and they all made for camp.

A couple of horses were left nearby, ready to go if the cattle decided to move, and then everyone stopped for dinner. Matt got a small hand ax to break open the 'roast rocks'. The ones who had fish the previous evening said this was even better, and Matt told them of the salt, pepper and smoked bacon. There was a lot of lip smacking and finger licking going on. They ate the last of Dawn's bread and Matt's biscuits as well as what the cook had ready. Everyone stuffed themselves with the good food, and then decided they had better get back to work to wear some of it off.

It was going to be slower work separating the cattle now, as the herd hadn't gotten much smaller but the cattle they wanted were fewer and farther apart. As the men would gradually work one or two cattle out of the main herd, Matt and Spud would slowly push them down the valley to the holding area. Dawn and Angela were riding back and forth to keep them from trying to rejoin the herd, but none of them did. It was slow, but not very hard work separating the cattle this way. If they could keep the cattle from getting excited and start running, slow and easy was the best way to go. When Spud left to get supper ready, Dawn helped Matt push the separated cattle down the valley. Angela patrolled back and forth, even though it wasn't really necessary.

When supper was ready everyone rode down to the shelter and supper and the job was discussed as the meal was eaten. Everyone agreed there were more cattle in the valley than was originally estimated. They now figured there was more than three hundred head before they started. Over fifty head were at the bottom of the valley now, and ten to twenty left to pick out of the main herd. There would be sixty to seventy head to move out when the job was completed. The boss told Dawn, "I think we can get you ten cents a pound on the hoof, when we get these cattle to the railroad. They will weigh no less than six hundred pounds each, most quite a bit more. You should have between three and four thousand dollars coming to you and Matt."

Dawn looked shocked, "That is more money than I ever dreamed of having. We never had that much altogether since we came here. Whatever will we do with that much money?" Angela said, "Well, it isn't all profit. There is going to be some expenses. You still have to pay someone to help drive them to the railroad. There will probably be some other expenses, but you will still have some money to work with. Instead of having to do everything yourselves, you might be able to hire some help. You will also have cattle to sell every year now, though maybe not as many."

Shorty spoke up, "In this valley the cattle will probably be in good shape year round. You might be able to ship earlier every year and get a better price. You won't have as many cattle to sell, but a better price will make up for it. At least you are sure of some money every year!" Dawn said. "If you hadn't found this place, we probably would have had to sell off all our cattle out on the range, just to live. You have done so much for us already and then you found all these cattle for us, which makes our life a lot easier. We could never pay you enough for what you have done for us. I can't even thank you enough!"

"Yes, I've helped you and Matt a bit, but the meals you fed me more than made up for the work I did. As for these cattle, Gus was in on that, remember? Besides we were just doing the job we get paid to do. It could have been Slim or Red here that found them.

I'm not a hero. I'm just a regular cowhand." About this time the boss decided he had something else to say. He began, "We won't be branding these cattle before the drive. The buyers decided to take them as they are. Because they are fully grown and in such good shape, he figured it wasn't necessary. He knows the Axe and the R-R are the only brands in the immediate area and that these cattle belong to Dawn and Matt. Also, I'll be there at the sale so there won't be any problems."

Angela spoke up at this time and said, "I think we better get some sleep so we can finish this job tomorrow, I don't know about the rest of you, but I think I could sleep on rocks, I'm so tired. I guess I'm not used to being in a saddle all day." It was a unanimous decision to crawl into the bedrolls and get some sleep.

The next morning everyone was up at daylight, anxious to get the job finished. The boys were on the job and had half a dozen cattle moved before breakfast was on the table, but no one needed a second invite when breakfast was called. Working and sleeping in the fresh air makes even plain food taste good. The crew was busy pushing more cattle out of the main herd. The cattle had spread out overnight, which made it easier to pick out the older cattle that they wanted. One at a time the cattle were pushed out to the side and two riders drifted them slowly down to the other bunch. It took a lot of time but it was easier on everyone, including the cattle, than roping them. That would get the whole herd upset and possibly cause problems with the ones already separated. With no corral or holding pen, it would be almost impossible to hold a lot of excited cattle.

When noontime came the job was still not completed. Everyone rode down to the camp for chow and there was the usual discussion over the noon meal. The boss decided, since the separated cattle were giving them no problems, it would be best to leave them in the valley overnight. First thing in the morning, they would start pushing the cattle into the notch and out into the open. They would continue working until suppertime and if they didn't have all the older cattle by then, the rest would have to stay. It would probably take three days to get them to the railroad without pushing them too hard. The slower the cattle moved the less weight they would walk off.

Angela and Xavier were leaving right after supper, to go back to the ranch. The boss would go to town first thing in the morning and have word sent to the buyers, when to expect them and they would rejoin the herd when it went past the town. Now it was time to get back to the herd and pick out as many more cattle as they could before suppertime. Someone suggested Matt catch and cook a few more trout for supper. The agreement was unanimous!

They worked steadily throughout the afternoon and it looked like they would have all the older cattle out before supper. Matt received a couple of reminders about supper, so about mid afternoon he went to camp, replenished the fire and headed for the lake with fishing gear and pail. In ten minutes he was on the way back to camp with two large trout. A few more minutes had them cleaned and ready to cook, including the bacon and salt and pepper. With the fish cooking, Matt went back to work. Dawn would stop at camp often to keep the fire going. Spud left the crew to get water heating and make biscuits to go with the fish. The crew was coming with the last animal they could find, when the cook signaled for supper. The final tally for the herd to be shipped was seventy six. This was more than anyone had expected and the news was welcomed by all. Matt and Dawn were very happy, as this meant there was no danger of losing the ranch! Now, everyone was eyeing the 'roast rocks' Matt had prepared for supper and with Spud's hot biscuits and plenty of tea and coffee it was a good meal.

Angela and Xavier left right after supper for the ranch, and the others sat and talked until sundown, they then shook out their bedrolls and turned in. Who knew what tomorrow would bring when they started moving these cattle to market. It was a quiet night and the cattle gave them no problems. At first light the cooks were at work on breakfast and when the meal was ready everyone ate quickly. Several people helped the cook pack up his food and tools and he started on his way. Matt had borrowed a shovel and dug a hole to bury the baked clay and anything else that didn't belong in the valley, including the ashes from the campfires. Nothing would be left to mar this beautiful valley, except tracks, and these would soon disappear.

When the cook led his packhorses past the cattle, they seemed curious, so Shorty and the crew started to crowd them a bit. Soon the cattle were following the cook, single file, down the gully. At least the start of the drive was going to be easy! The cattle slowly wound their way down the gully and out onto the open prairie. Here they bunched up and the cowboys kept them moving in the right direction. The chuck wagon was parked a short distance away and the cook was transferring his supplies and utensils on board. Meals would be easier to prepare now, with more equipment and food, plus a better place to work from. The drive was now underway and, hopefully everything would go as smoothly as the start. It seemed they had hardly got started until they were going past the town where Angela and the boss joined them. Three days would put them to the railroad where the cattle cars waited.

The chuck wagon caught up to them and went on by. When they came upon it just past noon there was a good meal waiting for everyone. The cook had picked spot where the grass was good, so the cattle had dinner too. When the cattle had fed for an hour or so, the drive went on. Soon the chuck wagon went by again and the next time the herd caught up to it, supper would be ready. The drive would spend the night near the supper stop. The next two days would be very similar to the first one. The second and third days were as uneventful as the beginning, and a bit monotonous. A boring cattle drive is the best kind; that means no trouble and the best beef.

When the drive reached the railroad, the cattle were herded into a holding pen. The buyers came down to inspect the beef they were buying. They were very impressed with the quality of the beef, for this time of year. One of the buyers said, "We would buy all the beef you have if it's in this condition. Beef is scarce right now and will be for the next month or two." Dawn told him,

"That's all we have right now, but this time next year we may have some to sell." The buyer told her, "Since you have prime beef, better than most ranches have in the fall, I think we can give you another cent a pound." Dawn was surprised but pleased to hear this news. Xavier went with Dawn and Matt to finalize the deal. Dawn found she would get half the money now and the rest in about two weeks when the cattle had been shipped to the final market. This money would be sent to the bank in town, for the owners of the R-R, Dawn and Matt Ryan! They were sure of the ranch being theirs for a long time now.

Now that the cattle were off their hands, there was very little to keep them occupied. This place called Medicine Hat was much bigger than their hometown. Dawn and Matt didn't feel up to facing the crowd that was on the streets. They decided to find a place to have a bath, change their clothes and get something to eat. Food that someone else prepared was going to be a treat for both of them! The whole crew was thinking along the same lines, so they decided to all eat at the same place. There was a small café on the outskirts of town, not very far away and everyone was to meet there at seven thirty for supper. Dawn and Matt arrived first and Dawn talked to the owner about holding three tables for her crew. She also made arrangements to pay the bill for everyone. This was a small bonus for all the help they had received from everyone in the past week. As the crew came in they ordered what they wanted as they took their places at the tables. The meal was good, but Matt thought his mother's cooking was better. Shorty, who Dawn insisted had to sit with them, agreed with Matt. Spud, the cook, said this was a fine meal but Matt's 'roast rock' was better. This brought a chorus of agreements and a gale of laughter. When the meal was over, Dawn and Matt decided to head outside of town and find a good spot to camp overnight. After what they had gone through in the past year or two, Dawn just couldn't bring herself to pay money for a place to sleep. A few of the men stayed in town for a while, but most decided to follow Dawn's lead and leave town. Next morning would bring a fair day's ride back home.

Sleeping in the open, everyone was awake when daylight arrived. The chuck wagon was nearby, so Dawn helped the cook get breakfast on the go. It didn't take long to put the meal inside themselves, so it was only a short time later everyone was packed up and ready for the ride home. The crew was in good spirits after a successful drive and an even more successful sale for Dawn and Matt. No one was in a hurry, so they rode along slowly enough so the chuck wagon could keep up. The crew rode along in groups of two or three so it was easier to carry on a conversation. Dawn usually rode alongside Shorty or Angela, sometimes both. She enjoyed Shorty's company, and Angela wasn't above trying to get them together as much as possible.

Just before noon, Shorty rode alongside the chuck wagon so he could talk to Spud. He said, "I'm going on ahead to look for a spot to stop for dinner. If I can find a spot with water and wood, I'll get a fire started. I'll take along the coffee pot and have water hot for coffee. Surely there will be a good spot in the next ten miles. Shorty told the others what his plans were. It would save a bit of time to have a fire going and water hot for coffee. Angela spoke up and said;" Dawn, why don't you go along to keep him out of trouble? We wouldn't want our prize cowhand getting lost or hurt!" This brought a few chuckles from the crew, but Dawn agreed to ride ahead with Shorty to look for a good spot for dinner.

They trotted their horses up the trail looking for a dinner spot. Usually when a person found water there was at least some wood. With the horses trotting, it was hard to carry on a conversation so talk would have to wait. Eight or nine miles up the trail, they found what they were looking for. It was a small hollow, with a tiny spring at one side. There wasn't a great supply of wood, but more than enough for their purpose. This spot had been used before, as there was a circle of rocks ready for a cooking fire. Shorty gathered wood and got a fire started while Dawn filled the coffeepot with spring water. The pot was set on the fire to heat as Shorty gathered a few handfuls of green grass. He figured the crew would be almost half an hour behind them. Twenty minutes later the coffeepot was pushed back a bit and the grass tossed on the fire. This made a small column of smoke to guide the others, as the hollow was slightly off the trail. In less than five minutes they could hear galloping horses, as the boys all took part in a race to the campsite; no one knew who the winner was.

When the chuck wagon pulled up a few minutes later, several of the boys helped carry what the cook needed, down to the fire. Water was put on for tea and as the cook prepared a meal everyone found a soft rock or patch of grass to sit on. With a cup of coffee in their hand, the boys were content to wait for their dinner. A filling meal was soon on their plates and the conversation tapered off as everyone was busy eating. As the plates emptied and bellies filled, the talk picked up again. Someone asked Dawn what she was going to do with her new-found wealth.

"I don't know yet," she said, "Matt and I will have to talk about it when we get home. We haven't had money for so long. It will take a while to get used to the idea of having some to spend. We aren't in a big rush anyway, but I think we would both like to have a horse for riding. I might be able to give you a better answer in a year or so." The meal was over and the coffeepot empty, so everyone helped Spud stow away the equipment he had used for dinner and a few minutes later they were on the trail home.

It was about seven o'clock when their hometown showed up. Dawn offered to pay for everyone's supper if they would let her. They appreciated the offer, but since it was still a twelve mile ride to the ranch, they all thought they should push on to the ranch before dark. Dawn thanked everyone for their help as they rode off. Dawn and Matt were going to have a bite to eat before going home as they lived a lot closer. They enjoyed a quick meal, and then headed for the R-R, as there were things to be checked over before bedtime. Now that the excitement had worn off, they realized both of them were very tired. It would be good to sleep in a bed for a change.

When they got to the ranch they found everything as they had left it. The horses were unsaddled and put into the pasture. Matt went to the chicken pen and found them closed up tight. When Dawn entered the kitchen, something smelled good. There was a pot of stew sitting in cold water in the sink. On the table was a note from Randy. It read, "When I got here the place was deserted. I remembered the cattle drive and figured that was where you had gone. Not much food left so I made some biscuits. I made the stew for dinner Saturday. I had to borrow some vegetables from the garden as I hadn't brought any with me. A man has to eat even if he isn't working. I just loafed around as there was no one to tell me what to do. I will probably see you all next weekend, a friend, Randy."

Dawn could just imagine Randy loafing all weekend, there was the pot of stew, biscuits and the kitchen was spotless. Dawn and Matt both felt it was time for bed as neither could hold their eyes open. Almost a week of riding and living outside was catching up to them and they were soon in bed asleep.

When the rooster sounded off the next morning, telling the world it was time to rise and shine, breakfast was already underway at the Ryan household. With breakfast over Matt went outside to turn the chickens loose and check the other stock. Everything seemed to be fine but there were no eggs in the nests. When he went to the barn, he found everything in order there too. As he was looking around, he saw the fence he and Shorty had been working on was nearly finished and his pigs had been watered and looked after. Matt also noticed the roof of his pig shelter was well covered with soil. If Randy had been loafing around all weekend, someone else must have been doing all the work! Matt thought of the bunkhouse and the clay still to be put in the cracks. He went up there but the small amount left was too dry to work with. He took the handbarrow and went to the house to ask his mother to help him carry some clay up to the bunkhouse.

She said, "I'll be with you in a few minutes, Matt. It won't take long to finish up what I'm doing." Matt told her, "I'll get the clay dug up and be waiting for you. If we make two trips it will be enough to do me for quite a while." Matt headed for the creek where he and Shorty had dug the clay the last time. In a few minutes he had the handbarrow loaded and some dug loose for the second load. Dawn arrived shortly to help him carry the load up to the bunkhouse. It was only a few minutes work to carry the clay up the slight incline to the bunkhouse. Matt got the tub and put it about midway along the side facing the house. The clay was emptied into it and another load was brought up. Matt decided to leave this load in the handbarrow and use it first. Dawn went back to the house to finish a few things she had started, but she was going back up to help Matt as soon as possible.

Matt was working away at pushing the clay into the joints as smoothly as he could manage. He would fill a few cracks before he would take the wet sacking to make it smooth and shiny. He thought he was doing a pretty good job of filling and smoothing the joints. When Dawn arrived she was quite impressed with the beautiful job Matt was doing. She asked Matt: "How do you get it so smooth? Even with the paddle, there would be lines and bumps in the clay." Matt showed her how to wet the feed sack and smooth the joints to get a good finish. She began pushing the clay into the joints the way Matt was. She didn't get it as smooth as Matt, as Shorty had showed Matt how and explained the process better. He told her to keep trying and she would soon be as good as him. He showed her how to use the feed sack to smooth all the marks out of the clay. In a short time she was almost as good as Matt. With the feed sack she could make her joints look as good as the ones Matt was doing.

Dawn had put wood in the stove before leaving the house. After working for a while she went back to the house to put more wood in the stove and put the pot of stew, which Randy had made, on to heat for their dinner. She went back to the bunkhouse to help Matt while their dinner was heating. They were soon as high as they could reach from the ground, so Matt got the sawhorses and a few wide boards. This made a stable platform to work from so they could reach the rest of the wall. When they had the front wall finished the stew was hot, so the job was shut down so they could eat. The reheated stew Randy had made was very good and disappeared in a hurry. During the meal Dawn asked Matt what his suggestions were on using some of their money. "Well," Matt answered, "you suggested possibly buying some saddle horses. I like that idea. We could even ride back to lost valley now and then to camp out and catch some fish to eat. I think that is the prettiest place I have ever seen."

"OK, Matt, we'll ask Xavier and Angela about buying the horses we are using now. We have been riding them a lot and have gotten to know them quite well. It would be a lot better than starting out with horses we don't know." Now that they had some money, getting them each a horse would be the first order of business. After the meal they went back to the bunkhouse to work. There was a space between the top of the wall and the underside of the roof, between the rafters. This had to be filled in but Matt wasn't sure how to go about it. He got a narrow board and trimmed it to fit snugly, and tapped it into place. He then drove a nail into each end so it couldn't shift. He kept trimming and fitting boards until that side of the building was finished. As he put the boards in place, Dawn would plaster them with clay. These joints were up under the roof and couldn't be seen easily, so they didn't worry about getting clay on the wood. The most important thing was to have the joints sealed tightly. When they were finished, all the spaces between the rafters were filled in and sealed with clay.

Dawn was thinking as she worked. Today was Monday, and she planned to have a dance for the hands at the big ranch. Maybe she should pack a lunch for her and Matt and ride over to talk to Angela about it. They would need someone to play music, even if some of the hands could play. It wouldn't be fair to them if they had to play the music and not be able to dance. She and Angela should be able to work out something, and find someone to help out with the music. She told Matt what she was thinking and he thought it was a good idea. He agreed they could ride over to the Axe and maybe they could find out about buying the horses. Matt was finishing up a bit of work while Dawn went in to make a lunch for them. When he finished, Matt went to the barn and saddled the horses. A few minutes later they were on the trail toward the Axe.

Before they got to the ranch, they found a nice spot to eat their lunch. They could have ridden on to the ranch and had supper, but they enjoyed the picnic by themselves. Arriving at the ranch, Angela was the first person they saw. "Well," she said, "long time no see! It must be almost twenty four hours isn't it? What brings you two cowhands over this way?"

Dawn told her what her plans were and Angela thought it would be a great idea. Cowhands always enjoyed a dance. Dawn said she planned to have some food ready and a lot of her 'bearsign,' Angela told her a few of the hands played guitars, but she also knew some people in town who would be glad to help out with the music. They would also need a few more ladies for the men to dance with. It wouldn't matter if they were married or not, as long as they would dance with the boys.

Angela told Dawn, "I'll ride over to your place either tomorrow or the next day and we'll go into town and talk to a few people. Since it won't be a really big 'do', I'm sure we can get it all arranged before Saturday. When you get back home be sure to make a list of everything you think you might need. Between Spud and I, we'll have a lot of sliced, roast beef to take along. You can make lots of biscuits and maybe a few loaves of bread. They will probably eat more of your doughnuts than anything else. I'll start on my own list too. Shorty and Matt can build some benches and a couple of tables to eat at. We are going to have a real party, eh sis?"

After visiting for a few more minutes, Dawn and Matt were ready to leave. Dawn told Angela to be sure to tell the hands and that every one of them was welcome to come. They were half way home before they remembered they hadn't asked about the horses. Oh well, there would be lots of time for that later. Now, they had to do some more planning and get everything ready for Saturday evening. By the time Dawn and Matt got back home, it was almost time for bed. The horses were unsaddled and put into the pasture. Matt checked the stock and closed in the chickens before going inside. Dawn had a paper and pencil and was making a list. Thanks to that extra bag of flour Shorty had got them; there was plenty to bake with. She did need some spice and a few other small items. Matt thought if they didn't have too much to bring from town maybe she could pick up some hinges. He said two pair each of small and large strap hinges and two pair of tee hinges should do. They would need them for the bunkhouse, root cellar and the table at the bunkhouse. Dawn decided to take the pack with her and any bulky items would go in it, the hinges and smaller things would fit in the saddlebags. Dawn put the list where it was handy and they got ready for bed.

In the morning it was busyness as usual. Matt opened up the chickens, milked the cow, and looked after the other stock. Dawn was getting breakfast ready, which was waiting when Matt came to the house with the milk. As they ate breakfast, they worked on the list, which Dawn kept handy. Matt thought they should make a big pot of beef stew. If they made it on Friday and heated it at least once more, it would be nice and thick for Saturday evening. Dawn agreed that was a good plan and there were now plenty of fresh vegetables in the garden. They couldn't think of anything else for the list, but it was kept handy, just in case.

Matt decided to go up to the bunkhouse and find something to work on. They would need two or three tables and some benches to sit on, but Shorty would have a better idea of how to make them than Matt would. He decided to move some of the short logs and lumber that was scattered around. He thought he would pile most of it at the low side of the woodshed. As he was moving the logs he was thinking that a person could make a good sturdy table from these short logs. He was thinking of how it could be done, until he could see it in his mind. First, two short pieces about seven or eight inches through. Then, two longer pieces set in notches in the bottom logs. The long logs would be about thirty inches apart. Next would be two smaller logs about seven or eight feet long and only four or five inches through for the seats to go on. Two more long logs, with two short ones on top to make it the right height for a tabletop. That will work, he told himself as he set about building a log table on a level spot.

When dinner time rolled around, he had the area cleaned up and a good sturdy table built. The tabletop was about four feet wide and ten feet long, with seats on both sides and a block of wood at each end for a seat.

He then got four small rail ends about four feet long and sharpened the ends. He drove them into the ground on the house side of the bunkhouse. They formed a rectangle thirty inches wide and six feet long. He nailed two seven foot long, six inch wide boards across the narrow ends about eighteen inches off the ground. The boards protruded just over two feet on each side of the stakes. Two narrow boards were nailed at the tops of the stakes so they were level and just slightly above the tops. Wide boards were nailed onto the long boards for seats and nine foot boards were nailed on for a tabletop. A couple of more log ends were trimmed for seats at the end of the table. Matt gathered rocks to make a fire pit where it was safe to do so. They could burn any brush that was in the area, plus some of the short log ends, giving some light to see by. He thought he had done well, as he had places for at least twenty people to sit and eat or just to talk, but right now it was time for Matt to eat, or at least his stomach said so!

As they ate dinner, Matt explained to his mother what he had accomplished up at the bunkhouse. She decided to go up to see what he had done, as soon as they had finished eating. Neither one had come up with anything else for the list, but it looked like Angela wouldn't be coming until tomorrow. Matt told Dawn he had just planned to clean up around the bunkhouse and wait until Shorty came to build the tables. He had been moving the logs and came up with the idea for the log table. He had cleaned up around the bunkhouse and built a table at the same time. "I was just thinking of what Shorty might do and I came up with the idea. Shorty always explains everything he does and why it should be done that way. He must be the smartest man around here!"

Dawn said, "Well, Shorty always says it's not how smart you are, it's how you use your smarts. Look at you, not even eight years old yet and you come up with some very good ideas. Do you think you are as smart as Shorty? He explains how and why to do something and gets you thinking. If you are around Shorty long enough, you will be able to come up with almost as many ideas and be able to do almost as many things as him. You are right though. Shorty is a smart man, no matter what he says!"

"I hope he stays around here for a long time," Matt said. "I wish he was my dad!" Dawn said with a faraway look in her eyes, "I do too Matt, I do too!" When the meal was over, they put the dishes to soak and walked up to the bunkhouse. Dawn was amazed at what Matt had accomplished. She said, "The tables are so sturdy and in just the right places. When the dance is over, they can be taken apart and nothing is wasted. The lumber can be used again as a few nail holes won't hurt it."

Dawn gave Matt a hug and said, "I've got two very smart men around here! I hope they are always here with me!" Her eyes were shining and she seemed to have trouble speaking. She decided it was time to go back to the house and get her dishes washed. As she was leaving Matt said, "I just thought of something we need. Shorty said he was going to use small rope in the bottom of the bunks. It will take a lot so we better get about two hundred feet. It doesn't have to be very big, but it has to be strong. Maybe you could get something to make a mattress out of too. Maybe something like a big bag to fill with straw or hay, maybe four, but at least two as we will soon have two bunks ready to use." Dawn said, "That is a straw tick you are thinking about. They are just a big bag made out of heavy material. I'll put small rope and straw ticks on our list."

Dawn went back to the house to do her housework, after putting the rope and straw ticks on her list. It was so nice to be able to buy a few things they needed and not have to worry about running out of money. She didn't plan to buy anything that wasn't important, but at least now they could buy the necessities.

Chapter 11

DAWN WAS LOOKING forward to the trip to town with Angela. It had been quite a while since she had been to town, except for the stop on the way home from the drive and the quick trip earlier for the seeds and supplies for the bunkhouse. As she thought of this, she realized it had been a put-up job by Matt and Shorty, to get her away from the ranch while they surprised her with the sink and running water. Thinking back about this, her eyes filled up with tears. Shorty had done so much for her and Matt since that day in the spring, when they had met in the hills. It seems as though it has been longer than that, she thought. It seems like he has been here forever and I hope he will be here forever. She said to herself, 'I better quit daydreaming and get some work done around here.'

Matt was looking for something to do around the bunkhouse. He was used to keeping busy and the time seemed to pass by faster when a person had something to keep them occupied. For the past year and more, both Matt and Dawn had been busy most of the time! There wasn't really very much he could do, at least until after the upcoming dance. He knew his mother was going to have hot beef stew, tea, coffee and doughnuts; lots and lots of doughnuts! He thought, 'if the stove was set up it would help to keep things hot. It would be in the way in the bunkhouse, but what if it was set up outside, maybe just under the roof of the woodshed, with the pipe going up past the roof.' He decided to run that idea past Shorty when he arrived. Also, if the window was removed, the musicians could be on the porch and the music could be heard better inside. The door could also be taken off for that night, as it wouldn't quite swing back flat against the wall.

Matt decided to take down the staging they had used at the back of the bunkhouse. It was no longer needed, but it would only take a few minutes to do. When this job was done, he would start filling in joints again. He couldn't think of anything else to do at the bunkhouse. He could work at the clay inside anytime, even when it was wet outside. Matt dragged the tub of clay over to the porch and slid it up a short board onto the floor. He started filling the joints, taking a bit more time and being more careful here where it would be seen more. He filled the cracks and smoothed them until he was up past the bottom of the window, he then sealed around the window frame and the doorframe. This end of the bunkhouse was receiving very careful treatment. With the wet sacking he would smooth the clay until there wasn't a mark showing, he then took a wet rag and wiped any clay off the logs. He was going to do a job he could be proud of, here where it would be seen the most. He was working at the top of the window when Dawn came out to see how he was getting along. They set up the sawhorses and Dawn helped Matt finish the end wall. They made sure it was well sealed where the wall logs touched the rafters. They would have the tightest bunkhouse in the country!

When the outside was all sealed, they moved inside and began sealing the joints in there. The end wall was where they started as it was closest and would be seen the most. This wall was finished when Dawn went in to get something for them to eat. Matt kept working along to the second window and past, just doing what he could reach easily; he would do the upper part from the sawhorses later. As he worked he was thinking of the upcoming dance and all the people that would be here. It wouldn't be like a dance in town, but it was still a big event here at the ranch. He was almost finished on the lower part of the wall when Dawn came out to tell him supper was ready. She helped him smooth out the clay while it was still soft. She told him he was doing a wonderful job on the wall, considering he had never done a job like this. They were both pleased with their work when they went to supper, which was the last of the stew Randy had made.

Dawn asked Matt if he was going to town with her and Angela tomorrow. Matt replied, "I don't think so. I can get a little more done here if you don't need me. There isn't really a lot I can do by myself though, except chinking the bunkhouse. I'll get you to help me get another load of clay after supper, though and then I'll keep working away at it by myself."

They both tried to think of something that should be on the list but couldn't. Matt reminded Dawn, "Just don't forget the hinges and small rope. Ask about loose pin hinges, but Shorty said he could fix up one of the regular ones if he has to. I think I know what he was going to do, too. If the big end was filed off the pin it could be pulled out and dropped in easily. Maybe I'll do that after supper. I'll get a big file then and with the door partly open, the file will go through on edge. I'll have a surprise for Shorty when he gets here.

Dawn said, "You are thinking more like Shorty all the time. Even I can come up with some good ideas, after Shorty taught us how to think. Well, I guess there isn't much more to put on the list. If Shorty comes up with something, one of us might have to ride into town for it on Friday or Saturday."

When the meal was over Matt went to the barn to get a big file, went up to the bunkhouse to start work on the hinges. It would have been easier with the hinge off the door, but Matt figured he could do it even if it took more time. He began to file the top of the hinge pin through the narrow crack between the door and the wall. It would have been much faster if he could put one hand on each end of the file, but he was making progress. About fifteen minutes later he could see he was filing on the top of the hinge. He got a four-inch spike and tapped the pin out with it. He filed the sides of the pin smooth and dropped it into place from the top. He thought, 'One down, one to go.' After resting his hands for a few minutes, he started work on the lower hinge. In less than twenty minutes he had the second pin loose. The bunkhouse now had loose pin hinges on the door!

Dawn had finished her housework and came out to help Matt carry more clay from the creek. He showed her what he had accomplished. He lifted a bit and got Dawn to pull the bottom pin and then the top one. Matt moved the door to one side. The door could be stored in the woodshed, or even used as another table when placed on the sawhorses. It wouldn't be in the way of people going in and out the night of the dance.

Matt said, "I think when we build the inside door, we should do the same. Then either door could be taken off so it wouldn't be in the way. If we build the frame in past the logs, it would swing back against the wall, unless another bunk was built. Four bunks should be enough for our ranch hands, seeing as how we don't have any!" Matt and Dawn both laughed at this, and left to get another load of clay for the bunkhouse.

They decided to get two loads as Dawn would be away with Angela tomorrow. This would keep Matt busy and maybe finish the bunkhouse as well. There was still the front of the root cellar and the front of the pig cellar to do, but neither would have to be done as carefully as the bunkhouse. Matt worked until it began to get dark, then checked the stock and went to the house. He and his mother talked as they ate a bedtime snack. It wasn't very long until they were in bed, as there was a busy day waiting for them.

When morning arrived, they were up and busy as they usually were. Matt turned the chickens loose, checked the other stock and milked the cow. Breakfast was waiting when he walked through the door. As soon as the meal was over, Dawn rushed t get her housework done before Angela arrived. She wanted to be ready and wasn't sure what time she would get here. Matt had Dawn's horse in the barn, ready to put the saddle on. Dawn was checking the list for the fifth time when she heard Angela ride into the yard. She grabbed her hat and the pack and headed for outside, where she almost collided with Angela in the doorway.

"Where are you going in such a rush?" Angela demanded. "Don't I even get a cup of tea after my long ride? There is always time for a good cup of tea." Dawn answered, "I thought you might be in a hurry. The tea is still hot so have a seat and I'll get a cup for each of us."

Angela asked, "And how are you and that short, fat cowboy getting along?" Dawn replied, "You have probably seen him more in the last few days than I have. I haven't laid eyes on him since we got into town on Sunday. Are you still trying to play matchmaker?"

"Well," Angela said, "Somebody has to! I bet you hardly say a word to him when he's here. I'll have to have a talk to Matt sometime. Maybe he can work on the two of you when I'm not here. He needs a man around here and so do you!" Dawn stated, "He has a man around here on the weekends, sometimes two and one time there was five!" Angela said. "OK, I'm just a meddling older sister, but you know you need a man around here and I don't mean just for work! Now, finish your tea and we'll be on our way to town."

In a few minutes they were on their way to town, to do some shopping, and visiting. The first thing they would do was to round up a few more people to help out with the music for the dance. They stopped at the hardware store and left the list of things Dawn needed. They also asked the owner, George Connors, if he knew of someone who would like to play music for a small dance. He said, "Well, I play a pretty mean fiddle and my wife does too. The schoolteacher plays just about anything that makes music and she has a guitar. With a bunch of cowhands wanting a dancing partner, she probably won't get to play much music though! Tell you what I'll do, we know a few other people who play music, we'll get a group together and provide the music for you. No charge, except for some food!"

This was better than they had expected, music and probably a few dancing partners too! Angela took Dawn's hand and practically dragged her to the ladies wear store. "Now," Angela said, "we have to get you something fitting for the 'Belle of the Ball'."

Dawn agreed she needed a new dress, but nothing too fancy, just a plain, pretty dress. As they were looking at the dresses, they mentioned it was for an upcoming dance. They also told the owner they would like to get a few more female dancing partners. She said almost any woman in town would go to a dance, but she knew of a couple of single ladies who would be interested. They explained it was only a bunkhouse and they didn't have room for a lot of people. She said, "The more the merrier, I always say, if you're going to have a party, you might as well have a real party!"

Dawn found a dress she liked and paid for it. Angela decided they were going to take time for lunch before heading back to the ranch. Dawn wanted to pay for the meal but so did Angela. She said; "When Matt and I were in town, he insisted on buying our meal, so I bought desert. OK, we'll have lunch and desert and split the cost. Fair enough with you?"

After the meal Dawn got the few things she needed at the general store, along with the straw ticks. The store only had three small ones but lots of doubles. She decided to take one double size tick. Next they went to the hardware store for the hinges and small rope. Mr. Connors said it came in five hundred foot coils, but a full coil wasn't much more than a two hundred foot piece, so Dawn bought the full coil. He told Dawn he would see them just after supper on Saturday. With all their business completed, Dawn and Angela mounted up and turned their horses toward home.

The girls were quite pleased with what they had accomplished. Dawn had a new dress, they had musicians and dancers coming, and so it seemed everything was ready but the food. The food situation would be taken care of on Friday and Saturday. Shorty arrived in time for a late supper on Thursday evening. He said Angela had practically run him off the ranch at gunpoint. "You are needed on the R-R," she said, "Now vamoose!" He usually did as he was told, so to keep peace in the family, he vamoosed.

As they shared the meal, they talked about what had taken place throughout the week. Matt could hardly wait to show Shorty what he had done. When supper was over, all three went up to the bunkhouse. Shorty was amazed at the tables Matt had built, as they were so solid, yet they could be dismantled easily. Matt showed him the door hinges and explained that the door could be removed for the dance, so it wouldn't be in the way. He also asked Shorty what he thought about taking the window on the porch out so the music could be heard easier. Shorty agreed if the musicians were on the porch, the open window would let everyone hear it better. He thought Matt and Dawn had done a great job on the clay chinking. Matt told Shorty how he had thought of using the stove for keeping the food hot. Shorty thought that would be better than running to the house all the time.

"Matt," Shorty said, "you are getting better at coming up with ideas than I am. Pretty soon you won't need me here at all!" Matt got a shocked look on his face. "I think I'll stick around for a while though," Shorty said, "maybe you can teach me a few things." Being that Shorty had arrived late it was now nearing bedtime. They decided to hit the hay now and get an early start in the morning. One last donut with a cup of tea and it was dreamland for all.

When the rooster announced it was time to rise and shine, all three were out and about doing the usual morning ranch work. The rooster and his harem were turned loose, the cow milked and the other stock was looked after. By this time the cook was ready to do her part and feed the crew. Breakfast disappeared in a hurry and soon everyone was busy with last minute jobs to prepare for the dance. Dawn was going to bake bread to have on hand for the dancing crew, but would wait until tomorrow to make fresh doughnuts. There is something about 'Bearsign,' which cowboys just can't resist!

Matt was going to work with Shorty for a while, before getting the vegetables from the garden and help Dawn make a big pot of beef stew. They would have some for supper to check it out, and then it would be reheated tomorrow night. The more times homemade stew is reheated, the better it is. About the time the bottom of the pot is showing, the stew is delicious. With an endless supply of tea and coffee, stew, bread, biscuits and roast beef, that Angela and Spud were bringing, there should be enough to feed a small army. The doughnuts Dawn was going to make tomorrow would be a sure hit with everyone. Even hard dancing cowpokes should be able to find enough food to fill them up! Shorty and Matt were up in the bunkhouse looking to see what should be done. The door had been taken off the bunkhouse as Matt had suggested and the window beside the door was removed also. Shorty suggested Matt should put a couple of narrow boards over the other window to protect it from elbows and shoulders. Shorty got a couple of small stakes to extend the small table Matt had built, and they used the door for a top. It wasn't going to be needed as a door but another table might come in handy. The stove would be set up as Matt had suggested, but extra light would be needed for tomorrow night. There were two lamps in the house and a lantern in the barn. With the fireplace that Matt had built outside to help light things up, they could probably get by with a couple more lamps, a few candles might come in handy too, for the tables outside. Dawn or Matt could make a quick trip to town later. Shorty started cutting some of the short, large logs for seats around the extended table.

The porch railing would make seats for some of the music-makers, the bench a couple more and the tables for those not dancing at the moment. Just about everything was ready now, except the lamps. The door could be put back on its hinges if it was needed, which was unlikely. Shorty took another look around before going to help Matt with the vegetables for the stew. They planned to use the biggest pot Dawn had, so hopefully there would be enough to go around. Shorty went to the garden to help Matt harvest the vegetables. Matt was pulling carrots, one here and there. He told Shorty, "I always try to pick the biggest ones where they are thick. Also while the potatoes are still growing, I don't dig them I just pick one from under each plant." Shorty said, "That's the best way Matt, if you thin out the carrots the others will grow bigger. If you take just one potato from each plant, the others will grow bigger to make up the loss. I see you have turnips planted where the other plants didn't grow, too. If all the space is filled in, it makes for less weeding. Of course, in the spring those young weeds sure make good eating too. I guess we better get busy or our company will be here before we're ready!"

They finished picking the vegetables and Matt carried them to the house, while Shorty took the tops to the pigs. They were much bigger than they were in the spring, and Shorty could see a slight difference each time he came. He went to the house to help Matt cut up and peel the vegetables. Dawn had about four pounds of beef cut up and browning in the frying pans, which would go into the big pot with all the vegetables. Matt and Shorty were soon busy peeling and cutting vegetables for the pot. By the time they were finished, the three gallon pot was brim full. It was almost dinner time and the stew would be kept boiling most of the afternoon. They would sample the stew for supper and the remainder would be set aside for Saturday evening. The boys cleaned up the mess they had made and the peelings were taken out to the pigs. They enjoyed the fresh vegetables for their dinner too.

Dawn got them a quick bite to eat as she had bread to get in the pans and bake. She would make biscuits and doughnuts tomorrow, so they would be fresh. Shorty asked Matt if he would like to ride into town to pick up a couple of lamps for the bunkhouse. He thought a hanging lamp for the center and a wall lamp for the end by the doorway. With the lamps from the house and the lantern from the barn, plus Matt's fireplace, they should have enough light. Matt agreed to go and asked if there was anything else that was needed. There was still plenty of kerosene in the can in the barn and no one could think of anything else. Shorty suggested Matt take a pack and a light blanket to wrap the lamps and chimneys in. A few minutes later Matt was on the way to town. Shorty decided to put the hinges on the table in case it was needed. Two hinges would hold the table to the wall and he decided to use a strip of leather to hold the braces to the tabletop. There wouldn't be much pressure on the leather as the braces hooked behind the front board under the tabletop. He got a couple of pieces of lumber to make a button to hold the table against the wall. With this done there was very little more work to be finished at the bunkhouse. He went down to the house to see if there was anything Dawn needed help with. Shorty helped with whatever he could, until Matt arrived with the lamps. They went outside to fill the lamps and get something to hang the ceiling lamp with. The lamps from the house and the lantern were filled at the same time.

Except for the biscuits and doughnuts there was very little left to be done. This evening, there might be a little time to relax, but tomorrow would probably be a busier day than even normal days were. All three spent a short time sitting on the open porch at the bunkhouse before going to bed.

In the morning everyone was up and busy as this was the big day or maybe the big, long night. Dawn was busy making doughnuts, (bearsign, to us cowpokes), and Matt was making biscuits. Shorty went outside to make sure there was a supply of wood for the stove and the fire pit. There were some short end pieces of logs that would make good firewood. Shorty split and stacked a good supply in the woodshed and against the bunkhouse near the fire pit. There seemed to be enough to do to keep them from getting bored.

They were just finishing up an early supper when Angela and Xavier arrived. They had ridden over on horseback, to see if they could help with any last minute preparations. Angela told them Spud was bringing the chuck wagon with some food supplies and plenty of cold roast beef. They sat and had a cup of tea with a doughnut, to visit for a few minutes, as there would be little time for that later.

When their tea was finished Matt took his uncle out to show him what they had been doing recently. He was impressed with the job everyone had done on the bunkhouse. Next he showed him the root cellar. He thought it would hold a lot of vegetables, plus anything else that had to be kept from freezing. The 'pig cellar' was next in line on the guided tour. Matt told him of needing a shelter or building for the winter months. He came up with the idea of building a root cellar, but on a smaller scale. Matt's uncle Xavier could hardly believe how big they had grown since they had been brought home in July.

He could see the sluice running water to the barn and said, "I'll bet that was Shorty's idea. He must be awful lazy to think up all these ideas to save work. He'd rather use his brain than his brawn to do everything!" Shorty smiled and said, "Well, I guess I'll have to admit I'm lazy then. You will have to admit though, if it wasn't for us lazy guys, we would all still be living in caves and chasing animals with a sharp stick." Matt and his uncle both agreed that thinking people like Shorty, made the world a better place to live. Matt explained to his uncle how they had made the sink and pipe to put running water in the house. Now he didn't have to carry water to the house or to the livestock. That gave him more time to do other things.

At this time the hardware store owner, George Connors and his wife Violet, arrived in a light driving wagon and they had the schoolteacher, Miss Carter with them. Their instruments were wrapped in blankets on a bed of straw behind them. They had a few extra instruments in the wagon, belonging to others who would arrive later on horseback. There was hellos and handshaking all around, until the music makers headed up to the bunkhouse to tune up their instruments. Every few minutes some of the Axe hands would arrive in groups of two or three. Everyone cheered as the chuck wagon came in sight. Matt thought he should get a fire started in the stove at the woodshed so water could be heating for tea and coffee. The hands all inspected the root cellar and bunkhouse, as some of helped to dig the root cellar and split shakes for the bunkhouse. Those who hadn't helped out here had done Shorty's job at the ranch so he could spend more time working for Matt and Dawn on the R-R. In a roundabout way, they had all helped to get the work done and this evening was to show how much it was appreciated.

After inspecting the work, the boys grinned and said it wasn't a very good job, but Shorty always did the best he could and they would give him credit for trying at least! No one paid much attention to what they said, as everyone knew they were impressed with the work that had been done here on the ranch. The horses were unsaddled and unhitched and put in the corral and the fence was lined with saddles. There were several light wagons in the yard, as well as the chuck wagon, which Spud had parked quite close to the bunkhouse. The owner of the ladies wear store had arrived with the two young ladies she had mentioned to Angela.

It wasn't dark yet, but there was a lot of music, foot stomping and laughter coming from the area in and around the bunkhouse. It seemed as if the party was underway already. There were more people here than they had expected and every now and then, someone else would show up. Then, out of the blue, Randy Ripley showed up. He unsaddled and put his horse in the pasture and headed across the yard. The first person he met was Shorty. He said, "So, you lazy lout, you're having a party and you didn't invite me! I do most of the work around here and this is the thanks I get. Maybe I should just leave." Angela snickered and said, "I wonder what we will do with all those doughnuts Dawn has made? I guess we could always feed them to the pigs. They would probably enjoy them!" Randy spoke up, "Well, maybe I will hang around for a little while, at least while the doughnuts last. I wouldn't want Shorty to eat too many." At this time most of the crowd moved up to the bunkhouse, where it sounded like there was a party going on. The cook had brought an iron grill from the chuck wagon and placed in on the fireplace Matt had built. He had a pot of coffee on the end where it would stay hot, as well as a pot of tea Matt had made on the stove. There were cups, plates, and eating tools on the table nearby. Everybody seemed to be enjoying themselves, with all the good food, tea, coffee, and the music coming from the bunkhouse porch. Some people were singing along with the music, others sat at the tables and clapped their hands.

Gus went up on the porch and clapped his hands and called a halt to the music. When everyone was quiet he told them, "The boys at the Axe have been working on a new song for a while now. We finally got it to the point that it is almost good enough for the general public. Now, if you will be quiet and listen for a few minutes, we will try it out on you.

Shorty's Song

Short 'n stout has been about,
And everything's just dandy;
He will tackle 'most any job,
Because he is so handy.

No matter what the job you have,
He'll do it mighty quick;
Because he works so easily,
It makes us look kinda sick.

He will climb your tall windmill,
Just like a birdie winging;
As he is working up on high,
You might hear him singing.

Don't you insult no ladies,
When Shorty is around;
Because if he ever hears you,
You might wake up on the ground

He soon has the windmill purring,
And pumping like it should;
It doesn't take him very long,
Because he is so good.

So here's to Shorty Stout from us,
He's always on the go;
A better man you'll never meet,
Because we told you so!

He can mend all your fences,
Or work in your garden green;
He is the most efficient man,
That you have ever seen.

When the music stopped, the whistling, clapping, foot stomping, and cheering started and kept up for almost five minutes. When the noise finally died away, Shorty said, "Gus, you guys should know better than to make up lies about people. You're lucky I don't get upset too easily!"

Gus answered, "Shorty, it wouldn't matter how big a lie we told about your work, it would still be the truth. I don't know how you do it, but just about everything you tackle, you do better than everybody else. Anyone who knows you will agree we didn't stretch the truth!"

Xavier then got to his feet and said, "Gus is right, they didn't stretch the truth about Shorty. Just look around you at some of the things he's done here. Normally I wouldn't argue with Shorty, because he is usually right. This time I will though, because I feel Gus is right: Shorty Stout can do more things better than most other people. Case closed!"

The cheering, clapping, and foot stomping went on for a long time, it seemed as though everyone agreed with Xavier and the Axe hands. When the noise died down to a dull roar somebody shouted, "OK, let's get this party underway!" The music picked up and the floor was packed with dancing couples. It was getting dark, but with all the lamps, lanterns, and the open fire outside, there seemed to be plenty of light. Most of the dancers didn't worry if it wasn't to light, so they could snuggle up close to their dancing partners. Dawn hardly had a chance to sit down, as every man there wanted to dance with her at least once but it looked as though Shorty was getting his share of dances with her. The schoolteacher helped with the music until she got pulled away from whatever she happened to be playing at the time. Once she was out on the floor, it was almost impossible to get away from the men looking for a partner. The schoolteacher, Karen Carter, and Dawn, were the most sought after partners at the dance. The other ladies weren't feeling left out though, as they were outnumbered at least two to one. These people had come looking for a good time, and it seemed as though they were finding it! There was plenty of good food, hot tea, and coffee and no lack of music. Scarcely an hour would go by without someone requesting they play 'Shorty's Song'. By now everyone knew the words so they all joined in the singing.

A few people left shortly after midnight, but most of them kept dancing until daylight crept up on them. By then everyone was ready to call the dance a success and the musical instruments were packed away in preparation for the ride home. As they left, everyone thanked Dawn for giving them such a wonderful time. The Axe hands were pleased to think that Dawn had done this to show how much she had appreciated their help. It was a tired but happy bunch of people leaving the R-R at daylight.

Chapter 12

THE FOUR PEOPLE left on the R-R were tired too. Everyone agreed that a little shut-eye was just what the doctor ordered. Shorty and Randy headed for the barn, and Dawn and Matt went to the house. A few hours of sleep and they would be ready to tackle some light work at least.

Matt was the first one to be up and around, but the others were only a few minutes behind him. No one was really hungry, but Matt had started the fire and put water on to heat before going out to check the stock. Dawn soon had tea ready and a light snack for everyone. Shorty decided this was going to be a lazy day for him. He said, "I'm going to go up to the bunkhouse and finish my bunk. When I get it built, I just might have to try it out to make sure it's comfortable."

Randy snorted and said, "That's all you have done since you started coming here; eat, sleep, and tell people how hard you have to work. If all you are going to do is loaf around, I might as well go somewhere else and find something to do!"

Dawn said, "Well, Randy, I'm sorry to hear that this ranch is getting too tame for you. We will miss having you around, but I guess Matt and Shorty will be able to eat my doughnuts before they get too stale. By the way, where are you headed that is more exciting than here?" Randy got kind of red in the face as he admitted, "Uh . . . actually, that pretty schoolteacher invited me to go on a picnic with her this afternoon."

It was now Shorty's turn to snort. "Now who is going to be loafing around? You slept half the day and now you're going on a picnic! All I can say is, have a good time and thank that schoolteacher for coming to play music for the dance, that is, until you kept her too busy dancing to play music. Go on, get out of here!" Shorty said with a smile.

"By the way," Randy said, "I won't be able to get here next weekend, and no, I won't be with the schoolteacher! I promised to help a friend of mine put up a building next weekend. It's the same guy I helped the last time."

Dawn said, "Thank you for everything you have done for us, Randy. I hope you have a good time on your picnic. I think the schoolteacher is a very nice person. Say, I've wanted to go camping in lost valley again. Why don't you invite her to go with us next weekend? She could come out here on Friday evening or after dinner on Saturday. I could have some bread and biscuits ready to take with us, and maybe Matt could have some 'roast rocks'. You haven't tried that yet, have you? You haven't even seen the lost valley yet!"

Randy said, "I'm supposed to help my buddy next weekend, but this sounds like more fun. You tell me where to meet you, and I'll be there Saturday evening. I can help my friend on Saturday and take Sunday off. If the schoolteacher is willing, I'll send her out here either on Friday or on Saturday." Shorty explained where to meet, and either he or Matt would be waiting for him at seven o'clock on Saturday evening.

Randy rode off to his picnic, and Shorty went up to turn the new bunkhouse into a real bunkhouse. Matt got the rope and went up to help Shorty get a bunk ready to sleep in. In a very short time, this would be an actual bunkhouse!

It was only a few minutes' work to get the frame of the bunk fastened solidly in place, since it had been prepared the previous week. With the frame in place, Shorty told Matt, "We have to have this rope tight so it won't sag too much. Could you get a couple of small saplings about three feet long? We'll put them at the bottom to keep the sides from bending in." Matt got the saplings and trimmed them to just over three feet long. A small hole was bored at one end and a nail was driven partway into the board on the wall. The end with the hole in it was placed over the nail, and the sapling was bowed down in the middle until it would fit inside the sideboard of the bunk and nailed in place. A second sapling was placed about two feet away in the same manner. The bowed saplings divided the base of the bunk into three equal spaces.

Shorty said to Matt, "You see, Matt, these poles act almost like springs. They hold the sides from bending in, but they are bowed down so the mattress doesn't touch them. Now, when we get the rope laced through the notches and pulled tight, we will have a nice, comfortable bed." Shorty showed Matt how to lace the small rope through the notches, starting in the middle and working both ways. He took a straw tick and went to the barn to fill it with clean straw. When he returned, Matt had the rope woven through all the holes and snugged up.

Shorty told him, "Now you tie the end, and we'll pull it up tight." Matt tied the rope, and Shorty told him to pull up on the second strand, while he pulled up on the first one. Matt kept a steady pull on the rope, and as Shorty let his go slack, it was pulled to Matt's area. Shorty then took hold where Matt was, and he moved to the next strand. This was repeated until they reached the end of the bunk. They repeated the process until the rope was almost tight enough to play a tune on. The rope was woven from end to end under the cross ropes and tightened as well. They now had a sturdy but springy base for a bed. The straw tick was wrestled onto the bunk and spread evenly. Matt tried the new bunk, and he thought it would be a great place to sleep.

Dawn arrived to see what the boys were doing and inspect their work. She tried the bunk and agreed with Matt that it would be a comfortable place to sleep. Dawn said, "When you get more bunks built, I'd like to sleep up here myself!"

Shorty said, "Well, we have most of the outside work nearly done now. We should have time to do more inside jobs. Since the days are getting a bit shorter, we could always work here in the evenings."

Dawn told the boys supper would be ready in a short time. It would be leftovers for supper as there was a bit of stew left and a few biscuits. There was tea but no doughnuts; apparently, they had been quite popular with the dancers last night. "Supper will be ready by the time you are," she told them as she headed for the house.

It was Sunday evening, so when supper was over, it was time for Shorty to head back to the Axe.

He told Dawn and Matt to make a list of things they might want to take to Lost Valley next weekend. If the schoolteacher arrived, they could leave by mid afternoon so there would be lots of daylight for setting up camp. Shorty then rode away, and Matt and Dawn would be left on their own for the next four days. After Shorty left, Matt went out to make sure everything was secure for the night. After a previous night with no sleep, both Matt and Dawn were ready for a good night's rest, and shortly after Matt reached the house both were in bed and asleep.

In the morning, it was work as usual. When the morning chores were done, Matt decided to seal the joints in the root cellar. He gathered more moss and stuffed the cracks full. He then gathered up all the small poles he could find and nailed them in the joints. The clay that was left was too dry to use, so it was emptied out, and he carried the tub down to the root cellar. He then asked Dawn to help him carry a load of clay from the stream. He was soon busy plastering the joints with clay. On the inside, he filled the joints completely until the wall was as smooth as a board wall. When the clay was dry, he would build a hollow wall on the inside and fill it with moss or straw. By the time he had the outside finished, Dawn had come out to get him for dinner. She thought he had done a good job, and the root cellar would be tight and warm for the winter.

As they ate dinner, Matt said to Dawn, "I think I'll fill one of those ticks with straw and sleep in the bunkhouse tonight. You can have the bunk. I can sleep on a tick on the floor. We helped to build it. Now we can sleep in it!"

Dawn liked Matt's idea, so they both planned to sleep in the bunkhouse that evening. She thought they should also start on their list of things to take on their camping trip this weekend. Matt said he was going to look in the barn for more of that harness thread. Dawn would bake bread on Friday, so they would have fresh bread to take along. Dawn said, "We can take some bacon too. It makes a good breakfast, and we want some for your fish. I have a small Dutch oven, and I'll make some biscuit mix to take so we will have fresh biscuits. We can take along some new potatoes and bake them in the Dutch oven or right in the coals. We will have a few really good meals while we are there!" As they thought of something, they would add it to the list. They kept busy throughout the days and before they realized it, Thursday was here! Shorty would arrive in the evening and the schoolteacher would be here either Friday evening or on Saturday. Matt had most of the things they would take either packed or ready to pack. The bedrolls were on the saddles and the saddlebags were fully packed. He had the tarp shelter rolled tightly and a small hand ax and short shovel ready to go. Most of the food would go in the pack to be carried on someone's back.

Even Shorty seemed anxious to go back to the valley when he arrived. It was getting late by this time so they had a snack and checked over the list to see if anything else was needed. Dawn and Matt told Shorty they had slept in the bunkhouse a couple of nights. Shorty snorted. "So, I build myself a new bunk and someone else gets to use it before I do? That doesn't seem fair to me!"

Dawn said, "Well, someone had to test it and see if it was suitable. My personal opinion is that it passes inspection. I just might have to test it a few more times, though!" It was bedtime, so Shorty figured he would try out his own bunk. Sleeping in the hay wasn't too bad, but sleeping in a new bunk in a new bunkhouse should be even better. Everyone headed for bed and a good night's sleep as weekends were always busy on the ranch.

Dawn was the first up as she planned to bake bread today. They would have a good supply of fresh bread to take to the valley with them. Breakfast was cooking, and she was mixing bread as it cooked. Later she would make biscuit mix to take with them. They were all busy throughout the day, each with their own work. At noon, as they ate dinner, the list was looked at and items added or subtracted. Shorty had brought another tarp, so there would be another shelter, one for the boys and another for the girls. Just as they were finishing supper, the schoolteacher arrived. She said Randy had told her about the trip to the valley and invited her to come along. She was welcomed by everyone and sat down for a cup of tea with them.

Dawn asked, "Why can't we go to the valley tonight? We will still have enough daylight to set up camp and it will give us more time there. I think we have everything ready to go, don't we?" Shorty and Matt agreed they were just about ready to go and thought the extra time there was fine with them. There was a flurry of activity as everyone put the last few things in order before leaving. The livestock was checked over, horses saddled, and they were ready to go!

Dawn and the schoolteacher, Karen Carter, rode along side by side so they could talk on the way. It wasn't a long ride to the valley, so they arrived at the entrance well before dark and a ten-minute ride put them at the bottom of the valley. Karen was quite taken by the beautiful valley. Dawn told her, "You just wait until we take you to see the small inner valley. This is beautiful, but words just can't describe that place. It is even hard to speak while you are in that beautiful spot!"

They decided to go farther up the valley to camp this time. Last time they had camped close to the bottom so they would be close to where the cattle were going to be held. They found a nice spot to pitch camp and everyone was busy getting things setup. Karen went with Matt to get some poles for the shelters, while Dawn and Shorty unsaddled and tethered the horses. Shorty tied a rope to a bush and drove a stake to fasten the other end to it. The horses were about seventy-five feet from the sleeping shelters. With the horses secured, Dawn began gathering rocks for a fireplace. Shorty thought if they dug a shallow pit for the fireplace, it would be better for cooking on. Some food would be cooked on top and some, like Matt's fish, would go in the pit to be covered with coals. When Matt and Karen came back with the poles, Shorty helped Matt put up the shelters, about twenty feet apart, with the fire pit in between. Dawn had the rocks ready, so she and Karen gathered dry, dead trees for firewood. By the time darkness had settled in, the camp was complete with a fire in the fire pit.

Karen was told of Matt's 'roast rocks', and she thought it sounded very tasty. For a while they sat around the fire and talked, but soon it was time to hit the bedrolls. The only sound to be heard was the occasional calf bawling for its mother. It was a lovely, peaceful place to camp.

When morning came, the fire was teased into life again. Shorty sliced some bacon, Karen was making biscuits and Dawn was getting out the fresh eggs and slicing bread. Matt was taking the horses to water at the lake. By the time the camp chores were done, breakfast was almost ready. Shorty had shoveled some of the coals from the fire pit, put in the Dutch oven with the biscuits in, and covered it over. The bacon and eggs were frying and the tea was keeping hot by the fire. When the bacon and eggs were almost gone, Shorty took the Dutch oven from the fire, and they ate hot, golden brown biscuits with their tea. This was a good start to a beautiful day!

While the girls cleaned up after breakfast, Shorty and Matt climbed the bank to find some bigger wood for the fire. If the fire was kept going, the pit would be full of coals for baking Matt's fish for dinner. They found a couple of good-sized dead trees and chopped them up short enough to carry back to camp, where they were chopped into shorter lengths. There would be a good supply of coals to cook their dinner with.

They wondered if they should show Karen the inner valley now or wait until Randy arrived and show them both tomorrow. In the end, they decided to go to the inner valley now and again tomorrow with Randy. Shorty untied the rope used to tether the horses and took it along as they went up to the small stream that came from the inner valley. The horses were retied here where the grass was especially good due to the good supply of water.

They tried to prepare Karen for what she was about to see, but they knew it was impossible to do. She would just have to see it for herself. Shorty thought maybe they would go farther up the valley, right to the waterfall. All agreed to this plan and started walking up along the small stream. When the narrow cut opened up into the smaller valley, they could hear Karen gasp in disbelief. They all stood for a few minutes looking around at this beautiful spot they were in. Shorty led the way farther up the little valley until they were at the pool formed by the waterfall. Looking in the pool, they could see dozens of huge trout, some probably weighing ten pounds or more. As they stood looking at these trout, Shorty walked up to the side of the waterfall and disappeared behind it. A minute later, he emerged on the other side of the fall. He then retraced his steps and was back with the others. He took Dawn's hand and led her toward the waterfall, with Matt and Karen following behind. Behind the waterfall was a dry cave, reaching back into the darkness. They looked around for a minute and then continued on to emerge on the other side. They followed the edge of the rock wall through scattered trees, where they saw a couple of deer. The animals didn't appear afraid as they had never seen people before. They moved slowly down the valley, into the narrow cut the stream had made in times long ago, and came out at the top of the main valley. Even here, large trout could be seen in the small stream. At one point, where the water was about a foot deep, Shorty motioned for the others to stop. He rolled up his sleeve and lay down on the bank. Moving very slowly he put his hand in the water, moving his fingers carefully. He moved his hand over a trout and slowly stroked its back. He then took hold of the fish behind the head and lifted it from the water. It was over two feet long and probably weighed ten pounds. He held the fish for a few seconds for the others to see, and then carefully put it back in the water. They mounted up and rode back down the stream to the lake.

Here he stopped and asked if anyone else would like to catch a fish. Matt thought he would like to try. Shorty told him in a low voice, "Move very slowly so you don't scare them. Put your hand in the water and let your fingers move like the grass you see waving in the water. Let your hand slide lightly over its back before taking hold behind its head." Matt did as he had been instructed and soon had a fish above the water. After a few seconds, he put it back and stood up. The girls decided to try catching a fish later when Randy was here. They went back to camp and over a cup of tea, talked about the inner valley. Dawn asked, "What made the cave behind the waterfall?"

Shorty told them, "Quite often there are hollows or small caves behind waterfalls. After a lot of years the water hitting the bottom splashes and wears a hole in the rock. Eventually the rock breaks off to form a bigger hole. Sometimes, there is a crack in the rock and the water gradually wears it bigger. The stream is then running through a cave or tunnel. For some reason the end gets closed off, and the water has to run over the top, where it probably did many years ago, and it makes a waterfall again. This cave looks deep as far as I can see, so that might be the case here. If I had the time and a good light, I might be able to find out, but I don't plan to go poking around in a cave without a good light!"

The others agreed that it wasn't a good plan to go into a cave without a good source of light. There was a short discussion on whether Matt should have fish for dinner or wait until Randy arrived. It didn't take long to suggest Matt have fish for dinner and again tonight when Randy was here. There seemed to be an endless supply of trout in the lake, so taking a few shouldn't deplete them too quickly. Matt took his fishing gear and went to the lake to get dinner. He had a longer line this time so it shouldn't be too hard to get a trout. He wasn't looking for too big a fish with only four people to eat it. In about twenty minutes, he was back with a good trout, which he soon had cleaned and ready to cook. He sprinkled the inside with salt and pepper and put two slices of bacon inside also. It was then wrapped in fresh grass and plastered well with clay. He removed some of the coals from the fire pit, put the trout in, and covered it with coals. Water was put on to heat for tea, and more wood was added. All four then sat in the shade of the shelter and talked about the inner valley.

Karen stated, "You were right about that place. There are no words that I know of to describe it. When I'm in there, I get such a peaceful feeling I don't want to leave. If Heaven is more beautiful than that, it must be a beautiful place indeed!" Karen agreed with them that, lovely as this valley is, the inner valley was far more beautiful. She told them how grateful she was to be invited to come along to this beautiful spot. She had expected to find a nice place, but nothing to the extent of what she had seen.

Matt figured his fish must be about ready to eat. He was trying to decide the best way to get the trout out of the fire. Karen said to him, "Bring your axe and come with me, Matt." They climbed the bank and found a thicket of berry bushes. Karen looked for a few seconds until she spied what she wanted. She told Matt to cut that one about two feet below the crotch and about eight inches above. She soon found a second bush much like the first. When both were cut to the proper length, Karen took them and put one stick in the crotch of the other. They were both curved, with the curved ends in. As she pulled them together, she pinched a piece of wood between them and picked it up. They went back to the fire, and Mat used the wooden tongs to pick the fish from the fire. He broke it open with the hand ax and called, "Dinner is served!"

As they ate the delicious fish with fresh bread and leftover biscuits and lots of tea, Dawn asked Karen where she had learned to make the wooden tongs. She said, "I grew up with a lot of brothers. They were elder than me, and I used to follow them around a lot. I saw them take things from the fire that way, plus a lot of other things most girls don't learn. Until I was about twelve, I was more like a boy than a girl. I can cook on an open fire, catch and clean fish, hunt, and clean and cook rabbits and other small game. I can track animals and build a shelter if I have to stay out overnight. I was a real tomboy when I was growing up, and I learned a lot of useful things. I'm not just a helpless schoolgirl when I'm outside of town, and I really enjoy getting away from civilization now and then, just like this."

Dawn said to Karen, "It's always good to know how to look after yourself, especially for us women. After Matt's father died, I had to do a lot of things I never did before. It is always so much easier if you can learn from someone else instead of just doing it wrong until you learn. Matt and I had to do everything, usually the hard way, until Shorty showed up and taught us the right way to do a lot of things."

About this time Shorty thought he should say a few words. He said, "Everybody thinks I'm awfully smart, but I'm not. I just had someone to show me how to do things and explain why and how to do them. I'm trying to show Matt some of the things I have learned. Everybody has a brain, but lots of folks don't know how to use it. I was taught how to use my head to think my way around or out of a problem. Matt, here, is a good thinker. Look at how he caught these fish and then cooked them. He catches on fast, and he can solve lots of problems with his head. He will probably be a far better man than I ever thought of being!"

The teacher, Karen, spoke up; "No, Shorty, you are the kind of person who never stops learning. Matt will be good with his head someday. He is good now, but you keep learning new things every day. Matt, no matter how good he gets, will never be quite as good as you are. I've taught school for a few years now, and I've seen some kids who are good at schoolwork, but take them outside, and they are lost without someone to guide them. On the other hand, some of the kids who have a problem in school can, like Matt, think their way out of all kinds of problems. Some people are doers and others are followers. You and Matt are the doers and like to be doing something. You are never really satisfied to just let things go. You think up ways to do almost everything better. Thank God for people like you, who improve the world for the rest of us!"

Shorty thought he should say something else, but didn't know quite what. He knew some of what Karen had said about him was true, but it was kind of embarrassing to be praised so highly. If people wanted to think he was smart, that was their problem, not his. People just wouldn't listen when he tried to tell them different. Well, he knew he wasn't very smart, but he had learned to use his head for more than just a hat rack. He had met people who were educated but hardly knew enough to come in out of the rain. Education was OK, but he thought commonsense would take him just as far.

Everyone was still eating as this conversation was going on, so by now all of them had enough to hold them until supper. They had the afternoon ahead of them and were trying to decide what they should do. Someone suggested going for a swim, and the others agreed. Dawn and Karen would go to the pool under the falls, and Shorty and Matt would swim in the lake. That was settled so the girls headed up the valley to their private pool. They all enjoyed the water and spent about an hour getting cooled off and clean.

After the swim, Matt thought he would try catching a few fish. He had brought a few fishhooks and a longer line and wanted to see just how big some of these fish were. He made sure there was no barb on the hook so the fish would be easier to release and wouldn't be hurt. He didn't plan to keep any; he just wanted to see what was out there in the lake. He went to the bushes and cut a small crotched twig about half the size of a pencil. It was trimmed down until there was hardly any crotch left, and then he rounded the ends. If a fish was hooked deep in the mouth, he could slide the blunt crotch down the line and dislodge the hook. This went into his shirt pocket, where it was handy if needed. He had cut a long, slim sapling for a fishing rod. With rod, line, and shovel, he set out for the lake. A few minutes of walking put him at the edge of the lake. He turned over a clump of grass to get a fat worm for bait, and he was in business. Before he left the lake, he would put the clump of grass back in place and leave very little sign that he had been here. His hook was baited, and he threw it as far as he could out into the lake. Before it had time to settle to the bottom, there was a fish on the hook! He pulled it in to shore and gently unhooked the fish and let it go. It was a big fish, but he knew there were bigger ones out there. He kept on catching and releasing trout for almost an hour. The smaller ones were about five pounds, and the biggest one he had hooked had been over two feet long and weighed at least twelve pounds. It seemed as if there was an endless supply of fish in the lake. Just before he decided to stop fishing, he had caught a fish of about seven or eight pounds. It was hooked so deep in the throat he didn't think it would survive if released. He decided this was their supper. He hooked and released a few more trout before calling it a good day of fishing. With the amount of fish in the lake, he didn't feel he was depleting the population too badly.

Dawn and Karen had returned from their swim earlier, and they told Matt and Shorty of the huge trout they had seen in the pool under the falls. They could swim right up to them and touch them before they would swim away. There were dozens of these huge trout in the small pool. As they talked, Matt was getting his trout ready to cook. He asked the others what they thought of delaying supper until Randy got there. No one had been working very hard, and they had been eating well so they weren't very hungry. They had new potatoes from the garden and thought of baking them in the Dutch oven. There were more biscuits to be made also. Randy might arrive late but there would be a good supper waiting for him. Karen suggested that since biscuits cook quickly, they could bake the potatoes in the oven, and then while the biscuits were baking, they would be eating the fish and potatoes. The fish and potatoes could be started at about six o'clock so they would be ready to eat when Randy arrived.

SHORTY'S STORY | 213

Matt volunteered to go to the meeting spot and guide Randy to the valley. He would trust the others not to eat all the food while he was gone. The rest of the afternoon was spent doing very little except exploring along the top of the former lake bank. All of the explorers had brought an armful of wood when they had returned. There would be a good supply to keep the fire going for the evening.

The time came for supper to be put on the fire to cook. After Matt got his fish in the coals, he saddled up and rode out to the meeting spot to look for Randy. He had barely reached the proposed site when he saw Randy coming. When he got closer, he announced, "I could smell supper cooking for the last three miles. I've got a big hollow spot behind my belt buckle, and I hope there is enough grub left to fill it. Lead the way, pardner. I'm ready to see this 'lost valley' that ain't lost no more!" They rode up the rocky gully and were soon out in the main valley. A few more minutes put them at the campsite. There were greetings all around and then Randy said, "Where is all the food? I could smell it for miles, and I'm ready to put away a lot of it!"

Dawn told Randy, "We weren't expecting company and supper is all over. It was good, and we ate every bite. Didn't you bring any food with you?" Randy knew she was just teasing him and supper would be ready soon. Karen got the Dutch oven from the fire and stacked the potatoes in the frying pan. The biscuits went into the hot oven and back on the fire. Matt used the tongs to remove the clay lump from the fire. Randy had his first look at Matt's 'roast rock,' and he said, "I've heard of these things but it just looks like a hunk of rock to me. I hope you have lots of salt if you expect me to eat that!" Everyone laughed at Randy's remarks.

Matt broke open the clay, and Randy decided he had changed his mind about the food. Plates were loaded with fish and baked potatoes. There was plenty left over for seconds, or even third helpings. A pot of tea sat beside the fire keeping hot. There was very little talk as everyone seemed to have an appetite like Randy's.

When the edge had been taken off their appetite, the conversation revived again. Randy commented that this was a real pretty spot, tucked away in the hills like this. It was pointed out to Randy that most people who had seen this valley thought it was an ancient lake. The bottom was flat and the banks of the lake could be seen on all sides. The soil was composed of rotted vegetation deposited over uncounted years. This was why the grass was so rich as well as having an abundant water supply. The gully which he had ridden up to get here was the outlet from the lake. In some bygone time the water had worn the rock away until the lake disappeared, except for the present lake, which had been a deep section of the original lake. As he looked around, Randy had to agree that was probably how this valley came to be here. Karen then said, "Randy, we have something to show you tomorrow that is so beautiful, you will hardly believe your eyes. There is a small hidden valley where that small stream comes from, which is so beautiful, it is beyond description. After you leave that beautiful place, it seems unreal, like you have just dreamed about it. I think from what I have heard so far, anyone who has seen it feels the same way. Apparently no one has been able to come up with a good way to describe it except beautiful, peaceful, and quite. No one can say, 'seeing is believing,' because even after you see it, you hardly believe what you saw. We'll let you try and tell us what you saw when we return from there."

Everyone felt stuffed from the meal they had just finished. They sipped at a final cup of tea as they talked of various topics. Darkness was beginning to creep into the valley and more wood was added to the fire, even though it wasn't needed for warmth. They sat and watched the flames dancing until darkness was complete, and then everyone made their way to their bedrolls. Morning would bring their final day for this trip to the valley, but it certainly wouldn't be their last trip to the valley.

Matt was the first one up and about in the morning. He added wood to the coals and soon had the fire burning brightly and water on heating for tea. The last of the biscuit mix was used to get two small biscuit for each. There was still some bacon so Matt sliced enough for breakfast. He could see everyone else was just lying in their blankets watching him. He grinned and said, "I've got my breakfast cooking, but I don't know what the rest of you are going to eat. There are still lots of fish in the lake and beef on the hoof. I always say, 'the early bird gets the breakfast,' and I guess that's me!"

There was some good-natured grumbling as the others crawled out of their blankets and checked to see if Matt was telling the truth. Soon all five were enjoying a hot breakfast on their last day in Lost Valley. Everyone was in agreement that there would be other trips to this beautiful place. When breakfast was over, it would be Randy's turn to look in awe at the beauty of the tiny inner valley.

Breakfast was soon over, and the girls made short work of the few dishes that had to be washed. The campsite was picked up clean and neat so everything would be left unspoiled by people as nature intended. They had camped farther up the valley so it was only a short walk to the entrance of the inner valley. Though some of them had been here three or four times before, all were still spellbound at the breathtaking beauty of this little corner of Heaven. Randy, too, was speechless as he gazed around him at this beautiful little valley. After about fifteen minutes, though not one word was spoken, they all began to walk slowly toward the entrance. Randy, like everyone else who had ever visited this valley, was speechless. A few minutes after they had left the inner valley, he asked, "Did I really see that or was it just my imagination?"

Dawn answered, "Every person who has been in there feels the same way. It seems as if it is too beautiful for words. I've been in there five times now and each time I feel the same. It's enough to make you believe in Heaven, isn't it?"

They walked slowly down the little stream to where Shorty had showed Matt how to catch the fish by hand. Dawn decided she was going to try it this time. She lay down on the bank and slowly lowered her hand into the water. Soon she was stroking the back of a large trout, and then grasping it behind the head, she lifted it clear of the water. She held it for a few seconds and then lowered it into the water. A few seconds later, she brought a second trout to the surface. She had a big smile on her face as she got up from the grass beside the stream. Next the schoolteacher had her turn at catching a fish with her hand. Soon, she had a large trout in the air and smiled almost from ear to ear. Randy also caught a couple of trout so he could say he had caught a fish with his bare hand. Karen said she had heard of people doing that, but she had never seen it done before. Now she had done it herself! What a wonderful spot this valley had turned out to be! There was still most of the day ahead of the campers. It was unusual for them to have idle time on their hands. Normally they would be busy at something. It was looking mostly like a lazy day so they decided to make the most of it. They sat or lay under the tarp shelters and talked most of the time.

There wasn't much food left so Randy suggested that maybe Matt should catch a trout for dinner. This time Matt went to the stream where they had caught the trout by hand. In this way he could catch the size of fish they wanted so nothing would be wasted. He was soon back with the fish and the clay to bake it with. There was a good bed of coals in the fire pit so in a matter of a few minutes dinner was baking. Water was put on to heat for tea, and then they just had to lie back and wait for dinner to cook.

Everyone agreed this was a lovely place to camp, but they all would like to come back again and spend at least one night in the little inner valley. On one hand, they thought they shouldn't intrude on that beautiful spot, but again they felt compelled to do so. That would be in the future and maybe not until next year, as it was getting late in the summer now. The valley would be there for when they decided to come back. Matt told everyone dinner was ready as he removed the fish from the coals. Dawn still had some bread to go with the fish and although it might lack variety, the meal didn't lack quantity or quality.

After the meal, everyone pitched in to help break camp and get everything packed and ready to go. The fire was wet down well and the baked clay was put in the pit and covered over. The next time anyone was here, the signs of a campsite probably would have disappeared. No one wanted any signs of their being here left behind.

When they mounted up, they rode side by side down the valley to the narrow gully, where it was single file only. Once out in the open, good-byes were said all around as this was where they would part company. Randy and Shorty went in one direction, as Dawn, Matt, and Karen turned toward the R-R and home. Shorty didn't have as long a ride from here, and Randy's trip was shorter also. When the others got back to the ranch, the schoolteacher still had a five-mile ride back to town. She had thanked all of them for allowing her to share this lovely weekend with them, and she hoped to be able to do the same thing sometime in the future.

When they arrived at the ranch, Dawn invited Karen to come back anytime. She told Karen, "Now that we have the new bunkhouse, we have plenty of room. When they get more bunks ready, we could chase them out and sleep there ourselves. Matt and I have slept there a couple of times last week, and I really enjoyed it!" Karen told them how much she had enjoyed the weekend of camping. She said, "I'll be sure to come back and visit soon. As I said earlier, I grew up with a lot of brothers and there was always a lot going on. You have a beautiful spot here and a lovely new bunkhouse. All of you have made me feel like I was part of the family. I would like to live in the country, but while I am teaching school, it is easier to be near town. Someday, I hope to have a place like this. You will probably see me in a couple of weeks time, until then good-bye and take care!"

The schoolteacher then rode away toward town, and Dawn and Matt went to the house to see how everything had fared in their absence. Matt looked over the livestock and it seemed as though everything was in the same condition as when they left. As usual they kept busy around the ranch and the time passed quickly. The week had passed, and Shorty had arrived on Thursday evening and had been welcomed home. A lunch had been prepared by the cook and eaten at bedtime. Soon all were in bed and asleep.

Chapter 13

AFTER THE MORNING meal was over, the boys went outside to work. It was cloudy and looked like it would rain so they were trying to finish up a few small projects before it got too wet. They finished up just ahead of the rain and hurried up to the dry bunkhouse, where they knew there were a few dry jobs waiting for them. There was no point in getting wet as there were lots of inside jobs to do and most of the outside work was completed now.

Shorty was working on the bunk above the one he had been sleeping in. He was trying to cut a small piece of board when it shifted, and the saw hit the back of his hand. It wasn't deep or serious, barely breaking the skin, but it bled a lot. Matt thought he should get Dawn to clean it up and put a bandage on it. Reluctantly Shorty went to the house to get Dawn to patch him up. She held his hand under the cold water and carefully wiped the dried blood away. She could see it wasn't too serious, but it was better not to take any chances with it. When she got the blood stopped, she dried his hand. She then got a bottle of whiskey and poured a few drops into a small dish. With a small, clean cloth she dabbed the whiskey on and around the cut. Shorty winced as the alcohol took hold of the raw flesh. When the cut was thoroughly disinfected, she got a strip of clean cloth and wrapped it around his hand above and below the thumb. When the bandage was secured, she put a few more drops of whiskey on the cloth directly over the cut. Shorty could feel it sting, but not near as viciously as the first time.

Dawn told him, "If that bandage gets loose or dirty you be sure to come back in here so I can clean and rebandage it." Shorty agreed that he would and went back up to the bunkhouse to work. He thought it was a lot of bother for a small cut, but he didn't really mind having Dawn make a fuss over him. He and Matt went back to work building the upper bunk.

This time he was going to use a six-inch board split lengthwise for the notched pieces. This would make it stronger with less bow in the sideboard. He marked the board, and Matt split it with the ripsaw. At the same time Shorty planed the sideboards. He then fastened the split boards together, and Matt cut the small notches in them, every four inches. These notched boards were then nailed securely to the planed sideboards. When all was ready the back sideboard was nailed solidly to the wall. The front board was nailed to the upright and the end board which was in place on the end wall. The final end board was put in place, and the frame of the bunk was complete. All that was now required was to put the small rope through the notches and pull it tight.

The rain that had been falling steadily had now stopped, and it was dry enough to work outside. The bunk could wait until the next wet day or the evenings to be finished. When it wasn't wet, they would rather be working outside. Without looking too hard, they could usually find something to keep them occupied. As they ate supper, Dawn suggested the bandage on Shorty's hand should be changed as it was getting very dirty. Shorty decided to wait until bedtime as they had a few things to do outside. After supper, Matt and Shorty went back outside to work until dark.

Since the bunkhouse was complete with one bunk useable, Shorty had been sleeping there instead of the barn. The bunkhouse now boasted of a hanging lamp near the center of the building as well as a standing lamp on the table. These had been bought just before the dance was held here two weeks ago. The boys had been working outside, but when darkness had arrived, they moved to the bunkhouse to do a bit with the lamplight to help them. A short while later Matt went to the house as darkness was usually bedtime for everyone.

Dawn had put on her cotton nightgown and a robe and sat and talked to Matt for a bit. She thought about the bandage on Shorty's hand and remembered she was going to clean and rebandage it. She knew that it should be done before bed as the old bandage was very dirty.

Matt suggested, "I could go up and bring Shorty down here, but he might not want to come at this time of night. Maybe you should go up there and fix his hand up." Dawn thought about this for a minute, then said, "I guess that's what I'll have to do then, as the cut might get infected if it stays dirty. I don't want him to have a sore hand and not be able to work at the Axe next week. I won't be gone very long." "I'm going to bed any way," Matt said, "I'll see you in the morning."

Matt went into his bedroom and closed the door. Dawn got some warm water, clean bandages, the bottle of whiskey, and headed up to the bunkhouse. She could see through the window that Shorty wasn't in bed yet so she knocked on the door and went in. Shorty was surprised to see her and got to his feet. Dawn put everything she was carrying on the table and told Shorty she was going to put a clean bandage on his hand. He told her it was fine and would be OK until morning. She insisted she was here and was going to clean and rebandage his hand right now! Shorty sat on a bench while Dawn removed the old bandage and soaked his hand in the warm water. When his hand was clean, she dried it and wrapped a new bandage on it. She then put more whiskey on the bandage over the cut. Dawn kissed the back of his hand above and below the bandage. "There," she said, "that

SHORTY'S STORY | 221

will make it better in no time!" "I'm sure it will," Shorty said, "it feels better already!"

Dawn then put her arms around Shorty's neck and kissed him on the lips. Shorty wasn't too sure what he should do, but he pulled her toward him until she was sitting on his knees. He put his arms around her to help with what she was doing. They sat like this for a few minutes, both enjoying the feeling of being this close together. After a few minutes, Dawn said, "I think I better go back to the house. I can trust you, but I don't think I can trust myself. I really enjoyed the last few minutes though!"

Dawn gathered up the things she had brought and started for the door. Shorty got up and went over to open the door for her. He tried to lift the latch to open the door, but it wouldn't budge. He shook and pushed on the door, but it was solid! He said, "I don't know what happened. That latch has always worked perfectly until now! I can pull the sticks off the window and go out and see what's wrong." "No," Dawn said, "That won't be necessary. I'll just have to sleep here for the night. There is lots of room for the both of us!" Shorty was a bit flustered as he said, "You can sleep in my bunk, and I'll sleep on the floor. I've slept in plenty of worse places in my life." Dawn turned down the lamp on the table and said, "No, this was supposed to happen. Turn out that hanging lamp, and then we are going to sleep in that bunk. Two of us, not just me!"

Shorty said, "But Dawn, I'm just a cowhand, and you are the owner of this ranch. I'm not really good enough to be working for you, and I have nothing. I believe you should stop and think about what you are doing!"

"I've been thinking about this for quite a while," Dawn said, "And I'm not going to think about it anymore! Now, if you won't get undressed and get into that bunk, I'll do it for you!" With that she started to unbutton Shorty's shirt.

Shorty protested, "But Dawn . . . !"

Dawn spoke up, "If you open your mouth once more, it better be to kiss me! If you say one more word, you will be leaving and not coming back! Now which is it going to be, me or the trail?"

Shorty kept his mouth closed and blew out the hanging lamp. Dawn helped him get undressed, and then she tossed her robe and nightgown over the frame of the top bunk. The three-foot-wide bunk was wide enough for two, but they had to stay close together. There was a faint glow from the lamp on the table, but it gave them some light. A few hours later after they had made love several times, Dawn said, "I should go back to my own bed, but I'm not going to. I'm going to spend the rest of the night right here!"

Shorty spoke for the first time in several hours. "The door is stuck solid and there is no way to get it open from in here! How can you leave?" Dawn giggled and said, "Go try the door and see if it will open!"

Shorty got up and walked over to the door. He took hold of the latch and . . . the door opened easily! Shorty closed the door, walked back to the bunk, and asked, "What is going on here? The door was stuck solid before and now it isn't! How did you do that?"

Dawn asked, "Why are you blaming me? I've never been out of your sight, or at least not far enough that you couldn't touch me! I did hear something outside when I was sitting on your knee, and I heard it again just after we got into this bed. That reminds me, you better get back in here before you get cold!" Shorty did as he was told, and it felt good to have a nice, warm bed to get back into. They got some sleep but were still sound asleep when the rooster began yodeling.

Dawn woke up and stretched as she looked at Shorty and said, "Well, I guess it's time to get up! It would be nice to stay here for a bit longer, but someone has to get breakfast ready." She got out of bed and started to get dressed. "You know," she said, "I like sleeping in this new bunkhouse! I think I'll sleep here some other time. I didn't know it would be so nice!" Shorty smiled and said, "What if the tenants objected to having company?"

"Well," Dawn said, "I could always pull rank. I am the owner, you know! Really though, I don't think I would hear one word of objection if I moved in here permanently!" Shorty grinned and said, "There wouldn't be any objection if anyone was in their right mind. I know I sure wouldn't object to that!"

Dawn gave Shorty a big hug and then headed for the house. As she went through the door, she noticed a small, round stick that was just the right size to go through the two rings on the door latch. She was smiling as she went down the hill to the house.

When Dawn got to the house, Matt had the fire going, water heating, and was mixing pancakes. Dawn went over to him, gave him a hug, and said, "Thank you, Matt!" He looked at Dawn and grinned. "It worked," Dawn said. "It worked really well, thank you."

Since Matt was making breakfast, Dawn let him continue with his work. He soon had pancakes cooking and tea ready. When Shorty came in, Matt had a stack of pancakes ready to eat. They all sat down and had a good breakfast of pancakes and molasses. Dawn and Shorty kept smiling at each other, and Matt grinned at them both. He was beginning to think his trying to get his mother and Shorty together was finally paying off. It was a very happy trio at the breakfast table today!

After breakfast, the boys were working on the root cellar, building a thick door to be insulated with dry moss. A regular door was built for the inside and then a frame of five-inch boards was fastened to the door so it fitted closely inside the door frame. Starting at the bottom, it was boarded up part way after putting tar paper on the frame.

Shorty said to Matt, "You can fill it with moss and finish boarding it up when you have some time. We'll get a start on the frame for the inside wall for the other side. You can trim the boards and nail them on as you fill up the space. We'll put tar paper under the boards so the moss won't get damp from the inside, the same as we did for the door." They were doing mostly what needed more than two hands to do and then moved on to other jobs. Matt could finish these jobs later when he was alone, now that they had the 'two-man' parts done. Dawn came out to tell them dinner was ready, so work was halted while they filled the hollows behind their belt.

Dinner was another enjoyable meal with lots of smiling from everyone. It was a good, tasty meal, but the smiling faces made it much more enjoyable. As soon as the food was eaten, the boys were back outside working, this time on Matt's pig shelter. They made a door for a person to walk through, but the bottom half was just a frame of boards with a big hole in the middle. A light door would be built later that would swing both ways. A pig could just push it with his nose and go either in or out, depending on where he was at the moment. Matt's pigs would have a nice, warm, and dry bed to sleep in this winter!

The outside jobs that had to be done around the ranch were beginning to get scarce! They had worked all summer and didn't seem to make much headway. Now, all of a sudden it seemed like most of the jobs were done. It made them feel good to run into a scarcity of jobs. Shorty decided he would split some wood. It would be nice to have the woodshed full before winter, and there was still quite a pile of wood to be split. He started to split wood, and Matt carried it inside and piled it in neat rows. Shorty worked with practiced ease, and the straight-grained wood seemed almost to fall apart on its own.

A person who works with an axe often picks up a lot of little tricks to help to get the job done easier. For instance, if the end of the stick is checked open, the axe man always hit in that small crack. If the wood is freshly sawed, he splits from the freshly cut end, not from the dried, tough end. Split with the knots, not across them. Some old-timers say to hit it in the toughest-looking spot you can find; if it gives a bit, the stick will split. Also, if a stick is cut on an angle, try to split it from the square end. Sometimes this is not possible as the stick will not stand on the angled end.

Shorty and Matt worked steadily but not hurriedly. A man who knows what he is doing doesn't seem to move fast, but he gets more done than a man working fast but not efficiently. It seemed like they had just gotten started when Dawn called them for supper. The pile of unsplit wood wasn't nearly as big as it had been, but the pile of split wood in the woodshed had grown considerably.

Another of Dawn's delicious meals disappeared in short order. A last cup of tea and a couple of doughnuts were a fitting end to a fine meal. Even plain food tastes much better when a person has worked up an appetite. The boys decided to go up to the bunkhouse and build an inside door. Shorty trimmed the boards, and Matt planed them smooth, only doing the wide sides, as Shorty would do the edges with the rabbet plane so the boards would touch on three sides instead of just one. With both of them working at different jobs, the door was soon ready to put together. As they were working, Matt stopped work, looked at Shorty and asked, "Are you going to be my dad now?"

Shorty put his hand on Matt's shoulder and said, "No, Matt, I can't be your dad. It would make me very proud to be your father but that isn't possible. You see, Matt, in this life, we only get one mother and one father and no matter if they are good, bad, or in between, they are the only ones we can have. A man would have to look a long time to find a son who could measure up to you, Matt. You are the kind of a son for a man to be proud of. Even if someday your mother saw fit to marry me, I could never replace your father. Maybe, if you want to, we could pretend I was your dad." Matt put his arms around Shorty, and he did the same to Matt. They stood this way for five minutes or more. Both had eyes that were shining and bright with tears.

Dawn had been about to step up on the porch when she heard Matt speak. She had stood quietly and listened to the conversation. Dawn had tears on her cheeks as she went back to the house without entering the bunkhouse. A few minutes later, Shorty suggested maybe it was time to get back to work, as they still had a door to get finished.

The boards were laid out on the sawhorses and nailed solidly together, the brace was inserted, and the hinges were nailed in place over the cross boards. Matt told Shorty of his idea to build the frame out past the logs, so the door would swing back flat against the wall out of the way. Shorty thought this was a great idea and the frame was soon extended. The door was then put in place and fastened, with two tight doors the bunkhouse would be snug and warm.

It was getting late so Shorty said he was going to the creek to wash off the sweat he had worked up splitting wood. He took some soap and went up the creek until he was out of sight. While the boys had been working on the door, Dawn had taken a bath in her bedroom. She had used lovely warm water, while Shorty was bathing in the cold creek. When she had finished scrubbing herself all over and dried off, she dabbed on some of the perfume Matt had bought for her, way back in July. When Shorty left for his bath, Matt had gone to close up the chickens and check the other stock. Shorty had since returned to the bunkhouse and lighted a lamp. In the house Matt and Dawn each ate a doughnut before going to bed. Matt looked at Dawn and said, "Maybe you should go change that bandage for Shorty again. It was getting dirty, and I know he got it wet!"

Dawn smiled and hugged Matt tightly and said, "Yes, Matt, maybe I better do that. We wouldn't want him to think we forgot about him would we? I'll get the things I need and take care of it. It might take a while though!" Matt grinned and said, "That's OK. Just do a good job even if it takes a while. See you in the morning, I'm going to bed!"

Dawn gathered up what she needed to take to the bunkhouse and was on the way in less than two minutes. She knocked on the door as she went through it. Wet clothes had been hanging on the porch as she entered. Shorty was sewing on a shirt as he sat in the chair he and Matt had made for Dawn, and he jumped to his feet as she came through the door. He said, "I didn't expect to see you tonight, as you can see, my hand is almost healed."

"Matt thought I should come up and take care of it for you," Dawn answered, "He wanted to make sure you don't have any problems with your hand. I don't think we will have any trouble with the door though." Dawn cleaned Shorty's hand and put a small bandage on it, even though it wasn't necessary. When she was finished, she got up and sat on Shorty's knee and put her arms around him. They sat like that for a few minutes and then she said, "I think I should go back to the house." She walked over to the doorway and closed the newly built inside door and leaned a short board against it to hold it closed. She turned around with a big grin and said, "The door won't open, so I guess I'll have to stay here. I don't want to be a bother, so I'll just sleep on the floor."

Shorty was smiling from ear to ear as he said, "Then I guess I might have to sleep on the floor too. If we try, two of us might fit on that narrow bunk." Dawn turned out the lamp on the table but left the hanging lamp lit. They helped each other get undressed, and then lay on the blankets on the bunk.

Dawn said, "I heard you and Matt talking earlier this evening. I was just about to come in to see what you were doing. I liked what you told him and how you said it. Now, I'm going to ask you a question, but I don't want you to answer it yet. You think it over for a few weeks then I'll ask you again. Remember, no answer for at least two weeks!"

She looked him in the eye and asked, "Will you marry me, Shorty? Don't say anything. I don't want to hear a word from you about it right now! I might have to go back to the house though. It's starting to get chilly in here." Dawn woke up just as it was starting to get light. She got out of bed and started to get dressed. Shorty started to get up, but she pushed him back down. "You stay there for a few minutes while I get breakfast started," she told him. Dawn kissed him and pulled the blankets up over him. She then headed out the door and down to the house. She had the stove hot and breakfast cooking in a short time. Shorty had made the rounds outside to be sure everything was OK. He washed up by the barn before going to the house. Breakfast was about ready as he walked through the door. Matt was just sitting down to the table, and he smiled at Shorty.

Shorty said, "You know, we're getting the work around here pretty well caught up now. Maybe we should get a few loads of wood for the woodshed. Winter will be here sometime, so we better start getting ready for it. We should have at least one load for the bunkhouse too." Dawn spoke up, "That's right. We don't want to run short like we did last spring. I feel a lot better with lots of wood ahead. We have some of the tops from the logs to cut up yet, but that can be done even after it snows. We never did get back to get the load you helped us cut up in the spring. The load we brought home plus the small ends that were cut off the logs kept us going. The weather will start cooling off any day now. You boys have worked so hard all summer, there are only a few small jobs left to be done."

When breakfast was over, the tools were loaded in the wagon, the team hitched up, and they started out to get some wood. When they got to where the wood had been cut the tools were unloaded, and the wood was loaded on. Shorty and Dawn tossed the wood on the wagon and Matt piled it neatly. With three of them working, it didn't take long to get a load on the wagon.

Shorty asked Matt, "Can you unload this by yourself, Matt? If so, your mother and I can cut more and maybe have a load ready when you get back. Just toss it in a heap close to the woodshed, we can split and pile it later." Matt said it wouldn't be too hard to toss the wood off at home and that he would be back by the time they had another load ready. Matt left for home with the load of wood, and Shorty and Dawn began sawing up more wood. There were quite a few trees blown down right here, and they would make plenty of firewood for the winter. When the tree was small enough to handle easily, it was limbed out, cut about ten feet long, and tossed aside. The small tops would be taken home long to be cut up later. It wasn't far to travel, so they got three loads hauled home before noon. Shorty and Matt unloaded the last load at the bunkhouse. This was piled just under the roof so it could be split later. When the second load was on the wagon in the afternoon, Dawn called a halt to the woodcutting. Shorty had to work tomorrow, and she didn't want him working too hard today.

Dawn told Shorty, "Matt and I can come out here through the week and get the small tops. We can even limb and cut the tops off some of the others here. There are also some of the small tops left where we cut the logs too. Another weekend's work should give us plenty of wood for both the house and bunkhouse."

Dawn got supper ready while Matt and Shorty unloaded the last of the wood. When supper was over, Shorty rode toward the Axe. He had four days' work waiting, as did Dawn and Matt.

On Monday, Dawn and Matt cut and hauled two loads of long wood. Some was cut already and some they limbed and cut up themselves. It was hard work, but they felt good that they were doing their own work. Tuesday, Dawn was baking, and Matt was working at the root cellar. Just before dinner, Angela rode into the yard. They sat and talked as they ate dinner, and when the meal was over, Matt went back to work in the root cellar.

As soon as Matt left, Angela asked, "OK, how are things going between you and that cowboy? I heard you went camping in Lost Valley last weekend, but why didn't the two of you go alone?" Dawn answered, "We get along just fine, not that it is really any of your business. Maybe we will go camping alone sometime." Dawn was trying hard not to smile, even though she wasn't being very successful.

"I'll be glad when the two of you get some sense in your heads," Angela stated, "Maybe you have already, because you look and act like a teenager. Sometimes, I think Matt has more sense in his head than you and Shorty combined. I came over here to tell you that they plan to start branding your cattle next week. Xavier wants to know if you and Matt want to help to keep the cattle separated. It would be just about the same as the last time, saving you from paying two more men. You and Matt have done it before, and you know it isn't too hard. I'll be there to give you a hand too. When they finish branding your cattle, they will start the roundup on the Axe also."

Dawn answered, "Well, we do know a little bit about what to do, and as you said, it isn't too hard. We might as well pay ourselves as someone else. We have most of our camping gear ready, so it won't take much work to get prepared. Just let us know when you get a day set to begin. We'll be there!"

Angela said, "We are giving that small horse to Matt, as it's too small for anyone on the ranch. If you want the one you are riding, we can work something out later." Dawn said, "Matt has to go back to school when it starts in the fall. His small horse will be better than walking or riding a workhorse. We've been planning to ask about buying them, now that we have some money. Before you go, let Matt show you what they have been doing all summer!"

Angela and Dawn went out to where Matt was working, and he showed her the root cellar, his pig shelter, and another look at the bunkhouse. She thought they must have been working very hard to get so much accomplished, since Shorty was only here on weekends. Matt explained that he and his mother worked all week while Shorty was away. They hauled wood, chinked the bunkhouse, and split shakes to have them ready for the weekends. Randy was here most weekends and one weekend, three of the Axe hands were here to help out. Matt and Dawn tried to do their share, but they had a lot of help too.

"Matt, you and your mother work too hard," Angela stated, "but I can see that Shorty has done a lot of things to make it easier. Shorty should be here all the time, and now that you have a good bunkhouse for him to live in, maybe he will be!"

Angele decided it was time to head back to the ranch. She would let Dawn know as soon as they had a definite date set to start the branding. All three called good-byes as she rode out of the yard. Dawn and Matt thought they should spend another day hauling wood before they went on the branding roundup. They worked around home the rest of the day and planned to go and get at least two more loads of wood tomorrow. In the morning, as soon as the regular chores were done and breakfast was over, they headed for the hills to get more wood. Dawn thought if they got a load of long wood first, they could start cutting up wood for the next load. They could work until it was time to go home to eat, take the first load home, and come back and finish cutting up the second load. The first load would go to the bunkhouse and the second one to the house. It was a tiring day, but they both felt good at having two more loads of wood home.

After a good supper, they thought they should celebrate by sleeping in the bunkhouse. The second bunk wasn't completed yet, but Matt thought they could put the rope in the bottom and pull it tight. Matt wove the rope through the holes and pulled it up snug. He then got Dawn to hold it while he pulled it up tight. After pulling the rope tight twice, they figured it was tight enough and the straw tick was placed on top. They now had two bunks ready to sleep on!

After a good night's sleep in the bunkhouse, they were ready for work again. Dawn was going to make a lunch, and they would get another load of wood. It would take them longer to cut and load it themselves, so a lunch would mean they could stay until they had a full load. The full day wouldn't be needed, but the time that was left over could be used around home.

When Shorty arrived, he would be surprised to see how much wood they had hauled. Dawn thought when they got back with the wood, they should get some fresh vegetables ready for supper. If they didn't have supper until later, Shorty would be there in time to eat with them. The day was spent cutting the wagonload of wood and hauling it home. The wagon was parked by the woodshed to be unloaded later. Dawn got a fire going in the stove, and then she and Matt went to the garden to get the vegetables. A good meal would be waiting for Shorty when he arrived.

Shorty rode into the yard about seven o'clock that evening. Before he got unsaddled, he could smell supper cooking. He washed up by the barn, and then he followed his nose to the house. Dawn was just filling a plate with potatoes, carrots, turnips, a few greens, and a quarter of cabbage. There was homemade butter for the vegetables, and Dawn had just put a pan of biscuits in the oven. When they finished eating the vegetables, there would be hot biscuits and tea and as always, a few doughnuts. Nothing tastes better than vegetables fresh from the garden, so it took very little urging for everyone to dig in and eat.

As the keen edge was taken off their appetite, they began to talk about their week's work. Shorty said, "I can see someone has been busy at the woodpile. It won't take much more to fill the woodshed out back. I could also see there is more at the bunkhouse too."

Dawn and Matt took turns filling him on what they had been doing throughout the week. They had cut up one load of wood and got a couple of loads in long length. They were both anxious to hear about the branding that was to take place next week, so they decided to let Shorty have his say.

Shorty then began to speak, "We plan to start Monday morning. Everyone will be in the valley Sunday afternoon and be ready for the morning. Spud will take the chuck wagon over to the entrance of the valley and use packhorses to take everything in. Your job will be about the same, to keep the branded cattle separated from the unbranded ones. It will probably be harder work for the hands, but it shouldn't take much longer. We've been thinking of making a squeeze fence and chute. We would find a spot where the bank is too steep to climb and build a wing fence to crowd the cattle toward the bank. Then there would be two fences side by side, getting narrower until only one cow fits between them. At the end would be a couple of gates, one in front and one behind. The cattle are crowded up to the first gate and the one behind is closed. We should be able to brand them without much roping and it would be much faster. We are going to give it a try and hopefully it will work, it should, as the cattle are very quiet."

From the way Shorty described it, Dawn and Matt thought it would be the fastest and easiest way to brand the cattle, compared to roping every animal. It shouldn't take very long to build a fence and squeeze chute and if it worked it would save much time. They decided to take along the bucksaw and a couple of axes to help cut poles for the fence.

When the meal was over, Shorty thought he would go outside and split some wood until dark. When Dawn finished the dishes, she went out to help with the wood. Shorty was splitting the wood, and Matt carried it into the woodshed and piled it neatly. Dawn would place a block of wood on the chopping block and Shorty would split it. If the halves needed to be split again, she stood them up one at a time. Dawn would then toss the split wood into the woodshed for Matt to pile. Since Shorty had been late arriving, darkness wasn't far away. As dusk arrived, the work was halted, and Dawn went in to make a cup of tea.

Shorty went to the bunkhouse and got his cake of soap and headed for the creek to wash off the sweat. When he was done, he went back to the bunkhouse and lit a lamp. He was surprised to see the second bunk completed. Shorty went back to the house for his cup of tea and a doughnut. He commented on the bunk being finished and thought it was a very good job.

Matt said, "Well, we both like to sleep in the new bunkhouse so we finished the bunk and each had a place to sleep. Tonight I'm sleeping in my own bed, so Ma can have the bunk. If we get another bunk ready, maybe we can all sleep there tomorrow night!"

Dawn looked at Matt and said, "You want me to sleep in the bunkhouse tonight with Shorty?"

Matt said, "Why not? You slept up there last weekend, so why not now? You both seemed so much happier after last weekend, and we both want Shorty to stay. I'm going to bed now so blow out the lamp when you leave. I'll see you both in the morning!" Dawn and Shorty looked at each other and smiled, then blew out the lamp and went up to the bunkhouse. Once there, they stood with their arms around each other for a few minutes. Shorty grinned and asked, "Which bunk do you want, top or bottom?"

Dawn answered, "Tell you what, you sleep in the top bunk, and I'll sleep in the top bunk! If you want to sleep in the bottom bunk, I'll sleep in the bottom bunk! How does that sound to you" "Sounds good to me!" Shorty said, "Now, we better get in that bunk and get some sleep!"

Matt had the stove hot and breakfast on the way when Dawn and Shorty got to the house in the morning. All three had big smiles on their face. As they ate and talked, they decided to get at least one more load of wood for the woodshed. If there was time before noon they would get two. That would be more than enough, but having extra wood made a person feel warmer. With breakfast over, the horses hitched up, and the tools loaded, they set out for the hills to cut more wood. Shorty and Dawn began sawing the wood while matt tossed it on the wagon and piled it in rows. They worked steadily with only a couple of short breaks and soon the wagon was loaded. Matt said he would haul it home and unload it while they worked at cutting another load. When he returned for the second load, more than half a load was waiting for him. The wagon was more than four feet wide, so Shorty suggested making the rows lengthwise in the wagon bed. In this way, when they got home, they could run the wagon up on a grade and the wood would roll out when the tailgate was removed. Matt began piling the wood in three long rows in the wagon. When the wagon was loaded, all three workers were ready for a break, and some food.

Back at the ranch, Dawn went inside to get a meal ready, while Matt and Shorty unloaded the wood. Shorty backed the wagon in toward the bunkhouse woodshed. Matt got two short boards and laid them on blocks of wood in front of the front wheels and removed the tailgate. When Shorty moved the horses ahead and up the ramps, most of the wood rolled out on the ground. Matt climbed up on the wagon and tossed out the dozen or so sticks that remained. Unloading the wagon this way saved a lot of time and effort. When the horses were unharnessed and turned into the pasture, Dawn had dinner on the table.

Chapter 14

A S THEY WERE eating, a light rain began to fall. They didn't want to work in the rain, so it looked like a good time to work on more bunks. Shorty and Matt went up the hill to get started while Dawn did her housework. The boys went to the barn to get some lumber Shorty had picked out. The sawhorses were set up, and Matt started planing lumber as Shorty measured and trimmed. He measured and marked where the upright two by four would go and put a cross piece on top of the ceiling joists to hold the top in place. Shorty planned to make the bottom bunk so it would slide out and make a double bed which was four feet wide. With the upright nailed solidly in place, he then nailed a short two by four from the wall to the upright. A planed six-inch board was nailed to the end wall at the proper height. A two by four was notched one and one quarter of an inch deep and sixteen inches long. This was nailed solidly to the board with the notch to the back, and the notch was filled in with boards. The boards would be the bottom of the bunk when it was used as a double bed. Shorty then built two light triangular brackets to support these boards at two foot intervals. Two more, three foot two by fours were laid flat and notched on both ends, one inch deep and six inches wide. Six-inch boards would be nailed into these notches to form the frame for the bunk. These two boards were placed one on top of the other and a row of holes were bored in a line down the middle. The two by fours had holes bored about one and a half inches from the inside. The frame was nailed together and placed on the two by fours already in place. A narrow board was nailed above the two by four with a slight clearance so it would slide easily. A sideboard was placed on the front and end of the bunk. When the rope was laced through the holes and pulled up tight, the bunk would be ready to use. When Dawn had gone to town to get four straw ticks, she had to take one four foot tick in place of a three foot one. The four foot tick would work fine on this 'convertible bed'

Shorty and Matt then started work on the top bunk. It only took a short time to get this one completed; as each time they built a bunk, it got easier. Soon the bunkhouse would boast four bunks. The rope was laced through the holes in the bottom and pulled up tight, all that was needed now was to have the straw ticks filled, but that could wait until after the rain stopped falling. Later in the afternoon, when the rain had stopped, Shorty and Matt went outside to split some more wood. The wood at the bunkhouse was going to be stored at the back of the woodshed. This would leave the front end for storing anything else that required being under shelter. Matt got a few small poles and laid them on the ground to pile the wood on. This would keep it slightly off the ground and away from the dampness. Shorty began splitting wood, and Matt carried it in and piled it in rows. They worked at the woodpile until Dawn called them to supper.

After another of Dawn's good meals, they went back outside again. They thought this would be a good time to fill the straw ticks for the bunkhouse, so they would be ready to sleep on at a moment's notice. It only took a few minutes to fill them, but it was awkward carrying them back to the bunkhouse. Finally the bunks were ready to sleep on. They went back to the woodpile to work until dark. When Dawn finished her housework, she came out to help Matt carry and pile the wood. A bit later they could see a rider in the distance. Soon they could see it was the schoolteacher, Karen Carter. She had a bedroll behind the saddle, full saddlebags, and a pack on her back.

She said to Dawn, "You invited me to come and visit, so I decided to take you up on your offer. I brought along my bedroll and a few things I might want in the next day or two. I can see you are all hard at work, so as soon as I get unsaddled, I'll give you a hand."

She removed her saddlebags and bedroll, and Shorty took the horse to the corral and unsaddled it. Karen took her things into the bunkhouse and was surprised to find all the bunks were useable. Soon all four were busy cutting, splitting, carrying, and piling wood. Karen could use both an axe and bucksaw and wasn't afraid of either one. With four people working, there was soon a big pile of wood in the woodshed. It was beginning to get dark, so Dawn went inside to make some tea. Karen stayed to help with the wood until Dawn announced tea was ready. Karen and Dawn carried the lunch up to the bunkhouse where the lamps had been lit, and tea was served.

Over tea, Karen was told of the upcoming roundup at Lost Valley. She said school didn't start for a couple of weeks and asked if they would like some more help. Dawn told her no help would be refused, so they now had an extra rider to work at the roundup. Karen said she hoped Matt would have time to cook some more fish while they were there. They all thought they would work extra hard to give Matt enough time to go fishing at least once. There were only a few cups to wash, so Dawn and Karen took them to the house. The two girls were on their way up to the bunkhouse when they saw a rider coming. It wasn't long until they recognized Randy Ripley. They all had forgotten Randy might show up.

They told him to put his horse in the corral and come up to the bunkhouse. Randy too was surprised to find all four bunks ready to use. Dawn explained to Randy that everyone was anxious to try out the new bunkhouse. Randy looked around and grinned as he said, "It looks like one of you girls will have to share a bunk with me!" Dawn laughed and said, "You are the last one here, maybe you will have to sleep in the barn! If you don't like that, Karen and I can share a bunk."

With that, Dawn took hold of the bunk and pulled it out a foot. Randy looked kind of surprised when she did that. He asked, "How did you do that? I thought all these bunks were built the same!"

They explained to Randy that this bunk was built to be used double if necessary, and this appeared to be the time. This was going to be the first time more than two people had slept in the new bunkhouse. Shorty claimed the bunk he had slept in a few times already. The two girls would use the double wide, and Matt would sleep on the one above them. Randy was left with the bunk above Shorty or the floor. He thought the bunk would be just fine for him!

They sat and talked for a bit before bedtime and Randy was filled in on the latest happenings on the ranch. They told him of the upcoming branding to take place in the valley. Randy informed them that the ranch where he worked had given the hands a couple of days off before the roundup started. He could help with the Lost Valley roundup for two days before heading back to his own roundup. Shorty figured he would have to ride to the ranch on Sunday to tell the boss how much help they would have. It wouldn't take as many hands from the ranch and would save Dawn some money. They planned to leave for the valley tomorrow to start building a fence and squeeze gate. They would take the tools they needed and maybe have the fence built or at least a good start on it before Monday. Now it was time to get some sleep so they could get everything ready in the morning to leave for the valley. The lamps were blown out as goodnights were said all around and soon silence settled on the bunkhouse.

When the rooster woke them in the morning, there was a flurry of activity as everyone found something to do. The girls went to the house to get breakfast ready, and the men looked after the animals and got tools ready to take with them. Shorty found an old cowhide in the barn and took it to the creek to soak. Strips of wet rawhide would be used to tie the rails to the posts and it would be easier to take the fence down later. The girls weren't very long getting breakfast ready and soon the meal was being eaten hurriedly. With the meal out of the way, everything was cleaned up, and the tools loaded. A couple of pots, frying pan, Dutch oven, and a coffee pot should do for cooking. A large batch of biscuits was mixed and the last of the bread and a slab of bacon were packed. Matt had also dug some potatoes for roasting. A short while later they were on the way, with the horses well loaded with the necessary supplies.

Before noon they were in the valley, looking for a good spot to camp. On the left side of the lake there was a narrow place where the lake was a lot closer to the bank. This would be a good place to put the fence as it would take a lot less work. Just before they reached the narrow point, there was a small cove in the original lake bank. It was about forty feet wide and ran back into the hill for fifty or sixty feet. This would make a good campsite as it was back out of the way and wouldn't alarm the cattle. There was enough room for the rest of the crew to camp also. The bank was very steep here and the canvas shelter could be tied to stakes driven into the bank and stretched out. The two shelters should make enough room for all the crew to sleep under.

Everyone was soon busy setting up camp before work began on the fence. A fire pit was dug and a fire started so water could be heated for tea. Everyone climbed the bank and began cutting poles for the fence. The rawhide had been put in the lake to keep it soft until needed. In a short time, a lot of long poles had been slid down the bank near where the fence was to be built. The two women cut some of the poles in five-foot lengths for fence stakes as Shorty and Randy sharpened them. Matt was carrying them to the approximate spots where they were needed. When a bunch of stakes were sharpened, Matt would hold them as Shorty drove them in solidly. The fence was built like a wide vee with one side against the steep bank and the other side running out into the lake. When the two fences were about ten feet apart, they were gradually narrowed until there was only room for one cow between them. Matt and the girls were carrying the poles and holding them in place, while Shorty and Randy tied them with the soft rawhide. As the rawhide dried, it shrank and become almost as hard as iron, holding the fence together better than nails. Braces were placed on the posts where it was narrow, as this part would get the most strain and punishment, as two or three animals tried to get through at once.

Everyone had stopped for tea and a light lunch after the poles had been cut. Since then, they had been working steadily and it was now nearing time to put on the nosebag. A suggestion was made that Matt roast a couple of rocks for supper. Matt grinned and got his fishing gear to catch supper. Since the lake was close by, a few minutes later, he was getting two nice trout ready to cook. He put two slices of bacon in each fish and sprinkled them with salt and pepper. When they were coated with clay and in the fire pit, he took a few slices of bacon and chopped it up small and put it in the frying pan. He then chopped half a dozen potatoes into small pieces and put that with the chopped bacon. While these were cooking, he mixed up some biscuits and put them in the hot Dutch oven. With water heating for tea, he kept stirring the meat and potato hash until it was cooked to a golden brown. He figured the fish should be nearly cooked, so supper should be about ready. He went to where the others were working and called out, "Come and get it before I feed it to the fish!"

Everyone dropped their tools and ran for the tarp shelter and the waiting supper. Matt had cut some crotched sticks for tongs to remove the fish from the fire. The fish and potatoes were ready and the biscuits would be ready when the diners were. When the fish were broken open, everyone lined up to fill a plate with hot potatoes and steaming fish. Tea was poured, and everyone began to shovel the food into themselves, talking very little as all were hungry. When the biscuits were removed from the fire and passed around, with refilled cups, talk began again. Matt was praised for the good meal he had cooked for them. They had all eaten Matt's baked trout before but told him again how good it was.

He was pleased with the praise being heaped upon him but he said, "My mother is a better cook than I am. It's just that the first time we were here I caught the fish and we had no way to cook it. I had to do something, so I thought about using the clay. I guess it turned out pretty good!"

Everybody thought the fish had turned out better than 'pretty good'. His mother might be a better cook, but with a few more years of experience, Matt would be a very good cook too. They all thought it was a good thing for boys to learn to cook because not all men would have a woman to do it for them. At least Matt wouldn't go hungry for lack of a cook. When the meal was finished, the crew went back to work on the fence. By the time darkness began to settle in, the fence was nearly finished. Tomorrow they would finish the squeeze and build the gates. When darkness began to creep up on them, they took time for a cup of tea before turning in. Soon after the stars began to shine, all were in their bedrolls and asleep. Tomorrow would be fairly easy, but the real work would start on Monday.

Daylight caught a few of them still in their blankets, but there wouldn't be much done today anyway. They would build a good fire pit near the squeeze and have a good supply of wood nearby. This would be necessary to keep the branding irons hot. If all went well, the branding might be completed in two or three days. Today, someone would ride to the ranch to let the boss know how big a crew they had already. It shouldn't take too many more hands to get the job completed.

A fire was started in the fire pit and water was put onto heat for tea. Dawn mixed up some biscuits, and Karen sliced some bacon. When the oven was hot, the biscuits were put in the fire to bake. With the bacon and biscuits ready and tea poured, the bystanders were ready to dig in. When the meal was well underway, they began to discuss the day's proceedings.

Dawn thought she and Karen could ride to the Axe and inform Xavier and the foreman of what they had accomplished. Leaving the boys to clean up around camp and finish the fence, the two girls set out for the ranch. Where the terrain permitted, they rode side by side so they could talk. Karen said she was hoping to get to know Randy better. She had heard some about his past, but he now seemed to be a real gentleman. Dawn told her what she knew about him, but since the dance in town, he was a hard worker and a gentleman. She didn't think there was a better man in the area except Shorty.

Karen smiled and said, "I don't think I would have much of a chance with Shorty. As far as I can see he is already spoken for!" Dawn blushed a bit as she said, "What gives you that idea? I don't see a ring in his nose!"

Karen spoke up, "I'm a woman too, you know! I can see there is something between you two. If I were you, I'd grab hold of him real quick before someone else tries for him. Shorty is probably the best man in the country, so you better grab him and hold on tight!"

Dawn told her that everything seemed to be working out right between them. She told Karen, "I've asked Shorty to marry me, but I told him to think it over for a few weeks before he gives me an answer. I think he is afraid because we own the ranch, and he is just a hired hand. If it wasn't for him, Matt and I would be in a very bad spot right now. You've seen some of the work he has done for us, and Matt thinks of him as his father. He has done so much for us, especially Matt. He even has us thinking almost as good as good as he does. I almost had to order him to sleep with me, but everything is working out fine now. I don't want you to tell anyone what I just told you, everybody will know what is happening soon enough!"

They rode along steadily and it wasn't long until they were at the ranch. As they rode into the yard, they were greeted by Angela. She was surprised and delighted to see them and invited them in for a cup of tea. Over tea they told her why they were there. Angela went to the office to get Xavier so he could hear what they had to say. Dawn explained to him that they had a crew of five people ready for the branding. She told him of the fence and squeeze gate they had built already. If the branding went anywhere near as easy as the job of separating the older cattle, it should be a fairly easy task.

Xavier thought with him and of course, Angela, two more hands should be plenty. The cattle in the valley seemed very quiet, so if they could be slowly pushed up to the fence the same way they had pushed the older cattle out of the herd, it should be a smooth operation. With the branding, every animal would go through the gate, which would be simpler than trying to separate them. The entire herd should be branded in two days. Spud was going along with a couple of packhorses to take the food and utensils that were needed. He would be able to help out some of the time, if needed.

The girls decided to go back to the valley as soon as they shared dinner with Angela and Xavier. They would all arrive at the valley before dark and get an early start in the morning. After the meal and visit, Dawn and Karen mounted up and rode back to the valley. The ride took a little more than an hour and gave them some time for more 'girl talk.' Karen said she had danced with Randy quite a bit at the, bunkhouse dance and had invited him on the picnic the next day. They both seemed interested in each other, and she said he was always a gentleman. Dawn said since he had been staying away from the alcohol, he was a very nice person. He was a good worker and had helped to do a lot of work at the ranch.

When the girls arrived back at the valley, they could see the boys loafing around the camp. The fence and gate were completed and a good supply of firewood was piled near the branding fire pit. Dawn told them that Xavier and Angela, with Spud and one other hand, would come over that evening. Somebody made the suggestion that Matt get supper ready for them like last night. Matt agreed with that and got his fishing pole and headed to the lake. It was only a short distance, and he was back soon with two trout. It was early yet so he was in no rush to get them on the fire. He began cutting potatoes into small pieces so they would be ready to put into the frying pan. He then sat and talked to the others until it was time to put supper on the fire.

Karen said to Matt, "Matt, there is something I want to ask you and Dawn. I would like you to help me some weekend. I want to take a group of school children on a trip to teach them how to survive in the wilderness. I could show them a lot of things, but I think they would pay more attention and learn more from you. I just want to teach them how to build a shelter, start a fire, cook food, and a few other simple things. Nothing too complicated, just enough to help them if they ever needed it. You could probably go out in the wilderness and survive on your own. A lot of the children don't know the first thing about being on their own. If I can get enough together, maybe we could go out next weekend."

Dawn thought that would be a great idea and told Matt it would be up to him. If he wanted to help Karen, it would be fine with her. Matt thought it would be fun to show others some of the things he knew and it would be even better for them to learn how to look after themselves, in case they ever got lost. They would take some time to make up a list of things the others should bring along. They could continue talking about it as they worked and maybe get some ideas from the others also.

Matt said if he was going to be cook tonight he had better get busy before he got fired. First he got the fish ready and put them in the fire pit. He then got water on to heat and chopped up some bacon to add flavor to the potatoes and also grease the pan. While he stirred the potatoes, Karen mixed up some biscuits as the Dutch oven was heating. It soon began to smell like suppertime. When the potatoes were done he moved them back just enough to keep them hot, the water was boiling so he added the tea and slid that back also. He thought the fish was about ready so he removed one from the fire and moved the other one back a bit. The clay was broken open and everyone was called to supper. Plates were filled with fish and potatoes and the business of eating began. It was a mostly silent crew as they filled up on this hot, tasty meal. It was just about time to start on the biscuits when somebody saw riders coming up the valley. They decided to hold off on the biscuits until the others arrived. Shorty and Randy looked after the horses while the four riders tackled the fish and potatoes. As soon as Shorty and Randy had the packhorses unloaded and the others unsaddled, they went back for biscuits and more tea. In a short while there was nothing left except fish bones and crumbs. Matt was praised again for the tasty meal he had prepared.

Everyone went to inspect the fence and squeeze gate and pronounced it satisfactory. With lots of help, the cook soon had everything set up to his liking. He had brought a tarp with him so this was erected over the kitchen area. All was in readiness now to begin the branding the next morning. The crew sat around the fire and talked until the sun went down and then all found their bedrolls to get some shuteye.

At daylight next morning the camp was a busy place. A fire was started in three fire pits; two for cooking breakfast and one to heat the R-R branding irons. With Dawn, Karen and Spud all working breakfast was soon on the 'table,' and the meal disappeared in a hurry as everyone was anxious to get started. The horses had been saddled while the meal was being prepared so they were soon out on the range working. Four of the riders went to where the cattle were scattered and slowly pushed about fifty head down to the fence. They were crowded into the narrow part and the branding got underway. As a cow was pushed up to the gate, a few poles were pushed through the fence behind it. This prevented it from moving in either direction. The poles of the squeeze were situated so there was room to brand the animal on the left hip. As soon as one animal was branded, it was released and another was pushed into its place. After branding, the cattle were pushed to the lower part of the valley to be kept separated. This job was given to Matt, Dawn, and Karen. It wasn't a strenuous job but important nonetheless. Keeping them separated made for a lot less repeat work. When there were a few branded cattle to be moved down the valley, two of the herders would ride up to the branding area and help herd them down. The whole crew was again amazed at how docile they were, for not having been around people. It was simply a matter of pushing them down to the fence

246 | R<small>ON</small> H<small>ERRETT</small>

and holding them until they were eased through the arrangement provided for branding. Of course, being white-face or Herford, they had a reputation for being easy to work around.

Nearing noon, Spud went to the kitchen area to get a meal ready for the cowhands. The others continued working until they were called to eat. A few cattle were left from the last bunch pushed from the main herd so they were branded before stopping to eat. Matt stayed with the branded cattle, riding slowly back and forth so none would try to rejoin the main herd. The first person to finish eating took over for him so he could eat. When the meal was over, it was back to work moving cattle. They continued with the work until past a normal supper time. The job was going so well, they expected to finish in two days. Dawn and Spud left to get supper ready while the others continued working. When the last one of the latest bunch had been pushed through, a halt was called for the day. By the time supper was ready, everyone felt as though they had done a good day's work.

As they sat devouring supper, including gallons of hot tea and coffee, they discussed the day's progress. It was believed by all that at least half of the cattle had been branded. It felt good to relax and have something besides a saddle to sit on! The evening was spent talking and joking until time to crawl into their bedrolls. A few of the men would sleep spaced out across the valley again to keep the cattle separated.

With the sunrise, it was business as usual. Someone suggested Matt take a few minutes to get more fish for dinner. The decision was unanimous, so the main course for dinner was to be Rainbow trout. The cattle were being pushed steadily through the branding chute. About midmorning, Matt put more wood on the fire and went shopping for dinner. In a matter of minutes two hungry trout were on their way to being the main course. He got these ready and also chopped up the last of the potatoes they had brought. He then went back to work for a while before putting the fish on to bake.

When Matt left the roundup the second time, Karen went with him. She was mixing up some biscuits as Matt got the fish in the fire pit. He then got the bacon chopped up and the potatoes frying and the tea and coffee pots heating. Matt left Karen to look after the cooking food, and he went back to ride herd on the cattle. When the last of the present group of cattle had been pushed through the chute, work was halted for a lunch break. It was a cheerful group that sat around the fire and ate Matt's baked trout, potatoes, and biscuits with plenty of tea and coffee. The branding was going well and should be wrapped up by late afternoon. After a well deserved rest and a good meal, everyone was back in the saddle to finish the job at hand. Just past mid-afternoon the last of the cattle were pushed through the gate and branded. Everyone sat down for a cup of tea or coffee and discussed the job they had just finished.

Xavier said they would head back to the ranch and get ready for their own roundup and branding. Everyone helped the cook load up his supplies and get ready to leave. Dawn, Karen, and Matt decided to stay another night and go back home in the morning. When Angela heard their plans, she told Xavier she was going to do the same. The others got ready to leave amid many good-byes and thank-yous. Soon it was just Matt and the three women in Lost Valley with the newly branded R-R cattle. They still had bacon and biscuit mix, but it looked like trout would be on the menu again.

Matt went to the lake to get a trout for supper. While at the lake, he found a dozen meadow mushrooms along the shore. He wondered what they would be like if he put them in the fish with the bacon strips. He decided to surprise the girls and kept quiet about his plans. Back at camp, he got the fish ready, stuffed them with bacon and mushrooms and covered them with clay. With the fish in the fire pit, Matt decided to do some exploring along the bank above the camp. Dawn was making biscuits to go with the trout for supper.

Matt climbed the bank behind the shelter and began looking around. He hadn't gone very far before he found some Saskatoon bushes hanging with berries. He began picking and eating them as fast as he could. He stopped eating them and picked as many as he could carry then headed back to camp. He showed the three women what he had found. They helped themselves to his handful of berries and asked if there was many more. He told them the bushes were loaded down heavily and thought maybe they should pick some for jam for next winter. All four got something to pick berries in and followed Matt to his treasure. They all picked hurriedly for about half an hour and then went back to camp for supper. All three commented on the flavor the wild mushrooms added to the baked fish.

After a good meal, they picked more berries until it was too dark to see. By this time they had a lot of containers full of fruit. They all had a lot of fruit for making jam, but everyone wanted more of this ripe fruit. They all decided to spend a couple of hours in the morning picking more. The containers that had been brought full of food would now be filled with fruit. As they crawled into their bedrolls, they were thinking of the sweet jam they would have for next winter. In the morning, after a quick breakfast followed by fresh fruit for dessert, they were back in the berry patch picking more ripe fruit. When the last available container had been filled, they began filling the only containers that weren't full—their stomach! When even their stomach would hold no more, they decided it was time to head for home and get all this beautiful fruit put away for the winter.

When the last of the equipment had been loaded up, along with the many pounds of fresh fruit, they were ready to hit the trail. The evening before, the fence had been dismantled and the poles and stakes stood against the bank of the camp area. There was a trampled area where the fence and squeeze had been situated, but the fast growing grass would soon cover over all signs that people had been here. The fire pits had been buried and everything cleaned up except the tracks. Everyone wanted to keep this valley as natural as possible. They rode single file out through the winding gully until they reached the open prairie. Here Angela said good-bye and turned toward the Axe, while Dawn, Karen, and Matt went toward the R-R.

When they reached home, Dawn invited Karen to stay and help make jam. Dawn had enough sugar for both of them and Karen could return her share at a later date. If the kitchen was going to be a mess, a little more mess wouldn't hurt anything. Karen agreed it was a lot easier with some help, and they soon had huge pots of berries cooking on the stove.

In the meantime, Matt went out to check on the livestock and gather the eggs. He found over a dozen eggs as they had been away for three days. They now had two hatchings of chicks, with each hen having twelve or fourteen young. There would be young roosters for the oven later on! The calf had been keeping the cow milked, but he decided to see if he could get a bit of milk for the house. He got some, but would get more in the morning. When he had checked everything over, he went back to the house.

Before Matt got to the house, he could smell the sweet jam. The house smelled like a candy store, only better. There would be plenty of jam for bread and biscuits next winter. He asked his mother about making biscuits for dinner, and, as they made jam, Matt mixed up biscuits and put them in the oven to bake. When the biscuits were done they all ate biscuits and jam for dinner with lots of tea. The fresh jam made a good lunch after which Matt went out to the garden to get fresh vegetables for supper. Potatoes, carrots, and turnips, fresh from the garden, would make a good supper, with maybe a few biscuits and jam for desert. He washed the vegetables outside and left them by the step. He would have put them in the sink, but there would probably be lots of washing and cleaning up after the jam making was done.

Matt went looking for something to do and settled on cutting and splitting wood at the bunkhouse. There wasn't much wood to be split, so he began to cut the long wood with the bucksaw. The wood was hard to hold on the woodpile, so he used his head to come up with a way to hold it while sawing it. He thought of the sluice he and Shorty had built to run water to the barn. If he drove two small stakes in the ground in the shape of an X, the wood would be easier to hold while sawing. This worked well until the wood got short when it was hard to hold. He got two narrow boards and nailed them in the shape of a vee. These were fastened in the top of the two crossed poles. Now a long stick was easy to hold and when it got short he could hold it solidly with one foot while cutting it with the bucksaw. He would cut wood until it was piled up in the way, he then put down the saw and carried the wood into the woodshed and piled it. They had been cutting some of the long wood when Karen had arrived, so a couple of hours finished the job and made a good supply of wood for the bunkhouse. With another job completed, Matt went to the house to get the vegetables ready for supper. He found that the girls had finished the jam making and the kitchen was all cleaned up. Karen was just about finished getting the vegetables ready to cook. Since he wasn't needed in the kitchen, he went out to split some of the remaining wood for the house. He kept himself busy until he was called for supper. The vegetables tasted good with lots of homemade butter to go with them. After the meal there was biscuits and fresh jam to fill any hollow spots. All that was missing was a doughnut, but Dawn would take care of that problem in the next day or two.

Karen decided she would stay overnight as she had nothing to hurry home for. Dawn suggested sleeping in the bunkhouse again. When the housework was finished, the two women went up to the bunkhouse. Matt had been splitting wood, but he put the axe away and joined them. They sat on the porch and talked until darkness began to make its way across the land. They moved inside and a lamp was lit. Karen thought the bunkhouse was the nicest building she had ever slept in. Dawn agreed with her and with a wink at Karen, said some times were nicer than others. The girls took the bottom bunks, which left a top bunk for Matt. He didn't mind where he slept; he just liked to sleep in the bunkhouse. The lamp was blown out and soon all three were asleep and dreaming of the Lost Valley.

When the rooster announced it was time to rise and shine, all three were awake. Dawn and Karen went to the house to get breakfast ready, and Matt went to milk the cow and check the other livestock. This time he was ahead of the calf and got the most milk. The two women soon had breakfast ready and it disappeared almost as fast.

Karen was going back to town today, but before she left she said to Matt, "I'm going to make a list of things to take on our trip this weekend, I would like you to make a list also. I will probably come out on Thursday so we can compare lists. We can also make a list of the things the children should bring. Dawn, I was wondering if we could go back to the valley to camp overnight, I mean just the main valley, not the inner valley. Matt can show them how to put up a shelter and how to catch and cook a fish. They aren't going to learn everything on one trip, but it will be a start."

Matt and Dawn thought Karen had a good idea and they had no objection to them going to the valley. They didn't own it; their cattle had found it and seemed to have claimed it for their own. Karen headed for town with a few bottles of jam wrapped up and packed in her saddlebags. She didn't want to take any chances on the bottles of jam getting broken on the way.

Matt decided it was a good time to build some shelves in the root cellar. He got some boards, saw, hammer and nails and went to work. At the back of the root cellar, he nailed two boards upright on each side. To these he nailed short narrow boards for the shelves to set on. He put three shelves about a foot apart, starting at the top. These shelves would hold a lot of jam and pickles or whatever had to be kept cool, but not cold enough to freeze. There was still plenty of room underneath for bins to hold the potatoes, carrots, turnips, and cabbage or whatever else they had to store for the winter. When it got cold enough to butcher a hog, some of the meat could be pickled and stored in the root cellar also. It was going to be useful for storing many things throughout the year.

Matt went to the woodshed and began splitting wood for the kitchen stove. As he worked, he was thinking of the trip he and Karen would be taking on the weekend. He was making a list in his mind of what would be needed. Most of what he needed personally was ready now, as they had been camping quite a bit recently. He was trying to think of what the others should bring. A bedroll would be the first thing, with a plate, cup, fork, and a pocket or belt knife. The knife would serve different purposes, at mealtimes and for preparing food, cutting branches, fishing poles, and many other uses. He and Karen would take the main things that would be needed, such as a tarp for shelter, hand ax, frying pan, Dutch oven, teapot, and the bigger items. He would use his improvised fishing gear that he had used the first time to show the others how to use what you have to provide food and shelter if necessary. He would keep working on his list until Karen showed up. Between the two of them, they should be able to come up with a small list of necessities for the children to bring along. What he and Karen provided would be used by everyone. It promised to be an interesting weekend. He had never planned to be a teacher, but this weekend he would be one!

Dawn came out at this time to tell him it was time for dinner. He got a piece of paper, and as he ate he wrote down the list of things he had been thinking of. He had made his list in three parts; what must be taken, what should be taken, and what could be taken, depending on how much each wanted to carry.

Chapter 15

MATT WAS STILL thinking of the beautiful valley and wishing he could live there. He asked Dawn; "Would it be possible for us to live in Lost Valley? I know in some places people can still file for a homestead, or maybe we could see about buying the valley. It would probably be more than we could afford, but I would like to try and find out something about it."

Dawn answered, "You know, Matt, I've been thinking the same thing. It would be a wonderful place to live, just think of the garden we could grow in that soil! When Shorty comes, we can talk to him and see what he can tell us about it. It won't cost much to check into filing on a homestead or buying it. You know, I bet Karen could help us find out something about that! When she comes tomorrow we can ask her to see what she can find out about filing on a homestead."

They both felt good just talking about the valley, but would make them feel a lot better if they owned it and could live there. Neither of them was expecting to see Shorty before Friday evening or even Saturday, maybe not at all this weekend. The roundup at the Axe was underway, so he might be too busy to leave the ranch. Matt would be going on the trip with Karen and the school kids, but Dawn was expecting a long weekend without Shorty being around. She decided she was going to remedy that situation right away!

Matt had his list completed to the best of his knowledge. As he thought of something, it was added. He went outside to split more wood; a job that gave a person a lot of time to think. Matt was getting to be a thinker, just like Shorty.

Matt worked at the woodpile for an hour or so, when he decided to get everything ready for the overnight trip to the valley. He planned to take his fishing gear, but use the improvised setup he had used the first time. He put the tarp and light rope in the bottom of the big pack, and checked over his bedroll and tied it behind his saddle. He knew Karen would bring enough biscuit mix for everyone, and he could probably take enough bacon for breakfast and to cook a couple of trout. Before they left, he would get some potatoes to take along too. With the Dutch oven, frying pan, and something to heat water in, they should be able to get a meal ready.

Matt kept the list in mind as he worked around the ranch buildings. Just about everything he would need was packed or ready to pack. When Karen arrived they would finish the list for the others to bring. Time passes quickly when a person is busy and soon Dawn called Matt for supper. They discussed the valley again as both were anxious to start checking into owning it. When supper was over Matt went to the garden and pulled all the weeds he could find to take to his pigs. They liked the fresh juicy weeds and the carrot and turnip tops. Matt now owned two big black and white pigs, which it seemed only a short time ago, were only small pigs. He was working away when he heard a rider coming. He was hoping it was Shorty, but it was Karen instead. He went to meet her and she asked Matt if he could unsaddle her horse and put it in the corral.

When Matt had the horse unsaddled, he went in the house where Dawn and Karen were talking. Karen was going to stay overnight, so Dawn was getting a snack and tea ready to take up to the bunkhouse. As they ate, Matt and Karen compared lists and added to Matt's list of what the others should bring. There were going to be seven others, from seven to twelve years of age, two of those were girls. Karen had asked a couple of them to bring some bacon and a couple of others to bring biscuit mix. If they could come up with something for the others to bring, it would be great.

Dawn said they could use her Dutch oven, frying pan, and teapot, so Karen wouldn't have to bring hers from town. When it was time to hit the sack, they had just about everything figured out. Karen would go back to town tomorrow, and they would all be back here Saturday morning. Maybe another time they would stay out for two nights, but the first trip one night would probably be enough. Karen suggested taking some containers to pick more berries for jam. They could give each child a bottle of jam and make more from the berries that would be picked this weekend. Karen said she would supply the sugar this time and also bring some jars. It was time for some sleep, so the light was put out and they would think on things as they slept.

When morning arrived they were all up and around, busy as usual. Dawn suggested maybe Karen could bring the campers here to sleep in the bunkhouse that night and then leave on Saturday morning. Karen liked that idea, as they could still cook breakfast over the open fire in Matt's fire pit. When breakfast was over, she set out for town but said she would see them later in the day. Dawn and Matt were busy as usual at the everyday jobs around the ranch. Dawn baked bread so Matt would have a fresh loaf to take on the camping trip. She also made doughnuts for Matt to take along as a surprise.

Matt had just about everything ready to go, so he went to the garden for some potatoes for either frying or baking, either way seemed to go good with trout. Keeping busy seemed to make the time fly for both Dawn and Matt. Soon it was supper time, and Karen would be here shortly after. When he finished eating, Matt went to the barn and filled a few feed sacks with hay; this would be a lot better than sleeping on the board floor.

When Karen arrived, it was a busy place for a while. The horses were unsaddled and put in the corral, while the bedrolls and food were carried up to the bunkhouse. The two girls weren't very big so Karen said they could sleep in the double bunk with her. Two of the smaller boys would share a bunk, and two would sleep on the feed sacks on the floor. This left a top bunk for Matt and the biggest boy from town.

Matt started a fire in the fire pit and everyone sat around and told stories and sang a few songs. Dawn came out with a doughnut for each one as a bedtime snack. It was soon time for bed as they would all be helping to cook breakfast early in the morning.

Matt had a good fire going in the fire pit when the rooster began to sing in the morning. He also had a bucket of water, soap, and a towel waiting on the porch. Very soon, everyone was washed up and helping to get breakfast ready. Dawn had mixed up pancakes, and one of the girls was cooking them. Bacon was frying also, along with biscuits in the Dutch oven. There was tea for those who drank it, and Dawn had cold milk, too. Most of the children helped with cooking the meal, and those who didn't would get their turn at the next meal. A short while later, breakfast was over and everything cleaned up. Everyone put away their eating tools and got things packed up ready to saddle up and set out on the survival trip. They were all excited about camping out a long distance from home. Matt and Karen helped the smaller ones get saddled up and made sure nothing was left behind. A bunch of very excited children were waving wildly at Dawn, who smiled and waved in return.

They rode slowly, looking all around, and stopping often to look at things, and Matt or Karen would explain different things to them. They were looking for tracks, but saw mostly cow tracks with a few deer tracks and a coyote print now and then. When they got to the entrance to the valley, Matt told Karen to lead, and he would follow along behind. When they reached the valley, a line of riders sat and looked across the beautiful valley. Matt and Karen agreed the branding camp would be a good spot, so that was where they headed. Arriving at the camping place, Matt got a fence stake and drove it solidly to fasten a long rope to. They decided to unsaddle and any exploring to be done would be on foot. When the horses were unsaddled and tethered, camp had to be set up before anything else was done. Matt and Karen asked the others about their ideas for making a shelter. The bigger ones set about building a shelter, while the smaller ones gathered wood and helped arrange the camp properly. Rocks that had been used before were collected and a shallow fire pit was dug. A fire was started and since it was nearly noon, water was put on to heat. Biscuits and a slice or two of bacon would do, as they would have fish and potatoes for supper. Soon a light lunch was ready and being eaten by the campers. When lunch was finished, the camp was cleaned up thoroughly. Karen explained that probably no one had ever been in this valley until just a few weeks ago and everyone wanted to keep it natural with no sign that people had been here.

With the camp chores out of the way, it was time to start educating the students. Matt got a couple of small containers and the group spread out along the shore of the lake to look for mushrooms. He told them if they found any to let him check them out before picking any. Soon a couple was spotted and Matt showed them how to identify the right kind. He picked the mushrooms and explained how to be sure they were good. Meadow mushrooms were usually white, sometimes light brown on the top. When turned over, the underneath was pink if they were very fresh and the older ones were darker pink or brown and sometimes almost black. There were other kinds that were safe to eat, but if a person picked only the ones they were sure of, there would be very little chance of getting something that might be poisonous. They gathered mushrooms until they had about half a peck or one gallon. The mushrooms would be taken back to camp washed and trimmed and cooked for supper. Karen took them up on the hill where Matt had found the Saskatoon berries and they picked some for dessert after supper. Karen explained that before they left for home, they would pick many more for jam and when they got back to the R-R they would each get a bottle of jam to take home. While in the bushes, Matt and Karen explained how to make a shelter of poles and brush. Maybe at a later date, they would take a partner and each pair would build a shelter and sleep in it. It was past mid afternoon and time to start thinking of supper. Matt asked one of the boys to get him a long slim pole, and he would show them how to catch a fish. Soon Matt had his rod set up with the original line and improvised hook. They all walked to the lake where he pulled up a clump of grass and found a couple of worms. He showed them how the hook could be pushed together until a fish pulled on it. Without baiting the hook, he showed them how he swung the line as far out into the lake as he could. He then baited the hook and asked one of the girls to try it. When a fish grabbed the hook, it stirred up a lot of excitement on the shore. The fish was pulled up on the grass and Matt showed them how to kill it quickly. He explained that a fish out of water was like a person in the water; neither could breathe. If you have to kill something, do it quickly so it won't suffer. Karen picked one of the boys to catch another fish. It only took a minute for him to land another trout for supper. Two of the boys volunteered to clean the fish, so Matt got some clay from the lakeside to coat the fish with. When the fish were ready, he got some bacon and some of the mushrooms to put inside of the fish. After a generous sprinkling of salt and pepper, he wrapped it in clean grass and coated it with clay. Several of the students were following the procedure with the other fish.

Matt and the biggest of the boys took a hand ax and went to get more dry wood, and the others helped carry the wood back to camp. Some of the group was getting the mushrooms ready to cook, while others were cutting up some of the potatoes. Matt made sure to keep one big potato for each to bake for the next day. It wasn't long until the smell of frying potatoes and mushrooms filled the air. Water was heating for tea and there was cold water for the non-tea drinkers. Karen showed them how to make tongs of crotched sticks, curved if possible, to remove the fish or other items from the fire. When the clay was broken open, everyone lined up to fill their plates with the mouth-watering meal. For a while, there was no sound except the sound of food being eaten. Camping and eating out in the wilderness was a new experience for most of them. Matt had produced a loaf of his mother's bread to eat with the meal. When everyone was almost completely stuffed, the container of berries was placed where they could all reach it. Before it got dark the dishes were washed and the camp made neat and tidy. A couple of the boys went with Matt, and the horses were led to the lake to drink. When darkness settled in, the camp was clean and neat and the stock was looked after and secure. Now they could relax around the fire and finish off the fruit. Matt and a couple of the older ones had put their bedrolls just outside the tarp to make room for the ones who wanted to be underneath. It wasn't long until it was time to say goodnight all around and crawl into their bedrolls.

Meanwhile, back at the ranch, Dawn had decided to sleep in the bunkhouse. After she had eaten supper and cleaned up around the house, she took some sewing and sat on the porch at the bunkhouse. She sewed until it began to get dark, and then she went inside and lit a lamp. She sat in the chair that had been made for her and read a newspaper at the table. When she finished reading, she turned the lamp down low, undressed, and crawled under the blankets on the double bunk. She was almost asleep when she thought she heard a horse outside. She listened for a bit, but she decided it must be one of her own horses moving about. Again she was almost asleep when she heard someone approaching the bunkhouse. The door opened and closed and footsteps went to the table and the lamp was turned up a bit. Shorty went to the bunk opposite her and got undressed to crawl into his customary bed.

Dawn said, "There might be room for two over here, unless you prefer to sleep alone!" Shorty was startled for a second before he said, "What are you doing sleeping here? I thought you were probably asleep in your own bed, and I didn't want to disturb you."

Dawn said, "Well, it is still my bunkhouse so I decided to sleep here. Matt and Karen took a group of school kids to the valley to camp overnight. We didn't expect you as we thought you would be busy with the roundup. Actually, we didn't expect to see you before next weekend at the earliest."

"Well," Shorty replied, "Your sister insisted I ride over here to make sure you and Matt were getting along OK. I tried to tell her you got along before I met you and would probably be getting along fine now. I seem to get the feeling she thinks there is something is going on between us. I might have to thank her for sending me over here though, since you are all alone with no one to protect you!"

Dawn smiled as she lifted the blankets and said, "Well, I'm all alone in this big bed, so maybe you better get in here where you can protect me!" Shorty didn't need a second invitation.

Morning caught some of the campers in their blankets, but Matt, Karen, and a couple of others were out and about. The fire was burning, water heating, and biscuits were being mixed up. Bacon was sizzling in the frying pan, and two campers were picking Saskatoon's for desert. A handful of leftover fruit was tossed into the biscuits as a surprise for breakfast. In a short time, breakfast was ready and being eaten by a hungry bunch of people; it seemed like camping was good for the appetite.

Matt told them he was going to show everyone how to catch a fish with their bare hands, when the camp chores were done. While some cleaned up the campsite, Matt and a couple of helpers led the horses to the lake for water. Enough firewood was gathered for the noon meal, after which they would all head back home. They walked up to where the stream entered the lake, and Matt demonstrated how to catch a fish with your hand. He explained that they must be very careful and not hurt the fish, because although there was plenty of fish in the lake, none should be hurt or killed unless it was necessary. The campers lined up to take their turn at catching a fish with their hands. When everyone had their turn at hand fishing, it was time to pick more berries to take home for making jam. Later two more children would catch a fish and these would be prepared for dinner. Soon after dinner was eaten and the campsite cleaned up, it would be time to go home.

Everyone had a great time on this trip and hoped to do it again sometime in the near future. They had all learned a lot, but there was much more to be learned. If they asked the right questions, they could learn a lot of helpful things around home. Karen would always be around town to help out and show them more. They all had a good start at learning to look after themselves when away from home. It was fun and interesting and just might help save their life, or the life of someone else, someday.

It was a tired but happy group that turned their horses toward home about mid afternoon. When they reached the ranch, they each received a bottle of jam before going home. Karen asked Dawn if they should make the jam now or wait until tomorrow. Dawn decided tomorrow would be soon enough as the berries were fresh and they would have more time. Karen and Matt were surprised to hear that Shorty had arrived last night. The smile that Dawn gave Karen answered the question that she would never ask. Karen decided she would ride into town with the young people, but told Dawn she would be back early tomorrow with sugar and bottles for the jam. They would both have a good supply of jam for the coming year. Matt unsaddled his horse and put away the equipment he had used on the trip. He had enjoyed showing others some of the things he had learned so far in his life.

Matt was outside looking for something to keep him occupied. For more than a year, he and his mother had to do everything that needed to be done on the ranch. He now felt lost if he didn't have something to do. Since Shorty had been coming every weekend, plus all the other help they had, there was very little work that absolutely had to be done except for a small amount of wood to be split.

Dawn was busy in the kitchen and as she worked, she thought back to last night. She had been surprised and pleased when Shorty had arrived unexpectedly. When Shorty had gotten in the double bunk, they talked for a bit. Dawn told Shorty, "I hope you have been thinking about what I asked you a couple of weeks ago. Now, I'm going to ask you again, will you marry me, Shorty?"

Shorty grinned and said, "I think I'm supposed to ask you that question, but since you have already asked me, I guess I'll have to answer you. Yes, Dawn, I would like to marry you! I'm just a cowhand, and you own this ranch, but if you think I'm good enough, I'll marry you. I know there isn't another woman in the country that would come close to being the person you are. Now, when do you plan to get married?"

Dawn said, "There isn't any rush that I can see. Maybe later in the fall when the work starts to let up. I don't want a big wedding, just something simple and quiet. What do you think about that?" Shorty answered, "I would say the smaller the better, but what about afterward? Your sister is going to want a big party, I'll bet!"

To that Dawn said, "If she wants a big party that will be up to her. We don't have room here, so it would have to be at the ranch. She will have to decide that later!" Neither knew what the future would bring, but when Angela got wind of the upcoming wedding, she would make her own plans. If Angela wanted a big party, then she would have a big party!

Dawn and Matt worked along at their own jobs for the remainder of the day. When suppertime arrived, they talked over what they had done since yesterday. Matt told Dawn about their trip and what they had done. He thought the kids from town had enjoyed the trip and wanted to do it again. Dawn told Matt some of what had taken place while he was away, but decided to wait until Shorty was here before telling him about getting married.

After supper was over, they went to the bunkhouse and sat on the porch until it was too dark to see. When a lamp was lit, they moved inside. Sleeping in the bunkhouse was a popular pastime for everyone, it seemed. They weren't long in crawling into their bunks, as Karen would be there early to help make jam.

Karen was true to her word and arrived in good time in the morning. Dawn had the stove hot and was ready to start the jam making. Soon after Karen arrived, the kitchen was filled with the wonderful aroma of cooking jam. Matt had offered to help, but Dawn said the two of them could handle the jam making. Matt was busy outside, as there was always something needing to be done. As they worked, Karen said that all the children were very pleased with the trip they had been on and some of the parents had even stopped by to thank her for what she had done. She told them Matt had done most of the teaching and the work.

Dawn told Karen she had something to tell her about Saturday night. She said, "I don't want you to tell anyone for a couple of weeks but I asked Shorty again if he would marry me and he said, yes! We don't know when it will be yet, but probably in three or four weeks, when the work begins to ease off after the roundup. I don't want word to get around, because Matt doesn't know yet. The next time Shorty is here, we are going to tell him. I am sure he will be very pleased to hear we are getting married though."

Karen was excited and hugged Dawn and danced around the kitchen. She said; "I'm so happy for you! There isn't a better man than Shorty anywhere. There will probably be a lot of jealous girls when they find out you got the best of the herd." The girls continued working at the jam throughout the morning. Just before noon, Karen made a pan of biscuits so they could have fresh jam and biscuits for dinner, with a cup of tea. Since the kitchen was so hot, they decided to eat in the bunkhouse. They called Matt and carried their meal and eating utensils up the hill. They chatted as they ate, and Karen told Matt how pleased everyone was about the camping trip and that they were all looking forward to going again. Karen also told Matt school would start in two weeks. Maybe after school started, they could make plans for another trip. Matt suggested maybe they could go to the place where they cut their wood. There was lots of brush they could use to build shelters, although they wouldn't find much to eat later in the fall. Karen thought that was a good idea for them to learn how to build shelters. As for food, they would have to learn what to take and how much. She said, "We could give them some ideas of what to take and maybe they could work together in pairs. I think they would learn faster if they do everything for themselves, but we could help them if they need it. Matt, we will soon have a group of young people who know how to look after themselves!"

The two women went back to the house to clean up after jam making. Matt went to the root cellar to start getting ready for the fall harvest. He got some small poles to use to put the vegetables on. The bins would be three feet wide, so he cut five of the bigger butt pieces three feet long to put on the ground. He then trimmed the poles and laid them on the short ones. This would keep the vegetables just barely off the ground. He then nailed a short board upright on the wall at each end. He drove a short stake in the middle in line with the two upright boards. Later he would get some boards to place inside to hold the vegetables. The carrots would go in a separate bin so they could be buried in clean soil or sand. If a carrot began to dry out it would soon spoil, so they were better kept damp and they would store a lot longer. The garden had done well this year and there would be a good supply of vegetables to store for the winter. Next year the garden could be made larger and grow even more. If they had more than they could use, they could always sell some in the spring.

There is always plenty to do around a ranch or farm so Matt and Dawn kept themselves occupied, and no one ever heard anyone say they were bored. Soon the week was gone and it was Saturday. They both hoped Shorty would come, but they knew he would be busy at the ranch. Just before dark they heard a horse, and who should they see coming except Shorty! Both ran to meet him as he dismounted to unsaddle his horse. Dawn gave him a hug and a kiss, which made Matt grin from ear to ear. Soon they were having tea and doughnuts and catching up on the news. After a while, Dawn got up and went over to stand behind Shorty's chair. She put her arms around his neck and said to Matt, "Matt, Shorty and I are getting married soon!" Matt's eyes got very big, he jumped straight in the air and yelled, "Yippee." It seemed as if he bounced off the walls and ceiling a few times before he went over to put his arms around both Dawn and Shorty. At last they were going to be a family! Matt was smiling from ear to ear and so excited he couldn't keep still. He asked them when they were getting married, but he never heard a word they said. Matt thought he was the happiest person in the whole world!

All three were too excited to sleep, but it was bedtime. Matt said, "I'll sleep in my room. You two go up to the bunkhouse. There isn't too much work to be done around here now, so we don't have to get up too early in the morning. I'm going to bed, so goodnight and I'll see you at breakfast." He was still smiling as he closed the door to his room.

Dawn blew out the lamp, then took Shorty's hand and headed for the bunkhouse. At the bunkhouse, Shorty lit a lamp and they got ready for bed. He was grinning as he said, "Why do I get the idea Matt is happy when he found out that we are getting married?"

Dawn answered, "I think he has been hoping for this for quite a while. He has been trying to get us together for months. Do you remember the night I came up here to bandage your hand? He locked the door so I had to stay here! What about the talk you and Matt had that night here in the bunkhouse? I think you have an eight-year-old son!"

Shorty smiled and said, "I sure hope so! Even my own flesh and blood couldn't make a better son than Matt. I just hope I can live up to what he expects from me!" Dawn replied, "I think you are far better than what he expected. You are a lot better man than I expected or feel I deserve. Now that's enough talking for tonight. Let's get some sleep . . . later!"

Next morning Matt was up before the rooster had made a sound. He got a fire going in the stove and water heating for tea. He mixed up biscuits and put them in the oven. He then made pancakes and got some bacon frying. The wonderful smells made him hungrier than he already was. When everything was ready, he packed it all in a shallow wooden box, with a bottle of the new jam, covered it with a towel to keep it warm, and carried it to the bunkhouse. He knocked on the door, opened it, and walked in. Shorty and Dawn were still in bed but wide awake.

Matt said, "Rise and shine, it's breakfast time. Are you going to stay in bed all day? I couldn't eat all this by myself, so I thought I might have to give it to the chickens." He carried breakfast over to the bed and set it down. He took off the towel covering everything, and the smell of breakfast filled the bunkhouse.

Dawn said, "Thank you for making breakfast in bed for us, Matt, but if you don't mind, I would prefer to eat at the table. I don't want to spill my tea on the blankets." Matt took the box over to the table and began setting things out. Shorty slipped into his pants and reached for his shirt. Dawn dropped her nightgown over her head and shook it into place as she got up. When they reached the table, Matt had breakfast all set out ready to eat. There was bacon and eggs, pancakes and molasses, and hot biscuits with butter and fresh jam. A pot of hot tea was ready to finish the meal. This was the first breakfast to be eaten in the new bunkhouse, and it was a meal fit for a king! Dawn and Shorty thought they must be very special to have 'their' son prepare a wonderful meal like this just for them.

After eating the big meal Matt had cooked for everybody, they all felt kind of lazy. Shorty was working hard at the roundup all week, so Dawn felt he shouldn't have to work on the only day he had off. Matt suggested they go fishing. He asked Shorty if they could smoke or dry some of the fish from the lake in the valley for winter.

Shorty said, "I'm sure your mother has a big crock that we could pickle some in. We could build something to smoke some, or even just a rack over a smoky fire like the Indians do. I've never dried fish before, but if they are cut in thin strips and sprinkled with salt, they should dry well. If we are going to take the day to go fishing, we better get moving!" Dawn took the few dishes to the house to wash, and Shorty and Matt started getting everything ready to take for drying and smoking the fish. It wouldn't be too hard to catch the fish, for if necessary, they could be caught by hand, but they would need some containers to bring them home in. If they could get some smoked and some partly dried, it would save a lot of work at home. The fish that were to be salted would be brought back and put in the crock here. Dawn sliced and buttered some bread and got the teapot and tea ready to go.

She also put a few pounds of salt in a container to take along. A short time later they were in the saddle and on their way to Lost Valley.

When they arrived at the valley, Shorty thought their old branding camp would be a good spot. He set about to cut some small green poles to build a smoking and drying rack, while Dawn got a fire going. Matt went to the lake to start getting some trout. Everyone was busy, and soon there was fish smoking on the rack. Green alders are preferred for smoking meat or fish, but almost any green wood, except maybe poplar, which gives a very strong smoke. Shorty built another rack where there was a breeze blowing for drying the trout. All the fish were cleaned and skinned, and salt was rubbed into them. The fish to be dried were cut into thin strips for faster drying. In a short time there were two racks full of fish, drying and smoking. Matt arrived with a couple more fish and began cleaning them. He told Dawn, "I've been having all the fun catching the fish while you two did all the work. Now I'll look after things here so you can do some looking around. We can catch some fish just before we leave to take home for pickling. Now, leave me alone so I can get some work done here!" he said with a grin.

Dawn and Shorty were smiling as they held hands and walked up the shore of the lake. It was early fall, but the weather was beautiful and warm. They walked along slowly, talking and looking around as they went. Dawn saw something interesting over by the bank and went over to investigate. What she saw was a small hole in the bank at the back of a small cove, like the one where they had camped. There was a shelf of rock, about four feet above the ground, and at some time in the past, an animal had dug a den there. It was about eight or ten feet deep, but they could see there was nothing in there now.

Suddenly Dawn got a silly grin on her face and began to take off her clothes. Shorty had a wide grin on his face as he helped her to get undressed. When all of her clothes were on the ground, she helped Shorty get rid of his. They stood looking at each other while grinning from ear to ear. Their clothes were spread on a soft patch of grass and they lay down on them in the sun. The warm rays of the sun felt good on their bare skin as they tickled each other with blades of grass. It was half an hour later when they decided they should get back into their clothes and continue their stroll.

They went up the lakeshore until they came to the small stream coming from the inner valley. Here they stopped and looked at the huge trout lying on the bottom. One fish was much bigger than the others, and Shorty said if he could get his hands on it, they would have a good start on the fish they planned to pickle. He rolled up his sleeve and put his hand in the water. Five minutes later he had a huge trout flopping on the grass. He used his knife to kill it quickly, and then held it up to show Dawn. He figured the fish had to weigh at least fifteen pounds. He put it on a stick for easier carrying, and they walked back down the lake to where Matt was hard at work drying and smoking fish.

Matt was surprised to see the big trout Shorty was carrying. Shorty held the fish up and said, "I've got the biggest one yet!" Matt laughed and asked, "What did you use for bait?" Shorty grinned and said, "*Me!* We were just walking along the stream, and it jumped right out on the grass. I think it was going to eat me!" All three had a good laugh at the 'fish tale' Shorty had told.

Matt had another fire going and a small trout baking for dinner. After the big breakfast they had eaten, they had forgotten about dinner. Now, the afternoon was half gone and they were starting to think about food. Dawn got water on to heat for tea, and then all three sat and talked as they kept the smoke fire going and turned the drying fish occasionally. Dawn told Shorty he might as well go to the Axe from here, as he was a few miles closer than he would be at the R-R. Shorty agreed that it was closer, but he had planned to help them get the fish pickled and the others hung up to dry.

He told Dawn and Matt, "When you pickle the fish, put some salt in the bottom, a layer of fish, more salt, and more fish until the crock is full or all the fish are used. Next, get a piece of clean board and shape it to fit in the top. Put on some weight to hold the fish under the brine and cover it with a clean cloth. When it comes time to cook them, they will have to be heated and the water changed a few times to get the salt out. After a few weeks, they could be dried so they could be carried anyplace or they could be left in the crock. These fish will be smoked enough so they can be dried same as the others. I think the best place would be under the porch roof at the bunkhouse. You could use small poles or a string to hang them on. I know you two can make out without me, but I'm just making you a few suggestions."

More green wood was put on the fire for the smoking fish, and the drying fish were turned again. Supper was now ready, so the baking fish was broken open and the bread was passed around for a good meal, mostly off the land. Matt had even found a few berries for dessert.

When the sun was only an hour from the horizon, they packed up the fish and the few dishes they had brought. The fires were put out and the fire pits were filled in with the sods that had been removed to make them. The fish racks were moved back into the bushes out of sight, and they were ready to leave. They rode slowly down the valley and out through the gully. When they reached the open prairie, they stopped to say their good-byes; Shorty rode toward the Axe, and Dawn and Matt turned toward home. All three were hoping it wouldn't be very long until the R-R would be Shorty's permanent home.

When they arrived home, Matt got some string and went up to the bunkhouse to hang the fish up to complete the drying process. He decided to sleep in the bunkhouse with the door open and his clothes on the railing seats, just in case any four-legged thieves came around. When he had enough strings to hold all the fish and it was all up and drying, he went to the house to help Dawn get the other fish pickled. They had over thirty pounds of trout and the three-gallon crock would hold about thirty pounds. They could probably find a use for any leftover trout, if there was any. He would leave the crock in the house overnight and carry it up to the bunkhouse and put it in a corner tomorrow.

Chapter 16

HERE IT WAS Sunday evening, and a week from tomorrow, Matt would have to go to town to school. At least he would have friends he had made camping last weekend. Karen seemed like more of a friend than a teacher, so going back to school wouldn't be too bad. Also, everyone was anxious to go camping again, so that was something to look forward to. Matt was also looking forward to showing everyone more of the things he knew about the outdoors. He didn't feel he was especially smart, but he had just had a better opportunity to learn different things which would come in handy throughout his life.

As usual Matt and Dawn kept busy all week and the time sailed by. Suddenly, they realized it was Saturday and they both hoped Shorty would be here, at least overnight. Dawn had baked bread and made fresh doughnuts, just in case Shorty should arrive. She wanted to make him feel welcome, which wouldn't be too hard to do when they were alone together.

Shorty arrived at the ranch before dark. He told them the roundup was going well, and it should be finished before the next weekend. Dawn and Matt each gave him a hug and welcomed him home. For the first time since he had left his parents home, he felt as if he was really coming home. Never before had a place felt so much like home as the R-R. They say, 'Home is where you hang your hat,' and from now on, the R-R would be where Shorty Stout would hang up his hat! They decided to have another easy weekend of doing very little. After keeping busy from daylight until dark every day since spring, it was different to have time to do nothing. After a light lunch and a couple of doughnuts, it was time for bed. Again Matt insisted that they go to the bunkhouse, and he would stay in the house. Shorty and Dawn walked hand in hand up to the bunkhouse. Shorty lit the table lamp so they could see to get ready for bed. Dawn got a block of wood, used as a bench at the table, and carried it over in front of the bunk to set the lamp on. She told Shorty, "I liked last weekend at the valley in the sun. We can pretend the lamp is the sun!" They helped each other to undress and lay down on the double bunk. Dawn said, "It sure was nice that someone built this wide bunk, it's been handy to have recently." Shorty didn't say anything, he just smiled. An hour later, the lamp was put out so they could get at least some sleep before morning.

When morning came, Shorty felt it was his turn to get breakfast ready. Dawn usually got breakfast ready, and Matt had done so a few times. He was out of bed at daylight and had a fire going in the kitchen stove a few minutes later. He had water on heating for tea as he fried bacon. He broke half a dozen eggs in a shallow bowl and dipped bread in it and fried it in the pan he had cooked the bacon in. He had just enough for three slices of fried bread for each one. With a few pieces of bacon each, bread to toast if it was wanted and plenty of jam too. Just as he was finishing up Dawn arrived; Matt would be here shortly as he was checking the stock. Soon they were all sitting down and to a good breakfast.

Since this was to be a lazy day, they decided to saddle up and go riding. There was no particular destination in mind, but eventually they arrived in town. A stop at the teacher's residence seemed like a necessity, so their mounts were pointed in that direction. As they neared the house, they could see a horse tied nearby and Shorty recognized the horse as belonging to Randy Ripley. Karen came to the door, followed by Randy, amid many greetings. She told them they were just about to have a lunch and asked if they would join them. A few minutes later, they were all seated around the table enjoying a nice meal. Afterwards, as they sat and talked over a cup of tea Randy asked Dawn, "When are you going to put a ring in this old bull's nose and tame him down? He's been hanging around eating you out of house and home, so you should put him to work, if you think you can get any work out of him!"

Dawn grinned and answered, "Well, I don't know about his nose, but I'm going to put a ring on his hand. We are getting married in a couple of weeks. If you talk really nice and behave yourself, you might get an invite."

Randy was shocked! He hadn't really expected to hear that Shorty and Dawn were getting married. After a few seconds, he began to recover and congratulated them both. He told Shorty he was getting a woman who was one in a million. Karen spoke then, "I think Dawn is getting a good man too. He is probably the best man in five hundred miles. I think they were meant for each other, don't you, Matt?"

"Yes, I do," Matt replied, "I know they are very happy when they are together, and I am too. We are going to be a family. I hope someday to have a baby brother or sister so I can show them some of the things I have learned," Shorty said. "Matt, when I marry your mother, I'm getting the best son a man could ask for. I'm going to be very proud to tell people you are my son!" Matt got up and walked over to Shorty and put his arms around him. His eyes were bright and he couldn't speak; Shorty's condition was almost identical to Matt's. Not one word was spoken, by anyone, for a full two minutes, and then Matt released Shorty and slowly walked outside.

There was silence in the room for another minute or two, and then Dawn said, "I think it's about time for us to hit the trail. We will let you know as soon as we get a date and time set. Matt will be coming to school so he will keep you informed. Thank you for the lunch and I'll probably be talking to you soon."

Everybody went outside as they mounted up and turned toward home. As they rode along, Dawn said, "I will have to tell Angela of our plans, but it's a long ride to the Axe and back for today. I can write a note for you to give to her but you will have to explain the rest to her. Maybe I should wait until tomorrow and ride over to talk to her. What do you think I should do?"

Shorty smiled as he said, "You just write the note, and I'll deliver it to her. I guess I'm going to find out sooner or later how to talk to my sister-in law. If I tell her tonight, I can guarantee she will be on your doorstep before nine o'clock tomorrow morning to get all the details!"

Dawn laughed as she said, "I guess you know my sister as well as I do. You can tell her everything, but she will still be over here to get it from me! The whole country will know before the week is out!" All three had smiles on their face as they rode into the yard at the ranch. After the horses were unsaddled, Dawn thought most of the jam she and Karen had made should go out to the root cellar. It was carefully packed in boxes to be carried to the underground storehouse. Shorty commented on the shelves Matt had made and also the vegetable bins. The jam was placed on the top shelf as Dawn would soon be making pickles to fill the others. When the vegetables were all in, it would look like a small store.

Later, all three went to the bunkhouse and sat on the porch. Dawn and Shorty talked of their upcoming wedding. Both wanted just a simple ceremony, but they knew that whether they wanted it or not, there was going to be a party afterward. If the bunks hadn't been built in the bunkhouse, it could have been held here, but there was no room now. Dawn went to prepare an early supper so Shorty could get a good night's sleep when he returned to the Axe. The meal was eaten slowly, but soon it was time for Shorty to leave. He got a hug from Matt and a hug and kiss from

Dawn. It would be only four or five days until he returned, but it looked a lot longer to all three of them.

Dawn had given Shorty a note for Angela, telling her of their upcoming wedding. She knew Angela would be here in the morning if she got the note from Shorty tonight. When Shorty rode into the yard at the Axe, he unsaddled and put his horse in the corral. He then went to the main house to give the note to Angela. When he knocked on the door, Xavier invited him in while he went to get Angela. Shorty passed her the note and stood, hat in hand, by the door while she read it. She came out with a scream that stood everyone's hair on end. She then jumped at Shorty and wrapped her arms around him and kissed him. Xavier tried to find out what was going on, but with Angela crying and laughing at the same time as she was trying to talk; he couldn't make out a word. Finally he got the note from Angela and read it. He shook Shorty's hand and gave him a hug. Shorty was congratulated and welcomed into the family. He was asked if a date was set yet and where the wedding would take place.

Shorty answered, "We are thinking of Saturday, two weeks from yesterday. We both want just a small wedding at the church in town or at the minister's house. We can't afford and neither of us want a big expensive wedding."

By now Angela was able to talk and asked Shorty, "When did you ask Dawn to marry you?" Shorty answered, "I didn't. She asked me a month ago, but told me to think about it for a couple of weeks. She asked me again last weekend and I agreed. I still don't think I'm good enough for her but she must think I am. Now, I better get out to my bunk and get some sleep before work tomorrow. Good night, all."

About seven thirty the next morning Angela mounted up and rode toward the R-R. School had started so Matt was in town attending school. Angela tied her horse and went to the house to see Dawn. "Why didn't you tell me you were getting married?" were the first words out of her mouth, "Shorty could have told me a week ago!"

"We didn't know until last weekend," Dawn answered, "I could have ridden over to tell you today, but I had a lot to do here. We want a small wedding that we can afford. We don't have room for a party or dance afterwards because we have bunks in the bunkhouse now."

"But Dawn," Angela insisted, "There has to be a reception and dance. Maybe we could have it at the ranch, but that is a long way to travel from town. We'll come up with something before then!" They talked for a while longer before Angela mounted up and left. When she hit the main trail, she didn't go to the ranch, but toward town. She got there at noon, just as the children were going home for dinner. The schoolteacher was on her way home to get her own dinner. Angela stopped to tell her the news, but found she had heard about it yesterday. She invited Angela to her home for a cup of tea and Angela told her she was trying to find a place to have a reception and dance after the wedding.

Karen said, "I have to talk to the school board about some things for the school. When I do, I can see about using the schoolhouse for the reception and dance. It would be a community event, so I don't think there will be a problem."

Angela agreed the school would be the ideal place for the reception and dance. There hadn't been a dance since the small one at the R-R bunkhouse. She told Karen she would be in to see her later in the week, so they could finalize their plans. Angela said good-bye to Karen and mounted her horse and turned toward home. Going past the school, she saw Matt talking to some other children. She stopped to visit for a minute before continuing on her way. She could see Matt was excited and happy that his mother was marrying Shorty. Soon she was on her way back to the ranch to do some more planning.

Everyone was busy throughout the week, some with work, some with everyday chores, some with school, and some with planning a big after-wedding party. Shorty arrived at the R-R on Friday evening and announced that he had the weekend off. He also said while doing the branding, they had separated all the R-R stock. There was about thirty head in a holding pen at the ranch and the three of them could go over tomorrow and drive them to Lost Valley with the others. A lot of them were younger cattle, which would replace the ones sold, with breeding stock.

Shorty looked at Dawn and asked, "How would you like to take a couple of days to ride up north to find a land office? We should find out about claiming Lost Valley before we get married. I don't know if a wife can claim land or not. If we could each file on a quarter section, we would have the whole valley. I was going to suggest doing this after we got married, but we should do it before, just in case. Matt, do you think you could look after things here if we were away for three days? We shouldn't be any longer than that!"

"Sure!" Matt said. "I can do that. There is very little to do now anyway. The grass is still good and there is lots of water. There are just the pigs and chickens to look after. Even going to school, I can look after everything here. You two go ahead and get that valley for us, even if it takes a week!"

Dawn said, "I don't like to leave you alone, Matt, but I know you can take care of everything. I won't worry about a thing because I know it will be in good hands. Now, let's get to bed, we have a cattle drive ahead of us tomorrow!" Matt went to his room and Dawn took Shorty's hand and went to the bunkhouse. Less than an hour later, they were both sleep. They would be spending a couple of nights camping and they would be alone then too.

On the R-R, early rising was normal and the morning of a cattle drive was no exception. Matt had a fire going and starting breakfast, so Dawn gave him a hand, while Shorty fed the horses and checked the other stock. Dawn packed a lunch for them as it would probably take most of the day to move the cattle. Breakfast was soon over and the three cowhands were on the way to a cattle drive. When they arrived at the holding pen, it was only a few minutes work to open the gate and push the cattle out where they were turned toward the valley. With one rider on each side and one behind, the cattle were moved slowly toward the valley. These range cattle weren't as quiet as the valley cattle, but by moving slowly they gave very little trouble. It was just a matter of letting them move at their own speed, with a little push now and then. Dawn had made sandwiches and would pass one to Shorty and Matt occasionally, so they could eat as they rode and keep an eye on the cattle.

It was getting late in the afternoon when they came in sight of the valley entrance. This would be the ticklish part if the cattle decided not to cooperate. Once a couple of cattle decided to start into the gully, the rest were sure to follow. If the cattle refused to enter the gully, they could have a real problem on their hands. They crowded them as much as they dared without having them panic. About all they could do was to wait and see and hope for the best. Several were sniffing around the entrance, but seemed to be in no hurry to take the first step. After half an hour, one cow started walking slowly up the gully, several minutes later two more followed. Ten minutes after the first cow entered the gully; all were strung out single file going up the dry streambed. The riders breathed a sigh of relief and followed the cattle up to the valley. Once into that lush valley, there would be little danger they would ever want to leave. As they entered the valley the cattle dropped their heads and began eating the rich grass. It looked like these cattle were at home on the range. Shorty looked at Dawn and said, "You have a good herd of cattle, on the best grass in the west, and no work to look after them. You are one lucky lady!"

Dawn replied, "Yes, I am a lucky lady, because one day you found Matt and me in the woods. If you hadn't found this valley and these cattle, we would have nothing. These are not my cattle. They are *our* cattle! They belong to you and me and Matt, one ranch, three partners!" Matt agreed with his mother on that point!

Now that the cattle were moved, it was time to head back home. They talked as they rode along, and Shorty wondered if they should leave tonight or wait and get an early start in the morning. Matt said, "If you leave tonight you can probably get ten miles, that's a lot more than you would get with an early start tomorrow. One day should put you where you want to be, so you would be there on Monday morning. You should only have to camp one night each way. Most of the camping supplies are ready to go and I can look after the ranch and go to school."

Dawn agreed that would be the best plan. They would pack some food, bedrolls, and eating utensils. That would be enough for the distance they were travelling. As soon as they reached home, Matt started getting all the things ready for Dawn and Shorty to take with them. There was no hot water, so Dawn and Shorty had a bath in cold water. They changed their clothes and took a change of clothes with them. When they were ready to go, there was still two hours of daylight left. Matt got a hug from both Shorty and Dawn; they mounted up and rode off into the sunset. This was true, as they had to ride west to hit the main trail north. They both knew Matt could take care of everything so they weren't going to worry about anything except getting the Lost Valley.

They didn't rush, but kept the horses at a fast walk. They would cover a lot of ground without tiring the horses too much. When there was about half an hour of daylight left, they began to look for a good spot to spend the night. They could sleep almost anywhere, but a place to make a fire and get water would be good. They found a small hollow with some bushes, some of them dead, which would supply them with firewood.

Shorty stretched a rope between two bushes to put the tarp over. Dawn moved any sticks and rocks from this area, so they would have a smooth place to sleep. They found a few stones and made a fire pit, so they could have a fire. They had eaten just before leaving, so they weren't hungry, but a fire in the morning would be handy to make tea and fry bacon over. Dawn spread the bedroll tarps, one on top of the other and put the bedrolls on top, making one bed for two people. When darkness was complete, their camp was too and they were soon under the covers. Dawn had pulled their bed toward the fire pit so they could see the sky. They lay on their bed watching the stars, until Dawn thought of something more interesting to do. Half an hour later, the camp was quiet and both were asleep.

At first light, the fire was going and bacon roasting on a stick. Tea was just about ready, and Shorty had saddled the horses. They had finished breakfast, broke camp, and were in the saddle by the time the sun began to shine. In the late afternoon, they came to the city of Medicine Hat. It was a big place of about ten thousand people. Neither one wanted to be in a town with this many people, but they were here and had a job to do. A stable was found on the outskirts of town where they could leave their horses, and they hired a hack to take them around town. The driver was asked to take them to the nearest land office. This was Sunday, so they knew it would be closed, but they wanted to know where it was located. The driver said the office would be open at seven thirty or eight o'clock in the morning. They went back to the stable where their horses were and asked the driver if he could pick them up in the morning and take them to the land office. He was paid for the ride they had taken, and Shorty gave him an extra fifty cents to be there in the morning.

They asked about sleeping in the hay in the stable and were told it was OK, since their horses were being boarded here. They asked about a place to get a bath and were directed to a place not too far away, where they each had a bath and Shorty shaved also. They decided to wait until morning to change into their fresh clothes. They walked around the local area, not going far so as not to get lost, until it was time to hit the hay.

They were awake at daylight and found a place to eat. Soon the man they had hired the day before arrived to take them into town. At the office they explained they each wanted to file on a homestead. They were shown a map of their area and could see the Axe and the R-R were marked on it. They told the man there was a small valley in the hills they wanted to file on, or even buy.

He told them, "That area is mostly wasteland, just trees, brush, and hills. You could probably find better land someplace on the open prairie!" They insisted this was the spot they wanted because of the valley. He told them since it was poor land it hadn't been surveyed and probably wouldn't be.

He said, "I'll tell you what we will do. Because it isn't good land, you will need more to make a living off it. You can each file on a half section, or three hundred and twenty acres. We will pay fifty dollars to have it surveyed, if it costs more you will have to pay the extra. It will cost you ten dollars each to file for a homestead. Since it isn't farmland, you won't have to break ground or plant crops, but you will have to build and be living on the land before five years are up. You will also have to have at least fifty head of cattle on the land inside of five years. Now, any questions?"

Dawn said, "We are going to be partners on this project. Do we have to build two homes or can we just build one home for the both of us?" He answered, "Since you are going to be partners, we can have it surveyed as one block, and one home would be sufficient! If you kept it as two separate lots, you would each have to build on your respective lots."

Shorty then asked, "How soon do we have to have it surveyed? It's getting late in the season, and it will be rough going in winter. We probably couldn't get it surveyed before spring!"

The agent said, "Since it is late in the season and it is rough land, I will allow you until the end of July of next year to have it done and the information from the surveyor sent to me at this office. Anything else?" Neither Dawn nor Shorty could think of any other questions. They got the land agent's address, and he told them if they thought of any other questions, feel free to write to him, he would be glad to help if he could. The papers were signed and the fee paid, they got a copy of the contract to show the surveyor. They thanked the man for his help and shook hands all around. Shorty and Dawn walked out, the prospective owners of a big piece of land in the hills. They were trying to get a ride back to the stable when their original driver showed up.

He said, "I thought you would be through in there by now. I got a couple of fares in the area and passed by here a couple of times looking for you. Climb aboard, and I'll have you back with your horses in no time!" When they arrived, Shorty paid the fare and gave the man an extra dollar. They were so happy with the way everything had turned out, he thought they should celebrate and buy a meal for themselves.

The driver told them, "There is a good place to eat just down the street, I'll take you there for free." In a couple of minutes he dropped them off at the place he had mentioned. They thanked him again as he drove off. Inside, they ordered a meal they didn't have to get ready and enjoyed it thoroughly. On the way back to the stable, they bought a few small presents to take to friends and family. Their business in the city was complete, and they both wanted to leave. They paid for their horses keep and turned them toward home. It would be good to get back to the R-R, where they would meet only people they knew. Cities might be OK for some people, but these people wanted very little to do with them!

They rode steadily until the sun went down and then started looking for a camping spot. They found a spot that was suitable and soon had a camp set up to their liking. The shelter was put up, a fireplace prepared, and the bed was made. Under full darkness they crawled into the blankets and discussed their good fortune in being able to homestead the Lost Valley. They had to laugh when they thought of filing on 'wasteland'. The valley was the richest land to be found on the prairies. They knew Matt would be very pleased as well!

Dawn said to Shorty, "We won't have time this week, but after we are married, we should spend some time back around the lake. We should decide roughly where the lines of our property will go. Outside of the valley, the land is rough and not much good, but we should do some exploring to see if there is anything out there. If we find groves of trees or something useful, we can include it in our claim, and as soon as we get back, I want to look into hiring a surveyor. I would like to have the land legally ours as soon as possible!"

Shorty agreed they would have to do some looking around to see if there was anything in the area they would like to include in their property. He also wanted to get it surveyed as soon as possible. It was going to be theirs, and they wanted everything legal. Soon both were asleep and dreaming of building a home in Lost Valley.

When the sun made its appearance in the morning, they were already in the saddle. They had eaten breakfast, broken camp, and now were homeward bound. There wasn't really any rush, but both were anxious to get home. The only stops that were made was to rest and feed the horses and themselves. Even then, it was late evening when they hit town. They decided to make a short visit at Karen's to tell her the news and maybe get a cup of hot tea. Karen was glad to hear the news and told them Matt was doing fine. She also told them almost everyone in the country was looking forward to the party after they got married.

After a quick visit and a hot cup of tea, they were back in the saddle again, heading for home. They were both anxious to tell Matt the good news. It was dark when they reached the ranch, but they could see a light in the bunkhouse. The horses were unsaddled quickly and they both hurried to the bunkhouse where Matt was waiting in the doorway.

He was glad to see them and waiting for their news. Dawn said, "Matt, we were hoping each of us could file on a quarter section of land, covering the valley. We didn't get a quarter section each." Matt's face fell and his jaw dropped almost to his chest. Dawn continued, "We each got a half section with Lost Valley included!" Matt's face lit up and he grabbed his mother in a bear hug. When he let go of her, he grabbed Shorty. All three were laughing and dancing around the bunkhouse.

Shorty began to speak, "There are some conditions though. Because this is 'wasteland' we don't have to break ground and plant crops, but we do have to have at least fifty head of cattle on this land and build and be living on it inside of five years!"

Matt let out a whoop and began dancing around the bunkhouse all over again. It didn't take a genius to see he was very happy! Everyone was too excited to sleep, but it was late so they crawled into their bunks and closed their eyes. It seemed like only a short time later the rooster told them it was time to get up. Excited or not, they had all slept soundly.

Matt didn't want to go to school, but both Dawn and Shorty insisted it was important to get an education. Shorty told him, "We are all partners on this ranch, and someday it will be yours. There will be records to be kept and bills to be paid. If you can't do it yourself, you will have to hire someone to do it for you and that is expensive. Better to be able to do it yourself, and then you know it's done right. It is always safer to do things yourself, so you know exactly what is going on." Reluctantly, Matt agreed he should go to school.

Shorty had to go over to the ranch and explain why he missed work. He felt it was important to keep working as the money would be needed until they had more cattle on the ranch. As soon as he had eaten, he saddled up and set out for the Axe.

Angela was the first person he met when he rode into the yard. She smiled and said, "Starting married life early are you? If so, why are you back here?"

Shorty explained why he had been away and that they were homesteading the lost Valley and surrounding area. She gave him a hug and a kiss and congratulated him on getting the valley. He explained that since it was considered 'wasteland,' they had been allowed to file on a half section each. He also told Angela he wanted to keep working so they would have some money coming in. She assured him there would always be a job for him here if he wanted it.

Shorty said, "We need to find a surveyor to mark out the land we want. We will also have to spend some time looking around to see what we want to cover with our claim. Is there a good surveyor in town?" Angela told him there was a good surveyor that they had hired a few times. When they had a rough outline decided, he would be a good man to get.

Shorty decided he should get to work so Angela directed him to where Xavier and the crew were working. He knew the hands would give him a rough time about missing work. As he expected, when the boys saw him they all had something to say. Gus was first with, "A Diller, a dollar, a ten o'clock scholar, what makes you come so soon? You used to come Monday morning, but now you come Wednesday at noon!" Another said, "What happened? You overslept till half past Wednesday?" They all had a good laugh and got in a dig of their own. He explained to the boss that he and Dawn had left Saturday evening and rode to Medicine Hat and filed on a homestead taking in the Lost Valley. It was described as 'wasteland,' so they were allowed to claim a half section each, covering Lost Valley and the surrounding area. "Next weekend Dawn, Matt, and I are going scouting around to see what area we want to include in our piece of ground," Shorty explained. "We have to get it surveyed ourselves, but the government will pay fifty dollars and if it costs more we will have to pay the rest."

Shorty was congratulated by all the hands for getting the homestead for Lost Valley. Somebody said, "Now, don't you forget you have a wedding to attend this weekend. We don't want you going off and getting lost so we have to call off the party!" This brought a wave of laughter from the whole crew.

Work went on through the week and since Shorty had missed two days, he worked on Friday to make up for one day. He arrived at the R-R just in time for supper. They talked as they ate and brought each other up to date on their weeks work. Matt told them everybody was talking about the dance being held at the school after the wedding. Most of the students had stayed after school to help move the desks to the woodshed and clean up. A lot of them would be at the dance also, at least for a while. Dawn added that Angela was looking for a place to hold the dance, and Karen got permission from the school board to use the school. They might have a small wedding, but it looked like a big party afterward.

Their plans were to have Xavier and Angela, Karen and Randy, and Matt with them when they got married at the minister's home. The wedding was to take place at 4:00 p.m. on Saturday. It looked like there would be a reception and dance afterward. They decided they could live with that, after all, nobody said they had to stay all night. They had plans to sneak away by themselves and leave the others to party as long as they wanted to.

They discussed the homestead also and planned to go looking around next weekend if possible. They could leave here on Friday evening and camp in the valley. They were claiming a section, or one square mile. One weekend should allow them to explore enough area to decide roughly where they wanted their boundary lines. The main thing was to ensure they covered the main valley and the small inner valley as well.

Right now they decided it was time for bed because, although it wasn't late, it looked as though there would be very little sleep for them tomorrow night. All three went to the bunkhouse, where Matt claimed the top left one and Shorty and Dawn got to use the double wide one. Soon all three were asleep and dreaming of the future, together, in the Lost Valley.

Chapter 17

DAYLIGHT CAUGHT NONE of the three in bed. Matt and Shorty were looking after the stock while Dawn got breakfast ready. When the chores were done and the boys washed up, Dawn had breakfast on the table. As breakfast disappeared they discussed their plans for the day and evening.

Dawn had bought a new pair of pants and a shirt for Matt on their trip. Shorty had bought a new shirt, but he had new pants he would wear for the wedding. Dawn had a new dress she had worn only once that she planned to wear as working on the ranch she didn't get dressed up very often. They planned to ride to town and leave the horses at Karen's and change clothes there as well. By doing this, when it came time to sneak away by themselves, they could do it unobserved. It was looking like a beautiful day and evening, so their bedrolls would be taken along too. Karen already knew of Dawn's plan and was going to help them pull off their escape. No one was in a hurry to do much today, they were just finalizing plans for the evening. After the noon meal, all three planned to have a bath and get slicked up for the wedding.

Every big pot Dawn had was on the stove full of heating water. Matt and Shorty had shined up their boots and everyone was just about ready for the trip to town. All three were looking forward to being a family.

Time passed slowly when they weren't busy but it was getting close to lunchtime. After a light lunch, everyone got soap and hot water and went in separate directions, Matt and Dawn to their rooms and Shorty to the bunkhouse. It didn't take long to bathe and put on clean clothes and shortly all three were ready to go with their wedding clothes wrapped up to keep them clean. The horses were saddled and soon three riders were on their way to town.

When they reached town, they went directly to Karen's. The horses were left here where they were out of the way, but ready for a quick getaway. They took a few minutes to wipe off any dust they might have picked up and change their clothes. Shortly after their arrival, Angela and Xavier came looking for them as it wasn't long until they were expected at the minister's home. Shorty and Dawn wanted a short, simple ceremony and the minister respected their wishes. In half an hour, Dawn was Mrs. Shorty Stout! They went back to Karen's where she prepared a wedding supper. Later they sat and talked as the celebrating wasn't due to start until about seven o'clock. Once things got underway, the party would probably last all night! The newlyweds didn't expect to see the finish as they had plans to disappear shortly after midnight.

Teams pulling wagons, riders, and people on foot were going past Karen's door heading toward the schoolhouse. It seemed as though it was time for the newlyweds to go and face the music. A small procession, led by Mr. and Mrs. Stout, walked down the street to the schoolhouse. Everyone was waiting outside to greet Dawn and Shorty. The wedding party lined up outside to accept greetings, handshakes, and congratulations from everyone. A lot of the well-wishers Shorty had never met before and some Dawn didn't know, although she had been around here a lot longer than Shorty had been.

The musicians were among the first to congratulate Dawn and Shorty and they soon had the music underway. It seemed as if the whole country was there, from grandparents to children and newborn babies, no one was going to miss out on a good party!

The dance had been going on for only a short time, when someone requested the musicians to play Shorty's Song. Every musical instrument was used during the rendition of this tune. Everyone who had heard the song before joined in on the singing and when the song ended, the cheers and applause went on for five minutes! When the cheering dropped below a dull roar, the schoolteacher, Karen, went to the middle of the floor and finally got everyone to be quiet. She said. "If everyone will just be quiet for a few minutes, I think we all would like to hear a few words from the newlyweds. I know we have a party underway, but just bear with us for a few more minutes, and we will all get back to the party. Now, here is Mr. and Mrs. Stout, Dawn and Shorty to most of us!"

Shorty started by saying, "The schoolteacher wants us to say a few words. Well, you will get very few from me!" At this, everyone cheered and clapped. Shorty continued, "First I would like to thank the boss, Xavier and his wife, Angela. If they hadn't hired me I probably never would have met Dawn. Next, I guess I have to thank Matt and Angela. It took them a while, but they finally got us together like they wanted. I also want to thank the hands on the Axe, Randy, and everyone else who helped to get the R-R in shape and the bunkhouse built. I can't name everyone, but I want you to know we appreciate everything everyone did to help out. Now I better let my new wife have a few words."

Dawn smiled and began, "I too would like to thank everyone for all the help they have given us. I would like to give a thank you to my elder sister, who, although she is sometimes a pain in the neck kept trying to push Shorty and me together. I guess Angela and Matt could see that we were meant for each other, even though it took us a lot longer to realize it ourselves. Most of you probably don't know about it, but Shorty and Gus found a lot of our cattle back in the hills in a lost valley. We have taken homestead claims on the valley and some of the surrounding area. Now, a very special thank you to a very special man who stopped one day to help a woman and her son cut some wood." With this Dawn threw her arms around Shorty and kissed him. Matt put his arms around both of them. There was a roar of applause and cheers for a few minutes before the music could be heard again.

Now, the musicians got down to some serious playing as there was hardly a break between tunes. The floor thundered to the tune of stomping feet and the windows probably would have bulged if they hadn't all been opened wide. There were mothers dancing with babies, grandfathers dancing with school girls, and everyone who could find a partner was dancing, or at least trying to as the room was almost too crowded for anyone to move. This was one wedding and dance that was going to go down in history as the biggest party ever to be held in this part of Alberta, and it would be remembered for a long time to come!

Shorty and Dawn danced together a few times, but they were much in demand as dancing partners. Once in a while when a waltz was played, they were pushed together and allowed to dance. They enjoyed the few times they got to dance together, but they also enjoyed seeing everyone else having a good time. Matt had danced with his mother, Angela, Karen, and also most of the girls he was going to school with. He was almost as popular as the star attractions!

There was no end to the food to be eaten. Tables had been setup against the school and everyone was expected to help themselves. As always, there was some alcohol around, but a few of the men were trying to see that no trouble got started. This was too nice an occasion to let a few people with alcohol spoil it.

Many people had commented on the great time they were having. So far, there had been no problems, and it looked as if it would stay that way. About midnight, Matt sneaked away in the darkness and hurried to Karen's place. He saddled his horse and put a bridle on Karen's horse. Shorty and Dawn had slipped outside to the food tables to get something to eat. Matt rode slowly down the street until he approached the schoolhouse and then galloped away toward the R-R, leading Karen's horse. Most people thought the galloping horses belonged to the newlyweds. A few cowboys jumped on their horses to give chase and bring them back. Dawn and Shorty had stepped back into the shadows, and when Matt went by, they headed for Karen's place. Shorty saddled their horses after they had both changed their clothes, and when in the saddle, he and Dawn walked their horses slowly away, but not in the direction of home. About twenty minutes of ride brought them to a sheltered hollow they had been hoping to find. The horses were unsaddled, and they spread their bedrolls on the ground.

After Matt had led the chase for a mile or so, he slowed down to a walk and turned off the trail and then back to town. He was soon back at the school, and with a grin and a wink to Karen, he rejoined the party. No one was really surprised or disappointed that the newly married couple had given them the slip, and the party continued as before.

The party was beginning to slow down by the time daylight arrived. Some people had left earlier, but there are always a few diehards that just won't quit as long as there is music being played. When the musicians started packing up their instruments, everyone decided it was time to go home. The last twelve hours would go down in history as the best time anyone had ever known in the area!

When daylight arrived, Mr. and Mrs. Stout were still in their blankets. They didn't have to be anyplace at a certain time and couldn't come up with a reason to rush. After all, a couple didn't get married too many times in a lifetime. Eventually they decided to get out of the sack and go back to the ranch. Matt was probably headed in that direction by now, and the snack they had eaten at midnight had pretty well worn off. They would go home and start their first day of married life with a good meal.

There was no sign of Matt when they reached the ranch. Dawn started a fire while Shorty unsaddled the horses. Water was heating for tea and bacon was frying when Shorty came through the door. Very soon, there was bacon and eggs, toast, jam, and plenty of hot tea for the newly married couple to eat, and before they were finished eating, Matt arrived looking pleased and hungry. He had stayed to help Karen get the school back in shape for classes the next morning. Matt sat down and helped to finish off the breakfast that remained.

He told them the dance had continued until cockcrow before finally winding down. He hadn't heard of any trouble, and he thought everyone had enjoyed themselves. Shorty told Matt, "I am going to keep working at the Axe for a while at least. We are going to scout around the area surrounding Lost Valley next weekend. I will probably be here Thursday evening as the roundup is finished. If so, we will probably go to the lake on Friday to start looking around. I think you should be there with us as it's as much yours as ours."

They talked of what they would need so it would be ready when they were. Each would carry a small axe and a knife. They should also have some brightly coloured rags to tie on bushes or trees. At first they would just look around and see if there were groves of trees which would be useful or even other small valleys. When they had checked over as much land as possible, they would start marking a rough outline of the area they wanted. If they could get a general outline for their section, the next step would be to get a surveyor to line it off properly. They all hoped to get it surveyed this fall, but if not, they would at least have a start on it.

Shorty and Dawn went up to the bunkhouse to catch up on some of their lost sleep, while Matt began to check over their equipment they would need for camping. He hunted up a couple of small hand axes and sharpened them a bit more. He then got a piece of leather and made a sheath for them so they could be carried on a belt. These would come in handy for blazing trees or cutting brush or for cutting small sticks for tying rags to, if there were no trees. Matt unpacked the big pack and repacked it again. First in were a couple of raincoats; their metal camping utensils went in next, followed by a piece of small rope like they had used on the bunks. He found a piece of red rag, which he tore into strips, bundled up, and tied in a loose knot. In his head he was making a list of things to be taken from the house, including the food. The Dutch oven, frying pan, and teapot, plus a small pail for carrying water would be the most important items. For food there would be bacon, biscuit mix, salt, pepper, and tea. Bacon and eggs were good for breakfast, and the bacon would be used in the trout he would catch. He would also get a few potatoes from the garden to eat fried or baked. He checked over the shelter tarp, rolled it tightly, and had it ready to be tied behind a saddle. He had just about everything they would need, but he would add to the list through the week as he thought of something else.

As he was working, he thought he should do something nice for his mother and Shorty. He was thinking of a nice meal and figured he would get some vegetables from the garden and have them for supper. He went to the garden and got about a dozen potatoes, some carrots, a turnip, and a cabbage of about five pounds each. Matt checked the corn and saw some of it was ready to eat, so he picked six big ears, which made him quite a load to carry back to the house. He stopped by the barn and washed everything well before taking them inside. He would like to have some meat to go with the vegetables, but all they had right now was the dried and smoked fish. He decided the vegetables would make a fine meal by themselves and was working away at getting the vegetables ready when he heard a horse outside. He looked out and saw it was Karen, so he went out to help her unsaddle her horse.

She asked Matt, "Is your mother and Shorty here? I brought them a nice roast of beef so they wouldn't go hungry." Matt told her that they were up at the bunkhouse having a nap. They headed for the house, and Matt explained what he was doing. With the roast Karen had brought and the vegetables Matt was preparing they would have a fine meal ready before long. The roast was put in the oven with salt, pepper, and a chopped onion. Matt went out to get a couple more ears of corn while Karen kept working at the vegetables.

As they worked, Matt told Karen about the trip to the valley next weekend. He said they wanted to explore around the valley to see what they wanted to include in their homestead. Karen thought that sounded interesting and wanted to know when they were going. She thought the valley was a beautiful spot and would like to go along. It would be interesting to see what was in the hills surrounding the valley.

Matt said, "If Shorty gets here on Thursday evening, we are going on Friday. He plans to keep working on the Axe for a while anyway. If we can decide what area we want for ours, we will try to get it surveyed this fall if possible."

Karen was thinking and said, "Matt, don't say anything about me going along. I'll come out here Saturday or possibly even Friday evening. If you aren't here, I'll go to the valley and surprise Dawn and Shorty. I would love to go exploring around there. I guess because the country is so rough, most of the travelling will be on foot. I have another tarp at home that I'll give you tomorrow. That way we can put up a shelter for us and give Dawn and Shorty some privacy. We can discuss it more next week at school."

The vegetables were ready, and the meat was just about done. About three thirty, the vegetables were put on to cook. They were hoping Dawn and Shorty wouldn't show up until the meal was ready, as they planned to take it up to the bunkhouse and eat supper there. The roast was taken from the pan, and Karen made gravy with the juice left behind. When all was in readiness, they got the dishes they would need and put them in a box. Matt went up to the woodshed at the bunkhouse and got the handbarrow Shorty had made. The meal, dishes, and teapot were all loaded up and carried up to the bunkhouse. As Matt was about to open the door, it swung open for him. Both Shorty and Dawn were surprised to find supper being delivered to them. Matt went to get another chair as Karen set the table and began dishing out the food. The wonderful smells made everyone even hungrier than they already were. Everyone dug in, and the food began to disappear in a hurry. When everyone was filled and having a final cup of tea, Matt and Karen gathered up the dishes and leftovers to be returned to the house. They sat and talked for a while until Shorty said it was time for him to return to the Axe. It would make a lot of riding to come home every night so he would stay there and come home on the weekends.

After Shorty was on his way, Karen and Matt washed the dishes and put everything away. Dawn suggested Karen stay overnight and ride into town with Matt in the morning. They could leave a few minutes earlier so she would have time to change her clothes before school. Karen liked Dawn's idea because she could sleep in the bunkhouse again. A short time later, they were all in bed as no one had gotten much sleep the previous night. In the morning, after a good breakfast, Matt and Karen rode into town together to begin another week of school. The week seemed to pass quickly, and soon it was Thursday evening. If Shorty arrived from the Axe, the three R-R owners would be heading to the valley in the morning. Shorty arrived late as he had eaten supper at the ranch. They got everything packed and ready to start with first light. Dawn made a big batch of biscuit mix to take along and bake in the Dutch oven. All three hit the sack early for a good nights sleep and to get an early start in the morning.

Dawn had the stove going and cooking breakfast, and as soon as it was light enough to see, Shorty and Matt looked after everything outside, saddled the horses, and went in to eat. Breakfast was a hurried affair, as all three explorers were anxious to be moving. A quick cleanup and the horses were loaded up and they were off to the valley. They didn't rush, but kept their mounts moving at a brisk walk. It was only a short time later when they approached the entrance to the valley. A ten-minute ride put them at the bottom of the valley, which was beginning to feel like home. The branding camp was chosen as a base, as it was close to water, wood, and the grass was still good for the horses. Camp was laid out quickly, wood secured for a fire and the horses tethered where they could reach water. With the rough, hilly terrain, the scouting would be done on foot.

Dawn had brought along some white rags, Matt had the red ones and each carried a hand ax. The red rags would be used when they had an approximate border to be marked off, the white ones would be used to show something of interest to be checked over later. With the axe, they could chop a trail through tangles of brush or blaze a line where trees or bushes were plentiful.

They were on the east side of the valley so that was where they would start exploring. Where possible, they would travel about a hundred feet apart so more ground could be covered. Dawn suggested using a white rag to mark the outside of the ground already gone over. This would show where they had been and the markers could be picked up on the next sweep. They spread out and tried to keep the person next to them in sight as they negotiated brush thickets, hollows, and other obstacles. By noon they had gone south past the end of the valley and returned to their original starting point. They had found berry patches, a few small groves of pine, and a lot of rough country. It was time for a rest and to get some food inside them. They discussed their progress, which wasn't bad at all and decided to use the afternoon to explore farther east. So far there was nothing very promising, but they wanted to look farther east, just in case. It was hard to say what they might run across farther out. The afternoon passed with similar results to the morning. There was a few hollows with some grass, a few small groves of trees, several small ponds or potholes, and trails made by deer and other animals. By late in the day, they had covered about a quarter of a mile east of the valley. They decided to call it a day, get a good meal, and rest up before another day of exploring.

At the campsite, a fire was started and water put on to heat. Matt went to the lake for a trout as Dawn mixed up some biscuits. It took Matt only a few minutes to get a trout for supper and he soon had it ready and baking. Biscuits were put in the fire to cook and to be ready when the fish was. A short time later, they were sitting around the fire enjoying a hot meal.

Supper had been late and before it was finished, a rider appeared in the lower valley. Karen soon approached the camp, to the surprise of Dawn and Shorty. Matt and Karen grinned knowingly at each other. They explained they had planned this on the wedding weekend while they were getting the meal ready. Karen said she had come to help them explore their homestead. There was still some food left so she helped herself, although she had eaten a bit before she left home.

When the meal was over, Matt and Karen used Karen's tarp to put up a shelter about forty feet away from the first one. The side toward the camp was pegged tightly to the ground, over a pole about five feet off the ground and stretched tight and fastened securely. When they were finished, Karen announced that the Honeymoon Hotel was ready for occupancy. The newlyweds said that wasn't necessary, but Karen and Matt insisted it was. Shortly after darkness settled in, Shorty and Dawn moved their bedrolls to the new shelter. It was time for all to get some rest for a new day of exploring.

When daylight arrived in the valley, Matt and Karen had a fire going and biscuits in the oven, water heating for tea, bacon frying, and eggs waiting to go in the pan. When Dawn and Shorty poked their head out, breakfast was almost ready. No one wasted any time in helping themselves to a good breakfast. As usual, the first few minutes were devoted to eating with hardly a word said. Gradually the eating slowed down and the conversation picked up. They told Karen about yesterday's exploring and what they had found. Today they decided to look beyond the north or lower end of the valley. With breakfast over, they gathered up what they would need and started out. Each carried a small hand ax and a few strips of rags. Shorty thought they should start at the gully, which was the entrance to the valley, and work eastwards at least as far as they had gone yesterday. Everyone found their places and they began. It was slow going, what with trying to keep each other in sight in this rough country, where sometimes a person could be twenty or thirty feet higher or lower than his neighbor. Again they found grass, trees, and a few small ponds, some of which looked to be very deep. They were half a mile east of where they had started when they decided to turn around. When they reached their starting point, they stopped for a short breather and a chat. Karen suggested Matt should take some time off in the afternoon, so he could make supper for them. There was enough time to make one more sweep before stopping for dinner. When this trip was finished, they were all ready for some food and a short rest. After a well-earned rest, they were back at the job of exploring the countryside. One more sweep put them back at the start in the late afternoon. They would make one more trip while Matt was preparing supper for the crew. They all told him to have plenty, as they would be half starved when they got to camp.

First Matt got the fire going and put on lots of wood before going to the lake for a trout. When ready, it was salted and peppered and two slices of bacon placed inside before being well coated with clay. He put the fish in the coals to bake while he chopped bacon very fine and put it in the frying pan to cook. While it was browning, he chopped four or five large potatoes and one large onion and put these in the pan with the bacon. He then made enough biscuits so there would be two for each. These were put in the Dutch oven which was buried in the coals to bake, and he got water heating for tea. Now all he had to do was keep an eye on the cooking supper and wait until the others arrived. He was just moving the Dutch oven back a bit, when three hungry people arrived. The fish was removed from the fire and broken open, the potatoes dished out, and tea poured; biscuits were waiting for when anyone wanted one. Matt had prepared a simple meal that was tasty and filling and enjoyed by everyone. The only thing that could have improved on it was a few of Dawn's doughnuts. They sat around the fire with a last cup of tea and discussed the day's travels. Two sides of the valley had been checked out, and they hadn't found anything of great interest. Shorty was thinking they should make their north line to take in the entrance to the valley, which started north and then turned west. If they ran a line about one hundred yards east of the valley and far enough north to take in the entrance to the valley, if there was anything of interest on the south or west sides, it would be theirs. They would check out the west side tomorrow, but probably wouldn't have time to check out the south end too. Dawn and Karen agreed with Shorty on the north and east boundary and their one square mile would take in whatever there was on the other sides. They still planned to do some exploring on the west side tomorrow, but the time they had left wouldn't be enough to cover the whole area they would claim.

Shortly after the meal was over, darkness began to slip into the valley. It was getting into fall and the days had shortened up considerably. The nights would soon begin to cool off and a warm fire would be welcomed. A good supply of wood had been gathered for their camp and now everyone sat around the fire and talked before bedtime. The explorers soon hit the sack in order to get an early start again in the morning.

At daylight, Karen and Matt were up and about and getting a start on breakfast. There was a bed of coals in fire pit and a few fresh sticks soon had a cheerful blaze going. The Dutch oven was put on the fire to heat while Karen got biscuits ready. Matt was slicing bacon for the pan, and there was one egg left for each camper. Shorty had gone to check on the horses and move them to another area so one spot wouldn't be grazed too closely. Breakfast was ready by the time the camp chores were completed. Breakfast was a hurried affair as they were all anxious to do as much exploring as possible on the last day available to them. The gully, which was the entrance to the valley, would be used as the north boundary for their search area. Again they lined up about a hundred feet apart and marched southward. This side of the valley wasn't quite as rugged as the other sides, in some places there were hollows with good grass and others full of trees. They had made two sweeps before they stopped for a lunch break, and they decided to make one more trip before calling it a day. Shorty would be going to the Axe when he left here, and the others would be heading to the R-R and town. Tomorrow would be another day of school for Matt and Karen.

When the final pass had been made, they decided to go with their original plan of claiming about a hundred yards east of the valley and far enough north to take in the entrance to the valley. The western side of the valley looked more promising and less rough than the eastern side and they would take what came with the southern end. Karen would talk to the surveyor in town and if he was available, she would send him out to the ranch at his earliest convenience. There was a possibility they would get a start on the surveying this fall and if all went well, it might be completed. All were hoping this would be the case. After a final meal, their camp was dismantled and everything packed up ready to leave.

When they had negotiated the twisting gully and came out on the open prairie, they stopped and dismounted. Shorty got a hug from everyone, including Karen. Good-byes were said, and Shorty rode toward the Axe and the other three to the R-R. As before, Karen decided to stay overnight and ride to town in the morning with Matt.

It was a typical week, with Matt busy doing chores at home and riding to school each morning. The weather was warm but the nights were beginning to cool off. It would soon be time to move the vegetables into the root cellar.

Karen had contacted the surveyor and he was going to be at the R-R the following Saturday morning. He wanted to have a look at the area he was going to be surveying and get a general outline of the section he was to survey. When Shorty reached the ranch on Thursday evening, he was pleased to hear the news; it looked like part of Saturday was going to be spent at the valley again.

Shorty decided Friday would be spent getting the potatoes dug and safely in the root cellar before the weather got too cold. The turnips, carrots, and cabbage could stay in the garden for a while yet as they seemed to grow better when the weather was cool and wet. The onions and dried beans would be harvested now, as onions prefer warm, dry conditions. Most of the corn had been eaten, but there was still plenty to be dried for seed. When she had the time, Dawn had been making cucumber pickles to add some flavor to the meat and potatoes next winter. There had been a few pumpkins which had been picked and stored in the bunkhouse until Dawn had time to make pies. Next year she had plans to try cauliflower, broccoli, and parsnips by starting them inside until the weather was warm enough for them.

When the root cellar had been decided upon, Matt had put manure on the ground beside the garden and ploughed it in. He had kept the new ground worked up to prevent weeds and to sprout any weed seeds in the ground. By preventing the weeds from going to seed this year, it would save a lot of work next year. With the garden produce, Matt's pigs and venison or beef, they would have lots of food this winter. Maybe later when the weather was colder, they could go back to the lake and get some trout to be kept frozen outside.

When the day ended, Shorty, with some help from Dawn, had just about everything out of the garden. The turnips, cabbage, and carrots would continue to grow even if it froze a bit. They seemed to like the cool wet fall better than the hot dry summer.

When the weather got cold enough so that meat would keep well, Shorty would go hunting and try to get a deer or two. He knew Matt could shoot, but he planned to show him a few tricks he had learned about hunting. They would have to build a meat house to keep the meat in. It would be a small building made of poles similar to the bunkhouse, but with a space between the poles. This would keep the animals away from the meat and if it didn't warm up too much, the meat would stay frozen.

When Matt got home from school, he helped to pick up the small potatoes for his pigs These were stored in the root cellar, and the pigs would get a few everyday while they lasted. The cattle, horses, and pigs would enjoy the carrot and turnip tops, as well as the cabbage leaves when they were harvested later. The animals would eat them now and they would get it back later in the form of work, milk, and meat. Besides helping Shorty in the garden, Dawn had prepared a meal of fresh vegetables, straight from the garden. It was time now to go inside and sample the fare and see if it was up to their specifications. It was hard to find a better meal than fresh, homegrown vegetables.

When the meal was half over, the conversation started. Dawn and Matt wanted to go along to the valley when the surveyor showed up. They figured it would take them a few hours to show him the general outline of their section, so they would eat lunch in the valley. Matt planned to take some potatoes and bacon, some of it would go in the fish and some for frying the potatoes. Dawn would mix up some biscuits to be baked in the fire. With the trout, potatoes, biscuits, and hot tea, they would have a good meal at noon. After a last look at the stock with darkness approaching, it was time to get some sleep. First thing in the morning, they would get everything ready to take to the lake.

With first light all three were up and busy. Shorty fed the horses and checked the other stock while Matt milked the cow and Dawn got breakfast ready. They were all ready to go when the surveyor arrived a short time later. He introduced himself as Bob White, owner of Quail Surveyors. He explained when he told people his name was Bob White, a lot of people called him Mr. Quail so he had used the name for his company. They led the way from the ranch yard and turned toward the valley. It was a cool morning, but the sun warmed the air quickly. It wasn't quite midmorning when they reached the dry streambed entrance to the valley. When they came out of the narrow gully into the flat valley, the surveyor stopped.

He said to Shorty, "I can see why you want this valley. I don't think I've ever seen a more beautiful spot. How did you find this place and get the cattle in here?"

Shorty explained how he and his partner had been looking for strays and had followed some tracks up the wash. He said, "The cattle found it first. These were Dawn's cattle and apparently they found it years ago and stayed and multiplied. There isn't much of a reason for cattle to leave a spot like this, with plenty of water and grass. We wanted to file on it but the agent said since it was 'wasteland' he would allow us each a half section. As you can see it is very poor land," Shorty said with a grin.

The surveyor, also with a big grin, agreed it looked like very poor land. "Now," he said, "Where do you want me to start?" They all dismounted and tied their horses. Shorty said, "From here it will all be on foot. There are a few places where we could get the horses up there, but on foot will be the simplest."

They climbed the bank and made their way in a northeasterly direction. Shorty explained they wanted three or four hundred feet on the east side of the valley. On the north end they wanted to cover the entrance to the valley. The surveyor said to Shorty, "We will have to get a long pole with a red rag on it and put it just to the north of the entrance. I can sight it from here with a compass, and the rest of it will just be a matter of measuring and following a compass. I will need someone to help me carry things and hold the sight pole. Would you be available? If so, I might be able to start on your job a week from Monday."

Shorty explained he would still be working at the Axe. He was trying to think of someone he could get to help when Matt said, "I could do that couldn't I? If I could do the job, we wouldn't have to pay someone else!"

The surveyor said, "I could pay you two dollars a day to work with me. I have to have someone to help me regardless. I'm sure it wouldn't take you long to learn what to do. It's just a matter of going ahead with a sight pole to a place where we can see each other, and move the pole in the direction I indicate. After we get a straight line, we go back and measure it. After it is all surveyed, it would be a good plan to make small piles of stones every couple of hundred yards or so. If your mother and father agree, I'm sure you can do the job."

Matt felt good that he had called Shorty his father; he had considered Shorty to be his dad for quite a while now. Dawn asked, "How long do you think it will take you to survey this piece of ground? Matt is going to school, but I guess it won't hurt him to miss a few days."

The surveyor, Bob, answered, "I think we can finish up here in a week. If it was out on the flat prairie, it wouldn't take near that long. With the hills and rough ground to work through it will take a lot longer to get an accurate measurement. With a good man on the pole, I'm sure a week will do it."

Dawn spoke again, "You could stay at the bunkhouse so you wouldn't have to go back to town, if you want to. If we had a tent, maybe you could camp here. We camped here several times, but it was warmer, and we only had a tarp roof to sleep under."

Bob said, "I have a tent I take out on some jobs. I'll bring it, and we can camp here and save travelling to the ranch, unless it gets really cold. This valley seems like a nice, sheltered spot." They built up a pile of rocks to mark the starting point, and then they went to the valley entrance and put up a tall pole with a red rag tied on it. When the surveying was started, the north line would be the first one to be done.

When they left the first corner, Matt went to their usual camping spot and started a fire before going to the lake to get a fish for dinner. While the others were looking around, Matt was preparing a good meal for everyone. When the fish was in the fire, he put the Dutch oven on to heat, filled the teapot, and mixed up biscuits so he could get them baking. He started chopping up bacon and potatoes to fry to complete the dinner. When the others returned, dinner was almost ready to eat.

Mr. White was surprised to find a meal almost ready to be served. They went to the lake to wash their hands and a few minutes later, were enjoying a good meal of baked trout, fried potatoes, biscuits, and tea. After the edge was taken off their appetite, Mr. White told Matt, "I might have to get someone else to work with me and keep you as camp cook! How did you get such a good meal ready in such a short time?"

Matt explained how his mother showed him some things, and he learned a lot just by doing it. He also explained seeing the fish in the lake and making a fishing line to catch one. Once he had caught it, they had no way to cook it, so he had just coated it with clay, and they had 'roast rock' for supper.

When they had eaten their fill, they cleaned up around camp and climbed the bank to look for some dry wood. Each found a few dead bushes which they dragged back to camp. This would be some wood for a start when the surveying got underway. Matt planned to bring the bucksaw to cut wood with as it was easier than cutting it with an axe. Now that he knew what he was to do, Mr. White, who insisted he be called Bob, was ready to go back to town. He would get hold of Matt in town or leave a message with the schoolteacher, advising when he would be available. If he could make it for the following week, he would probably come out to the ranch on Sunday evening and stay at the bunkhouse. Back at the ranch, they all said good-bye and said they would probably see Bob next weekend.

Chapter 18

AFTER BOB LEFT, Shorty suggested he and Matt take the wagon and get a load of small logs for a meat house. They would want logs about four to six inches for building it. It would be just like a cabin, but with spaces between the logs. They would notch the corners just enough to make it sturdy and leave about two inches of space between the logs. This would keep out all but the smallest animals, but allow the cold winter air to go through. It would be built about eight feet square inside as that would hold a lot of meat for the winter. They could build some wooden boxes with tight-fitting lids to keep cut-up meat and also their salted and smoked trout, in. Maybe later they could get some fresh trout to freeze too.

Dawn wasn't about to be left behind when the boys were going to the hills, and she was ready when they had the horses harnessed and hitched to the wagon. Axes and saws were placed in the wagon and they were off for the hills. Once there, they began to cut and limb trees, no bigger than seven inches on the stump. They were cut about ten feet long and limbed until they were too small for firewood. As the logs were cut they were loaded on the wagon, the small tops were left until last and piled on top of the load; one load probably wouldn't be enough to finish the job, but it would be a good start. When loaded, they went back to the ranch, where the firewood was tossed off near the woodshed, and the wagon was parked where the meat house would be built as the wagon could be unloaded later.

With the shorter daylight hours now, when supper was over, there wasn't much time for working outside. Dawn, Matt, and Shorty decided to spend the evening at the bunkhouse. The stove had been set up inside, so a small fire was kindled even though it wasn't needed. Shorty thought they should have a checkerboard so they could play checkers to help pass the time when they weren't busy. He told Matt to find a short six-inch board and plane it smooth all around. Shorty was cutting one-inch-wide strips from another narrow board at the same time. He got Matt to plane the narrow strips while he took one and whittled it round. When Matt finished planing the strips, he nailed them on the ends of the two twelve-inch pieces of the board. This made a twelve-inch square board, with a one-inch strip all around. He then marked the board all around at one-and-a-half inches. These lines were drawn to make sixty-four squares. Shorty started to saw half-inch thick discs off his round stick, and Matt got a flat iron bar, heated it in the fire, and burned a black X on alternate squares on the board. Meanwhile, Dawn had a brick and was smoothing the checkers on its flat surface. When she had them smooth enough to suit, she laid some of them on the stove until they were black, turned them over to blacken the other side until she had fourteen black checkers, which made them a couple of spares. When the job was completed, they sat and played a few games of checkers.

Shorty and Matt had the first game which Shorty won. Dawn then played against him. The players were fairly evenly matched, and all three enjoyed the game. After half a dozen games, it was time to hit the hay. Matt bored a small hole in the board, and it was hung on a nail on the wall. A can would be brought up from the house to store the checkers in. With winter not far away, there would probably be many evenings spent playing checkers.

Matt was first out of bed in the morning, and he went to the house to get a fire started and begin cooking breakfast. It wasn't long until he had water heating and pancakes frying. When Shorty got up a few minutes later, he went out to check the stock, and turn the chickens loose. He also milked the cow and took the milk to the house. Dawn was helping Matt, and in a few minutes breakfast was on the table.

As they enjoyed their breakfast, they talked about what should be done today. Matt suggested getting more logs for the meat house. If all the logs were here, even if they got snow, the building could continue. It probably wouldn't take much snow to stop them from getting up in the hills. Shorty agreed with Matt's idea, so they went out to unload the wagon. They each took a long piece of firewood to pile the logs on so they wouldn't freeze to the ground. A short time later, they were hitched up and on their way to the hills. Before noon, they were back with another load of small logs and firewood. Dawn went inside to get them something to eat, while Shorty and Matt started building.

First they found a few small, peeled tamarack logs which were halved together and placed in a shallow trench for a base. Matt went to the barn and got some two by six for a doorframe. When this was in place, it was squared up and stayed securely. The end-base logs had been left a bit lower so the first logs were placed on the ends. The doorway was to be in the middle, so Matt cut short pieces of two by four for the logs to set on, on each side of the doorway. The short logs were notched and fitted and then spiked through the doorframe into the ends. Simple square notches were used as the building didn't have to be tight, except to keep out any roaming animals. A short piece of two by four was placed between the logs at the middle of each wall also to prevent sagging over time. The boys had two courses of logs on the walls when Dawn called them to dinner. As they ate, Shorty said, "Matt, I think we should get some gravel from the creek for the floor. We can do it now and just shovel it over the wall before it gets too high."

Matt asked, "Do we use the wagon, or do you have a better idea?" Shorty smiled and said, "We'll build a stone boat or drag, it won't be so high to shovel gravel onto."

After dinner they got two small logs about seven feet long. Shorty chopped the ends to resemble runners. A notch was cut about eight inches from one end and a smaller log was fitted into the notch and solidly fastened. Matt was cutting two inch lumber four feet long. These were spiked to the runners to form a deck six feet long and four feet wide, which overhung the runners a few inches on each side. A frame of eight-inch boards was placed on the top to hold the gravel. Matt harnessed a horse, and it was hitched to the stone boat. They hauled it to the creek where there was a gravel bar, and it was shoveled full of gravel. Two trips were enough to put a good coat of gravel on the floor, almost three inches deep. This would keep the floor from getting muddy if the weather warmed up. The horse was unhitched, and the stone boat was stood against a tree until needed again.

Matt bored holes through the logs in the corners and drove small saplings for pins. Every two courses, he did this to hold the corners solidly, even though the corners were notched. When they stopped for supper, the walls were about four feet high. Dawn had a good meal waiting for them as Shorty would be going to the Axe later. Matt had a week of school, then possibly a week's work as a surveyor's helper.

Through the week, Dawn kept busy making pickles and shelling beans along with her usual housework and looking after the pigs and chickens. Each night when Matt got home, he filled the wood box, which was a lot easier now that it could be done from outside.

On Friday, Matt got word from Bob White that he would be at the ranch on Sunday evening. Matt was going to be a surveyor for a week! As soon as he got home, he told Dawn and Shorty the news. He began making a list of things to take to the valley for the surveying trip. He liked the idea of having a week off school, but he was excited to be able to earn some money, doing something he knew he could do.

Shorty and Matt worked at the meat house on Saturday, and with the progress they were making, the walls would be high enough by supper time. Beams were placed on top of the walls at two-foot intervals to keep the walls from spreading and to hang meat on. They planned to have a two-foot peak with a good overhang all around so rain wouldn't blow in on the meat. Rain shouldn't be a big problem, as this building would only be used in the wintertime.

With the short days, not much could be done outside after supper. They spent most evenings in the bunkhouse, and when Matt wasn't playing checkers, he was working on his list of supplies or packing them in a backpack or duffle bag. After he had beaten Dawn and Shorty one after the other, he decided to hit the hay. He didn't want to have his winning streak broken!

It was a cool but nice day when they got out of their bunks. Dawn started breakfast while the boys did the chores. Matt collected the last of his tools and supplies and was ready to go. After breakfast, they worked on the meat house for the morning. Before noon they had the rafters in place and fastened solidly. Shorty thought if it was boarded in up and down, with tarpaper and then another layer of boards, it would make a good roof. Four-inch boards were used for strapping, and then the roof could be closed in with the boards up and down; even without the tarpaper, the roof should almost be watertight.

The carpenters stopped work about mid afternoon. Shorty and Dawn decided to go along too, when Matt and Bob left for the valley. In the morning Shorty would go on to the Axe, and Dawn would go back home. They were all packed and saddled when Bob arrived, leading a packhorse carrying all the equipment he would need. It was quite a procession that left the ranch yard late Sunday afternoon.

They arrived at the valley just before dark, and everybody was busy getting camp set up before darkness was complete. A fire was started and supper was soon underway. Dawn had brought some biscuits and stew, which was heated in no time. With supper over, it was time for bed. Matt suggested he and Bob sleep under the shelter, and Dawn and Shorty take the tent. Dawn objected, but Bob sided with Matt and the newlyweds went to the tent. When daylight arrived, breakfast was almost ready to eat, which when he finished, Shorty headed for the Axe. Dawn got the camp in order, and went with Bob and Matt to see what they were about to do. She paid close attention as Bob explained the signals he used and what each meant. Before she left, they were hard at work cutting brush, flagging, and marking out the line. She said nothing to them, but she planned to come back and help out now and then. She figured she could be a surveyor's helper too!

Bob had explained to Matt and Dawn, "When I put my right arm up and to the side, you move that way, when my left arm is up move to the left. When both arms are straight up, that is where I want you." Where they had made the pile of stones, the surveyor's stand was set up. Matt went a few hundred yards ahead and held up the pole. When Bob indicated he was on the right location, he stuck a stick in the ground with a rag on it. He then went back toward Bob, and the process was repeated, as they wanted to have a marker about every hundred yards.

Matt went ahead and put up another marker. He could look back the line of markers and put others in between. When they came within sight of the marker that had been put up to show the entrance to the valley, they were north of it. This meant with the north line running straight east and west, they were outside the entrance, which was ideal. By noon they had covered nearly half a mile. Whenever Matt had a few minutes, he gathered rocks to make a pile around some of his markers. Later, when time permitted, they would try to have a pile of stones every hundred yards or so; rocks were much more permanent than wooden posts.

They went back to camp to have something to eat. Neither one wanted to take the time for a big meal, so they settled for cold biscuits and tea. They decided to work until almost dark, and then make a good meal for their supper. Matt had been chopping brush out of the way to make a sight line, making posts and doing a lot of walking back and forth. They were marking off a piece of land one mile square, with a perimeter of four miles, but Matt would walk more than fifty miles before they were finished! At the end of a day, Matt would feel like he had earned his money.

After a quick lunch, they were back on the job. When time permitted, Matt tried to keep a clear path along the line. In some places there was very little brush, and it was easy to keep the line cleared. In other areas, he could only cut the taller brush so they could see, and they had to go through or around the standing bushes. Later they would cut the brush that remained, build more piles of stones, and cut the brush on the line every few years.

Matt and Bob worked until the sun was almost down; they figured this would give them enough time to get a good meal ready before dark. Some of their tools and equipment could be left where they finished work so there was less to carry back to camp. They weren't too far from the gully that led to the valley, so they headed south until they hit the trail. When they entered the valley, they could see three horses and knew they had company. When they reached the camp, Dawn had supper almost ready, this was a welcome surprise as they were ready to eat. Dawn said she knew they were working hard and decided she could help by getting supper ready. It was very much appreciated by Bob and Matt, who had been on their feet all day. Dawn told them, "Tomorrow I'll be here just past mid afternoon to take over for Matt so he can catch a fish and get supper ready. It's better to have enough time to get a good meal ready, than to try to get something ready after dark." Bob said to Dawn, "Tomorrow we will be working south, we will leave a marker where we cross the gully. You can tie your horse there and follow the line to us and Matt can come back and bring your horse to camp. That will save both of you a bit of walking."

Dawn thought that would be fine and she would be watching for their marker. Darkness was soon settling into the valley, as they finished supper and sat by the fire and talked. Soon it was time to hit the bedrolls and get some rest for the coming day of work.

Matt had a fire started when Dawn came out of the tent in the morning, she took over for Matt, and he went looking for more dry wood. Dawn soon had bacon and eggs ready, hot tea and the biscuits would be done shortly. She had made enough so there would be some left for dinner. She told them she would bring more mix when she came back later in the day. When breakfast was over, she cleaned up around camp, saddled up, and turned her horse in the direction of home. Bob and Matt were shortly at the end of the survey line and hard at work.

When they had gone what Bob thought was far enough, they went back to the starting point to measure the exact distance. Matt would stretch the measure tight and push a stick into the ground with a white rag on it. They would then move ahead and repeat the process. Bob had estimated the distance very closely, but he had a lot of practice over the years. At exactly one mile, they drove a substantial post and piled rocks around it. The north line was completed, so they began working south on the west line. Before noon, they came to the gully which was the entrance to the valley. Matt crossed to the other side, and they continued on, sighting, marking, chopping, and walking. There was plenty of sign where they had slid down the bank and scrambled up the other side, but Bob left a red rag, so Dawn wouldn't miss them.

When noon came, they were a few hundred yards past the gully. They decided to cut across country to the valley, instead of backtracking. This saved them a fair bit of time and walking. There was still coals left from breakfast, so a few small twigs soon had a fire going and water heating for tea. They toasted some biscuits and ate them with Dawn's Saskatoon berry jam. This would keep them on their feet, especially when they knew there would be a good meal at supper time.

They followed the same path they had made going for dinner and were soon back at work on the line. Matt and Bob continued to work steadily throughout the early afternoon. Matt would go ahead with the sight pole and watch for the signals from Bob until he was in the proper position. He would then push the pole firmly into the ground and then he would backtrack putting in smaller poles with rags on them. Matt could sight back the line and get the markers in the correct position. On his way forward, he would cut as much brush as possible and toss it aside. It was a lot of walking and hard work, but he was used to working and enjoyed it. He was pleased with the thought of owning this valley and someday living here.

About mid afternoon, he could see Dawn walking up the line behind them. Bob had moved ahead to sight out the next section of line. Matt stayed for the next leg of surveying to make sure Dawn knew what to do before leaving to get supper ready. Dawn had paid close attention the first morning, so she was almost as good as Matt, and she was as good with an axe. Bob was impressed with what Dawn could do. She had impressed more than one man with her ability to work. They continued to make good progress with Dawn handling the pole, the axe, and the rocks. They still had some daylight to work with when Bob called a halt. He decided they should go back to the corner and do some measuring. That would put them near the valley entrance when it came time to stop for the night. The tools to be left were all put in one spot for tomorrow, before they hiked back to the corner. Once again Bob realized Dawn was an efficient worker. They had crossed the gully with their measuring before it began to get dark.

Meanwhile, back at the camp, Matt was busy was usual. He had restarted the fire on first arrival and put water on to heat. He then caught a good trout and got it ready to bake. The Dutch oven was heating for biscuits, and he was cutting up potatoes to fry. He had the potatoes almost ready to go in the pan when he heard a horse coming and was surprised to see Shorty arriving. He left his horse saddled for the moment and gave Matt a hand by making the biscuits for supper. The biscuits were in the Dutch oven when he looked up to see Dawn and Bob coming up the valley. Both Dawn and Shorty had a big smile to greet the other with.

Shorty asked Matt, "Why didn't you tell me your mother was here?" Matt answered with a grin. "You didn't ask me and besides, I was busy!"

The trout was baked, and the tea and potatoes were ready; the biscuits would be available soon. All four sat down to a good, hot meal. When their appetite was partly satisfied, they began to discuss the surveying job. Bob told them, "I think we can finish by Friday, but if not Saturday will do it for sure. I've had a good ma . . . er two good helpers." He smiled as he looked at Dawn. "For the rough ground we've been covering, I think we've done very well. Another thing, the food is a lot better than I'm used to when camping out like this!"

"Well," Dawn said, "This is a hard job, and a person can do more on good food than otherwise. I figured if you have a good breakfast to start the day, and a good supper to finish it, a person can get along on a lighter meal at noon. I wanted you to see how Matt does the fish and potatoes, so that's why I took over for him. Some people come in time to eat but too late for work!" She was looking at Shorty with a smile on her face at the time.

Bob grinned and said, "Yeah, I see what you mean. He must be smarter than us and planned it that way!" Shorty just smiled and never said a word. Bob continued, "Usually, I charge five dollars a day for me and my equipment, plus a bit for food and travelling. Matt has worked so hard and the food has been so good, I'm going to take twenty five dollars for myself and the rest is for Matt. I haven't done nearly as much walking or hard work as he has, and the food is better than what I could buy in town. He will have to work something out with his mother, though!" he said with a grin. All four laughed at Bob's last remark!

They sat and talked over a last cup of tea until it was time for bed. Dawn and Shorty went to the tent, while Bob and Matt spread their bedrolls under the tarp shelter. A short time later all were sound asleep.

As soon as breakfast was over the next morning, Shorty saddled up and rode toward the Axe, after telling them he would be back here on Thursday evening. Dawn cleaned up around

SHORTY'S STORY | 315

camp and washed the dishes before leaving for home. She told Matt she would be back to get supper for them so they could work later.

Matt and Bob continued measuring until they reached the end of the surveyed line and then switched to the harder job, for Matt at least. He carried the pole, walked back and forth putting in stakes and markers, and chopped brush almost continuously. They mostly cut just the brush that had to be moved to provide a sight line, as the rest could be cut back at a later time. The most important project now was to get this section of land surveyed and marked off legally so it could be registered at the land office.

When noon came, Bob thought they were getting close to where the south west corner would be. After a lunch, they would measure the rest of this side, and then finish surveying to the corner. They left their tools and walked in a north easterly direction toward camp.

Before leaving, Dawn had put a couple of heavy pieces of wood on the fire, and a pot of water was near enough to be quite hot. In a few minutes the surveyors had hot tea and leftover potatoes and biscuits with jam. This would keep their stomach from complaining too loudly until supper time. Back on the job after a good lunch, they measured up the west side until they came to their tools. In a short time they had the west side lined off and measured to the corner. Again a substantial post was erected and rocks piled around it. This left the south and east sides to be surveyed to complete the job.

Bob decided, since they were already here, they might as well continue on from here. This area was mostly rolling hills, and Bob could sight from one to the next. It would be harder to get a good measurement, but faster to run a line. They worked steadily throughout the afternoon with Matt mostly walking and cutting brush. When mid afternoon came and went, they assumed Dawn was getting a meal ready for them and at least, they hoped that was the case. They worked until the sun was almost set before gathering up the tools to take back to camp.

As they neared the camp, their noses picked up a wonderful aroma. Dawn had made a pot of stew with dumplings and hot biscuits. Bob and Matt didn't realize how hungry they were until they smelled the mouthwatering stew. They needed no second invitation to fill a plate and dig in. The barley and dumplings Dawn had added had made the stew thick and tasty. For the first ten minutes, the only sound to be heard was the clicking of forks on their plate. After the second helping, they put down their plates with a contented sigh. It takes good food to let you know just how big your appetite really is!

The conversation began as they sat back with a cup of tea and a hot biscuit. Dawn was told they were about half way across the south end. Tomorrow would finish that side and get a start on the east line. If they could keep up the progress they had been making, the job should be completed on Friday. They sat and talked for a bit longer, and then rolled up in their blankets for some sleep. Dawn made pancakes with molasses or jam for breakfast. The surveyors were soon back at work, and Dawn cleaned up around camp before leaving for the ranch. Shorty would be here for supper, so she planned to have a good meal of fresh vegetables, maybe a trout and the leftover stew.

When Dawn arrived that afternoon, she had a load of fresh vegetables with her. Two sacks tied together and hung over the saddle had a large turnip and a cabbage, while the other held potatoes, carrots, and a couple of onions. She washed the potatoes thoroughly and put them in a large pot she had brought along with her. She then scrubbed the carrots and split the biggest ones lengthwise. These went into the pot with the onions, which were chopped a bit. The big turnip was sliced and peeled before joining the other vegetables in the pot. The biggest cabbage she could find in the garden was cut into eight pieces, which was crammed into the pot to fill it to the brim. She put the pot on the fire, took Matt's fishing rod, and went to the lake for a trout. A few minutes later a trout was prepared and in the fire baking for supper. She had brought a couple of loaves of fresh bread, but decided to make biscuits also. This was going to be a meal to be remembered, at least for a while. Everything was ready to eat except the biscuits, which should be cooked by the time the others showed up. The water was hot so she made the tea and set it beside the fire to keep hot.

The first person she saw was Shorty, riding his horse up the valley. Before he reached the camp, she could see Matt and Bob walking down the valley. Shorty was at the camp and unsaddled when the two surveyors arrived. All three wasted no time getting washed up and lined up to dig in as the aroma of the food almost made them drool. Dawn had moved the pot of vegetables off the fire to allow it to cool a bit, and shortly all four had a plate piled high with steaming vegetables and baked fish. A second helping went the way of the first before any talk was heard. Bob said they had all four corners marked out and just had the east line to finish. This should be completed easily enough tomorrow.

There wouldn't be much Dawn and Shorty could do to help, so they decided to brush out the line where necessary and make more rock cairns for permanent markers. In the future, any time they wanted a change of scenery, they could spend some time piling up more rocks. Tomorrow, the full section of land they were claiming would be surveyed legally. Bob would finish the paperwork and send it to Medicine Hat to be registered. He told Matt to stop at his office on Monday, and his money would be ready for him.

Matt asked his mother about putting it in the bank with the money they had received from the sale of their cattle. Dawn thought he should have his own bank account, as someday he might want to buy something for himself. If it was needed for the ranch, they would use it, otherwise it would belong to Matt.

Everyday darkness came a bit earlier, so it was soon time to hit the hay. Nobody wanted to waste any daylight, so bedtime was earlier, too and as usual everyone was out and ready for work at when the sun appeared. After breakfast, Matt and Bob left to finish the surveying, and Dawn and Shorty began cutting brush and piling rocks. They worked with Bob and Matt to help clear brush faster for the surveying. When there wasn't much brush to cut, they piled rocks to mark their boundary. An hour before noon Dawn left to get dinner ready, for which it seemed leftovers would be the main ingredient. It seemed as if the flavor was leftover also, as everything tasted much better after being reheated. After a good and tasty meal, it was back to work for the crew of surveyors. Just past mid afternoon, the job was completed!

Bob thought if it was OK with everyone else, he would like to stay and look around for a while and go back to town tomorrow. Dawn said that was fine with everyone, and they would have another good meal to celebrate the completion of the surveying. She thought they should show him the main reason for wanting to get this valley and the surrounding area. Matt said he would get supper ready, and Dawn and Shorty could show Bob the inner valley. They thought he should go with them as they could all pitch in and help to get supper before dark.

Everyone hiked up the valley to where the small stream entered the lake. Here they showed Bob the big trout lying in the water, and Dawn demonstrated how easy they were to catch. They then walked up the stream to where it came from the inner valley. They entered the tiny valley and walked up to the waterfall. They pointed out the huge trout in the pool under the waterfall. Bob too, seemed to fall under the spell of the inner valley, as he, along with the others found it hard to break the silence of this special, beautiful place. As they were making their way back down the main valley Bob said, "I can see why you wanted this place. The main valley is beautiful, but words cannot describe the beauty of that tiny inner valley. I felt as though I shouldn't speak while I was in there. I've surveyed some beautiful country over the years, but nothing comes close to that little valley!"

Shorty said, "Welcome to the club, Bob. Those are the exact words of everyone who has entered that valley!" Shorty explained how he and Gus had found this valley by following tracks looking for strays. When found, the valley was full of R-R cattle, all of which were sorely needed at the time. Now that the valley was going to be theirs, they had to build, and be living on this section of land before five years were up. This didn't seem like too big of a problem, as all three were anxious to be living here. It was going to be hard to get supplies and building material into the valley, but Shorty had been studying the entrance, and he thought with some work, maybe lots of it, a wagon road could be made in the gully.

Dawn and Matt had been busy getting a meal ready, and now it was just a matter of waiting for it to finish cooking, baked trout with a few leftover vegetables, bread and biscuits and of course, a good supply of tea. After a good meal, they sat around the fire and talked until later than usual as nobody had anything that was terribly pressing to be done the next day.

Breakfast the next morning wasn't as bountiful as the previous meals. It consisted of tea, a couple of slices of bacon for each, and biscuits. No one was complaining as they had eaten well all week and although biscuits might not last as long as heavier food, all had enough to eat. Before he left, Matt asked Bob if he would like a couple of trout to take home with him. Bob thought that was a fine suggestion, so he and Matt went to the lake to catch a few trout. Matt told Bob how it came about finding the lake held trout and catching one and cooking it in the fire. Matt gave Bob his pole and he soon had three nice trout to take home with him. These were cleaned and packed with his gear on the packhorse. When Bob was on his way, the three homesteaders went to work cutting brush and piling rocks to mark the boundary of their property. In places there was very little to do except pile up rocks, as when time permitted, Matt had cut most of the brush. Some of the low spots still had a lot of brush to be cut and moved back from the line. They wanted a good, clear line to mark the edge of their property. Their plan was to have at least three feet of clear area on each side of the line, even in the hollows where it didn't show. They would probably spend other weekends working at clearing the lines, as there was still plenty to do. They worked steadily throughout the day except for a short break for biscuits and tea. When they left for home they had completed the north line, with piles of rocks about every hundred yards. Some piles were bigger than others, depending on availability of material.

All three were tired, but felt good about someday owning this beautiful valley.

Work continued into the fall which was already here, some mornings were white with frost but most of the outside work had been completed. On one warm weekend, all three worked at getting the last of the vegetables out of the garden and into the root cellar. There was now a good supply of fresh vegetables to last all winter and beyond. The woodsheds were stacked with plenty of wood, although neither was completely filled. Shorty wanted to move another stack of hay to the barn, but it would be easier to do with some snow on the ground. He was still working on the Axe, but the work was getting less every day, and soon he would stay home and work on the R-R, at least until spring.

Shorty had bought a single horse sled from the Axe to use for hauling wood this coming winter. It wasn't being used there as, when hay was being hauled, the huge team sleds were used. On nice weekends, all three had gone to the hills and cut wood. It was stacked neatly on small poles to wait until snow arrived. The sled was lower and easier to load and unload. On these trips to the hills Matt took along his twenty-two caliber rifle. It was too small for big game, but just right for rabbits and grouse. He could use it very well, but Shorty gave him a few pointers each time out. He told Matt, "When I plan to kill a deer, I aim for the head. If I hit it, the deer usually goes down; if I miss the deer is gone and unhurt. If you hit a deer in the head, nine times out of ten it is dead, if it isn't, it will go down, and you can finish it off. I've seen animals hit in the shoulder or chest, that ran for miles before they dropped. I hate to see any animal wounded, and then die a slow death because the hunter couldn't find it. Another thing, when you fire a rifle, squeeze the trigger slowly. If you take a couple of seconds to squeeze it, you will probably hit what you are aiming at. If you pull the trigger too quickly, sometimes it pulls the rifle off the target. When the weather gets a bit colder, you and I will go out and get some meat with your twenty-two."

Matt had shot small game with his gun, but had never tried to kill a deer before. Shorty told him; "When hunting, look for male animals, one male can breed a lot of females, but if you kill a female, you kill a lot of future generations. If you are desperate, kill a female if you have to, but otherwise leave the females to reproduce."

When the snow finally came, about six inches fell overnight. The ground had been frozen solid, so it had been good getting around. Matt went outside and piled snow as high as he could get it around the house, and he also buried the water pipe to the house. The snow kept the house a lot warmer and easier to heat.

Shorty decided it was time to haul some hay from where it was stacked and put some in the barn. He had been working at home for the past couple of weeks, as work was scarce on the Axe at this time of the year. He and Matt got a couple of small logs about six or seven inches through and about twelve feet long. Shorty hewed the big ends until they looked like sled runners. Three smaller poles were lightly notched into the tops. The runners were about six feet apart and the small poles were ten feet long. Matt got some boards and nailed them on the poles about six inches apart, making a deck about ten feet square. Matt then got some small saplings and nailed them to the ends of the small poles, and then he nailed narrow boards to the saplings to form a square, open at the front. A chain was fastened to the back crosspiece and one turn was put around each pole up to the front. The strain would be on all three poles so the sled wouldn't be pulled apart. A couple of feed sacks were filled with hay for cushions, and they were ready to go. When they reached the hay stack, the weathered hay was removed from the top and put to the side. The sled was loaded until it looked like a haystack itself and hauled back to the barn. This hay was unloaded and put in the barn for the milk cow, saddle horses, and the team. Time was taken for a lunch, and then they went back for another load. The second load cleaned up the stack, and the weathered hay was put on top of the load. This load would stay on the sled and be put in the pasture for the stock to eat when they were outside.

Chapter 19

NOW THAT IT was cold enough for meat to keep well outside, it was time to think about getting some for the meat house. Shorty and Matt got their rifles and checked them over, and each put half a dozen extra shells in their pocket. The snow wasn't too deep so they didn't bother with snowshoes. Shorty carried the big pack and Matt had a smaller one. Each one had a hunting knife and a small hand ax on their belt. A package of smoked fish and a small rope was in each pack, plus each had a small, tight container with a few matches inside. They went prepared and in the event of an emergency, they could build a shelter, make a fire, and they had a small amount of food with them. Especially in winter, it is always better to be prepared; as they say 'better safe than sorry.'

They left the house after telling Dawn where they were going and when they would be back. Shorty had decided to go to the hills where they had cut the logs. Matt had seen two deer there, and it was a fair distance from home. The game that was near home would be left alone in case meat was needed later. The weather was cold but not bitter and walking kept them warm. When they reached the hills and trees, they slowed down and moved along carefully.

Shorty told Matt, "If we see a deer, you try for it and remember, don't rush your shot and make the first one count. If you don't get a chance to shoot, don't worry, the deer probably won't go too far. If you shoot and miss, the deer will probably go a long ways before stopping. Try to find something to rest your rifle on, even if it's up against a tree; it's easier to hold it steady if it's on or against something solid. If we see something, I'll be ready too in case you miss, but I don't think you will."

They walked along slowly, side by side but about ten feet apart. The soft snow cushioned their footsteps, and they did their best to avoid sticks and dead limbs. There were many deer tracks, so they knew this was a good area to be hunting in. After walking carefully for about twenty minutes, they came upon a small group of deer, eating twigs off a fallen tree.

Matt was behind a tree, with his rifle resting on a limb, while Shorty held his rifle against a tree and sighted the biggest buck. When Matt squeezed the trigger, the buck dropped in its tracks. The other deer left in a rush although the report from the twenty two wasn't very loud. Matt went to the deer and using his hunting knife, he cut the deer's throat so it would bleed out. Both rifles were leaned against a tree limb safely out of the way. The deer was rolled onto its back so it could be opened up and the insides removed. The heart and liver was set aside on clean snow to be taken home with them. Shorty estimated the deer would weigh between one hundred and fifty and one hundred and seventy-five pounds. They now had to decide whether to skin the deer and hang it in a tree, or drag it home with them. Matt thought if they had a small pole tied to the deer's antlers and rolled it onto its back, they should be able to drag it downhill at least and maybe all the way home.

Shorty thought Matt's idea was a good one, so they prepared to take Matt's deer home with them. The heart and liver was wrapped in a clean cloth Dawn had given them, and placed in the pack Shorty would carry. Going downhill wasn't too bad, especially after they hit the trail they had hauled the logs out of. They would drag the deer until they were getting out of breath and stop to rest a bit. They came in sight of the house about two hours after noon. The deer was hung up in the meat house and the hide removed before they stopped to eat. While eating, Matt told his mother about his first deer-hunting trip and the other events of the day. Shorty thought if they quartered the deer and left it in the meat house until later, then put it in the root cellar overnight, it would be cold but would not freeze. If they let it freeze solid in big pieces, it would be almost impossible to cut later. That night they would build some tight wooden boxes and tomorrow the meat would be cut up and packed in the boxes to freeze solid.

A fire was started in the bunkhouse and when it warmed up, they began to cut and plane lumber for the boxes to store the meat in. Narrow cracks would be left in the bottom to allow the juice to drain out. To start with, they built four boxes, sixteen inches wide and twenty-four inches long with the sides eight inches high. Each box would hold a lot of meat. Dawn suggested letting the meat freeze before packing it in the boxes, so it would be easier to get out, so Matt planed a couple of extra boards to put the meat on to allow it to freeze separately. The deer had been quartered and left to cool until bedtime, when it would be moved into the root cellar. A good start had been made on their winter supply of meat and fresh venison was on the menu for supper!

Hopefully the weather would warm up for a day or two so they could butcher one of Matt's hogs. Some of the pork would be pickled and the bacon and hams smoked. Some would be done like the deer, frozen to be used fresh throughout the winter. Shorty planned to get at least one more deer; this with the pork and fish should keep them eating well all winter. Matt would soon be through school until the weather warmed up in the spring. When school was over for the winter, they would start hauling wood. When there wasn't much else to do, they could always haul wood for next winter. It was always better to have too much than to run short, which had happened to Dawn and Matt last spring.

When school was over, they began to haul wood when it wasn't too cold. A week after Matt got his deer, the weather warmed up enough to butcher one of the hogs. Now there was fresh frozen pork so there was a variety of meat to choose from. When hauling wood, Shorty carried his rifle in hopes of seeing a deer. On the third day, while Matt was taking a load of wood home, Shorty killed a big buck, which he figured would weigh at least two hundred pounds. When Matt got back, they loaded the sled with wood and put the deer on the top. At home it was hung up and skinned, then quartered and left to cool. They now had a guaranteed supply of meat for the winter and into next summer. When spring came, any remaining fresh meat would be pickled so it could be used through the summer. Now, they would see about making a trip to Lost Valley to get some trout to freeze, this would make an even better variety for the winter.

Throughout the winter, when the weather permitted, they cut and hauled wood. When the weather was too cold and stormy, they worked inside. The bunkhouse was easy to heat and they spent a lot of cold, stormy weather there. They built shelves on the wall by the bunks and sliding drawers under them. They also built a wood box in the wall, so wood didn't have to be carried around to get it inside. They could usually find something to do to keep them busy.

When the weather began to warm up, they had a good supply of wood ahead, the woodshed at the house was almost solidly filled and half the storage area at the bunkhouse was packed full. A lot of little things had been done at the house and bunkhouse to make life easier.

One nice day, Angela arrived for a visit. As they were having a cup of tea she asked Dawn, "What have you been doing all winter? It doesn't look like there is a baby on the way yet! I was sure you would be expecting before now." Dawn told her, "Don't try to rush things. A baby will come when it's ready, and you worrying about it won't make it happen any faster. I'm not worrying because I'm not too old yet."

The conversation drifted to other less important topics. The Axe had lost very few cattle over the winter, so it looked like a good season coming. Dawn told Angela they had checked over the valley and didn't think they had lost any cattle. As soon as time and weather permitted, Shorty was going to start working on a road into the valley. They were all anxious to get started building and living in the valley.

Since the weather had improved, school had started up again. Matt was riding his horse to school every day now. Everyone had been too busy to take the school children on any more survival trips, but they hoped to do so in the near future. Matt had hoped to make a trip in the winter so they could learn how to build a shelter that would keep them warm. They would still have cold weather and maybe even snow before summer arrived. He was going to talk with Karen and maybe plan something for the coming weekend. Everybody had more time now before the busy summer season which was fast approaching.

The next day in school, Matt asked Karen's opinion on another trip. She told him all the ones who had gone before wanted to go again, and there were several others who were interested. They made a new list of the items they should take along and made a dozen copies. When school was over for the day, she asked who was interested in going on another survival trip. All the ones who had gone before were anxious to go, plus five others. Karen told them to ask their parents if they could go and bring a note giving their permission. Each of the interested children was given a copy of the list of items needed for the trip. The trip was planned for Friday evening, and they would be away for two nights. Karen explained they would probably be working together as groups of three, so they could pick partners and go together on the food supplies. It was an excited group of children leaving school that day!

On Friday evening, Karen led a long line of campers out of town toward the R-R. A couple of the elder boys would go directly to the ranch as they lived on ranches farther from town. They were going to the valley again this time, but would camp in the hills surrounding the valley. As soon as everyone had arrived, they set out in order to have enough daylight to get shelters built. The horses were tied to a long rope Matt had brought along and several of the elder ones would be responsible for looking after them. Karen and Matt found a sheltered spot, just off the main valley. The campers were divided into groups of three, and all were soon busy cutting poles for shelters. Matt was working too, showing them how to make a shelter that would keep them warm and dry in cold weather. On a slight slope, Matt pushed two poles into the ground at an angle, eight feet apart at the bottom and tied the tops together about five feet high. A long pole ran from these to the ground farther up the slope. Smaller poles were fastened to this, making a framework about five feet high in front and about three feet at the back. Matt put his big tarp over this and fastened it securely in place. He then got a lot of brush and placed it on the tarp, starting at the bottom. He explained to them, if it rained the tarp would keep them dry, but if it was cold the brush would help to keep them warm. He also told them, if it was snowing the snow would make it even warmer, but the brush would keep the snow from melting on the tarp. With a small fire in front of the shelter to reflect the heat inside, they would be fairly comfortable even if it was cold outside.

When any of the campers had a problem, Matt and Karen would help out so all the shelters were ready for occupancy before dark. Some of the younger ones were busy gathering dry wood and rocks for fire pits. They were all learning to work together and to think of others and not just themselves. Their canvas groundsheets were wide enough that three people could sleep on two of them. Matt took one of them and placed it over the front of the shelter with a three-cornered opening at the top. This would allow for ventilation and if a fire was needed for heat, it would allow any smoke that entered to escape. The evening wasn't very cold, so they would have only one central fire to sit around.

Matt and Karen had each brought a Dutch oven so two groups would make biscuits and share with the others. The cooking duty would be shared so everyone would have a chance to learn and be responsible. Two frying pans would also be shared for cooking bacon or whatever was on the menu. Shortly after dark, it was time to crawl into the bedrolls, as there would be a lot of things to do and learn tomorrow. Three of the youngest boys would share Matt's shelter, while three of the girls would join Karen in hers.

When morning came, it was a busy time getting breakfast ready for this many people. The large central fire pit was used for baking biscuits and a smaller pit was used for frying bacon. The groups cooking breakfast would have it a bit easier next meal, when different groups took over the cooking. It wasn't long before everyone had enough to eat and the rest of the days work could get underway. The camp had to be kept clean and neat at all times and a good supply of wood kept on hand. Next the horses had to be looked after; this normally would be done before eating, but there was really wasn't much to do in caring for them.

Matt explained to everyone he was going to be a partner in owning this valley and the surrounding area. They had filed a homestead claim on the valley, and it had been surveyed. He said anyone would be welcome here, but they would be expected to keep everything cleaned up and leave nothing behind to indicate anyone had been here. He told them, where they had camped before there was hardly any sign that anyone had been here. The fire pits had been buried, and the rocks had been moved back into the bushes.

Karen and Matt thought this would be a good time to show the campers how to catch a fish by hand. They hiked up the valley to the small stream. Most of the crew was excited to see so many huge trout in one place. With half of the crew on each side of the stream, Karen and Matt demonstrated how easy it was to catch a fish by hand. When it came time for the dinner crew to catch one, Matt told them theirs would be kept for the noon meal. When two fish were on the grass, Matt showed them how to kill one quickly. Before they left for camp, some cattail roots were pulled up to be roasted for dinner. After a bit more exploring, they returned to camp so the cooks could start working on the next meal. Matt showed them how he coated the fish with clay, after putting some bacon inside, and a generous sprinkling of salt and pepper. Biscuits were being mixed up to be baked and eaten with the trout.

The air seemed to be cooling off, so the ones not busy with preparing dinner were gathering wood for the fires. A fireplace was built in front of each shelter, with bigger rocks on the outside to reflect the heat under the shelter. At one shelter, Matt drove small green sticks into the ground and put pieces of green wood between them to form a wall leaning toward the shelter. This would work like the rocks to reflect the heat under the roof of the shelter.

After the meal, they did some more exploring. The air continued to cool off, and it began to feel like snow. Matt was showing the others what he had learned about finding directions. When the sun was shining, there wasn't much of a problem and on a clear night the North Star was always there to guide the travelers. Matt showed them how the moss on a tree or rock was usually thicker on the north side where it didn't dry out. This wasn't always one hundred percent reliable though, as in some cases a tree or rock was sheltered from the sun, and the moss was just about the same all around.

By now the temperature had dropped to below freezing and fine snow could be seen in the air. It was time to head back to camp and get prepared for a cold night. The horses were moved to a more sheltered spot although there was very little wind in this valley. Matt and two others went to the lake to get a couple of trout for supper. Most of the others were collecting wood as several fires would be kept burning throughout the night. The fish were cleaned and placed in the clean snow to keep cool until time to cook them. A tarp shelter had been erected by the main fire pit, so most of the campers were sitting there. A few branches had been placed over the fireplaces in front of the sleeping shelters to keep the snow out until time to start a fire at bedtime.

Matt had brought some potatoes, so the supper crew was busy getting them ready to cook for supper. The trout had been coated with clay and placed in the coals to bake. Two Dutch ovens full of biscuits were baking and water was heating for tea. Most of the children drank tea occasionally, and this was one time a warm drink would be appreciated. It wasn't too long until everyone had a plateful of hot food and a cup of tea. Karen had brought along some jam for the biscuits, and they all enjoyed the hot meal on this snowy night. Darkness arrived earlier due to the storm, and by this time there was four inches of light snow on the ground, and the shelters looked like big snowdrifts. The snow around the camp area was kept brushed back with branches so the ground wouldn't get muddy and wet.

It was time to get a fire started in the fireplaces to keep everyone warm while they slept. The campers for each shelter got a fire started, and it was their responsibility to see that it was kept going or suffer the consequences. Once in their blankets, they would probably be warm enough even without a fire. Matt and Karen explained to the campers how the fire should be tended and that it should be fed often. Too big a fire might melt the snow on the shelter and cause the tarp to leak. Soon the camp was quiet and almost everyone was asleep.

When morning arrived, the snow had stopped, and the sun was shining, the temperature was rising, and the snow was beginning to melt. A couple of pole racks were put up to hang the blankets over so they would air out and not get wet from the snow and dripping water. Matt decided to leave the frames for the shelters standing, but the brush had to be removed to get the tarps. The breakfast crew was busy frying bacon and baking biscuits. The campers were pleased that they had built a shelter that had kept them warm and dry, even in a snowstorm! After a good breakfast, most of them wanted to catch a trout to take home with them. Matt got his fishing gear and each one found their own bait and caught their own fish. When cleaned, the fish were packed in snow for the trip home.

Every one of the campers was pleased with what they had learned and they were glad for the snow to test their shelters. Karen thought they should talk to their parents or other elder people and see if they could come up with other survival tips to share with the others the next time they were out camping. They had all enjoyed their trip, but were now anxious to get home and share their experience with their family, so in a short time the horses were saddled up and the campers were on the way home.

When Matt arrived home, he explained to Dawn and Shorty how the weekend went. The campers had enjoyed themselves and had survived a spring snowstorm. They were already planning to make another trip in a month or so.

Shorty was trying to decide the best way to make a road into the valley. He knew there was a lot of rocks to be moved and dirt to be leveled. If the rocks weren't too big, they could be rolled onto the stone boat and hauled to a hole or wide spot in the gully. The scoop would work for a lot of leveling and for moving dirt, but it would be slow. He was trying to figure a way to make a scraper that could be pulled by a team of horses. It should have iron cutting edges so it would cut into the soil and not just slide over it. There was some iron in the shed, but no pieces long enough for what he wanted.

Dawn had been trying to think of something that could be used, and suddenly she said, "What about a wagon tire off a big wagon? It wouldn't be very heavy but you could put some weight on it. There must be some old wagon wheels at the Axe that you could get one from."

Shorty said, "That's just the idea I was looking for! It would be too light to cut deep, but one horse could pull it easily. We could bore a couple of holes in it so we could fasten some weight on it. It would drag some dirt and drop it in the low spots, and it would be ideal for leveling. There are places where we would have to use the scoop to get the gully wide enough for the wagon tire to go through. With a few weekends of work, I think we could have a road good enough to take a wagon over. I'll see what I can find out as soon as I get back to the Axe. We might have to take the wagon over to get the tire and scoop. The scoop will drag fine upside down, but the wagon tire won't.

This was Sunday, and Shorty would be going back to the Axe to work later. After supper he said, "I'll find out about a wagon tire as soon as I get there. I'll ask Angela to ride over and tell you if there is one I can get. You could hitch one horse to the stone boat and go over for the wagon tire and scoop and leave everything at the entrance to the valley. You wouldn't even have to walk home. You could ride the horse from there. Next weekend we can load everything we need on the wagon and start work on our road. We can haul some rocks and maybe try a wagon tire scraper. I'll drill a few holes in the tire before we bring it over."

Shorty kissed his wife and went out to saddle up to ride to the Axe. All three were busy through the week; Shorty on the range, Matt in school, and Dawn looking after the ranch and doing her housework. Angela arrived on Wednesday to tell Dawn that Shorty had two wagon-tire scrapers ready to be picked up along with the scoop. He had bored a hole in the tire and put a big spike through it with a washer under the head. He then got the blacksmith to bend it into a loop and weld it closed. At ninety degrees from the first hole, he bored two others. A bolt could be used to fasten a weight on the rim so it would cut better. Dawn would go over tomorrow and bring everything to the valley. With two wagon-tire scrapers, the scoop, stone boat, and picks and shovels, they were ready to start building a road!

They would camp at the valley to save time travelling, so Dawn began to get the things together that they would need for camping. The wagon would take everything to the entrance to the valley, from where the necessary items could be taken into the valley on horseback. She loaded the pick and shovels on the wagon, and then began getting the food ready. She got a box and put some potatoes, carrots, and a turnip in it, along with a few onions. The vegetables had kept perfectly in the new root cellar and there was a good supply left. She also got a couple of pieces of pickled meat to take along. In the evening she could make up a big pot of stew, which would be quick to heat up at mealtime. She then got a big batch of biscuit mix ready to take with them, which was much easier than taking all the ingredients and mixing it up there. The pots and pans she would need also went into the wagon, as well as the necessary eating utensils. When Shorty arrived on Thursday evening, Dawn had everything ready to go. The team was hitched to the wagon, and they set out for the valley and a road-building weekend. Matt would miss school on Friday, but he wasn't going to miss building a road to their valley!

Chapter 20

WHEN THEY REACHED the gully, the supplies that were needed were loaded on the stone boat and pulled into the valley with one horse. Everyone was busy setting up camp as they would be here for three nights. When the shelter was set up and everything was in its proper place, Matt got a fire started and began cutting up vegetables while Dawn got the meat ready to make a big pot of stew. With a pot of stew ready, it would only take a short time to reheat it for dinner tomorrow. All three were anxious to get a road made into the valley, so they could start building and eventually live in this beautiful spot. With three of them working, two or three weekends should make a passable road.

Shorty had put a couple of wide planks on one wagon tire. With the horse hitched to it, a person could stand on it to drive the horse and put some weight on it. He thought if Dawn could use the scraper, he and Matt would use the stone boat and start moving some of the rocks. They could be dumped in holes or piled on the wide spots on the corners where the stream had cut farther into the bank. As the scraper dug out rocks, they could be gathered up and hauled away. They couldn't really plan very far ahead until the actual work was underway. The camp was in good shape and tomorrow's dinner was cooking, so it was time to get some sleep. The next few days promised to be busy ones for the three homesteaders.

Daylight found the camp awake and busy as usual. When it was light enough to see, Shorty had watered the horses and given them some grain. Dawn and Matt were getting breakfast ready, which was hot biscuits, bacon, eggs, and tea. It didn't take long to get breakfast out of the way, and they were off to start the day's work. One horse was led to the lower end of the gully, while the other pulled the stone boat. Dawn's horse was hooked to the wagon-tire scraper, and she began leveling the floor of the gully. She couldn't go all the way through, so she would go partway and turn around. Where the surface wasn't too rough or hard, the wagon tire did a good job of leveling the soil. It shaved off the small ridges and filled in the low spots. Shorty and Matt were busy rolling rocks onto the stone boat and hauling them to the deeper holes and hollows in the gully. The bigger rocks went in first, then smaller ones, and finally some dirt would be scraped over everything to make a good road. Late in the morning, Dawn went to camp to get dinner ready, and Matt took her horse and kept scraping the outer end of the gully, while Shorty kept hauling rocks.

When they thought Dawn would have dinner ready, they unhooked Matt's horse and rode to the camp on the stone boat leading the second horse. The horses were looked after before the people ate as they were doing the hardest work. The team was given some grain and water, and there was good grass for them too.

Dawn had the stew heated and hot biscuits ready with jam for them if it was wanted. Matt and Shorty had been working hard and had a good appetite and two plates of stew disappeared in a hurry. A few biscuits went down with the stew, then a few more covered with jam were swallowed with some tea. The empty stomachs weren't empty for very long. They took a ten minute break as Dawn rinsed the dishes with hot water and put things away, then the three road-builders were back at work.

Shorty asked Dawn to bring in the scoop on her first trip, then he and Matt would cut back some of the corners where she was working. This would give her more loose dirt to level up where she was scraping. They cut and scraped and leveled for the rest of the afternoon. When it was almost supper time, Matt went to catch a trout for supper and put the stew on to heat. He restarted the fire and put the stew where it would start to heat without scorching and went to the lake to get supper. In a short time he had a trout baking, the stew and water heating, and was making biscuits. He was just about to move supper back from the heat when he saw Dawn and Shorty coming. Hard work makes for a good appetite, and the twice reheated stew was impossible to resist.

They were almost through eating when they saw a couple of riders coming. When they got closer Shorty identified them as Gus and Rusty. As they rode up to the camp, Gus said, "Smells like we are just in time. We left the ranch before feeding time, hoping we might find a bite to eat here. That stew and 'roast rock' smells good enough to eat."

They got their plate and dug into the thick, dark stew, some fish, and a biscuit and a cup of tea was passed to each of them. They were too busy eating to talk and until after the first plate was emptied, not a word was said. When the conversation started up, Shorty asked what brought them to the valley. Gus answered, "Well, we knew you were going to start work on a road in here, so we came over to help out. If the grub is all this good, we might even stay and work for a while!"

Dawn spoke up, "Well, if you came looking for work, we might be able to find you some. I don't know about the grub department though. We only brought enough to hold us for the weekend. We might all be eating trout for the next day or two!" Everyone there agreed there were lots of times they had eaten worse than baked trout. Dawn decided that since they were going to have extra help, she could ride home and get more vegetables and meat to make more stew.

Gus thought they had made good progress on the road building so far, but with a couple of 'real men', the job would go a lot faster. Over tea, they discussed the job and the best way to do it. Gus thought putting the big rocks in the deep holes was a good idea. It was too far to haul them away, and filling the holes and piling them in the wide corners saved a lot of time. In some places there was what, at one time, were small waterfalls. Not much of a problem for a saddle horse, but a major obstacle to a loaded wagon. After a bit more discussion, they all decided it was time to get some sleep as all had worked hard all day.

In the morning, just as the sky was starting to lighten, the fire was burning brightly and biscuits were baking. There was bacon and a few eggs left, so everyone had a good breakfast. As soon as Dawn had the camp cleaned up, she left for home. She would get more meat and vegetables and mix up more biscuits. Matt planned to catch a couple of trout to go with whatever was left for dinner. When Dawn got to the open prairie, she met Slim with a team and light wagon. He was coming to help out too and had brought more horsepower and a pick and a couple of shovels.

Dawn decided she had better get home and get some food ready, as she had a big, hungry crew to feed. From the looks of the crew, she would probably have to spend most of her time getting meals ready. When she got to the ranch, she got her biggest pot, and filled it with potatoes; she then got two turnips, some carrots, and a large cabbage. She didn't know how she was going to get everything back to the valley, but she would somehow find a way. She also got three large pieces of pickled meat to go into the pot with the vegetables. She mixed up enough flour, baking powder, salt, and lard to make about a hundred biscuits. She thought this should feed a small army, which was about what she had to feed. She put the vegetables in two feed sacks and tied them together, so they would hang over the saddle. The meat was put in the big pot which would go in the pack on her back. The biscuit mix would go in a container that she could carry on the saddle. She got a few more plates, cups, and forks in case someone hadn't brought theirs. She also collected the eggs and made sure they were well washed. The biscuit mix was unpacked and a layer was replaced in the container, some eggs were placed on top, a layer of mix and so on until the container was full. With the eggs safely packed in the flour mix, which now filled two containers, they would make the trip to the valley. She now had just about everything she would need to feed the road-building crew at the valley. She had picked up more bacon, and with the fish Matt would catch, they would all eat well. Dawn was all packed and ready to leave when she heard a horse coming; she was surprised to see Karen riding into the yard. As she dismounted, she told Dawn she was coming to see if there was anything she could do to help with the road building. Dawn told her of the crew that was working there already and that she had come for more food supplies to feed everyone. Karen was heading for the valley, but had stopped in to see if there was anyone here. She had her bedroll and tarp with her, so she took part of the food Dawn had ready and they set out for the valley. They hoped Matt would have enough for their dinner too, when they arrived.

When they reached the entrance to the valley, Karen was surprised at the work they had already accomplished on the road. At the lower end there was a smooth road, plenty wide enough for a wagon to travel over. When they got farther up the gully where everyone was busy working, she could appreciate how much work had been done on the outer end. It was time to eat and some of the crew had gone ahead to get ready for dinner. Matt had baked two big fish, the last of the biscuits, and everything else that had been leftover but it looked as if there would be enough to feed everyone. They took a short break after the meal to give the horses some time to eat and rest up a bit. It wasn't long though, until everyone was back at the road building. As soon as everything was cleaned up, Dawn and Karen began working on another big pot of stew. One piece of meat was chopped up fine and then fried until it was well browned. This went into the pot with all the vegetables which were chopped to about half-inch-square pieces.

The pot of stew was soon bubbling away and would be kept cooking slowly until supper time. A second piece of meat was put on to boil, the water being changed twice to remove the salt; it was then left to boil until it was cooked. With supper cooking, they had a bit of spare time, so Karen was going to go to the stream and get a trout to bake for supper. Dawn decided she was going to take over one of the horses and scraper for a while, thus allowing one of the men to do a different job for a change. They were making good progress with the road building, and Dawn felt she should be doing her share. She would work with the horse for a while, and then go back to camp to help put the finishing touches on the meal that was cooking.

Dawn took over driving a horse for Slim, so he went to work with a pick, digging the soil loose on narrow spots and sharp corners. The men had been trading jobs every hour or two. The ones moving rocks and using a pick would trade with the horse drivers, so everyone had an easier job now and then.

With two wagon-tire scrapers, one scoop, the stone boat, and picks and shovels, there was a lot of activity in the gully. Matt was leading the horse pulling the scoop, while Rusty was on the handles. They were cutting the bank back on a narrow corner. When the scoop was full, Matt would haul it to a low spot and dump it. The scoop was pulled back up the gully for another load which was taken up the gully to another low area. When there were small rocks, he would take a scoop full to a hole where they could be buried. There were two men with the stone boat, loading and hauling the bigger rocks, which were placed in the deeper holes or piled in the corners of the wider areas. Progress was steady and by supper time, they should be over half done on the road to the valley. It wouldn't be very long now until the first wagon would roll into Lost Valley!

Dawn returned the horse to Gus who had taken over the pick from Slim. She then went back to camp to help Karen, even though there was very little left to be done. With the stew cooked and a trout baking, supper was almost ready. Water was heating for tea and coffee, so Dawn made a big batch of biscuits. She was wishing she had some dumplings for the stew. Dawn thought to herself, 'I wonder what would happen if I put some biscuits in the stew for dumplings? I guess there is only one way to find out!' She covered the top of the stew with biscuits as a substitute for dumplings. The Dutch oven was full of baking biscuits and the two women expected the men to arrive shortly.

It wasn't long before a tired and hungry crew was seen coming up the valley. The horses were unharnessed and looked after before the men washed up in a pail of warm water the women had ready. The stew smelled wonderful, as well as the trout which was laid out on a wooden tray. Everybody lined up to fill their plates and began the serious job of eating. They were surprised to see dumplings on top of the stew. When they began eating them they found they were good, not quite like regular dumplings but still very good. When the plates were emptied and refilled, they began to discuss the day's progress. Gus said, "If we don't run into problems on the rest of the project, I predict we will have a passable road by mid afternoon tomorrow. It will still need some finishing, but it will be passable. Probably every spring you will need to do a bit of work on it, after the spring runoff, nothing major, just a bit of leveling." Dawn then said, "I agree with Gus that we will have a passable road before tomorrow evening, barring any major problems. And no matter if it does wash a bit in spring, it will never be as bad as what we started with. I've been wondering if it would be possible to make a shallow ditch along one side for the water to run in, if there is any. I don't mean too deep, just a few inches lower, so the whole road wouldn't wash and need repair."

The crew all agreed Dawn's idea was a good one and would probably save some work each spring. They began discussing various ways to dig a ditch the simplest and easiest way. Different ideas were talked about and discarded, until Matt came up with the idea of using a plough to make a ditch. There would be places where the plough wouldn't work, but most of the trail would allow the soil to be moved fairly easily that way. Slim came up with the idea of fastening a short plank to the moldboard to push the dirt farther away. He said, "If you fasten a handle to it, someone can walk alongside and put pressure on it to move the dirt. Then a wagon-tire scraper would level it without pushing the dirt back in the ditch. We won't get that done now, but when we are using the scrapers, we can stand on one side so it will cut deeper. That will leave a hollow for the water to follow until you can plow it deeper."

Everyone agreed that Slim's plan, coupled with Matt's, was the way it was going to be done, unless a better way was found later. Right now, everyone was enjoying the time to sit or lie back as they rested. Some were having a final cup of tea or coffee and the occasional biscuit. They all thought this was a beautiful, peaceful spot and could see why Shorty and Dawn wanted to get a road made so they could build in here. Tomorrow should make the road a reality and the first wagon to ever enter this valley should arrive tomorrow afternoon!

Dawn said, "Since this is our place now, I think our wagon should be the first one to come in here. The rest of you will be in the ranch wagon right behind us. If it hadn't been for all the help you've given us, we would have been a lot longer getting a road built. When we get our house built, it looks like there might have to be another dance to show our appreciation!" The boys all cheered, as it didn't take much of an excuse for a dance and a good time. The tarp Karen had brought had been put up, so there was plenty of room for everyone to spread their bedrolls. Shortly after full dark, everyone was in their blankets and most were asleep after a hard day's work.

When morning arrived it was busyness as usual. The girls were cooking bacon, eggs, and biscuits while the men gave the horses a bit of grain and watered them. By the time the chores were done, bacon, eggs, tea, and coffee was served and biscuits would follow. Soon the whole crew was busy at the road or camp chores. When the two girls finished their work, they took over driving the horses pulling the wagon-tire scrapers. They were travelling one behind the other, as there were very few places wide enough to meet. On the way out, they would stand on the far right side of the scraper so it would cut a bit deeper on that side. The return trip would deepen the hollow slightly more. Each trip would shave the outside a bit deeper and push the dirt toward the center. They would go up the gully until there was enough room to turn the horse and scraper and repeat the process. The boys were hard at work hauling rocks, picking, shoveling, and scooping soil. As another section of trail was completed enough to pull the scrapers over, the girls would extend their circuit to cover the new area. Karen gave her horse to Matt, and she went to camp to make biscuits, heat water, and reheat the leftover stew. Half an hour later, Dawn gave her horse to one of the boys and went to see if Karen needed a helping hand. As she left, she told them dinner would be ready in twenty minutes. Karen had everything just about ready, so Dawn took over heating the stew, which had to be stirred constantly so it wouldn't scorch. When it started to bubble, she moved it back just far enough to keep it hot. The biscuits were ready, and the tea and coffee were hot when the crew same in sight.

The whole crew was excited at the prospect of having the road completed. It was discussed as they ate, and all agreed two hours would provide them with a useable road for the wagons. Everyone ate quickly as they were all anxious to get back to work and complete the road.

With lunch out of the way, they were all back at work to complete the road. The scrapers were not going all the way out now, as they felt that end of the road was smooth enough. They were concentrating all their efforts on the uncompleted section. It wasn't very long until the girls were able to turn their horses at the lower end of the valley. The rocks were all buried or piled out of the way and the final widening and leveling was taking place.

Gus instructed Shorty to take their team out to the wagon and finish harnessing up. The remaining two horses would make a few more passes over the road and then follow Shorty's lead. As Gus had predicted, slightly after mid afternoon, Shorty, Dawn, and

Matt were on the first wagon to navigate the new road into the Lost Valley. The second wagon with Gus, Slim, Rusty, and Karen was close behind. A lot of effort had been put into building this road to the valley, and now it was ready for use. The wagons were taken to the campsite where all the camping equipment would be loaded. Although it wasn't thought necessary, a temporary barricade of poles would be put across the roadway to keep the cattle from leaving. With all the grass soon to be in the valley, the bare roadway wouldn't be very tempting to the R-R stock.

Everything that had been used for the weekend of camping and cooking was loaded on the wagons, along with the scoop and one wagon-tire scraper. At the entrance the horses were halted and there was many thank-you's and hand shaking all around. Dawn and Shorty told everyone how much their help had been appreciated and that they were always welcome at Lost Valley. Everybody then mounted their horse or wagon and headed for their home ranch.

Now that there was a good road to the valley, Dawn, Shorty, and Matt would spend some time deciding where to situate their future home. As soon as the trees began to grow and peel easily, they would be back in the hills cutting and peeling logs so they would dry faster. They were hoping to have a home built before fall, so they could live in the valley next winter. For the three of them, the future was beginning to look very bright indeed!

The next weekend Shorty, Dawn, and Matt went to the hills to get some logs to build a gate at each end of the newly built road. There wasn't much of a reason for the cattle to stray, but a gate at each end would ensure they stayed put. Already a name had been chosen to put on the outer gate: 'Lost Valley Ranch.'

When weather permitted, a large garden was planted as Matt had enlarged the garden area the past summer. When the trees began to peel, many hours were spent falling and peeling them, leaving some top on them to help them dry faster. A couple of overnight trips were made to the valley checking out prospective building site for their new home. They wanted a protected spot, which was almost any place in the valley, where they could dig into the bank for a root cellar. They also wanted a good garden spot near to the home site, and again almost any spot was suitable. Water should no problem, as a well dug to a depth of eight or ten feet should give them a good supply of water. A spot was finally chosen about half way up the valley, on the west side. A narrow cove ran back into the former lake bank, which with some work would make a good place for a root cellar. With a site chosen, plans could be drawn up, subject to change, of course. Their idea was to have the house close to the bank with a woodshed on the back end, connected to the root cellar. They would concentrate on getting the house up first, as the root cellar at the R-R would keep the vegetables protected and they could be brought to the valley as needed. Dawn, Matt, and Shorty were busy doing everything they possibly could do to get ready for the home building they hoped would come in the near future.

About the middle of July, Karen and Matt made another survival trip with the school students. They had talked to their parents and other elder citizens about survival tips they could use and most had an idea or two to share with the others. After this trip, several of the students planned to go on an overnight trip by themselves. They were camping at the site they had used earlier, as there was good water close by and there were fish to be caught. They were going to try eating cattail shoots and roots as survival food, and it being early summer, there was other plants growing that they could eat. Some might not be the tastiest, but if a person was starving, it would be better than nothing.

Back at the ranch, Dawn and Shorty had been busy as usual. The plans for their new home in Lost Valley were almost complete, subject to adjustment and minor changes. One good reason for not chiseling your plans into granite; it's much easier to change them. While Matt was away, they had been working in the garden. In the middle of the afternoon Dawn stopped work and said, "I want to go to the valley and spend the night in the inner valley. We've been planning to do that for almost a year now and we haven't done it yet. Let's get a few things together right now, and we can eat supper there!"

Shorty thought that was a good idea too, and he went to saddle the horses and get their bedrolls ready. He got the big pack to carry food and cooking utensils in. Dawn had gone to the house to mix up some biscuits and slice some bread. Most of the things they had used before were in one place, so it was easy to get everything ready quickly. When Shorty had the horses ready, he went to the meat house and got some bacon, which would make breakfast or it could be used to flavor a baked trout. They had found a few small potatoes and some greens, so they planned a small, private celebration.

With their tarp shelter, a good supply of food, bedrolls and themselves, they set out for the valley. It was a beautiful afternoon so they were in no hurry. They rode side by side talking and planning for the day they would live in the valley. Even when they reached the valley entrance, they could still ride side by side. There was now a log arch at the entrance with a new gate; hanging from the top log was a sign that read; 'Lost Valley Ranch.' After the road was built, this gate was erected to keep the Axe cattle from mixing with the R-R stock. At the lower end of the valley, where the road ended, there was a temporary gate to keep the R-R stock from leaving, which probably wasn't necessary, as the cattle in the lush grass of the valley had no reason to leave. They rode up the west side of the valley, close to the bank. This would be the road to their home to be built soon, they hoped. The trail up the valley would follow a fairly straight course, close to the steep bank, but not following each small indentation of the old lakeshore. Probably, in the future, they would fence off a small area of the valley to provide hay for their horses and milk cows. They stopped at their future home site to look around for a bit. It was nearing supper time, so they continued up to the valley to the entrance to the small inner valley. Here they dismounted and tied their horses to a bush and went on foot into the tiny valley to look for a good camping spot. When a good spot was located, they gathered rocks and got a fire started before going back to unsaddle and water their horses. With the horses looked after, they carried their supplies to their waiting campsite.

Dawn began to prepare supper while Shorty got some poles to put up their shelter, even though it was a lovely evening and a shelter wasn't necessary. They would rather sleep in the open where they could see the stars. Dawn had some biscuits in the oven and was boiling the few potatoes and greens, while water was heating for tea. Soon they were enjoying their meal of the first vegetables of the year, from the garden. They took their time eating, as there was no work waiting for them to do. When the camp was cleaned up and everything was neat, they decided to explore the inner valley once again. When they reached the waterfall, Dawn decided it was a good time for a bath, and she began taking her clothes off as she looked at the water. Shortly, she was standing under the waterfall, enjoying the feel of the water splashing on her bare skin. Once Shorty realized what she had in mind, he peeled off his clothes and joined her in the water. Soon they were both laughing and splashing like a couple of children. After washing each others back, they swam across the pool a couple of times. After another rinse under the falls, they were ready to get out of the water. Instead of getting dressed again, Dawn waded into the pool again and started washing her clothes with Shorty following suit. The clothes were thoroughly washed and wrung as dry as they could get them, they then walked back to the camp carrying their clothes and boots. The clothes were hung on small poles Shorty had erected near the fire, so the heat would help dry them. After being in the cool water, the heat also felt good on their bare skin.

Shorty picked Dawn up in his arms and carried her the short distance to where their bedrolls were spread, where they lay down and pulled a blanket over themselves. It wasn't long before the blanket was tossed off and they began the serious business of loving each other. This was repeated a couple of times in the night under the stars. When daylight arrived, Dawn crawled out of the blankets, restarted the fire, put water and the Dutch oven to heat, and crawled back under the covers. She tickled Shorty until he woke up and they made love once more.

Dawn thought it would be nice to have another bath before getting dressed in their freshly washed clothes. After a good shower under the falls, they went back to camp for breakfast. Dawn made biscuits while Shorty sliced bacon to fry, and soon a good breakfast was ready to eat. As they ate Dawn told Shorty, "You are going to be a daddy!"

Shorty was surprised and said, "When did you find this out? You haven't said a word to me about it before!" Dawn said with a grin, "It happened last night. I just found out!"

"What makes you so sure you are going to have a baby from last night?" he asked. "I thought it would be at least a month before you could be sure!"

Dawn grinned and said, "If you don't believe me, just wait nine months and you will find out! It's going to be a girl, and her name will be Allie!" They both stood and put their arms around each other. Both Mummy and Daddy were very happy and they knew that a certain big brother was going to be very happy also!

Right now it was time to load everything on their horses and head back home. There was a lot of work to be done if they were going to have a home built in this valley before fall. They knew everything was going to work out all right for them, and they would be living here in Lost Valley when their daughter Allie was born!

written nov 2009 to
Feb 2010

Edwards Brothers, Inc.
Thorofare, NJ USA
March 31, 2012